Jesse's Highway

Jesse's Highway

By
Barbara Miller

CFI
Springville, Utah

© 2007 Barbara Miller

ISBN 13: 978-1-59955-022-0

Published by CFI, an imprint of Cedar Fort, Inc., 2373 W. 700 S., Springville, UT, 84663
Distributed by Cedar Fort, Inc. www.cedarfort.com

LIBRARY OF CONGRESS CATALOGING-IN-PUBLICATION DATA
Library of Congress Cataloging-in-Publication Data

Miller, Barbara, 1939-
  Jesse's highway / Barbara Miller.
     p. cm.
  ISBN 978-1-59955-022-0 (acid-free paper)
  1. United States—History—Civil War, 1861-1865—Veterans—Fiction.
  2. Remorse—Fiction. 3. Illinois—Fiction. 4. Religious fiction. I. Title.
PS3613.I5247J47 2007
813'.6--dc22
                    2006103447

Cover design by Nicole Williams
Cover design © 2007 by Lyle Mortimer
Edited and typeset by Kimiko M. Hammari

Printed in the United States of America

10 9 8 7 6 5 4 3 2 1

Printed on acid-free paper

DEDICATION

This story is dedicated to Charles S. (Ottie) Spring, Union soldier, Ohio 64th Infantry, 1861–1865. He passed away January 1897. Thanks, Ottie, my own unknown soldier.

Prologue

THE PREACHER

This man, this prisoner, known as the preacher, walked
up and down the compound all day long. Where he got
the strength, no one knew. His body was emaciated and
weathered, he appeared never to eat or drink, and only heaven
knew if he slept with both eyes closed. The Union rags, which
once passed for a uniform, flapped around his rail thin limbs like
dry leaves stubbornly clinging to a dead oak. He had no friends,
for it was already widely accepted that he was more than a few
cards shy of a full deck. All but one of the worst ruffian gangs
left him to wander alone and unmolested. He had been captured
at Brice's Crossroads while serving under Major General SD
Sturgis after a surprise ambush by Forrest's Confederate troops.
He was dragged, with others of the splintered Union forces,
through the scorching open countryside of Georgia to the infamous Andersonville prison. He was older by ten or twelve years
than the ruddy-cheeked boys and pale young men who had
joined up for the adventure of blowing Johnny Reb to hell.

The nickname that followed him was earned by his prolific
use of scriptural language and a constant harangue against war.
Since his arrival at that odious camp, he would pace for hours
on end, muttering to himself, gesturing—revival style—toward
the blistering sky, stopping only occasionally to cast a bulbous
eye at some unsuspecting sick or dying Union man. He had his
favorite quotations and used them liberally.

They shall beat their swords into plowshares and the lion shall lie down with the lamb! He would hiss into the diseased man's face. *Wash you, make you clean; put away the evil of your doings from before mine eyes; cease to do evil!* His breath was stale and his presence as horrifying as the lone rider on the white horse. He was anti-sin and anti-war to the last syllable.

New prisoners were curious. *Hey, old man! If yer so agin war, what air ye doin' down here? Ain't ye carried a rifle and shot a man clean through? How come yer here a'tall?*

"*I am come that men might have life and have it more...*"

The preacher's sentence would be interrupted by a kick to the backside from some itchy new gang member, eager to show off and gain his dubious status. The words of Isaiah would then be mingled with the dust of the Georgia compound and muffled by the raucous laughter of that small knot of troublemakers.

The preacher's name was Davis Chancellor, but its significance was lost even to himself. There was nothing to a name anymore, nothing to a number or a rank in this hellhole. Even Lincoln's name was dim, and heroic causes had become remote. Noble intentions had been reduced to merely keeping body and soul together, picking lice out of a dead companion's shirt that might be bartered for a smoke or brass button. Tin cups became as chalices and a night's sleep free of bug bites or torturous dreams of home was a treasured event.

It was August 1864, the winding up of a summer of death and shame in Andersonville. Davis Chancellor was to remain there and miraculously survive another seven months, continuing the arduous torment of his fellow-soldiers, and directing his harangue toward the hapless Rebel guards, who were as eager to be rid of Andersonville as the prisoners themselves.

Chapter One

THE GUARD

I n February, when the compound was a year old, one Jesse Campbell, of some obscure Tennessee Campbells, was called up to serve the remainder of his time as a guard at Andersonville. The place was worse than anything he had imagined, since propaganda issued by the Confederacy tended to play down the seedy and filthy conditions. He had served nearly two years and thought to have already looked into the face of war, but what he saw and smelled and felt there turned his stomach.

A man who comes into this stink-hole had just as well shoot hisself at the gate, was a constant observation on both sides of the fence. *If'n a wound don't kill you, the scurvy will, so you might do better to save yerself some pain right off.* Trouble was, rifles were as rare as hen's teeth, so the prisoners could only pray for some special dispensation to come their way. In that regard, there was the constant talk of exchange. The men were sick of the word, but every time new prisoners were shuffled in the guards were grilled with questions of exchange. None came.

Jesse's post was an open air lookout box on the south wall, too often downwind of the long sinks, filthy latrines that ran parallel to the sluggish stream used for drinking and wash water. The stench gagged him, and he took to wearing a neckerchief over his nose and mouth when the wind was up.

Jesse counted the weeks until he would go home to Tennessee. There was not much as far as family went back there, but there was Jen. Jen and the clearest skies on God's green earth. Jen would be waiting, exactly as he remembered her, pretty and pale, and she would ask him to brush out her gingery hair while they sat on the porch of her daddy's house, just as he had the night before he left. It had been a long while since he had heard from her, but then, he had not written a great deal in the last few weeks. His sensibilities were so afflicted by the whole war that he hardly knew what to write. There was nothing to recommend his life as a soldier anymore, and this assignment was the bottom of the barrel to him. Then again, much of the correspondence was lost en route anyway, and questions and answers were so disjointed that most letters were one way monologues. He fought with all his might the feeling that they could be drifting apart.

Jesse was a romantic, but the war was taking the gentleness out of him and numbing his soul. He could not have seen it coming, having volunteered with some fiery notion of preserving a time-honored way of life. Hell, it was not really even his way of life. His own father was a print setter, and his mother was heir to a backwoods legacy and could barely read. She died one evening after a quilting party. She had just sat down in her chair and gone to sleep, leaving the boy Jesse and his daddy to fend for themselves.

When the war began in earnest, Jesse, being young and restive, felt it his duty to go against the Yankee menace and do his part. He and Jen had stood in the moonlight and talked of the future. *Jen*, he had whispered soberly, *I promise you I will return safe and sound and someday we will stand right here on this very spot and I will put a gold ring on your finger. You'll be Mrs. Jesse Campbell forever and ever, and we'll have us a little place down by the hollow, and everybody passing by will wish they was us.*

Jen had looked up into his green eyes and let the tears fall freely from her own. *Jesse, I'd be the happiest girl on earth if you'd just stay. I can't imagine my life without you. Once you're gone, I'm just going to wilt.* Then, catching herself, she put on the brave face of someone in the presence of the inevitable hero.

Never mind what I just said, she told him. *It wouldn't be right for me to stand in your way of duty. I'll wait for you Jess, if it takes forever!*

There in Andersonville, up in that forsaken lookout box, it felt more like forever than the previous twenty-two months combined. How long had it been since he heard from her? Three months at least, he calculated. Only two months to go though, and he would head home, marry the sweetest girl in all of Murfreesboro, and try to make something of his life. Maybe go out west, where there was no war, maybe strike out for gold country if Jen would go.

April came, 1865. The Union had claimed victory at the Battle of Five Forks, Virginia, the Federals began occupation of Richmond, and Lincoln himself would visit the Confederate white house. Surrender of the Confederacy was only a few days away, but in the Andersonville compound, life was drawn out, wrenching from its participants all will to remain human.

It was April 3, a Monday. Jesse Campbell stood for his last hours in the odious lookout tower, now weary and frayed from doing double duty. His replacement had come down with dysentery and could not make his watch. Jesse had daydreamed all the previous month about his release date. Now here it was upon him and he was dog-tired and irritable. The breeze that played around the tower was hot and laden with the familiar foul stench. Jesse covered his face with his worn bandanna and stared down into the haze of dust mingled with smoke, humidity, and insect clouds.

There had been a few disturbances throughout his watch, but nothing a shot fired into the air didn't straighten out. Unrest seemed to grow, however, as the day inched forward. His commanding officer had made the rounds and warned the guards not to tolerate any more skirmishes. "It looks like a nest of wasps out there," he growled. "If any group decides to swarm we're in trouble, and I command you to fire directly into the next group of dissenters and watch the maggots scatter."

The officer had just turned to make his way out of the tower when a tremendous uproar was heard almost directly below. Two large groups had confronted one another just beyond the dead line, apparently in a dispute over some coveted space. Blows were quickly exchanged, and a general tussle stirred the dust. Jesse and the officer stared into the fracas, disgusted and angered. Jesse raised his rifle but hesitated, wiping away the sweat that tracked down his forehead and into his eyes. The officer swore loudly and commanded Jesse to fire. "Blast the bastards to Kingdom Come!" he ordered, turned with clenched fists, and made his exit. "Do it, or I'll beat the living hell out of you myself!"

Jesse regretted the squeezing of his finger against the trigger. With little or no aim, he fired into the pitiful mass of humanity on the ground. Not once, but three times. Immediately, the crowd dispersed. Two of the men, injured by his shots, were dragged away, but the third, whose neck was torn by the searing ball, was left sprawled in the dirt. Seeing that he was dead, his comrades quickly abandoned him. From the settling dust only one prisoner emerged to approach the still figure. He was the preacher, Davis Chancellor.

The preacher had skirted the compound since morning, sermonizing and passing among the near-dead like a brother in arms, a comrade opening the gateway to the netherworld. *Hear counsel*, he repeated to each one, *and receive instruction, that thou mayest be wise in thy latter end.*

His visits were dreaded. The living withdrew from him, the dying had nowhere to go for escape, but those who still had wits about them feigned sleep. He moved through the camp like a dark shade, sometimes resembling a tattered scarecrow mounted on legs of straw and being driven by a bad wind from place to place. But Davis Chancellor was true to his calling, and all the jibes and kicks and final ostracism had little affect on him.

He was just passing the skirmish beneath Jesse's post when the shots were fired. He gaped into the crowd and watched the men scatter and drag away the two wounded soldiers. He seemed polarized for a moment before being drawn to the fallen man's side. He leaned down to him and saw that sermons would be wasted on those ears. Feverishly, he began to search the man's pockets. Such thievery was uncharacteristic of the preacher, though others indulged in it regularly. From the dead man's breast pocket he pulled a small black book. He looked into it quickly; then, clutching it in his fingers, he raised it high above his head and gestured to Jesse. With a surprisingly swift and strong movement, he pitched the book over the dead line and high enough to reach the tower. It came to rest at Jesse's feet.

Then the preacher spoke in a loud, hollow voice, his words flying up to Jesse with alarming clarity. "A man that doeth violence to the blood of any person shall flee to the pit! The Lord will not spare you and all the curses that are written in this book shall lie upon you, and the Lord shall blot out your name from under heaven!" Davis planted his feet firmly and raised his hand again towards Jesse. "Take the name of this man whom you have destroyed, lest the Lord remember you as a murderer and shedder of innocent blood. Read his name every day you live, and feel your awful shame! He that covereth his sins shall not prosper!" Then he repeated the words he had spoken all day long. "Hear counsel, and receive instruction, that thou mayest be wiser in the latter end."

Suddenly, other scavengers fell on the dead man, rifled his remaining pockets, and tore buttons from his shirt. Jesse stared down at the vultures in plain disgust. He dropped his weapon and slumped on the tower floor, overcome with fatigue and regret, weary of war and its hideous face. He removed the bandanna and wiped his cheeks and neck and wondered if his victim was old or young. Was he very young, like so many hot-heads, or was he older and not so idealistic? He wondered if the body below had boasted a family of offspring or left a pretty girl at home as he had. He reached for the small book, his hand twitching nervously, his fingers invading the privacy of the dead. He turned the first few pages and realized they were all a blur, the script unreadable and the paper grimy from much use. He saw water drops fall on his dusty brown hand and recognized them as his own tears. For the first time in nearly two years, Jesse Campbell was crying.

Jesse received an early discharge and was given a small medal of recognition. This he threw away at the first opportunity. He left his post and the compound at Andersonville and never looked back. Just before his return to Tennessee, the Confederacy surrendered, and Abraham Lincoln was shot in the head where he sat enjoying *Our American Cousin* at Ford's Theater in Washington, DC. These were the large events, the pictures painted upon the national scene, and each of them had an effect on him, but the disappointment that met Jesse on his own doorstep overshadowed any other of the post-war turns. He returned home to discover that Jen had married another man.

He did not even have the hope of visiting her or the dream of a chance meeting on the street. She had married in January and moved immediately to Ohio. Worst of all, she married a Union man. Jesse's father had learned of it through an announcement made in the papers. It was the first thing he told Jesse, figuring he should know that right away.

The ache that Jesse had felt occasionally now ground deep in the pit of his stomach. What he secretly feared had come to pass, and there was no altering it. He tried to hide the disappointment on his face, but his father read through it. "Son, it's best to forget what can't be changed," he advised. "Get on ahead with your life. You've got your health, you've got a good head on your shoulders, and, God willing, another gal just as fine as Jen will come along."

Jesse pondered these words as he tried to sleep that night. The fact was, now that he thought on it, it had become harder and harder to conjure up Jen's features through the long months. He could invoke misty images of a young, ginger-haired woman with pale blue eyes, but the whole portrait was never quite there. He put it down to time and distance, but always clung to the cherished dream of their union. He fancied that once they were together again it would be the same as before. After a while he fell asleep, and even dreams of war played on a blank sheet. He saw nothing and thought nothing until the morning came.

He slept late, at least late for a soldier, and awoke to wide streaks of sunshine pouring in through the shuttered window. He eased out of bed and stood to stretch. There, facing him, was his own full-length image. His mother's old oval mirror was leaned against the converging corner walls and offered a stark reflection. He had not viewed himself this way for a long time, and he noted that he needed a few more pounds of meat on those bones. Since Southern guards had eaten nearly the same fare as the prisoners in the compounds, scarcely a man came home overweight.

Pulling on an old pair of trousers and buttoning a white cotton shirt across his chest, he suddenly felt really at home. He studied himself again. A shave was in order, perhaps a trim. Certainly new boots. Stocking-footed he stood five feet eleven inches, and boots would raise him to over six feet—not as tall as the president whose stand had sent so many boys to their end, but taller than all of his friends. He wondered how many of them were gone, how many of them might be buried in common or unmarked graves along some remote and deserted highway.

Jesse's features favored his mother but took on his own masculinity. His hair was brown and wavy, just like hers, and his eyes were green, leaning toward hazel as he got older. His upper lip was thin, but the lower portion of his mouth was full. When he would pout, his mother used to tease him that his lip stuck out so far a rooster could come and sit on it. His cheekbones were high and chiseled, even more now that he had become thinner, and his eyes turned up at the corners in the same Swedish way as his mother's people. She always told him he was handsome, but he decided that was the way of all mothers, and didn't believe it.

He combed his hair and went down to the privy, noticing as he passed through the kitchen that food had been set out for him. His father went to his work early, when it was still dark, so they would see one another later. The morning was fresh, and early May was coming on sweet and fragrant. When he was a boy, on this kind of day, Jesse loved crawling out of bed early to make his way to a little stream running through the town. Spring rains always transformed the stream from a pleasant meander to a bubbling highway of rushing water. He would toss willow sticks and new leaves on the bantam crests and follow them until they became lost on the frothy water's edge. He was almost tempted to do the same now. Instead he sat in the big kitchen and savored the cold corn pone and sweet syrup his father had laid out for him.

When he finished he walked through the rooms of his boyhood home. Of course they all seemed smaller, and they might have seemed emptier except that they were filled with memories and memorabilia: the worn quilts, the tatted table runner, the cup and saucer collection. Shelf after shelf of glassware and walls plastered with cherished programs and posters whose type his father had set. One might have been surprised at a home so adorned with feminine treasures if his father had been a rugged man, a rough and ready sort. But Marcus Campbell was not either of these, and though he came from work every day with ink blackened hands, he kept a spotless home and stayed abreast of the theater and newly printed books. He always said, "Just because your mother is gone is no reason to become cloddish bachelors, living as if we fell out of a Kentucky cave or off a turnip wagon." After surviving under wartime conditions for so long a while, Jesse more than welcomed the comforts of such a home as his father kept.

At last Jesse could no longer avoid the task he had put off the night before. After his breakfast, he went to his room and pulled out the haversack that held his motley souvenirs of war. There was not much in it, certainly not the medal he had been awarded for, Heaven knew what. His extra clothing had been all but threadbare, so those few garments he had given to a man worse off than himself.

After tossing aside a comb, a buckle from his army belt, a shoe blacking kit that had seen limited use, and a collection of arrowheads, he pulled out the one object he dreaded most. It was the little black book the preacher had thrown him. He turned it over in his hands, feeling its worn leather cover. Its edges were frayed and looked purposely torn, like the feathery fringes of decorated stationery. He had not really examined it before, and he wondered why he had even brought it home. The truth was, it seemed to exert a powerful pull and possess a dark curiosity, and he was unable to toss it aside as he had the medal.

Now he sat on the straight-back chair by his window, turning the pages, noting the passages marked, all of them underlined with a fuzzy gray lead. They were scriptures, no doubt favorite ones, marked by the man or boy who met his Maker at the end of Jesse's rifle. Apparently he had been a religious man. This was his well-worn Bible. Jesse stopped flipping the pages and returned to the inside cover. A name was written there. The script was neat and even, the spacing precise and graceful. It looked as though it had been written by the hand of a woman. The name was Peter Beaudine. There was an address below the name. He was from somewhere in Kentucky, and the Bible had been given him in 1860, by whom it did not say.

A seedling of thought sprang out of those thin papers and looked for a bed in Jesse's muddled mind. He shook it off immediately, as if ridding himself of a shiver or some specter in the night. He put the Bible down and took up his shaving. He did not want to think just yet, for thinking involved too much pain. Unconsciously, he resolved to give himself over to feeling, to recapturing something of the freshness he had left in the boy who lived here before the war. He decided to go fishing.

The sun was now high, and the shadow pursuing him was almost directly underfoot. His familiar countryside was in bloom, recovering itself from the fierce trampling of battles that had taken place while he was away. Nearby Stone's River had been the scene of bloody confrontations in late '62 and early '63, and those fields boasted recovery with the passage of time. Nature was never beaten back permanently, and now she reclaimed her once bloodied bosom with flowerettes and springing green blades.

Just outside town, a bedraggled stand of cottonwoods offered him shelter by the stream side, and he slipped lazily down to the bank. Jesse looked forward to an afternoon of peace and maybe a little nap. Amazing, he thought, what a world of difference a few days can make in a man's life. The line dangled and drifted in the cool water for several minutes and he had no luck with fish, so he lay back on the mossy slope in hopes of some shut-eye. Warmth from the sun and the soothing flow of the water enveloped him. He relaxed, but sleep would not come. Instead, a haunting scene entered his mind, and a disturbing image wove its way through the cottony quiet of the afternoon. He saw himself lying upon a charred hillside, surrounded by fellow soldiers. His head turned to either side, and he saw that his dead comrades were all around, lying in a row, like so many railroad ties, their faces cast upward. Their hands, with palms turned toward the sky, seemed to reach up in silent supplication.

Smoke rose in the distance, and the trees on the horizon spread narrow and fingery limbs through the gray mists. Oppressive silence pushed on his eardrums, pressuring thoughts to a far corner of the scene. Out of the mist and the bare-limbed forest a rider came, silent and dreamlike, clothed in the war rags Jesse had seen so many wear. The horse came quietly toward him, raising dust and pebbles from the vast field. The soldiers had disappeared. He lay there alone, heavy, and unable to move. The rider drew his mount to a halt a few yards short of Jesse's head and walked slowly to him. There was a gaping hole through the man's neck, yet he walked on. Just as the figure came within a hair's breadth of touching him, Jesse shot up out of his hollow vision. "Peter Beaudine!" he whispered hoarsely in his half-wakeful state.

Jesse stared at the grass for a moment before realizing that he was indeed hearing hoof beats, and they were real. He heard voices from beyond the small rise where he lay. Looking up he saw two riders on the horse, one of them a young man, the other obviously a girl in full bloom, dressed in buoyant skirts and a tight fitting blouse. They did not see Jesse there, and jumped easily from the horse. The girl ran through the trees, quick and agile as a rabbit, and the young man's pursuit was purposely checked, letting her stay ahead just a little. He let her run for a bit, but with a sudden burst of energy caught her by the arm and pulled her close to him. They were about to kiss, when Jesse stood up straight and hollered.

"Cougar Rivers, I swear I saw you dead at Chickamauga! How is it you are come back to life?" He paid no attention to the girl wrapped in the man's embrace, and walked directly to them.

It was, in fact, Jesse's boyhood friend Cougar Rivers standing there, his arms around a would-be conquest. He released her immediately and threw both hands into the air. "Praise my great aunt's holy apron! If it ain't Jesse Campbell! I ain't no ghost, seein' as I was never killed. When did you get back?"

"Yesterday, just yesterday. And you?"

The girl, obviously disgruntled, stepped away from the two of them and folded her arms across her bosom. "Cougar?" she said. He ignored her and answered Jesse. "A month of Sundays and then some. I come back sick as a hound, but I'm fit and rarin' now." He tossed his head toward the girl and grinned widely.

Jesse, as if suddenly aware of the young woman, looked at her and nodded a slight greeting. "Miss," he said, acknowledging her. She smiled weakly.

"I, uh, was just fixin' to do a little fishin' here, but the good ones don't seem to be bitin'. Guess maybe I'll just head upstream a ways and see how it is there." He began to gather his few things to leave.

Cougar took his arm and said, "Don't go on account of us. Say, I was just thinkin' this mornin' about a good spot about a half mile from here. What say we all go on up there and see how they bite?"

The girl was clearly perturbed now and broke her silence. "Cougar, fishin' ain't part of my plan for the day. If'n you want to spend time with me, it ain't goin' to be on the end of a fish pole!"

Cougar looked at Jesse and winked. "Mary, if you ain't

bitin' on my fish line, there's plenty of others will. I ain't seen Jesse in over two years and me and him's goin' to spend some time catchin' up. If you don't like it, you can git right on that there horse and skedaddle on home." He nudged Jesse in the ribs and smiled at both of them.

The girl saw no other way out of her predicament. She huffed angrily, and an impressive pout covered her face. She stomped to the horse, gathered her many skirts, and leaped agilely to his back. Digging her heels into his side, she nosed the horse toward town and was gone in a few seconds.

"Easy come, easy go," grinned Cougar, and slapped Jesse's thin back with brotherly intensity. "Don't never mind her. They's plenty here for the takin'."

Jesse saw that war had not changed Cougar's inclinations toward females one bit. Cougar was like a bee, lighting on one flower after another, never staying in one place long. Jesse never could figure Cougar's charm. He treated women like so much dust under his feet and still they followed after him, hanging on his words, begging for his attention. He knew instinctively that the pouting girl who had ridden so quickly to town would be waiting for Cougar's return and be glad to see him. They walked along the shoreline a few hundred yards.

"Jesse! Gosh, I'da swore you was dead yourself. I beat it out of Chickamauga all right, but not on a death wagon. They had a hard time findin' me, but they only threw me in confinement for a little while. Hell, they needed every blessed body they could drag out to carry a rifle. Killed me a few Yankees and it felt good." Jesse stayed silent.

Cougar rattled on. "I guess you musta done the same, eh?"

Jesse's dream was agonizingly fresh in his mind. "The last one was the worst," he said, as if he were not aware of Cougar's presence. He spoke from the smoke of that recent vision. "He was some 'down on his luck' Kentucky boy in a Georgia prison camp. I had my orders to fire."

Cougar continued his own war speech with a string of colorful words and phrases he had picked up from a Georgia regiment. Jesse, hardly ever shocked at anything Cougar said or did, threw back his head and laughed for the first time in months.

"Coug, you are one shameless Confederate. What are you doing now to save your skin from starvation?"

Cougar's face became serious for a moment. "Shameless I may be, but I no longer call myself a Confederate. You got to stay on the winnin' side, Jesse, to keep your skin on your bones. I know you won't tell nobody here, but when I seen it was old man Lincoln and Grant and Sherman on the march, I took myself away from Jefferson Davis's army on a permanent basis. I sure as hell didn't want to wind up like my mess-mate. His name was Willie, blown to smithereens by a mortar shell. One minute he was right there in front of me, the next minute he was everywhere else!"

There was silence. Jesse tried to distill Cougar's words and find some justification for dismissing the awful realization of their meaning. He stared at the rough tufts of grass beneath his feet. Shortly he spoke. "You sayin' you deserted? How'd you get here without a parole?"

Cougar spit into the water and hardened his jaw. "I'm sayin' I got off the losin' side and I am settin' my course for as far away from Johnny Reb as possible. I'm headin' north as soon as I can get me some cash together, and I'm thinkin' to set myself up in some trade or such, and leave 'dem ole cotton fields' to rot. You saw what it was, Jesse. Can you believe the South is goin' to rise again, after what them Yankees done to it? The fields are nothin', the plantations are burned to the ground, the rivers run over with dead men." He kicked a knobby tree root with the toe of his cracked boot.

"That's all the war got me, Jesse." He growled, gesturing at the worn leather. "That and a few sweet morsels of southern calico. My clothes was in shreds and my belly was scratched from crawlin' pert near the whole way home. I swear! I got out of cracker country by crawlin' in my sleep! And, yessir, without no parole! Nobody knows though, except you, and it would kill my folks if'n they found out."

Deserter. Jesse had understood why some ran away. He had thought of it himself a time or two, but he still hated the word, the implications. Cougar had turned tail when other boys stayed and gave their lives. Jesse stared into the stream, his eyes fixed on the gentle water, while Cougar went on making excuses. The rider in his vision came to mind. Peter Beaudine had stayed and, thanks to Jesse, was one of those who paid the highest price.

Cougar shook him by the arm. "You won't tell them, will you? You been listenin' to me?"

Jesse's thoughts snapped back to the present. He answered his old time friend quietly. "I'd never tell them, Coug. That'd be your place to do. Naw, they'll never hear it from me."

Cougar appeared to be relieved. He went on. "I looked over my shoulder the first few days after I come home, but I figured since the war was over now and the Reb army was pretty much shot down, nobody would come lookin' for one little ole deserter like me."

He sensed Jesse's discomfort and jumped up to change the subject. "Them fish ain't goin' to bite now anyway, Jess. It's too hot of a day. Let's go on back into town and get us a drink of somethin'."

"I quit drinkin', Coug. I got some bad hooch down in Georgia, and even the smell of the stuff makes me sick now. I kinda wanted to drop by the *Register* and say hello to my daddy. Come on with me."

Cougar dusted himself off and hopped from one foot to the other. "You go on over and say hey for me. I got a power-ful thirst and printer's ink ain't goin' to fill me up. Say, if you wasn't so puny lookin' I'd double dog dare you to a race. Bet you couldn't beat me now!"

"Don't count on it, buddy. I wasn't county champ for nothin' you know." Jesse returned Cougar's good natured challenge with a broad grin. "Get on your mark, you no good, low-down, woman chasin' raider!"

"Set, *go!*" hollered Cougar, and sprinted quickly ahead of

Jesse. Jesse allowed it, knowing his friend was a short distance runner. He could easily overtake him in a few yards and throw the challenge back in his face. It felt good to run, it felt good to pass Cougar, and it felt good to welcome himself back home.

Marcus Campbell was finishing the leading on an article to appear in tomorrow's paper. In it were listed the men and boys who had served the Confederacy and returned home safely. He might have volunteered himself if he had been more convinced that slave holding was an inherent right of the southern gentleman, but, as in other matters as well, he was like a fish out of water in the South. The slave issue was not one with which he cared to attach himself. He believed that no given man had the right to indenture another for a lifetime. No family or landholder ought to hold a man's future in his palm simply because he had more means. On the other hand, he held that Jeff Davis had always been a man of honor, and Marcus would uphold Davis's presidency as long as it was viable.

Two years ago, when Jesse got fired up about joining the army, Marcus was displeased, but after one brief talk with him, kept his peace. Jesse had been so insistent, so sure it was the right thing to do, that all Marcus had left was good wishes and prayers. He watched his only boy march off with a rowdy gang of idealists and hot heads and become lost in the clouds of dust raised by dozens of young feet. That day, which now seemed so long ago, he went home calmly, nodding greetings to those who had come to see their boys off. Some were jubilant and hopeful, others were grieving, with dark countenances, and Marcus passed through them with the familiar serene look he always wore. When he got home he took down the crockery and cooking pots, set two places at the table, looked at them and left the room. He sat down in the bedroom, stared out of the open window, and watched the pale curtains flutter in the evening breeze. As the sun dropped to the western horizon, the shadows darkened, changing from a warm plum to deepest black. He did not light the lamp, but sat alone in the room, enfolded in the hard arms of the first of many dark and lonely nights. His boy had gone to war.

Chapter Two

PLANS

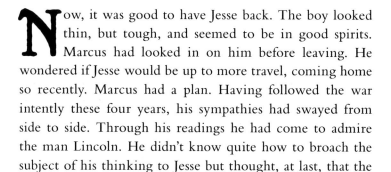

Now, it was good to have Jesse back. The boy looked thin, but tough, and seemed to be in good spirits. Marcus had looked in on him before leaving. He wondered if Jesse would be up to more travel, coming home so recently. Marcus had a plan. Having followed the war intently these four years, his sympathies had swayed from side to side. Through his readings he had come to admire the man Lincoln. He didn't know quite how to broach the subject of his thinking to Jesse but thought, at last, that the direct method was best.

Just as Marcus finished the article, Jesse strode through the *Register* office door. He heard him greet the others, and went out from the press.

"Jesse. You've come at the right time. I'm about to take lunch. Have you just come from the house? Do you mind sitting out under the tree here with me?"

"I've been down at the creek, having bad luck at fishin'. Guess it's too late in the day. I just came by to see you, check up on the old *Register*, find out what's happenin' in town."

Jesse sat on one of the impossibly worn chairs by the door and waited while Marcus washed up. He loved the smell of the press, and the familiar sight of the paper's rumpled office took him back many years. He had greeted Waldo Buchanan, the editor, and Jimmy Holmes, the apprentice, exchanging a few pleasantries. Seated under the massive sycamore outside, Marcus and Jesse shared the food in Marcus's leather pouch. Marcus approached his proposition quietly.

"Jesse, I know you've just barely come home, and maybe you're tired. Maybe you've seen enough of travel for a while, so if you don't care to do this thing I want to tell you about, why, I'll understand."

Jesse was intensely curious. The gleam in his father's eye was unlike any he had seen before. Something was afoot with Marcus, and Jesse urged him to continue. "Go on, Daddy. I'm all ears here," he said.

Marcus cleared his throat and continued. "Well, you know, that is, you must know, that I have read everything I could lay my hands on about this war that's finally coming to an end." Jesse nodded silently. "Mr. Lincoln is dead now, and it seems there will be another long journey for him before he's laid to rest. I've read about the itinerary and the funeral train going to Springfield." Marcus stood up nervously and continued. "Now, I know you fought for the Confederacy, and saw many of your compatriots die for that cause, but I also know that what is about to happen up north is as important an event in the history of this conflict as anything that took place on a battlefield."

Before Marcus could finish pleading his cause, Jesse looked his father in the eye and said, "Daddy, you're wantin' to go see that train, aren't you?"

Marcus nodded, "It's not just that, son. Now, I'm not saying that this means I've gone over and sided with the Union position, for that would negate everything you laid your life on the line for. I'm saying that all my life I've lived here, from a farm boy on up to the Register, and laid out type and sent out papers recording the news as someone else saw it, living second hand, so to speak, because of responsibilities here. Now that you're home safe, and we have a good apprentice down at the paper, I just have a great urge to finally go see something for myself."

"You want me to go with you, is that it?" Jesse asked.

"Now, don't be offended. You wouldn't have to go out of any admiration for the man, and I understand that. Just maybe out of curiosity and a chance to be with your old daddy. We'll be a couple of bachelors hitting the high road before you find some nice girl and settle down."

Jesse smiled outright. "I'm not offended, Daddy. In fact, I do have a natural curiosity about the man myself. It'd be an honor to go see history ride by on some tracks that wasn't all torn up by raiders and Yankees."

Marcus nodded his head and grinned. "Yes, by gosh, the two of us together. I'll tell Waldo right now. If we leave tomorrow sunup, we can get to Springfield in good time." He was nearly bursting with Jesse's answer. It was still the same Jesse, the best of the best, and they would be together a good long while.

"Springfield?" Now Jesse stood. "You're wantin' to go all the way to Springfield?" He paused a moment to calculate. "Why, that's almost three hundred miles. You have money for passage?"

"Better than that. I have two good horses, stabled out at Jamison's place. I figure pacing ourselves at twenty miles a day, we can be there in a hair over two weeks. We'll be there in time for the ceremonies and just take our time coming back."

Jesse was truly astounded. He had known Marcus to be careful and calculating, some said the typesetter was plain dry, and he never thought to see his father want to go any farther than the next county. That Marcus had bought horses, planned the trip, and probably had provisions already revealed to Jesse a different side of the daddy he had always known.

"How long have you had these horses, Daddy? Mr. Lincoln only just died last week. Have you become a seer since I went away?"

"Seer, no. Just started planning ahead when I saw things going worse and worse for the South. I figured you'd need a mount when you got home anyway. And guess what else." Marcus was animated beyond himself at this point. He pulled a small iron key from his vest pocket and held it firmly between his stained fingers. "When we get back to the house later I'll show you what this key opens. You won't believe it."

Marcus had been right. That evening Jesse gaped in awe as his father pulled a small chest from the back of a chifforobe that still held all of his mother's knittings and crochet work. The smells of rosemary and chamomile were sweet to him and brought instant memories of himself as a boy, cocooning his body in this place after her death. Marcus slipped the miniature key into the brass-washed lock and opened his treasure box. It was filled with Yankee currency, paper and coin, stacked neatly and piled in denominations. A low whistle slid from Jesse's lips and he felt transfixed. He had not ever seen that much money in his father's house, even in Confederate notes. Over the last few hours his evaluation of Marcus was taking a phenomenal turn.

"I want you to know, Jesse, that I came by this money honestly. Since it was just me here, it was easy to save. I only started converting my savings to Yankee dollars when I realized that the South was steadily losing ground. It's yours to share with me. We'll have plenty for the trip and for when we get back. What do you think?" Marcus's eyes danced as he watched his son. He had waited for this moment a long time, and was a little proud to see Jesse's reaction.

"Daddy, I'm just about speechless here. This looks to be a considerable store. And to think, I was sleepin' right next to it and never would have thought. Daddy, are you sure you didn't go without?" Jesse looked seriously into Marcus's eyes. "You didn't hide all this up and sacrifice so's I'd have somethin' when I got back, did you?"

Marcus dropped his smile and tears came quickly. "Jesse, I never knew for certain that you'd be coming home. I saved it for a lot of things, but most of all hoped we'd use it together." Then he uncharacteristically said, "I sure as hell didn't want to use it to bury you. That was the one thing I prayed I'd never use it for." Two years of being wrapped in the cold arms of uncertainty now melted away with the release of his long pent-up emotion. He threw his arms around Jesse and stood for a long while, hugging him and not even trying to keep back the tears.

Over supper, father and son talked of the death of Abraham Lincoln and other Washington gossip. Marcus poked the fire as he had a thousand times while Jesse was gone, but this time, not absent mindedly. He felt as if he could talk with Jesse the rest of his life and never tire of it. "Some pious men say it's a shame Mr. Lincoln was at the theater when the shot was fired. It would have been better, they say, that he'd been attacked on the street or at home or any place other than the theater. In my opinion, the theater is not as bad as they portray. These are high minded preachers, I'll grant, but sometimes I think the common man is lost on them. I'd dare say too, that none of them has ever even been to a production. Besides that, if Mr. Lincoln enjoyed theatricals they can't be all that bad. What do you say, Jesse?"

"I think that after what I saw in the war, it might be a pleasure to watch actors on a stage make fools of themselves without really hurting anybody. Besides, it's hard to know what's real anymore. Last month, Andersonville was the realest thing in my life, and the most awful. Now, here I am sittin' in the same chair Mama rocked me to sleep in, and drinkin' good, clean water out of a pitcher her mother passed down. I couldn't ask for more, and only a few days have made the difference."

"Do you think you'll ever be able to forget the war, Jesse?"

Instantly, the vision of Peter Beaudine riding the pale horse appeared to him. He thought of the worn Bible. "I don't know, Daddy," he answered. "Maybe most of it, maybe not."

Chapter Three

Courier— Another Story

Sometime late in that March of 1865, while Jesse was performing his assigned duties at Andersonville, another man, a courier, stood beside a Union commander's fire in another arena of the conflict. Wiping soft webs of sleep from his eyes, he awaited instructions. He had eaten a scanty meal of ash cake and coffee and had a few hours of merciful sleep since arriving in camp. One of the horse soldiers had attended to his mount, Buckshot, relieving him of that duty. After being allowed to sleep too little for his liking, he was awakened by a rough hand and told to beat it to the commander's quarters. He would soon be back on his horse and weaving through the thick Georgia pines to carry a message to the next command.

He rarely knew what messages he carried, and though besieged at times for answers from foot soldiers, he could honestly say that he was ignorant of the contents of these missiles. *I'd ruther not know myself anyway,* he'd say, and ride on to his destination. In these pre-dawn hours, it was no different. He was handed the rolled message, which he slipped into the weather beaten leather tube, took his orders, and leaped onto the waiting horse.

He headed out of camp under a thick blanket of stars and a moon just on the wane. There was enough light to see and take the proper direction, but no hint yet of the breaking dawn. The sun still slept in some depth to the east as he approached the woods, but he had gotten his bearings, so was sure he rode in the right line.

Just as the first pale tints of salmon warmed the sky, Buckshot stumbled. The courier went flying, sailed into a clump of pine stumps, and was immediately charged by a rowdy and filthy group of interceptors. There were five of them, laughing and cursing, tearing at his clothing, pounding him. "Scummy see-cesh! Yer goin' to learn a thing or two about bein' out in the woods alone. It ain't safe, 'specially if yer carryin' tradable."

Before he could protest that he was not a Confederate soldier, he was kicked soundly in the stomach by a size eleven brogue, and the courier saw pinpoints of red light as he crumpled. He vaguely recalled hearing shots and only slightly felt a ball tearing into his shoulder before he passed out.

The five robbers rifled through his clothing and tore off his boots and pants, leaving him to die in his underclothes. "No doubt they're loaded with vermin," growled one of the men, "and I wouldn't touch 'em with a ten-foot pole." After removing any trinkets or valuables, they tossed his bloodied shirt across one of the stumps and tied the pants to a long branch. One of the men hoisted the branch above his head and rode away, carrying the flapping pants like a banner. The five laughed and cursed, and then removed the message from its tube, never bothering to interpret it. None of them could read anyway, so they could not know that the courier was not a see-cesh, but a Union man, pro-abolition, as they themselves claimed to be.

The courier lay unconscious for a time and all became quiet in the woods. Morning light soon fingered its way through the dense and tall trees, and delicate patterns danced on the needled carpet as the sun rose. Hooting owls retreated deeper into the woods and high above, whippoorwills and thrushes began to make songs. It would be a beautiful day, warm and bright, but not seared with the blistering Georgia heat of summer yet.

A short while passed. The courier lay sinking, unaware of any changes around him. Soon, two figures emerged from between the close standing trunks and stepped gingerly to the wounded man's side. One of them, a woman, leaned down to look closer. The other, an older man, pulled her back and said, "Wait, he might rare up. Let me check him." The man then nudged the soldier and tried to jostle a response from him. He got nothing. He knelt close to him and put his cheek next to the courier's nose and lips. "Creation!" he whispered loudly. "He's breathin' still!"

"We better stuff somethin' into that wound," said the woman, "else he'll bleed out and be gone before we get him home."

They accomplished their work quickly, the man carrying the wounded courier under the shoulders, while the woman lifted both of his legs and moved forward.

His wounds proved to be serious. One shot, which had gone through the shoulder, bled profusely and caused nerve damage which would render his right arm useless for a brief while. He suffered severe trauma to the left rib cage and his stomach, where the raiders had kicked him. Luckily, the second shot was fired at him while the band retreated. It only grazed the wrist of his other arm and did not hit any nerves or major blood source.

He spent the next few days in a state of delirium and haze. He awakened to terrible burning pain and found breathing with several broken ribs an excruciating effort. His dreams were peopled with wild men and screaming horses, by visions of his mother and sister berating him for going to war. He saw angels swarming around him, bathing him in warm, soothing liquids, wiping his brow and smiling. On a few occasions he thought he must be in heaven. Then his dreams would turn on him, and he was sure that he now lived in hell. Many days passed before he realized he was lying in a low shed, on a bed of sweet straw, and hidden from all but two people.

Later that first day, when his rescuers had tended to the courier's wounds and were sure he would be safe, they stole out of the shed, the man leading. After a long interval the woman joined him in the large cabin a few yards away. When she had wiped her shoes and shaken the dust from her long skirt, she went over to the man and reached for the briar pipe in his hand. He gave it to her and she took a long draw, letting the smoke drift across her face. Then she squinted, closing her eyes against it.

The man spoke. "You reckon he's Union or See-cesh?"

"I can't reckon nothin' sure yet, but the unmentionables he's wearin' don't look like they came off a southern mam's clothesline. I thought sure he'd be cold as a wagon tire layin' out there as long as we had to leave him. I didn't have a mind to bury another one so soon."

She sat wearily by the cold hearth, leaned her head down, and shook out her hair. It was yellow, fluffed up and unruly. The man had long ago dubbed her Cotton. He liked her and respected her and treated her as he would his own daughter. She was Amy Sutter, his daughter-in-law, widowed when his son Calvin died at the Battle of Shiloh. She was a northern woman, at least in sympathies, and Jim Sutter had taken to her right away. Amy and Calvin's child lived with them. The child was just past three now and could talk a blue streak, as they said. Her name was Clarice, and when she stood in the open doorway, the gold from the morning sun passed over her head through the downy fluff that would someday be exactly like her mother's. Jim called her Cotton Two, and Amy called her Clary.

Amy peeked into the trundle where the child still slept on a little straw tick. "Good thing she sleeps deep. Will you take some breakfast before you go to the mill, Jim?"

"I believe so. Just some eggs if you don't mind. I got to hurry though."

Amy stood and began breakfast. She was a tallish woman, young, no more than twenty two, and long-waisted. Her face was open and honest, and her eyes a remarkable green, with lashes of long blonde brush. Her most unusual feature was that hair. She tried all manner of ways to tame the mass of yellow fleece, but unwilling tendrils wrapped themselves around her neck and across her forehead every time she warmed to any task. She wore simple clothing, stayed to herself, and worked hard. The neighbors knew her to be honest and strong and that she and Jim were just friends, just family, and there was no hanky-panky going on at the Sutter cabin.

Jim had lived in the area only five years and worked at the mill, grinding meal for Alva Wheeler. He was not a particularly ambitious fellow, but he attended meeting every Sunday and was one of the elders in the church. He and his boy Calvin had moved there after Mrs. Sutter passed away. Calvin had come home one day after a trip to Atlanta with Amy in tow. "This is my new wife, Pa. Her name is Amy. She's goin' to live here with us."

After the war started and Amy was expecting their first child, Calvin, ever adept at making rash decisions, walked in one day and announced that he was volunteering up to fight. He also informed them that since he was a great admirer of Mr. Abraham Lincoln, he would be joining the Union Army. Other fathers might have fussed and objected, other wives might have cried and cajoled. But Jim and Amy understood Calvin. Besides that, they leaned toward the Union position themselves. They kissed him good-bye, waved until he was a speck on the road, turned back, and set to the task that would carry them through the war.

They became Union sympathizers and slave smugglers.

Time would pass, Jesse would return home, and the courier would be watched and cared for attentively. Those who assaulted him in the woods would go on a short while longer. They were the kind who called themselves vigilantes, hoping to give their activities something of a higher calling. The fact was, they were no better than raiders. They scavenged and robbed, followed troops, and gleaned the remains of battle on the field and at deserted farms. They were not above theft, arson, murder, or rape. None of the five were fit for either army, for they had no real cause in mind. They laid claim to the Union side because their natural leader, one Tommy Jackson, fancied a medal from the Federals when the South was pulverized by Mr. Lincoln's superior troops. He had never bothered to actually sign up and be outfitted as a soldier. Front line conflict was not his dream, but he just knew that if he followed the boys and cleaned up after them, somebody would appreciate it and reward him.

It was Tommy who had lifted the courier's personal valuables and divvied them up back at camp. Each man took what Tommy decided he could use. Upon discovering that the man had been a Federal, he merely said, "Damn shame he was one of us, but he had no call to come bustin' through them woods and trippin' over our ropes." Agreement and laughter was heard all around. Amid the booty was a handful of brass buttons, an ax, a nice haversack supplied with dried food, a canteen, bedroll, felt hat, the leather tube, other stuff a soldier might carry. They took his horse as well, and the weather beaten saddle bearing the letters U.S. ARMY. The horse would be used to carry their accumulated plunder, and everything else went out pretty evenly. One last item was left, a small black book. Tommy figured to keep that himself, though he would be hard pressed to really get benefit from it, not being a reader. "I'll keep this right here in my breast pocket," he said. "You never know when it might stop a ball from tearin' through me someday."

As it happened Tommy and his little band were captured shortly after that incident in the pines and found their next camp to be Andersonville. He kept the book on him at all times, figuring one day to trade it for smokes or fresh meat, as the need might arise. He never got the chance to trade it. Tommy was blown away by a shot fired into his neck, and the book, a Bible, was tossed to the guilty guard by a crazy old man called the preacher.

The name written so carefully in the Bible was Peter Beaudine.

28

Chapter Four

THE ROAD

Jesse and Marcus finished up their preparations after a late meal that same evening. Provisions for the journey were packed in haversacks, and bedrolls were tied to the backs of two sturdy chestnut mares. They were just walking back to the house when Jesse heard the anxious voice of Cougar Rivers behind him.

"Jesse, buddy! Oh howdy, Mr. Campbell. How's it with you?"

Marcus recognized Cougar and politely nodded. "It's fine, Cougar. You taking the night air?"

"Afore it takes me, that's sure! I got to chew the fat with Jesse here for a minute, if'n you don't mind." Cougar unceremoniously grabbed Jesse by the arm and dragged him off the path to a clump of laurel bushes.

"Listen, Jesse! You got to let me hole up here for a while. I'm in a slight pickle on account of that Mary girl I was with the other day and I need a place to lay low in." Cougar's words were caught between little breaths, and whispered intently.

"You in trouble again, Cougar? Don't you ever learn your lesson?" Jesse felt slightly peeved. He was anxious to get to sleep and be fresh for the early morning departure.

"Me and Mary was havin' a frolic out in McPherson's hayloft just a few minutes back, and her cracker pa come lookin' at the wrong time. He let out a whoop fit to wake the dead and headed home to grab his musket, screamin' he was goin' to fix my flint in two minutes flat! I run home and grabbed some of my plunder and have been out here in back for a bit. I won't be no trouble, I promise. Just throw me a slab or two of fatback and some cakes and I'll make out all right."

Jesse shook his head in amazement. "If you've been out back for the last few minutes, how is it you didn't notice my daddy and me loadin' up those horses? We won't even be here for the next month. I don't think he'll want you hangin' around, especially if some girl's pa is on the lookout and carryin' a grudge."

"You ain't goin' to be here? Where in blazes are you headed? You just barely got home." Cougar seemed astounded, then, before Jesse could answer, questioned his friend. "Can I stay in your place? I'd sneak out at night and get my grub and . . . "

"I know what you'd be sneakin' out at night for, Cougar, and you'd be bringin' trouble right back here on my daddy's house. Sorry, but I got to refuse you." Jesse shook his head and Cougar scratched his.

Ideas tumbled wildly in Cougar's mind. "If I show my face t'home, Mary's pa will see to it I'm dead meat. He ain't above hidin' in the bushes."

Jesse laughed at Cougar's comment. "Seems you are not much above it yourself, old buddy. No, excuse me. It was the hayloft you mentioned, wasn't it?" He slapped the unhappy Cougar on his arm and stood back, waiting for the next desperate move.

"Damnation! Then I'm just goin' to have to go with you, wherever it is you're headed. What say I get me a horse and get my stuff together somehow and sleep here in the shed 'til mornin'?"

"I guess my daddy would a lot rather have you ridin' with us than holed up in the house. He's real particular about his house. I'll go talk to him about it." Cougar grabbed Jesse's hand and shook it vigorously. "Jesse, you're the best friend a man ever had. I owe you considerable, and I promise not to cut no shines wherever it is we're goin'."

Marcus agreed to have Cougar meet them at the Two Smokes junction at dusk. It was nearly twenty miles and the day's travel to get there, and if Cougar followed the river instead of the road, it would ensure that they wouldn't be seen with him. Marcus didn't want to appear to encourage a scoundrel. In truth, he had known Cougar since he was a small boy and always thought the young man was just a notch above worthless. Jesse's friendship with Cougar was always a mystery to him, and he was relieved to see that Cougar's wild ways had never rubbed off on his boy.

At an early hour Marcus and Jesse secured the house and mounted their horses, excited for the experience that lay before them. After a long day's ride, they rendezvoused with Cougar at Two Smokes, as planned. That night was coolish, but not shivery cold, so not much effort was made to keep up the fire after coffee water was heated and fat fried. Marcus hastily pulled out a notebook he had brought along. He licked the lead end of a new pencil and began to write the first of many pages detailing their journey.

Jesse observed his father, while Cougar went a few steps into some brush to relieve himself. Marcus sat close to the dying fire and studied what he might write before putting pencil to paper. He wrote a few paragraphs and reread them in the waning light. Satisfied with his descriptions of their first day out, he closed the book, said goodnight, and settled in to rest. Jesse was curious but didn't ask to see the journal. Instead his hand absently reached into his pocket and retrieved the little black Bible. It was too dark now to read from it, but in his mind's eye he saw again the neatly scripted name, *Peter Beaudine, Lone Oak, Kentucky*. He wondered exactly where that place was. They would have to travel through a section of Kentucky to get to Springfield, and the small seed of thought which he had repressed when he first read the name came to mind again.

No, he told himself, it would be impossible. He had a life to live and needed to get on with finding work and rebuilding his future. So the man was dead; it was part of war. It could just as well have been Jesse Campbell himself, shot through the neck and buried somewhere in Georgia. If Peter Beaudine had pulled the trigger on Jesse, would he have come looking for Marcus to apologize for killing his boy? The thought was ludicrous. How does a man go about doing that anyway?

"*Mr. Campbell sir, I'm awful sorry, but in the line of duty, I was forced to shoot your son and kill him. Never mind, he was in the middle of a fight already, and might have come to his end by a blade or some other prisoner, but he was unarmed and I fired blind into the crowd. Never mind, Mr. Campbell, he was your only son and it'll stick in my craw the rest of my life. I'm sorry, and, by the way, here's the Bible he probably got from you. That's right nice penmanship.*"

Jesse slammed the book shut and crawled under the blanket next to Marcus. They had made up their bedrolls soldier fashion, between two logs, with clumps of pulled grass beneath them for comfort and a canvas tarpaulin as a protection against heavy dew.

Cougar rolled out on the other side of the coals, thinking about Mary. Dang shame her daddy had showed up like that. Well, there's always another one out there. He went to sleep and dreamed once more about the dreadful sights of war. He had discovered that though he'd been able to crawl away from battle to save his skin, he was not yet able to crawl away from memories and haunted dreams. He was restless most of the night.

The following day they passed through Nashville, the capital of Tennessee since 1843. Last year it had been the site of bitter defeat, as the Union forces trampled Hood's army and claimed another victory for the North. The next two days were uneventful, aside from the saddle sores Marcus was feeling. He had thought he was ready for the long journey, but soon discovered that twenty miles a day straddling the back of a horse was not a walk to the river. He dared not complain, but spent as much time as possible off that mare. The fourth night out they came upon a run-down clapboard home just off the road, and advanced carefully. The place was backed by a thick orchard of trees, peach, by the smell of the blossoms. The scent washed over Jesse in soft and bitter waves. Many a time he had stood with Jen while they were courting in the old orchard behind her daddy's sprawling home. This house more closely resembled Jen's outhouse than anything. It was a cramped place, and seemed to have been thrown together by one-eyed carpenters using a witching stick for a level. A feeble yellow light wavered through the loosely boarded front door, where a miserable old hound lay watching their approach. He lay as still as one of those wrought iron lions seen in front of public buildings, but he never allowed his bleary gaze to wander from them. Jesse stood in his stirrups and ventured a greeting.

"Halloo in there! Is anybody home?"

His call was returned by a wild scuffling and a frantic shadow making for the door. A woman appeared, disheveled and feeble looking. Her eyes were wild with the fierce anticipation of one whose most anguished hopes might be realized. "Lewis, is that you? Is that you at last?" She came forward and aimed a wild kick at the dog, who had ambled away just in time. "Git outta my way, you mangy sack a waste! Lewis? Air you come home at last?" Her gaze passed beyond the three riders, as if they were not standing there at her doorstep. "I been waitin' right here all these months, Lewis. Ever'body else is gone but me."

A chill passed through Jesse as he realized the woman was stone blind, and probably crazy as well. He leaned toward her slightly and said in a calm voice, "Ma'am, we have not seen Lewis, but many folks are usin' this road lately, and maybe he will come soon."

She listened intently, then turned and entered the one-room house. The three men looked from one to the other, wondering what they ought to do. Their first hope had been to spend a night under a real roof, maybe get some fresh biscuits and milk from the owner. Suddenly the woman burst through the door, screaming and aiming an ancient blunderbuss straight at Marcus.

"I know who you air, you rotten, no-good raiders, back to burn us all out agin! Git yer fat carcasses off'n my property afore I blow you all to Kingdom Come! Now!" She hit the rickety porch firing.

Jesse, Marcus, and Cougar had wheeled their horses the minute they saw the gun and were pounding dust on the road before the first ball settled. They rode on for another thirty minutes before setting up camp.

"I don't care if we did look like yellow bellied cowards," said Cougar, "but her aim seemed pretty good for a blind woman. And bein' touched in the head, why you never know what a person'll do!"

Marcus was quiet as they ate. "I just hope Lewis wasn't her son," he said.

"That reminds me, Coug. What did your folks say when you told them you were leavin'?" Jesse asked as he finished a long drink of cool stream water.

Cougar slapped his forehead and fell back on the flattened grass. "I'll be jiggered!" he spouted. "I knowed there was *somethin'* I forgot to do! I suppose they're goin' to wonder about that. Well, I'll just have to write 'em a little note after we get to Springfield."

"You mean you pulled your gear together, loaded up the family horse, and never once told your folks what you were doin'?" Jesse was incredulous.

"Not exactly. They was out to meetin' over to the Baptist church, and I imagine, goin' the rounds with Mary's pa after. They just wasn't home. Besides that, this ain't the family nag anyway. That sway-back couldn't get as far as Two Smokes without bustin' a leg or two. That there's Mary's horse." Cougar motioned to the horse that Jesse now recognized as the one from which Cougar and Mary had dismounted at the stream.

"Well, it was awful nice of her to loan you a horse, rememberin' the trouble she must be in over you." Jesse said, fishing for information. He hoped his suspicions were false, but Cougar's answer verified the worst of them.

34

"Mary didn't exactly *know* she loaned me the horse. But by now she knows we are both gone, so she'll figger it out, and after she gets over bein' mad, why, she'll say to herself that if I'da took the chance of her daddy seein' me when I come to *ask* for the horse, he'da shot me, and I'd be dead, and so she'da loaned me the horse on the sly anyway, so I just went ahead and took it myself, knowin' she woulda said yes to begin with."

Marcus looked up from his writing and shook his head, resolving to leave Cougar somewhere along the way to work out his own life. Imagine! They had been on the road four days now with a womanizing scoundrel and a horse thief to boot. He was going to have to speak to Jesse in private very soon. He made a note of it in his journal.

Cougar sensed discomfort from his companions and jumped up, dancing. "Looka here. We're about eighty miles from there right now, and there's no way her old man's goin' to follow us, just to get his horse back. He don't even know which direction we took. Hell, if I ever git back to Murfrees-one-plow-boro, I'll bring him *two* horses! Meantime, we just keep on ridin' to Illinois and go see us a dead president."

Marcus did not like Cougar's constant use of the words *we* and *us* in this conversation. It made them sound like a gang of some sort, and his mounting displeasure caused him to clam up even further. Jesse read the dark mood coming over Marcus, and realized the same bleakness and disappointment in himself. He kept reminding himself that it was better than having Cougar sneak into their empty home, a thing he knew Cougar would have done, even against his wishes.

They retired at the fall of darkness. The uneasiness burrowing in Marcus caused him to be more careful than ever with the money bag he kept around his waist. Neither he nor Jesse had mentioned it in Cougar's presence, but he knew he would be cautious when the time came to take any of it out. He would make sure Cougar was nowhere in sight. That day they had made good time. A light rain had washed over them for a few miles, but it served to refresh the riders and bring up the green of the woods and fields. They were in Kentucky territory now. Foliage bloomed riotously on either side of the roads and traces they traveled, and the wildflowers danced in the freshening spring breeze. Marcus had never been out of Tennessee in his life, and he found the landscape pleasing in spite of the daily jangle on horseback. Writing in the journal, he did justice with his whittled pencil to the feel of the ripening land and the scenes he witnessed along the way.

He recorded in his diary the following: *I feel I would have made a decent journalist. My eye is good and vocabulary has increased over the years to the point that I can describe more than adequately all that I see. I am overwhelmed at some of the things I have seen of late. Today we rode a little off the main road and followed the trace northwest along the railroad tracks. A section of the tracks was torn up, by whom I do not know. The iron is unbelievably twisted and the ties are gone completely, probably used months ago for firewood. The object of this act was, no doubt, to cut off supply trains and thwart the purpose of the enemy. The South has been bitterly trampled by the war and her past glories are utterly lost. It occurs to me that the mad-woman we encountered a few days ago could well represent all of those whose lives were disrupted and shattered by the senseless conflict. And yet, was it senseless? How else could the question of one man's enslavement to another have been answered? How else could the Union have been preserved? What will happen to the South now that even Lincoln is gone?*

Each night he wrote until the light faded and the fire dimmed. Jesse could barely contain his curiosity, but he held firm against intruding on Marcus's privacy. He would wait until his father invited him to read or listen to the observations recorded in the journal. Cougar appeared never to notice the older man's writing at all, and he fidgeted with sticks or things in his haversack until finally settling down to a last draw on his pipe before sleeping. He was getting on his companions' nerves, and they often found themselves riding behind or ahead of him to be out of earshot.

Chapter Five

Cougar Disappears

On the fifth day out they awoke to discover that Cougar was gone. Neither of them had heard him leave. No hoof beats or neighing of the horses had awakened them. "He must have walked his horse out or floated on air," said Jesse. "I don't know whether to hope he comes back or not. He seems to be more bother than he's worth."

Marcus threw off his blanket and grunted. "That's not a question I have any trouble with. I've had my doubts about him since he was about seven years old, and none of this surprises me when I stop and think about it. The only thing that's ever surprised me is that you befriended him at all." Jesse smiled and shook his head.

"You know, it wasn't so much a situation of me befriending him. He just kind of latched onto me when we were kids and I always felt a little bit sorry for him. He may have been trouble to everyone else, but he treated me decent. He's kind of a mystery." Jesse stirred the dead ashes of their nighttime fire and threw some dried grass and twigs in for tinder. Lighting the fire, he said, "I never could figure out his charm with the girls. Seems the worse he treats them, the more they come runnin' after him. I've seen it happen time and time again. That Mary girl probably would have given him the horse, just like he said, and swiped a few bills from her folks as well if he had asked."

Suddenly Marcus leaped out of his blankets and grasped at the belt around his waist, slapping his side as if swatting angry bees. Jesse thought it comical until he realized that Marcus was frantically checking his money bag. A sinking feeling plunged to the pit of Jesse's stomach. Then his father smiled in relief. "Thank the Almighty," whispered Marcus. "It's still here!" Jesse was a little exasperated with himself. For a fleeting moment he had actually envisioned Cougar stealing from them and the thought made him sick. "Daddy, there's no way he could've even tried for that belt and you not wake up. Besides, neither of us ever mentioned it to him."

"Maybe you're right," said Marcus, shaking his head. "But I've lived long enough to just about believe anything can happen. I don't mean to insult your friend, but if he shows up again, I'm going to be watching my back and most of all, my money."

"Don't worry, Daddy. I'll be watchin' too. Come on and sit down. Coffee's boilin' and these cakes will be done shortly."

The morning light played through low, scattered clouds and caused father and son to speculate on the possibility of rain. It would surely help the poor, miserable cotton farmers and soldiers returning to reclaim their plundered properties. Marcus made the rare morning entry in his journal, and remarked the same out loud to Jesse. Just as they mounted for yet another leg of their journey, a rider was seen approaching from the east. It was not Cougar. The man, somewhere in his middle years, rode at a good pace and reined up quickly in front of them.

"Whoa, Molly!" he shouted to his horse. "Hello! Hello! I saw your smoke this mornin' and couldn't resist catchin' up to you!"

He was still shouting, smiling from cheekbone to cheekbone, as if he hadn't seen any living thing for a long while. He continued to shout. Jesse answered him with a friendly greeting, but obviously was not heard. "You're goin' to have to speak up, young fella! I lost my hearin' as a cannoneer last year, and I ain't much good at readin' lips!"

Jesse raised his voice. "Yes, I said hello. Are you from around here?"

"I am, that," bellowed their visitor. "I own the farm about five hundred yards that way! I was just out inspectin' my chickens for fox damage when I seen your smoke!"

"I hope we were not trespassin' on your property," hollered Jesse. "We're on our way to Illinois, and campin' out along the road!"

"Trespassin'? Land sakes, no! What would it matter anyway? As long as you ain't raiders or bummers, and keeps away from my wife and daughter, you're welcome!" The man's shouting continued. It was a little unnerving to Marcus, but he could tell that Jesse thought it amusing. The shouter went on. "You two travelin' by yourselves, are you? You didn't happen to see a scruffy lookin' young fella about your age on the road, did you?" He inclined his head toward Jesse. Marcus and Jesse traded glances.

"Well," Marcus, began, his voice too low to be heard by the farmer.

"Speak up!" the man shouted once more. "I'm practical as deef as a post!"

"I say!" Jesse continued. "We did see one yesterday, but today we have been alone on the road! What's the trouble?" It wasn't a lie, but a slight omission of having seen the scruffy man most likely to fit the shouter's description.

"Oh, no trouble atall, unless I catch up to him! He come walkin' up to the place last night, after dark, lookin' starved and down, so we offered him food and a place to sack out! All the time he was eyein' my daughter behind my back, and her bein' young took it fer a compliment! The wife told me in the mornin' she seen the low-life haulin' out of the back shed and our girl hangin' onto him fer dear life!" He looked around the campsite with a yellowed eye and spit a long stream of tobacco juice into the ashes of their dying fire. A slight sizzle popped off the live coal where the juice landed and a little whiff of smoke rose. The farmer continued. "If'n I ketch sight of that bad egg again I'm obliged by honor to string him up by whatever's hangin' loose! You sure you ain't seen him?"

"Swear on the Bible!" shouted Jesse, raising his right hand. The farmer grunted and seemed satisfied with that answer. Before he turned to go, Jesse yelled one last remark, which was a question that had been burrowing in the back of his mind. "Do you know of a place called Lone Oak?"

The man rubbed the morning stubble clinging to his elongated face. He wiped a trickle of dried tobacco juice from his chin, and thoughtfully shouted, "Up north somewheres I think. This side of Paducah. I never git up that way m'self!" He turned away from them and hollered a farewell.

"Keep yer powder dry, boys!"

"Looks like Cougar's on the loose again," said Jesse, as they headed up the road. "Someday he's bound to get his comeuppance. I don't think I want to be around when that happens."

"From the numbers of people he's managed to offend, it may be that you'd have to buy tickets for the event anyway," replied Marcus. Later in the day he voiced his curiosity about Jesse's question to the dishonored farmer.

"What's in Lone Oak, Jesse?"

Seated on a log, resting from the journey, Jesse answered offhandedly, "Oh, just somebody I came across during the war used to live there. I thought once of passin' through to see the family if I ever got anywhere near."

"Well, we'll be crossing the river at Paducah. We can ask for directions on our way back. Was he a brother in arms? Somebody in your company?"

"He was a soldier, yes. But a brother in arms, no. In fact, he was a Yankee, as far as I could see. I didn't really know him well." Jesse was reluctant to tell anyone the whole story yet. He regretted having told Cougar anything at all and didn't want to burden Marcus with it. Peter Beaudine had become a blur of sorts in his conscious thoughts, but continued to rumble quietly in his subconscious, a cloudy figure out of the gray mist of war. Marcus read discomfort and sadness in his son's eyes, but was reluctant to pry. "Maybe we can look it up on the way home. We'll see," Jesse went on. Then changing the subject, he said, "Do you think the *Register* would be in need of another apprentice when we get back?"

Marcus dropped the Lone Oak train of thought immediately and smiled broadly. "What? Were you thinking you'd like to try the printing business?" The notion made him nearly delirious. Jesse by his side! "We can ask Waldo as soon as we get back. Speaking of Waldo, I thought that after this adventure is over, I would show some of my journal to him and see what he might think about publishing a page or two in the paper. I'd say we are the only folks from Murfreesboro who are making this trip, and it might be of interest to friends and neighbors to read my impressions." Once again, Jesse was astounded. This was Marcus as he had never imagined him. First the trip, now wanting the public to share his thoughts. These were new and brilliant colors flying for Marcus, and Jesse was glad to see them emerging.

"I think that's a fine idea, Daddy. I don't see why the *Register* wouldn't agree to it."

"Well then, maybe before we get home I'll share some pages with you and you can tell me what you think." Marcus was clearly enthusiastic, though still suffering from a natural reluctance. Jesse could wait. He would discover at the end of his wait that his father's words would not disappoint and would eventually be cherished by generations to come.

When Jesse and Marcus reached the great Ohio River, they were impressed to stay overnight in one of the Paducah boarding houses, if such a thing existed. They arrived around suppertime, and cooking aromas from hometown kitchens reached out to them. Fresh beef and chicken, potatoes, and fried bacon on the side, maybe a boiled, mashed yam, with butter and salt. Jesse's hungry imagination leaped ahead of his stomach and brought water to his mouth. They reined up outside a fair-sized house advertising room and board. Easing off their horses, and not wanting to look like common hobos or mudsills, father and son dusted themselves off and ran their fingers through travel-tangled hair.

"Do we look half decent?" Jesse asked his father.

"Maybe half," answered Marcus, smiling, just relieved to be back on his feet. They tied the horses to hitching posts outside and stepped onto a wide porch, anticipating a basket of biscuits and some good fried chicken. After that, maybe a warm bath and a nice, soft, feather-filled tick. The front door was opened wide, welcoming them into a large dining room, perhaps three-quarters full of hungry men. None of them was any slicker than Jesse or Marcus, and some looked downright dirty. One such young man was belligerently addressing the girl carrying a tray of food. "Listen here, tomcat! I bin sittin' here long enough and I'm dang near starved. Haul it on over here and bring me my biscuits and gravy afore I have to take ya over my knee!" His two table companions laughed loudly and traded more rude remarks with each other.

Marcus was appalled at such behavior and averted his eyes from the girl, hoping some other male employee would come out and quiet the man. Marcus disliked confrontation of any kind, but was embarrassed for the girl. She was young, no more than twenty, and pretty. Her chestnut hair was piled on her head, under a man's slouch hat, and she wore clean coveralls which barely concealed a womanly shape. Jesse's eyes, on the other hand, were glued to her. Something in her demeanor was appealing. She didn't mince like a girl. She walked with a stride, taking long, measured steps. As she passed the heckler, he reached out and grabbed at her trailing apron strings. She veered away from him and went back to the kitchen.

The three detractors continued to amuse themselves with crude remarks until she reappeared in the dining room, balancing a heavy tray laden with hot chicken, biscuits, and gravy, intended for customers across the floor. As she passed, one of the men stood and gripped her arm, speaking loudly. "We're fresh out of the war here, woman! Show a little respect for them that fought Johnny Reb and whipped his fanny!"

The girl tried to pull away, but the tray teetered precariously in her hands and she could only fidget helplessly. Jesse was able to stand it no longer. He jumped up from his chair, knocking it over behind him. Marcus protested, "Jesse, no!"

He strode to the middle of the room where the trouble brewed and grabbed the standing man with a strong right hand. "I think you'd best let the young lady go and do her work! Looks like she'll get around to you when she can."

"Damn! Seems like we got ourselves a hero here, boys. I'm real scared."

Suddenly, the girl turned and stared Jesse straight in the face. "Look here," she hissed. "I don't need any pretty boy hero standin' up for me, thank you! I can handle myself just fine!"

The man let her go and all of them guffawed loudly. "Yeah, pretty-boy. Go on and sit down with grampaw over there!"

Jesse was astounded and a little embarrassed. He had only meant well, and was rebuffed and insulted in front of the whole dining room. The girl immediately returned her attention to the three others and said, "Well, if you fought in the war, you must've been heroes yourselves. Somebody ought to decorate you for it." The men looked surprised and smiled up at her with confused grins. Before they could respond, she gritted her teeth and poured steaming gravy into the lap of the first offender.

He leaped out of his seat, hollering obscenities and dancing around the chair like a man on fire. The girl put her tray down on a nearby table, ripped off her apron, and walked resolutely out the front door. In spite of the humiliation still burning in his cheeks, Jesse watched her stride through the door with admiration and not a little interest. Under better circumstances, he thought, this might be a girl he could cotton to. Then, he returned to his chair to dedicate himself to filling an empty stomach and silently daydreaming about a girl in boy's coveralls and a slouch hat.

After a good supper they made arrangements for lodging. It seemed they were lucky to get anything decent at all.

"All I got left is a room up the back stairs. Hit's small but hit's clean and free of vermin, since yestiddy anyhow. Hit's five dollar fer the night, and they's a pitcher and bowl with some soap on the chester drawers. Hit's cash up front, pree-ferable coin."

The house proprietor was a woman, they guessed, but it was no giveaway as far as her appearance was concerned. She wore men's clothing too, just as the girl in the dining room, but the shape beneath could obviously use the concealment. A bag of potatoes came to mind, with no differentiation between the breast region and the abdomen. The woman, Ruthann by name, sported one of the worst haircuts that side of the Ohio, and looked like a stranger to a brush and washcloth. As she spoke, a stiff black hair, prominent on the discolored mole dominating her chin, wiggled up and down, resembling a one-legged bug trying to escape some dark prison. Jesse was fascinated by the image of the rest of the bug and thought of how Cougar might describe it. I must be gettin' buggy myself, he decided, and looked forward more than ever to a good night's rest.

She held out a grimy, dried hand to receive payment and offered one last comment. "They's only the one bedstead in thayer but you folks is scrawny enough to fit if'n you go it spoon fashion. And, oh yeah, they's no spittin' out the winder when you gits up in the mornin'. Hit's the law!" The room was barely bigger than an army tent, but, by Heaven it was indoors and the two travelers crawled into bed grateful for small favors. Jesse might have fallen immediately to sleep if the picture of the mole, the hair, and saying chester drawers hadn't kept springing into his worn mind. He began to giggle and shared his humor with Marcus, whose state of weakness rendered him as silly as his son. They laughed and cackled like old women until a voice from the other side of the wall growled for them to shut it up or eat buckshot for dessert.

Just before Marcus drifted to sleep, the thought of his journal passed through his mind. He had forgotten to record the day's events. Ah well, he reasoned, tomorrow first thing will be soon enough. Before they left the next day Jesse chanced to see Ruthann once more and inquired after the girl in the dining room. She snorted and spit before answering. "That one," she laughed, "is a corker and you'd best quit your curiosity over her. She's in here slingin' hash all week, then goes out to her place in the woods to clear the north forty for her pa. She prob'ly does it one handed too, for she's the hard headedest and stoniest gal I ever seen. Them paps is made of rock as fer as I can tell, and ain't no fit place for no man to lay his head."

"I wasn't meanin' to marry her, Miss. I was only curious. Maybe see you on our way back to Tennessee. Good day, now."

"Same to ya!" she said, and shuffled awkwardly back to the boarding house.

Chapter Six

RECOVERY

Their guest had been sequestered in the Sutter shed four or five days by now, and with her day's work finished, Amy Sutter listened to the silence that blanketed their neck of the Georgia woods. Clarice slept soundly in her little trundle bed, although it was fairly early evening. Even Jim snored softly in his back room. Amy was restless, however, and sat in the doorway, turning the heart shape of a locket over and over in her hands, letting the gold chain fall loosely between her long fingers. She stared out into the woods and in her mind's eye saw the shadowed figures of some forty or fifty slaves who had passed through those same woods on the way to freedom. They had hidden them, Amy and Jim, and fed each one a good meal before sending them along. Most of these people would take an eastern route and flee to the sea, perhaps to continue their journeys up the coast or farther south.

Amy never knew what happened to any of the darkies she had sheltered. Most of them couldn't write and, for safety's sake, were never given an indication of who the Sutters were. There were one or two whose likenesses she would like to have had—children, each dark as coffee, whose round eyes had glistened in fear and gratitude all at once, while she nourished them and tucked them in. *Thanks to you ma'am*, was all she had now, and the tremendous sense of satisfaction at having saved another human being from a life of the indentured slave.

This evening as she remembered and considered her part in it all, she wondered if the always prevalent rumors of an end to the war were ever going to prove real. Her husband, Calvin, had been real at the beginning, she thought. She flipped open the locket to study his picture and gazed at a shadow of the man who had fathered her child, the impetuous southern boy who had swept her to this place and promised Christmas in July and a house full of babies. He was always a charmer, always on the move, and saw the other side of the mountain as clear as a bell. He thought he foresaw a swift end to the war between the states, and said he ought to hurry and join up so as not to miss his chance to say he fought in it. She wondered if he had seen death coming at him in Shiloh with the same clarity. Well, he had had his chance. He fought in the war all right, and for him, it did come to a swift end. His prophecy proved true, at least where he was concerned.

Now, where were the babies to come from? How were the promises to be filled? She would have to seek other means, other dreams when this was all over. Amy didn't feel she could live forever off the kindness of Jim Sutter. Jim needed a life of his own too, a woman to keep him company, someone to make him interested in the night and to bring cheer to him every day. With a determined clinching of her hand, she clamped the locket shut, vowing not to look at it again for a long, long time.

She knew the man they harbored now had to be Union. His presence in the woods so early of a morning told her he must be a messenger. She had seen Tommy Jackson and his band camped out there for two days. Even then, she feared for anyone passing through. Jim had called the band off attacking their place by allowing that he and Amy were dyed in the wool abolitionists, and feeding them supper. The men had eyed Amy, but drew away when she hinted that there were plenty of girls in town they wouldn't have to shoot first to get their way with. "Amy can nick the ears off a mockingbird at a hundred paces, gentlemen. I have seen her do it!" Jim warned them.

Amy was not a hard woman, but she could draw a line past which not a soul could cross unless she allowed it. The fact that she and Jim became a part of the infamous and so-called Underground Railroad grew out of this determination. Jim had been like-minded, but not bold enough to take action until Amy mentioned it one evening. Calvin was gone, buried now, the bones of his body splintered in many places by random shell fire from the musket of some Confederate soldier. Amy and Jim consoled themselves, as numberless others were having to do, in knowing that Calvin had marched into the war fired and fueled by enthusiasm and idealism. It didn't seem to matter whether a person mourned a southern soldier or a northern sympathizer; dead was dead and the lost were not coming home to either side. Southern women wept as long and hard as northern. But, by Heaven, Amy had declared when her mind was made up, "I'll do all I can to make sure some of these people Calvin fought for get their fair chance at freedom."

Jim admired Amy's strength and threw himself into the dangerous work, thinking always of his son, always of the last look he'd had at him, smiling, bursting with certainty that the highway he was taking was straight and would lead to a Union victory. Now, from all reports, it did that. Amy's musing ended when she realized she hadn't checked the wounded man since before supper. She slipped the locket back into a small cedar box on the shelf near her bed and walked to the shed outside.

He seemed to be coming around now and sleeping less. For the first few days it was touch and go, she thought. After they had cleaned him up and dressed the wounds she began to see how he might look without the swelling in his face and head. He wasn't baby-faced like Calvin, but he wasn't mean looking either. His hair was a dark blond, and the beard that continued to grow came in with a slight tinge of red. His eyes were that very strange blue, the color of turquoise stones the Indians wore, which varied in hue with the shifting light. He looked to be taller than Calvin as well, though not much heavier. She knelt beside him now, studying her patient. His eyes opened.

"I'm not dead, am I?" he said, his voice quivering notice-
ably and barely whispering. She pulled back slightly at his first
words. "No," she whispered in turn. "You are not dead, but
you came mighty close." They stared slightly off center of each
other's eyes. Then she shifted her gaze toward the low doorway. "Will you take some food? I got mush in the house. You
could probably tolerate that."

He chuckled quietly. "I'm famished as a locked up fox. I
expect a whole chicken would make me sick, so mush sounds
pretty good right now."

Amy stood up and brushed some straw from her skirt. "I'll
be back in a minute." As she turned to leave he spoke again.
"I felt like I was dead, you know. I saw my passed on relatives
and an old pet coon dog I had when I was just a boy. I was sure
they came to get me."

Amy chuckled, "Well, if they did come to get you, I guess
they were disappointed some, since you are still here. I'll be
right back."

The mush was still warming on the flagstone hearth, and
Amy spooned a little into a small wooden bowl. She poured a
splash of milk into the food and returned to the shed. Her patient had tried sitting up on his own, but found the effort too
much and slumped back into the straw bed. She saw what had
happened and scolded him in a gentle tone. "You have been
only slightly this side of death's door, soldier boy, so you can't
expect to run races right off the bat. Just lean on back and let
me help you this one time."

She spoon fed him in a dwindling light, as the sun dropped
slowly behind the Sutter woods. Taking no chances, she did not
light the oil lamp that hung on a nail by the door, but placed
her fingers on the young man's lips to direct the last bites of
mush into his mouth. The mere act of eating tired him, and
she heard him breathe heavily in the closing darkness.

"You'd best rest again," she said. "You've had a hard time
of it, comin' around, but you finally did it."

"Thanks, I guess, to the Good Lord and you. I don't

know what to say right now, except thanks." His voice was a mere whisper.

She could sense that he had relaxed as his body settled once more into the sweet smelling straw and hay. "There is one thing you might say before I go."

"What would that be?"

"You might tell me your name, so's I wouldn't have to keep callin' you soldier boy."

She felt his agreeable reaction, even in the darkness.

"I'm Peter Beaudine. Kentucky's my home."

"Well," she said, "I am Amy Sutter, and my home's just over yonder. Get some rest now."

"You do the same, Miss Amy. And, thanks to you, again."

An unexplained shiver passed over Amy as she returned to the house, and a queer, tender smile played across her lips as she repeated the name in her mind. Peter Beaudine. Tomorrow she would ask what he had been doing in those woods. She would see if he truly was a Union man. She would introduce him to Jim, but not to Clary. Her child was old enough now to let a word slip here and there about strangers in the shed and whispers in the black night.

Now, in the shed, the courier lay back in contemplation. He ached like almighty Hades, every muscle in him feeling contorted and drained. His right arm was almost totally useless, but his stomach was full and his mind was full. He closed his eyes and still the picture of the woman's frothy, bright hair entered his brain. *It's like a halo*, he thought, *a halo on the angel who saved my life. Maybe I just imagined it, maybe I only imagined her.* A gentle burp and the sweet aftertaste of mush and honey told him it had been real, and he turned as gingerly as possible to the position he would sleep in for several hours.

In the morning Amy awakened early, earlier than her usual hour, and lay on her bed considering the day ahead. She would fix Jim some breakfast before he went to the mill, and feed Clary if she were awake. She might eat something herself before visiting the young man outside. These immediate events passed quickly through her mind, but the sequence played only once. Her anticipated meeting with Peter Beaudine repeated itself over and over, in spite of her conscious attempt to get past it to the remainder of the day. She pictured him lying there, still asleep, breathing softly in the slanted rays of the morning sun. His hair would be tousled and fall over one eye, and he would resemble an innocent child caught in the middle of some pleasing dream. There would be a little smile on his lips. She remembered the feel of them while she fed him last night. They were curved and deeply colored and soft, almost womanly, though nestled in the prickly growth of beard. A small twist of emotion swelled in the pit of her stomach. She had not been touched this way by the thought of a man since Calvin went away.

Jim was already up, moving about the kitchen, starting a cooking fire. She could hear Clary turn in the trundle and then call her *Mama*. The sequence was interrupted now. Jim would be the first to go to the shed and take the breakfast out, while she attended to Clary. It was only proper, and she feared he might notice some new eagerness in her words which hadn't been there before. She jumped out of bed quickly and threw on her dress, thinking to give him the news that their charge had taken food last night. As she walked beside Clary's bed, the child looked up at her and said, "The man in the shed was callin' for somebody last night, Mama. I heared him."

Jim turned away from his fire building and watched her as she entered the kitchen. "I heard him too, and had to go out and shush him. He must've been havin' a dream, and he seems a whole lot more pert now than before. He was callin' out a name, but I didn't catch it. I told him if he wanted to keep on dreamin' he'd best keep shut at night. I don't care how fine the gal was. You should've seen his face when I walked in. I think he was expectin' his mama or somebody. Loo! I am sure glad to see him come around."

"I know he's come around, Jim. I was goin' to tell you he took some mush last night, but you were already asleep on your bed. I went to check him and he was wide awake. Even asked if he was dead."

"He don't look it now. Throw a couple more eggs in the pan and I'll see if he'll take somethin' this early." Clary peeped through the doorway, rubbing the night's sleep from her eyes and grasping a little crocheted coverlet tightly. Her expression belied slight fear. "Is there a dead man in the shed, Mama? Did he talk to me last night?" Jim crossed the room and scooped his grandchild into his arms, smiling broadly. "Ain't no dead men around here, Cotton, but there is somethin' you got to know and keep quiet about."

Amy was glad Jim was willing to explain the situation to Clary, and she reflected quickly that she would be sorry one day to take her away from her grandfather's influence. The fire was right now, the frying pan was hot enough to throw in some thick slabs of pork rind, and she whipped a dozen eggs into the grease. The smell of sizzling salt and fat filled the kitchen and drifted on the breeze to Peter Beaudine's eager senses. He felt crazy with hunger, feverish with curiosity about the woman and man who had saved his life. And he wondered if there were more than just the two of them who knew about his predicament.

Peter vaguely recalled the circumstance of his injuries. It had happened in the dark woods, and he seemed to remember Buckshot suddenly hurling forward, and himself flying back-side over head into the trees; then maybe some yelling and blows, followed by the hot flash of lead entering his body. After that, he could recall nothing. How many days had passed, he wondered, and how long before he'd be able to move his right arm and hand.

Filled as he was with questions, when Jim brought the pan of eggs to him, Peter's hunger overcame his curiosity and he wanted to eat like a man giving up a long fast. Jim urged him to slow down and withheld bites. "Take it easy, son. It'll all come back on you suckin' it up like that. There's plenty more when you are a little stronger."

Again, it seemed the very act of eating tired him tremendously. He stopped and lay back to rest. He reached out his good hand to Jim in a gesture of gratitude and spoke in a low voice. "I cannot thank you enough times for what you're doin'. I'd be a dead man by now if not for you." Jim grasped the young man's hand firmly and answered in a slow drawl. "It's the least we could do for a soldier, son." His thoughts reached back in time to Calvin, and he wondered if anyone had given solace to his boy before death came. He continued, "We feel you'll get your health back, though maybe not the use of your arm. That's hard to tell right now, but your fever seems to have broke and that's a good sign. I don't see no signs of gangrene and the wounds are healin' right well. You're still real weak, so you'll have to take it slow."

Peter was confused at the generosity of this southern woodsman, but decided against revealing his identity as a Union soldier at this point. The last thing he wanted was to wind up in a prison camp, and his hopes that the war was soon ending had been dashed so many times that he had given up thinking about it.

Jim finished spooning the eggs to Peter's mouth and wiped the little spills from his beard. When he went back to the house, Amy had changed into a clean apron and he noticed her hair was pulled behind her ears by some pretty barrettes that she rarely wore. The kitchen was righted already and his plate of food was covered by a pie tin, so it kept warm. Clary played with a rag doll on the doorstep.

"Well, he ate every bit and looks like he savored it down to the last lick. You might want to look to his bandages in a while. Seems like a nice boy, though he wasn't givin' away no name or rank yet. Never mind. Could be he's scared to tell us just now."

Amy was eager to speak. "His name's Peter Beaudine. He's from Kentucky," she spouted quickly. "He told me that much last night."

Jim did not look up from his breakfast, but sensed her excitement. "Kentucky, eh? Then he could be Union *or* secesh.

We'll just have to feel him out. Meantime, I got to go to the mill."

Amy bustled about before seeing Jim off. She dressed Clary in a fresh white smock, prepared her to meet the mysterious man in the shed, and gathered the clean linen to dress his injuries. "He has some wounds and that keeps him from bein' someone you can play with. Don't be jumpin' on his lap or throwin' your arms around his neck just 'cause he's friendly. He's still mighty sore."

She took Clary's hand in hers and walked slowly to the shed, deliberately checking her pace. When they reached the doorway she hesitated briefly, then rapped on the rough hewn wood. "Hello in there! I've come to check your bandages. Are you decent?"

She heard a slight shifting from within, then his response. "I'm as decent now as I'll ever get in my condition. Pass on through!"

Amy opened the door a few inches and peered into the dim corner where he lay. Clary did the same and squinched her eyes. "I can't see nobody, Mama," she said.

As Peter eagerly watched the door swing open, the morning light struck Amy and Clary's billowing curls, and illuminated them with delicacy. Their heads looked as though they were covered with golden, shimmering lace. Peter smiled. He thought he had never seen such a beautiful or welcome sight in his life. Then, as suddenly, his smile dropped, for he feared now that Amy and the man were somehow inexplicably married and this was their little girl.

Soon all eyes were adjusted to the dusty, dim light of the shed, and Clary was properly introduced to Peter. "She knows," said Amy, assuring Peter of secrecy. "She also knows we do not mention to anyone that you are here. But I need to ask you, though I am fairly sure already, if you are Union or Confederate."

Peter saw occasion to tease her. "If you are fairly sure, then you tell me."

Amy played into his tease and tossed her head slightly. "I say you are Union, and you need not be afraid because of it either."

"Either way, I'm not afraid, but tell me how you came to conclude Union."

"Well, if you must know, it was your unmentionables that gave me the clue." Amy turned her eyes toward the low ceiling and studied the webbed rafters overhead. Peter was incredulous, and nearly lurched out of his hay bed. "My *what?*"

Clary began to titter and slapped her hand over her mouth. Amy laughed as well. "I'm sorry, but when Jim and I found you, that's all you was wearin', and they looked to be newish, like someone had shipped 'em from up North. It's not like I peeped or anythin'. Besides that, there you were, ridin' through the woods, no doubt on a big horse, carryin' a message of sorts. I say you are a Union courier. Nobody else would have been in the woods at that hour."

"Except you and your husband, it seems." Peter interjected quickly.

"Jim and I heard the shots and figured it was Tommy Jackson and his gang up to no good, so we headed quick to the woods and saw them hie to the west with a big horse in tow and your pants flappin' in the breeze, tied on to a sourwood stick. We lay low for a few minutes to make sure it was all clear. Then we carried you back here and sweated like slaves at auction to stop your bleedin'. More'n once I thought you'd be a goner."

Peter was staring at her now, once more stricken with gratitude. "I can't believe you'd risk so much for a man you guessed to be Union. How long have I been here, anyway?"

"Goin' on seven days now. Like I said, it was touch and go."

"Well, besides my newish lookin' drawers, was there anythin' else of mine you found in the woods?"

"No, and Jim did go back and have a look-see later."

"I always did carry the Testament that Laurel gave me. I hope that whoever took it will one day read it, and maybe get some good from it."

Clary had been tugging at Amy's sleeve since midway through the conversation. "Mama," she said, "who is your husband? Who's he talkin' about?"

She smiled down at Clary, and answered seriously. "I reckon he's talkin' about Jim, little one."

Clary looked at Peter with disbelief. "Jim ain't nobody's husband. He's my granddaddy!"

Peter cocked his head and questioned Amy with his gaze. She reddened slightly and explained. "Jim's my father-in-law. Clary's daddy was killed at Shiloh, fightin' for the Union. I guess we'll stay here with Jim, until the war's over, at least."

"Oh, I am sorry to hear that. About your husband, I mean."

He lied through his teeth, and wasn't even going to ask forgiveness for it. "And you are right about me bein' Union. I was on my way to deliver a message at the next Union camp when my horse went down. I thought he'd just tripped."

"Not hardly. The lowlifes in the woods must've strung a rope across the path the night before so they could easy plunder anybody comin' through. They're nothin' but scum anyway."

"Rotten, lousy bastards!" Clary's high pitched baby voice seemed to stir even the dust particles playing in the morning sun. Amy and Peter both stared open-mouthed at her. She had jumped up and stomped her foot on the hay strewn floor, and thrust her lower lip away from her chin. Amy was aghast. She grabbed Clary by the shoulders and glared at the child. "Where'd you ever hear such talk, girl?

Clary's lip retreated quickly. "I heared it at church. It was Uncle Willie, when he was mad at the army." Peter forced himself to stifle a snicker. The little girl had suddenly brought to mind his own sister, Laurel, who seemed to pick up the same kind of language when she was about Clary's age. He watched as Amy composed herself and dealt with her child. "Well, we will just have to have a little talk with Uncle Willie next time we go to church." She rubbed her hand through Clary's hair and tousled the curls even further. "Why don't you run on up to the house and see to Bullseye? Bet he's real hungry by now."

Clary leaped at the chance to feed Bullseye. That hound was by her side most of the day, and she called him her best friend. She scurried from the shed and left Amy and Peter to shake their heads together and release their laughter.

"She puts me in mind of my sister Laurel. She was forever embarrassin' my ma, comin' out with the same kind of talk. Only she didn't hear it at church. My daddy is generally a quiet man, but he could swear a blue streak and cuss a coon out of a tree. She figured if Daddy said it, it was all right."

"Well, that's one thing I'm glad of. Jim is not a bad talkin' man. He's an elder at the church, and quiet, generally. I never even saw him cry when the news came about Calvin. He just went into the woods and stayed there a long time. When he came out he was dry eyed and did everything he could to console me. Only every so often do I see him stare off into the hills, and I know it's then he's thinkin' of Cal."

Peter sat up a bit and pulled a piece of straw, placing it between his teeth. "What do you do when you think of him?" He hoped the question wasn't intrusive.

"Oh, me? Why, I try not to think on it too much anymore. A person has got to get on with livin'. Besides that, I got Clary and Jim to look after. There's other things too, because of the war." She felt she should change the subject, so she began to unwind the fresh linen. "We'd best see to those bandages right now."

Peter nodded his head and let Amy do her work in silence. It felt right. It felt natural to have her gentle but firm hands wash his wounds. He still couldn't do much for himself with the arm hanging limp at his side, and the despairing thought came to him that if ever he were to embrace her, it would be with the one good arm only. He began to be tired again, and knew that when she left, he would sleep a little, maybe dream. And then what?

Chapter Seven

Just Two Now

Jesse and Marcus figured nine more days of good riding would get them to Springfield on schedule. Marcus talked of little else, unless Jesse steered him to some other subject. The newspaper they bought before leaving Paducah was filled with very little other news than the funeral procession, accounts of John Wilkes Booth, the hated assassin, and the effect of Lincoln's death far and wide. Photographs of the living and deceased president appeared on every page. Quotations from close cabinet members, ministers, foreign dignitaries, and friends of the family were crammed between advertising spaces.

The farther north they rode, the closer they got to Lincoln country. Kentucky claimed him as his mother state, but Illinois had sent him to Washington, and was now prepared to stretch out her arms and envelope him in eternal rest.

"You know," said Marcus, continuing his endless stream of observation, "they say that Mr. Lincoln suffered from melancholia his whole life and that he often dreamed of the future. Some reports have it that he foresaw his own funeral, actually looked into the coffin and saw himself in it! If even half the stories I have read concerning him are true, he was indeed a remarkable man."

Jesse was inclined to agree. "I can see now, that the war could have had no other outcome, Daddy. When I looked at all the boys dyin' around me, at the end it didn't matter if they wore blue or gray or butternut dyed shirts, or whatever; I knew the right would win. I guess I'm prepared to admit that the Confederacy's cause was lost from the beginnin'. Damn! Most of those southern boys who died never even owned a slave themselves." He regretted his slip of the tongue. "Sorry about the 'damn' there, Daddy. Too much time in the ranks, I guess."

Marcus said simply, "Son, I have heard a lot worse language than that. But I do appreciate your sentiments. I would never myself, even if I'd had the means, have kept a slave. It goes against the grain. I guess Mr. Lincoln felt the same."

He halted his horse within a few paces of a downed log at the roadside. "I just have to dismount for a short while, Jesse. My back is tied up in knots."

As they rested, he read aloud from the paper. "This is reprinted from the *New York Herald*. See what you think. 'Whatever judgment may have been formed by those who were opposed to him as to the caliber of our deceased Chief Magistrate, or the place he is destined to occupy in history, all men of undisturbed observation must have recognized in Mr. Lincoln a quaintness, originality, courage, honesty, magnanimity, and popular force of character such as never heretofore, in the annals of the human family, had the advantage of so eminent a stage for their display. He was essentially a mixed product of the agricultural, forensic, and frontier life of this continent—as indigenous to our soil as the cranberry crop, as American in his fiber as the granite foundations of the Appalachian range. He may not have been, and perhaps was not, our most perfect product in any one branch of mental or moral education; but, taking him for all in all, the very noblest impulses, peculiarities, and aspirations of our whole people—what may be called our continental idiosyncracies—were more collectively and vividly reproduced in his genial and yet unswerving nature than in that of any other public man of whom our chronicles bear record.'"

"That," replied Jesse, "is a mouthful." He sat for a moment, reflecting, then asked Marcus a question. "Do you suppose it's true all they say about Mrs. Lincoln? I've heard stories about her that would curl an Indian's hair."

"I don't know. At first I thought the tales were flying from his political enemies, trying to discredit him further through her. But over the years, several verifiable stories have been printed, by reliable sources, mind you, so that I am forced to believe she is not all put together. In fact, there's an article in this very paper telling about her hysteria at the president's bedside." Marcus began to shuffle the sheets of newsprint, searching for the same.

Jesse heard a whoop and a shout coming from the field to the south of them. A man was riding through the newly plowed loam, his horse kicking up clods and dust on every side. Jesse moaned, removed his hat and passed his fingers through his hair. Marcus looked up as well, and joined in Jesse's lament.

"Not Cougar again!" he said in near disgust. "I thought maybe that shouting farmer had caught up with him and settled the honor affair."

Cougar's horse slid to a halt just short of them. The unwelcome rider leaped off, smiling and slapping dust from his pants and boot tops. "Well, dog my cats! I knowed I'd catch up to you Campbells somewheres along the way. We're still headin' for Springfield, ain't we?"

If Cougar noticed any negative reaction from the father and son, he ignored it and began to rifle through the haversack slung over his horse. "Sucker! I'm clean out of smokes! Could I ask the loan of some tobaccy, Jess? I'm dyin' for a draw here."

Jesse handed him a plug and studied Cougar's horse for a long moment. "Say, Coug, that's not Mary's horse there, is it? Looks like a different color on it."

"Same horse, Jess. But you're right about the color. I had me a little trouble a short while back and so I got the loan of some stove blackin' and kinda gave old Hester here a dye job. Anybody lookin' for a man on a brown horse might just pass by one who was ridin' a black one."

Marcus shook his head in obvious displeasure. He buried himself further in the newspaper while Jesse ran the flat of his hand along Hester's flank. It came up sooty and sweaty. "That horse sweats anymore, she'll leave a trail. Where've you been since we last saw you, Coug?"

"Damndest thing ever, Jess. I had a supper invite that last night from a sweet little thing just across the field from where we was camped, and I didn't want to wake you fellahs up, and Jesse, I don't want to put down your cookin', but the promise of home baked bread and fresh ham was too much to pass up, so I just kinda walked out nice and quiet. When I come back in the mornin', why you two was already gone."

Jesse fiddled with the reins and the bit in his horse's mouth and answered Cougar innocently. "Well, I don't know how that could be. We stayed around quite a while waitin' for you to show up. We got worried when even the smell of bacon didn't bring you out of the bush. And then, the strangest old farmer came ridin' through the field, hollerin' his head off, lookin' for some young, scruffy type, I think he said. Seems the fellow he was after had taken some advantage somewhere on his property, and he was bound to . . . " Jesse hesitated, appearing to search for the farmer's exact expression. "Oh yeah, said he was bound by honor to string the man up by whatever was hangin' loose."

Cougar's eyes shifted from the horizon to his worn boots. "Must've been one of them Kentuckians. They're a dang strange bunch, so I hear." Then, changing the subject, he looked at Marcus. "What you readin' there, Mr. Campbell? Seems you always got your nose stuck in a book or paper." Marcus responded without looking up. "I am reading several accounts about Mr. Lincoln. The news is full of nothing else."

Cougar hunkered on the ground next to Hester and played with a stray twig as he continued. "There ain't nothin' in it about no mixup at a card game is there? I, uh, watched a game where a fellah got shot and I thought maybe there'd be somethin' wrote up about it."

Marcus stood abruptly. "No, there isn't. No card game news, no fresh bread and ham news, no wanted man on a brown horse news. Only important news." He replaced his paper and climbed onto his horse, speaking directly to Jesse. "It's time we got on the road again, son."

Cougar again ignored the slight and jumped back to his borrowed horse. "I suppose you two have been gettin' along fine since we parted ways, but to tell the truth, I get a might lonesome on the road. Hope you don't mind me still taggin' along."

Jesse glanced toward Marcus, who averted his gaze altogether. *I guess it's up to me,* Jesse thought, and answered curtly. "As long as we don't have any honor bound fathers showin' up or trigger happy card players followin' us, I guess it's all right. And I advise you to slosh Hester through the first creek we hit, because she's lookin' a little marbly around the flanks."

"Well, thanks, Jesse. I'll just do that. And, say, you wouldn't have a swallow of anythin' with you, would you?"

"Not the swamp water you're after. Plain well water is all we carry. You're welcome to some of that." Marcus rode as far ahead of or behind Cougar as he could, biting his tongue and trying to control his thoughts. The notion that the worthless trouble maker could put them in a predicament or delay their journey gnawed at him, and inspired him to devise wild plans in order to be rid of the millstone on the runny horse. He was ashamed of it, but he couldn't seem to stem the tide of erratic thoughts lodging in his mind. Mile after mile, he wondered what Jesse was thinking, and if together they could find a way to be rid of Cougar.

Marcus was still lost in this train of thought when his horse suddenly stumbled. The mare pitched forward and then rolled on her side. Marcus was not quick enough to leap free of the thundering animal, and fell beneath her, his leg caught from the knee down. He cried out in agonized pain. As Jesse reached them, the horse made an effort to rise, allowing him just enough time to pull Marcus free of the tremendous weight. The horse screamed wildly from her struggle and it was clear that her leg had snapped. Cougar joined them and made the final assessment.

"That horse has got to be shot. I'll take care of it, Jesse. You just see to your daddy, there." Jesse was grateful for the help, and glad now that they had not been alone when this happened. Reaching gingerly to inspect his father's leg, he discovered that the knee had probably sustained the worst injury, and Marcus needed immediate help.

The shot fired from Cougar's rifle rang over the meadow, and the mare was immediately still. Jesse turned and instructed Cougar to ride back to the last farmhouse they had passed and bring a wagon. Marcus had broken into a sweat but felt clammy to his touch.

"I'm shaking like a leaf, Jesse. It's shock. Cover me and get me some water. My whole leg feels crushed." Marcus was trying to remain calm, but could not control the convulsive trembling of his body. Even his teeth rattled.

"Read me something, Jesse, while we wait. Read me the itinerary of the train. Anything!"

Within the hour Cougar returned. Hester was at a full gallop, far ahead of a plow horse doing its best to escape the long leather whip of his owner. Cougar had enlisted a ragged looking farm couple on the road to help out. Marcus was loaded as gently as possible into the rattle trap wagon, which Jesse thought didn't look much more satisfactory than the infamous three-wheeled ambulances every soldier had come to fear. He rode as close as he could to the side of it and watched anxiously as Marcus flopped like a puppet in the rough board bed.

The physician's place was only a few miles north, but every rut and rock in the roadway caused Marcus jagged pain, as the wagon jolted beneath him. The farmer urged the old horse forward with cussing and shouts, while his wife tried to keep Marcus from rolling off the pile of quilts they had provided for his comfort. When they arrived at the doctor's home, Jesse realized the money belt would have to be exposed, so he asked for just a moment alone with his father. They removed it from Marcus's belt, and Jesse secured it around his own waist, letting his shirt flap over it. He had taken out a few dollars to offer the farmer and pay up front to the physician. Cougar glanced swiftly at Jesse's hand as the money was exposed, and swore in a whisper under his breath. When the doctor came in, Marcus refused the suggestion of brandy, but accepted the laudanum handed to him for pain.

"I'll examine him and let you know what we need to do. Just take a seat outside, if you would, and try not to worry." Jesse and the others were dismissed quickly and found themselves staring at one another.

"His horse must've stepped in a gopher hole," said Cougar.

"More'n likely a snake hole it was," countered the farmer. "Road's thick with 'em hereabouts. Where was you all headed before this happened?"

Cougar answered before Jesse could get a word out. "We're goin' to Springfield to see us a dead man." Then he laughed. "Like we never seen any before, eh, Jesse? The war 'bout did us in for that. But they wasn't none of them presidents, so this one's kinda different."

The farmer's face registered shock. "Are you speakin' of Mr. Lincoln that way?"

Jesse quickly interrupted. "Don't mind Cougar here. He's just back from the war and is not used to polite society yet. We, that is, my Daddy and I, are on our way to Springfield to pay our respects and he, that's Cougar here, wanted to come along." Then, noting the expression on the wife's face, changed the subject. "We surely do appreciate your comin' to our aid so fast. Will this cover your time and trouble?" He extended his hand to the man, offering a few bills.

The woman stepped forward and gaped. "This here's good cash money!" Then she reached out a brown, wizened, child-size hand and snatched it from him. She cast a hasty glance at her husband and turned to Jesse. "You and your daddy are welcome to stay with us while he mends. Reckon you might have to miss the ceremonies up north though, for he ain't goin' to heal overnight."

"Well," said Jesse, hesitantly. "I'll talk it over with him after the doc is finished. But thank you kindly for the offer."

She backed away and edged close to wagon. Moving to the horse and concealing herself behind him, she stuffed the money into the bosom of her dress. Her husband continued to glare at Cougar and began a harangue against the South, heaping praises on the Union army, General Grant, and especially the late, great President Lincoln.

It was determined that Marcus's knee would have to be opened up and bone fragments removed. He would spend the next two nights at the doctor's residence and then be moved to the farmer's house. Jesse was welcome to hold over with the farmer and Cougar could come along if he had no where else to go. The day began to wear away and after he was stitched up, Marcus slept. The farmer and his wife had returned to their home, leaving Jesse and Cougar to camp out behind the doctor's house. Cougar speedily found an excuse to wander into the small community and Jesse knew he'd be gone most of the night. He could do no more worrying about what ruckus might follow his erratic friend, and settled himself in for the night. He had Marcus's things slung over the back of his own horse, and pondered what to do with the extra saddle.

The night was clear and a slight breeze bore the heavy scent of spring blossoms across the orchards to Jesse's encampment. At any given point during the war he remembered thinking he might never find rest like this again. One such evening came to mind. It was after his regiment had been engaged in a hand to hand skirmish, and he, as a foot soldier, was already fed up with these face-offs. Hand-to-hand combat was dreaded. A man looked into another man's eyes while fighting like this and could feel his opponent's sweat on his skin. The battle had been brief but fierce, and he had barely escaped serious injury twice. He remembered lying down to sleep that night, surrounded by the sounds of suffering men and calls for relief when none came. He was awakened numerous times by his mess-mate, a boy named Charles, from the outskirts of Murfreesboro, whose dreams were full of fear. He had thought of Jen and other nights, and other circumstances, and believed they had all been illusions. When he had risen the next morning, he discovered that Charles had apparently deserted. It was the first time the thought had crossed his own mind.

Now it was April, and he feared he would finish his father's journey alone. Certainly Marcus could not continue the trip to Springfield, and even if Cougar went with him, Jesse knew they would be at cross purposes. For the first time in many months he let his eyes rest upon the stars as they punctuated the soft, black night. Some of his gentle nature was returning and, looking inward, he glimpsed the tender feelings he once had. The harshness and bitterness of war that had created a brittle shell around his spirit began to retreat little by little. It was being with Marcus that had initiated his rebirth.

Tomorrow, he thought, I will ask Marcus if I should go on ahead without him. Having come this far, it would be a shame if they both missed it, and Jesse was now fully embraced by the same mystique that had drawn his father. Sleep was not coming to him, although he was settled comfortably and felt dog-tired. He was now past thinking about Jen with regret. She had become a pleasant, warm blur, rather tucked away with other boyhood dreams, perhaps like the quilts in the quiet corners of his mother's chiffarobe. Instead his mind was filling with the most recent encounters he'd had. The strapping young woman in the dining room at the boarding house became foremost. She wasn't mannish, but she seemed to embody the same strong qualities a person might expect from a frontiersman or a homesteader. She had looked determined and hard in a way, but Jesse sensed something bewilderingly feminine in her victory over the troublemakers. Perhaps it was the way she strode from the room, the insulted air she bore. A man would have stayed and fought with his fists. She hadn't needed to do that, and still got away holding the upper hand. And, in spite of the insult she had slung at him, he was attracted to and moved by her. Overhead, a rush of bat wings charged from the eaves of the doctor's house, and he could see the darting, pointed wings pass across the face of the moon. Jesse had chosen purposefully to sleep on the green, fresh grass, although he had been invited to stay in the small parlor. It was stuffy inside, and smelled of formaldehyde, reminding him of the improvised hospitals, so quickly thrown up during the war. Most men who went in emerged feet first, and some, he recalled, with no feet at all.

At last he slept, and sleeping, he had hoped to dream of the girl in the dining room. In her stead came the vision of two men at Andersonville—the lanky, raggedy figure of the preacher and the haunting, faceless young soldier whose life Jesse had ended. Peter Beaudine, again.

Chapter Eight

ON TO SPRINGFIELD

When Jesse and Marcus were left alone the next morning, they both knew what the answer to Jesse's question would be. Marcus was adamant, overcoming the obvious pain gripping him. He spoke with intensity.

"Jesse, you've got to go on! Be my eyes and ears and my pen. I'll be following you in my thoughts the whole time. Take most of the money and get what you need and record everything you see. It's important to me, Jesse. If I can't make it, by Heaven, you've got to do it for me!"

"You want me to take your journal, Daddy? I don't know if I can do it justice. I have never been much of a writer."

"Just your impressions will be good enough for me. Just write down everything you notice—the trappings on the train, the way the houses look draped in respect, the faces of the people there, the smells in the streets. Record the feel of the air and the mood of the crowd. That kind of thing. Go ahead and read what I've already written. Your writing doesn't have to be like mine, but reading mine will help you see the things I notice and find important."

"Do you think you'll be all right? I really hate to think of leavin' you here alone." Jesse was torn with this decision before him, and knowing its finality didn't make it any easier.

"That farmer and his wife will be glad to have me stay over the while during your absence. Believe me, they need the money badly. Now, you go on. Leave the saddle and other tack for the doctor, and we can settle things all around when you get back."

He winced as he tried to shift his injured leg. One more thing. "If Cougar goes on with you, be sure to keep a close eye on the money. I don't trust him as far as I can throw him."

"That would be about two inches right now. Don't worry, Daddy. I'll be extra careful anyway. I have an idea you went without plenty to get this much together, and I'm not about to lose it."

There were several days of hard riding ahead for Jesse. He replenished supplies for the road, embraced his father, and took a cursory look around the small community for Cougar. Not finding him was something of a relief, and Jesse rode away determined to do justice to Marcus's journal and ride in peace to Springfield.

Every evening on the way, he took out the precious journal and after reading an account from Marcus's view-point, skipped to the next blank page and recorded his own thoughts. Jesse liked writing his observations about the sur-roundings. It was a restful thing to do at the close of a hard day's ride, and caused him to concentrate on more than the discomfort of being on horseback all those hours. If Cou-gar had attempted to join him on the way to Springfield, he was merely a shadow behind him, unseen and unheard. Jesse decided to give him no more thought, and, as he rode nearer and nearer the Illinois state capitol, the highway be-came more crowded with other pilgrims, bent on the same destination. He recorded their faces and paraphernalia, the size of their families, the entertainments of the children as they ran and played beside the wagons. There were child-less travelers, couples toting the generation before and after them, all piled in the ricketiest of horse-drawn wagons. They came from everywhere, on their way to see Old Abe for the last time, to savor the trip, and to tell the story over and again to future audiences. Jesse supposed this is what would happen to his and Marcus's account as well, even if it never was printed in the *Register*.

Chapter Nine

THE BEAUDINES

As the days of Peter's recovery passed, word filtered into Georgia that the Confederacy was lost, Negroes were indeed to be free, Abraham was dead. What? Abraham Lincoln dead? The worst blow for the south, many swore, for the vice president was surely not of the same magnanimous temperament as Father Abraham. It was said that Mary Lincoln, of the Kentucky Todds, had gone mad the moment she knew her husband was dead. John Wilkes Boothe, the assassin, was hunted like a dog and killed.

These events touched the lives of everyone in the divided country, but it was the personal stories that would live in memory. Where were you when Shiloh was lost? Did you hear Old Abe speak at Gettysburg with your own ears?

How'd you lose that leg? Come closer; my eyesight's about gone since the war. So much had happened to Peter since that rude interruption in the woods, but now he was actually grateful for Tommy Jackson's interference in his life.

While Jesse Campbell made his way to Springfield, Peter made his way around the Sutter cabin, and though he still slept in the shed, the days found him puttering dreamily inside the cabin. While Jim was alone with Amy one morning, he teased her. "Looks like Peter should be well enough soon to head on back up north. That's where the opportunity will be, and his family must be worried sick about him," Jim said. Seeing a slight pout cloud her face, he continued. "Though I must say, his healin' seems to be takin' a powerful long time for such a strappin' fella. Either he's seein' the advantages of a good situation or a certain cotton-haired young lady is causin' the slowdown."

He watched her squirm as she swept dust out of the door and into the filtered sun. She was nearly blushing, not a thing she was accustomed to doing. "Oh, Jim," she answered. "He's so good to entertain Clary and she just loves him. He keeps her out of my way while I work. I suppose soon enough he'll be goin' on up north, back to his own family." Jim studied her face and saw that the thought vaguely chilled her. True, Amy knew Peter must be anxious about seeing his family again. He would certainly have to write to them soon or have her write the letter for him if his arm didn't heal faster.

In her heart Amy hoped the actual writing would be strung out many more days. She had taken over almost the full care of her Yankee courier, and though he was able to manage the basic personal duties, he still needed some help. Though the regaining of mobility and usefulness in Peter's arm was taking a long time, anyone within yards of the two of them could have seen what was coming. Jim Sutter was no fool, but until now had kept his peace. At that moment they heard Peter's footsteps coming up the path, and the subject was changed to the weather—another hot one coming today; bet you could fry an egg on a flat rock.

Later that same day, while Jim was busied at the mill and Clary napped, the heat and humidity drew Amy and Peter to the spring house to eat their noon dinner. They had often eaten there, where the damp, cool shade and bubbling water invigorated an otherwise slow afternoon. Amy matched Peter's casual pace, so the walk was leisurely and pleasant, and her steps became graceful next to his careful strides. Letting her walk slightly ahead, he noticed the swing at the hem of her best gingham skirt and the shimmer of the sun through her hair. He had noticed before, standing beside her, he was just tall enough that she had to tilt her chin to raise her eyes to his, and when she raised her eyes, they seemed to pull the corners of her mouth upward. The tilting and the raising and the smiling became one single movement, so that each time he thought of her she was executing this same motion and expression.

Amy had drawn her impressions as well. She liked looking up to meet his eyes, and took note of the way his lids lowered sleepily and that his gaze was slow but playful. She often felt that gaze from behind, but purposely guarded herself from turning to face it. Today she felt it was no longer avoidable.

She led the way down the impossibly green path to the spring house. Peter's presence behind her was like a great blanket of heat as she sensed every movement of his body and felt his eyes studying her hair. She knew if she turned immediately she would see the crooked, boyish grin that she often had glimpsed as they talked. It was now a part of her day, that grin, and she looked forward to seeing it. When she thought of it, a burning tingle shot through her wrists, winding up somewhere in the pit of her stomach. Her feelings were intense. This new consciousness made her want to burst, and her sense of it was that Peter felt the same way. She believed she would explode if his hand touched hers, or, if he once brushed against her arm, she would faint dead away. They reached the spring house quickly, where inside the air was damp and the temperature was constantly several degrees cooler than outside. The effect always chilled Amy, and today she allowed herself to shiver openly. She had put down the basket and was just beginning to rub the goosebumps from her bare limbs when she found herself suddenly enveloped in Peter. Not just by his arms, but in the folds of his shirt, the hollow beneath his chin, by the warmth of his breath on her hair. He was wordlessly, wonderfully everywhere, surrounding her and flowing through her veins. Weeks of restraint gave way to powerful emotion and she responded by returning his fiercely warm embrace. She had not held a man in her arms or kissed anyone except Clary since Calvin had gone to war. Now, Peter was overwhelming. After a few moments, she pulled away, breathless.

Peter spoke first. "Amy," he whispered her name hoarsely. "I can't get around it anymore. I love you! I can't be here with you without wantin' you." His whole upper body shuddered with feeling. "I'm sorry. It just came over me. I didn't mean to insult you or anythin'."

Amy's composure was lost. She shook her head and straightened her apron, still trying to steady her own breathing. "Oh, Peter! I'm not insulted. It's just a little scary."

"I know. I'm not whole yet. My arm, bein' this way. I hate it!"

"Oh, please Peter. Don't think that bothers me. You'll heal with time. I just meant, you're the first since Cal left. I was all closed up after that. It's kind of like the dam busted open just now and the rush was more than I could handle." She reached for him gently. "The truth is, Pete, I've kept my feelin's bottled up too."

"Well, hey Amy, shall I go? Should I stay and court you from the shed?"

Suddenly becoming coy, she folded her hands behind her back and lowered her head. "Why, Mr. Beaudine, sir, you shall stay and court me until the cows come home if you like." She paused and raised her eyes to his. "Seein' as how I have no better prospects and have already glimpsed your unmentionables, I think that's the only honorable thing we can do."

Another long embrace and series of kisses committed them entirely to each other. The question of him returning home came up shortly after, when Peter began projecting a future for them together. It would, of course, include the family he had left behind in Kentucky. He wondered what their reaction would be, how they would accept Amy and furthermore, how she would accept them. In truth, he couldn't know that most of his family had given up on ever seeing him again. Back in Kentucky, his sister Laurel had resigned herself to his probable death and now saw him buried in one of those common ditch graves somewhere in the south. Her heart had been broken by his departure, so soon on the heels of their father's return with a disabling injury. She had begged him to stay home, not because she was afraid of the work he left behind, but because she loved him more dearly than anyone else in the world.

Peter's father, Clive Beaudine, expected now that his son was a war casualty as well. Even though Clive had served in the corps of engineers and built roads for the troops, he had seen so much of destruction that he often wondered how anyone came back whole or living.

Other misfortunes that struck the family after Clive returned were only enlarged by his eldest son's absence. Peter's younger brother, Arthur, had been the cause of their greatest misfortune when, while playing with hot cinders from the fireplace, he set the frame home afire. It wasn't something he thought of or dreamed would ever happen; Arthur rarely foresaw consequences in his actions. The Beaudines lost almost everything they owned and had to start all over. Left to his own devices, Arthur was not bothered one way or the other about Peter coming home. His mind darted from one subject to another with regularity, and the only subject that fixed itself upon him was the war. After Peter left, Arthur pestered his parents to let him join up too, and rattled on endlessly about what he would do to those Rebs or Yankees, or whoever it was they were supposed to be fighting. Arthur was sincere; he was fiery and impetuous. The problem was, Arthur was addled and, as his own mother put it, about as dumb as lint—as dim as twilight, she often said, and would smile at Arthur, who took all of her pronouncements as clever and witty.

Hattie Shane Beaudine held views of the world unfamiliar to most strangers and often insulting to those around her. She was also the lone optimist in the family, and clung to the notion that one day Peter would indeed return home. She saw it in signs all around and read it in the direction of the evening wind. A certain motion on the pond early in the morning would spell return on its otherwise smooth surface. Her eccentricities were legend in and around Lone Oak, and people pitied Clive at having cast his lot with her. She knew what they said and always had her own retort ready.

As often as she would hear a story bandied around about her she would seek the originator of the offending comment and face off against him or her. "You are a brainless stump-jumpin', clod kicker with yellow meat for innards. If you had any guts at all, and I'm not sayin' you do, you'da come to me personally with your tripe instead of noisin' it around town. Anytime you care to fling another complaint about me or my family to the wind like you did last week, you will do it at your own risk. I got me a few new spells I'm itchin' to try out on the likes of you!"

Everybody knew she was referring to witchcraft of some nebulous sort, and that she, as the territory dowser, threatened long-forgotten curses she claimed originated with her Scottish ancestors. If any of Hattie's three children inherited her queer ways, he or she was careful to keep it hidden, even Arthur.

Now, as Peter knew he must tell Amy somewhat about his family, he found difficulty in explaining them to her without portraying a clan of misfits. He knew he was part of them, but suddenly he began to feel as if he had grown up in the company of clowns. His father was quiet, he told her, and meant henpecked. His sister was outspoken and strong, he said, but he really meant tomboyish and rowdy. His brother Arthur—well, there was no getting around it. Arthur was slow and would probably always be a burden to his folks. Then there was the question of Hattie. How does a young man speak the unvarnished truth about his kind of mother without sounding outrageous? He was certain Amy had never known a woman like Hattie, and each time he envisioned the two of them meeting, he was filled with trepidation and a little bit ashamed of himself. Hattie was, after all, his mother.

Amy no longer walked to the shed with Peter's breakfast, since he was up early and joined her and Jim at the table. Every day she laid a cloth across the table which she had washed in the big wooden tub at the side of the house, and dried in the heat of the Georgia day. It was blindingly white and stiff, and the snap of it when she shook it out was like the crack of a sharp little whip. Clary always jumped at the burst of sound and begged her mother to do it over again, just so she could squeal and become the center of attention.

Now, with the promises silently made in the spring house, it would just be a matter of time until the sparks would fly out and hit Jim full on. Amy and Peter were not very well versed in the art of deception and it didn't take long.

It happened only a few days after they had openly admitted their feelings to each other. Jim had come in from the garden and found Amy and Peter, heads close together, composing the letter to his family. Peter held her left hand while she took his dictation with her right. Clary played with Bullseye at their feet. They did not notice his tread on the bare floor boards, so he mischievously decided to stand perfectly still to see how much time would pass before he was noticed.

Bullseye was the first to acknowledge him. The dog got off the floor and went to Jim, raising his big head for a friendly stroke from his master. Clary followed, calling out, "Grampa! Your feets is all dirty! You muck up the floor!" Amy and Peter looked up but did not unlock their fingers. It was time to tell Jim something he already knew. Amy began, "Jim, we're writin' the letter to Pete's folks. We're tellin' them that soon as Pete's well enough he'll be on his way back." He was now "Pete" to her and she would call him that ever after. She stopped and looked square at him, waiting for him to continue.

He cleared his throat and took up the conversation, his vocal chords trailing a slightly higher vibration than usual. "We're tellin' them that when I come home, Amy and Clary will come with me. That is, sir, if we have your permission. And you'd be welcome too, if you want to come." Jim was touched by Peter's polite and obviously sincere request and invitation.

"You're meanin' to marry then?" he asked, cocking his head a little and raising one eyebrow slightly.

"Well," said Pete, swallowing and clearing his throat. "Yes sir, we are."

Amy squeezed Pete's hand fiercely and looked directly into Jim's eyes. "With your blessin', Jim. I couldn't ever do it without."

"I'd be pleased to see your union. You know how I feel about you, Amy. And Peter, I've come to respect you. I couldn't come with of course, but thanks for the invite anyway." He hesitated a moment, and looked warmly at Clary. "I guess I'd better spend a little more time with baby Cotton-Two over there, before you'd all go." He walked over to his granddaughter and took her by the hand. "Let's you and me go down to the woods and see about pullin' some of the little blue flowers I saw there earlier this mornin'. Your mama and Peter's workin' on some mighty important stuff here."

He led her through the door quickly so that Amy and Peter could not see the moistness filling his eyes. His loss would be the Beaudines' gain, and he didn't know how long it would take for him to get over it. He would manage, somehow, this he promised himself. He had done it before, and he could do it again.

Chapter Ten

CEREMONY

Springfield was clothed in the somber garb of sorrow, as a brave widow facing the onslaught of public mourners. She must receive them—the honorable, the gauche, the sincere, the curious, the truly bereaved—and maintain a calmness which would soothe all comers. Her streets were etched in black. Her windows wept, flowing tears of inky crape and muslin. Juxtaposed were the red, white, and blue Union flags, hanging cheerlessly in heavy half-mast posture. It was as though the flags, unfurled, had not the heart to climb farther on the rigid poles, and did not welcome the May breezes.

Yet, nature still swelled and burst with life, as if nothing sorrowful had happened. Beneath the black moods and stunned reactions of the people, the earth did not still its season, and the greening of Springfield surged ahead. Tulips and lilacs and early cherry buds splashed brightness across the city, from dooryard to outbuilding, to the railway station that would welcome Old Abe and his boy Willie. Flowers would be heaped upon the coffins, as if to beg the president to smell them just once more before lying down for the last time.

Jesse arrived the day before the funeral train was scheduled. He could find no shelter in the swollen hotels and boarding houses on that third day of May, so he rode up and down the residential byways, hoping to see anything posted. He would take a hayloft, if available, or a lean-to shed in someone's back pasture. He rode a little north of town, in fact, following the rails, allowing that if he had to, he would sleep beside the tracks and not miss the train that way. There were travelers all along the way, from north and south, east and west, all seeking the same ends. About sunset he saw a man alone, driving a flatbed wagon along the same rutted road, coming from the opposite direction. They exchanged greetings and stopped to chat. Before long, they struck up an agreement, and Jesse tied his horse to the rear of the wagon and jumped on the bench seat beside its owner.

The man was about Marcus's age, but large and sunburned, and wore a stump where his lower left leg had been. As if to make up for the loss of his leg, the big man's shoulders were massive and his hands were about the size of boxer's gloves. Jesse decided to step around the subject of loyalties if it came up. It did. The man's name was Neils Hansen, and he had come originally from Wisconsin. "Wanted to enlist like all the younger men," he told Jesse. "Never could abide the idea of slavery, but more important was to preserve the Union, just like President Lincoln wanted. He never started the war, you know. Would've come no matter what Republican was elected. Went because I knew it was my duty. What about you?"

Jesse answered obliquely. "Duty was my reason too. I did my last tour in Georgia. It was awful hot and dirty, and I was sure glad to get back home. My daddy and I were on our way together to see the train and be in Springfield for the ceremonies."

Neils Hansen jiggled the reins above his horse's ears and clicked his tongue. "Must've had a powerful interest in Mr. Lincoln to come from as far as you have." Jesse's drawl must have given him away.

Jesse sidestepped the comment and went on about Marcus. "My daddy was the one with the idea. He's worked at a newspaper his whole life, settin' other people's news and copy, mainly, and just wanted to see a thing firsthand for once. He started a journal of our trip, and now I'm goin' to finish this part of it for him."

Neils was interested and curious. "Where's your father now?"

"His horse went down on him and busted his knee. He's stayin' a bit south with a farmer. He sent me on. I didn't really want to come without him, but here I am anyways. I hope to do justice to what I see. I do have a healthy respect for Mr. Lincoln, and think that in the end, the right won out."

Jesse's words were hint enough to Neils that here was a square young man, no matter which side he fought for. He decided not to explore attachments, and they bounced along another few minutes in silence. After a bit, Neils picked up the conversation once more.

"Interesting things happened after people heard about Mr. Lincoln's murder, did you know?"

Jesse nodded his head. "A little, not much yet."

Neils continued. "Read about it. Seems that there was a fellow in Maine that said it was good that Old Lincoln, the SOB, was finally shot and it shoulda been done long ago. Well, a mob got hold of him and painted him with tar, and feathered him good and made him salute the Stars and Stripes. Then somebody took a likeness of him to hang on posters around town. It was rich. Guess that kind of thing happened all over. A man daresn't mutter a word against Mr. Lincoln, unless he wants to suffer some consequence or another." Jesse thought of the antagonism Cougar had caused with his offhand remark about going to see us a dead president as they talked with that farmer three days ago. Now, listening to Neils Hansen, he began to expand his picture of the man, Lincoln. He would be certain to pass these observations to Marcus, and leave them imprinted in his father's journal.

The two new acquaintances had their supper on the road, like so many others who had hurriedly put together their pilgrimage. Jesse was to sleep on the flatbed of the wagon and

Neils lay out his quilt under its shelter. "Never did like looking at stars before I went to sleep. Seems they all died out before I did, and always felt like I hadn't slept noway."

That warm and enveloping night, while they slept and thousands like them in the city slept, Lincoln's funeral train moved at its steady pace over the rails. All along the route from Chicago to Springfield, bonfires burned through the darkness. One hundred, two hundred or more onlookers gathered from place to place, waiting for the spectral engine number 331 to appear as a pinpoint of light on the flat horizon. Some would put an ear to the track, eager to sense the heavy and distant vibrations around the long bend of night. When at last the train arrived these mourners stood reverently, some placing their hands over their hearts, others weeping openly or reaching out to touch the shrouded car as it bore its heavy burden homeward. In the years to come, children who had been allowed to sleep through the event would berate their mothers for not waking them. Travelers would speak of the nighttime vigil and interpret their vision of number 331, and none of them would be wrong or stand corrected in those recollections. Though a public occasion, the passing of Lincoln's train elicited the most private of emotions and reactions. It was a shared experience, but each individual's deeply felt turmoil contributed to the commonality of it.

Jesse and Neils arose early in the morning and decided to leave the wagon and go to Springfield on horseback. Upon reentering the city, Jesse grasped the enormity of the thing once more. Photographers who had followed the war and captured images too grim to leave to the imagination now clamored to immortalize this last lamentable chapter. The train had not yet arrived and there was a slight drizzle, but the streets were already thick with a mixed populace, townspeople and country folk alike, fitted in their own peculiar finest. Jesse could muster a clean shirt and pair of trousers, but nothing fancy.

Neither was Neils outfitted as well as he would have liked, but it was the best he had. He managed walking very well, in spite of the stump supporting his left side. They passed by the Lincoln home on Eighth and Jackson Street, where an assemblage of men had crowded in the yard and on the corner. The ever-present photographer set up in the middle of the thoroughfare, unflinchingly obstructing traffic and going about his work as if time stood still for him.

Jesse had heard some say that the long journey of the funeral train was morbid, that such ongoing public display of the man Lincoln was vulgar and gauche. Some said there was an undertaker riding on the train to make certain his face was presentable at the many stops along the way. Thank heaven, it was whispered, that the boy Willie had been gone too long to display. It was unnerving to many that Lincoln's son had been disinterred and toted all this way to be placed beside his father. Jesse and Neils spoke of this and related matters.

"Heard there was an invention by some fellah back east, to make sure people who maybe were buried alive could get help and get dug up. A little bell, attached to a rope inside the coffin, case the poor joker wakes up lookin' at the underside of the lid." Neils spoke quietly as they walked across the street to the Lincoln home. Then he changed the subject abruptly. "Read that Mr. Lincoln came back from a long trip one day to find out the wife had added onto his house. Another level," he went on, pointing upwards, "like it is now. Guess he liked it though, since it still stands. Live in a sod house myself and got no wife either. Some say Lincoln's missus is a few eggs short of a full basket and was a Southern sympathizer. Don't know myself."

Jesse hardly knew what to add to this colorful narrative, so he kept his silence. He absorbed what his ears offered, what his eyes scanned, and what his skin felt, and his nostrils breathed in the aromas of the city around him. Someone weaving his way through the crowd stopped them and raised printed sheets, hawking copies of a brief address Lincoln had delivered at Gettysburg. "Only five cents for these immortal words, given in solemn eloquence before the living and the dead on those hallowed Pennsylvania grounds. You'll not regret having your own personal copy, sir. Just five cents for a superb act of elocution, from his own lips. What do you say?" Thrusting the paper in front of Jesse's face, the man stared intently into his eyes. Jesse fished in his pocket for some change and became the possessor of a copy of the address, which had been hastily printed and embellished with a silhouette of Lincoln at the top. Neils bought one as well, and the hawkster disappeared into the swelling throng.

After much solemn jostling they secured a place in the line that would pass by the coffin at the State House. Jesse had never seen so many flowers in his life. They were potted, draped, woven in wreaths, strewn on the floor, crushed to brown beneath the shuffling feet of hundreds who went before him. There was a stifling and heavy scent everywhere as new flowers arrived and offerings of all varieties of pine boughs and homegrown lilacs were placed around the casket.

Lincoln's upturned face was expressionless, but not stony, and the pallor enveloping his skin was not unlike the description which had been given of him when he lived. The hair was stubborn, even in death, and seemed to have defied the undertaker's attempt to tame it. People moved in front of the coffin at a steady pace and generally in a reverent manner. Jesse walked behind Neils and was nearly past the foot of the casket when a sharp object jabbed him in the ribs. He turned to see Cougar directly behind him, still pointing an index finger into Jesse's back. He was surprised to see that his wandering friend had actually made it to Springfield. First, that he had any real interest, and second, that he hadn't gotten himself shot along the way.

"Looks like hell's froze over, man! I never thought I'd see you after you went off in such a hurry." Cougar half shouted.

A few heads swiveled at his irreverence. Jesse was not in the mood to be put on the defensive. He ignored the remark and simply replied, "Guess we made it."

They walked on as the long queue wound its way out of the capitol building and onto the warm avenue. Neils stood off a little from Jesse and Cougar, staring at the new arrival with a knitted brow. Cougar, oblivious as ever, rattled on in a vague manner, half bragging, half excusing himself for his off-and-on appearances. Jesse wearied immediately of Cougar's blathering and announced, looking directly at Neils, "We'd best grab a bite before they take it all on over to the cemetery at Oak Ridge."

Neils nodded in agreement, and Cougar invited himself to join them. They squeezed into a small dining room off the main street and ordered ham and eggs. Jesse's mind's eye immediately visualized the girl in coveralls, and thoughts of each image replayed behind the disinterested stare he cast about the room. Neils was quiet, and Cougar sailed into more variations of his trip alone.

"Goin' it alone has its advantages. For one thing, I can go as fast or slow as I need to, but it does tend to get mighty lonesome. I found out too that the north ain't suitin' me as much as I thought it might. I'm wonderin', Jesse, if you won't mind me taggin' along back to Tennessee with you."

Before Jesse could check himself, he blurted out, "I won't be goin' back directly. I have some business to take care of in Kentucky."

Had Jesse actually convinced himself he should go to those people? What was he thinking? He would have to see to Marcus first. Cougar skimmed over his companion's remark and took up his own train of thought.

"Well, never mind then." He was fast becoming an irritant to the big northern traveler. To divert the subject from Cougar to himself, Neils said, "Guess there'll never be such a tribute to another president in our lifetime. Never was a more revered man, I do believe."

"Old Abe?" Cougar responded, jabbing himself with a toothpick. "Damn! Am I bleedin?" He put a napkin to his gums and examined it. It was clean. He went on, "Well, for my money, it was the old man that started the war in the first place. Darkies'd been better off down on the plantation where they belong. You mark them words. They'll be out on their black ears and not know how to do a blamed thing except say 'yassuh' and 'no suh' and dance around. Lincoln made out like he was doin' them a favor, but he's goin' to be six feet under and don't give a damn now anyways."

Jesse could see the vexation rising in Neils. He hoped the man from Wisconsin didn't have a gun on him. Cougar took no notice of the reddening cheeks of the big man sitting next to him, and with his customary lack of tact he said, "Say, where'd you get that stump anyways? Off a maple tree?" He laughed loudly at his own joke and poked Neils playfully. Neils was near bursting. Jesse cringed as Cougar went on.

"Well, the old man looked like death warmed over, don't you think?" He laughed again. "I seen homely mugs in my life, but I never seen any to match that one. He looks like he was beat up with a ugly stick!"

In the middle of his next round of laughter, Neils' giant balled-up fist pounded Cougar's face to the back of his mouth. He sailed into the table behind theirs and tumbled over two men waiting to be served. When he came to rest in a heap on the floor, he felt the hot spurting of blood from his face and the explosive pain of his broken nose. He tried to open his eyes, but they were blanketed by a fuzzy black and red dome, and it was a few moments before he realized what had happened. He felt a sudden grasp on his shirt front and a jolting wrench as he was yanked off the floor. He opened one eye to see the twisted and angry features of his new acquaintance.

Neils pulled Cougar as close as possible to his face and growled fiercely at him. "No so-called man talks that way about Mr. Lincoln in my earshot! And if you want to laugh about ugly, get yourself a looking glass and chuckle at your own face. You ain't never going to look the same, pretty boy, and when your time comes there won't even be a yellow dog on the street stop and slobber on the likes of you!"

Neils wheeled around, still hoisting Cougar off the floor, and stumped his way to the door. People shuffled in their chairs and moved aside to let him through, some applauding and others jeering the battered Cougar. Jesse just lowered his head and shook it, knowing Cougar had at last got his just desserts. Still, it was hard to suppress a wince listening to the scuffle of Cougar's boots as he picked himself up from the planked porch.

Neils marched back to his seat, adjusting his shirt collar and hoisting up his belt. "Isn't your fault you run into a polecat like that, and don't think I hold your acquaintanceship with him against you. Got a brother-in-law myself of the same jackass persuasion. What say we eat and get on over to the cemetery?"

Jesse smiled, and with a gesture of new respect said to Neils, "Well, I heard they serve up a pretty good knuckle sandwich around here, but I think I'll just stick with ham and eggs like we ordered."

Neils laughed loudly and leaned back in his chair, now freed of the tension Cougar's presence had caused. "Guess you can put this in your father's journal, eh? Just can't abide a smart mouth ignoramus like that," he said, and looked up at the tray of food being placed before them. It was loaded with their orders and extra sausages and flapjacks with maple syrup. The young man waiting on them explained the surplus. "Some of the boys over there thought you earned a little extra for knockin' that kid's block off. Everything else is on the house as well. Eat hearty!"

They did, and Jesse chided himself for enjoying every bite.

The cemetery was jammed with thousands who strained to listen to the orations delivered on behalf of the fallen president. The day was warm and humid, the sun showering bright heat from the sky, and more than one person was assisted by ambulance nurses as the pressing crowds produced a few cases of heat exhaustion.

Jesse was filled beyond satisfaction of appetite with food, and standing in the heat of the day he suddenly felt a great urge to lie down and nap. A hawk circling overhead caught Jesse's eye, and he gazed upward to follow the bird's slow journey aloft. He wondered if such a bird paid any mind to what was happening below or even noticed the throngs of humanity passing in a body to this one spot. Did a hawk's eye view ever include anything more than scurrying rodents or other unwary prey? He decided to write about the procession to the cemetery from a sky born outlook, as if he were the sharp-eyed hawk high above. The words had already begun to form in his mind. The phrases he would use in Marcus's journal played over and over in his head. Making hasty notes, he impressed Neils with his concentration and seriousness. Neils was not one to beat around the bush, but only after he saw Jesse slide his notes into his shirt pocket and replace his pencil did he speak to him. His thoughts came as a total surprise to Jesse. "Jesse, you seem a fine young man. I like the way you conduct yourself. Got another sister back home who's just about old enough to match up with a good man. Like you to meet her, maybe see how things go. What say?"

Jesse was astounded. "Why, I, uh, you hardly know me more than a day, Neils. I'm flattered you'd think such a thing!"

Neils persisted. "Ain't the prettiest girl in Wisconsin but her face won't stop a clock, that's sure. And she's real strong and a good workin' girl. Been milking cows since she was a whelp. Taught her myself. Give it a consideration, won't you? You could bring your father on up when he was well enough."

Jesse felt a little squirmy and warm around the collar, and tried to ease out of the subject diplomatically. "Actually, before we go back home I have a little business to take care of in Kentucky. Somethin' I sort of promised myself I would do now that the war's over. Besides, I kind of have a situation in Tennessee."

"You have another gal already?" Neils was not giving up.

"Well, there was one . . . " Jesse hesitated to reveal that the girl had married and was out of his reach by now. "But, I'm talkin' about a job at the newspaper where my daddy works. I got to get on my feet before I take on any wife."

Neils nodded thoughtfully. "Suppose you have a point there. But then, if you liked dairy farming, I could set you up pretty good in my neck of the woods."

"I haven't seen the business side of a cow since I was knee-high to a grasshopper," Jesse laughed, "but I do appreciate the offer."

Somebody standing ahead of them shushed people in the vicinity and announced that services were beginning. It strained the hearing to catch every word spoken by the orators, but all spectators leaned forward in the effort. Old people cupped callused hands against long-lobed ears to capture the expressions carried on the May afternoon breeze, and children quietly twisted bits of grass or leaned lazily against the grown-ups' legs to stay awake. Parasols served to shield the women in the crowd from the sun, and they stood like stems supporting a forest of black mushrooms. Suddenly, it seemed to Jesse that the man Lincoln must be tired of all the frenzy and ceremony, and that the spirit of him was far from this place.

Jesse began to feel empty and wanted to get away too. Inexplicably, he thought again of the Yankee, Peter Beaudine, and a vision of Andersonville clouded the crowd around him. Neils Hansen melted from his side, and Jesse was again standing guard in the hot and humid Georgia prison tower. He could see the blackened faces of thousands of prisoners whose skin was darkened by smoke from their pine tar cooking fires. He sensed his fingers gripping the regulation army rifle, and the scene repeated itself behind his half closed eyes. He was suddenly jolted by the exploding of a firecracker at the back of the throng. The burst made him sick inside.

He turned toward Neils and mumbled softly, "I'm feelin' kind of woozy. I need to get out of the crowd, so I'll just go on back to the wagon and wait for you there." Neils nodded and directed his attention to the speaker while Jesse slipped through the packed mass of spectators, gripped in the vision of a falling Yankee soldier and the little black book sailing to the tower and settling at his feet. The great futility of it all enveloped him once more, and he felt blackness all around. War had made him careful and vulnerable and raw and stony all at the same time. He knew now that he must certainly go to the

Beaudines and somehow try to cleanse himself of the horrors of the conflict. By declaring his guilt to some tangible mother or father, by seeing their hatred or relief in knowing at last what had happened to their boy, he might be able to absolve a part of the blame he felt. The idea frightened him, made his blood run a chill course through his arms, and pound in his throat, but he was now committed to it.

Chapter Eleven

LONE OAK

eils stood outlined against a purple sky on the open road that led away from Springfield. The sun was slipping to the edge of the flat Illinois horizon and would soon give way to an expanse of prairie blackness, miles and miles of rustling, and wind-swept grasses. It seemed the wind never ceased its travels across those flatlands, and its murmuring was the speech of some living thing.

"Sure you won't come ahead with me just to get the lay of the land, eh, Jesse?" He pressed one last time. "It's beautiful country up there and the people's good too." This time he did not mention his sister.

"Like I said, Neils, I appreciate the offer, but I guess my heart's still in another place, and my future too. Maybe someday we'll meet up again, and I can write about you in the *Register*. Who knows?"

Neils shook his bedroll out and tucked it under the wagon. Crawling in, he answered, "Hope not. It's better to be just a common man who never gets uncommon attention. In spite of all the greatness of Mr. Lincoln, I wouldn't be him for love nor money. I'd like to live to a ripe old age and sit out on my doorstep just smelling new mown hay and hearing my cows mooing to be milked. Wouldn't be any man wanting revenge like that on a peg leg dairy man."

He snuggled under the wagon like a child in a trundle bed. "No, sir. Nobody'll ever want to write me up, not even when I'm finally dead and gone."

Jesse nodded and hopped onto the wagon bed, settling in for the night and staring at the now black sky. Shimmers of stars emerged with the swiftness of a sudden shower. "It's God throwing diamonds out of his hand," Jesse's mother used to say. He recalled other nights when he'd slept under acrid clouds of enemy fire, and had tried to find comfort in those same lights, with no success. Now he felt assured that he could become free of some of the stain and stared into the night once more before rolling to his side and falling asleep.

In the morning he and Neils parted with a warm handshake, and the big peg-legged man headed north, while Jesse turned to the south road with Kentucky on his mind. When he reached the farm where he had left Marcus, Jesse was met with the news that his father had already headed to Murfreesboro.

"A Tennessee man come by the farm to see about fixin' his busted wheel," the farmer explained. "It turns out they was acquainted, your daddy and him, so the man said your daddy had just as well go on down home with him as wait. Seein' as how he had a wagon and all."

Turning slowly and raising his arm, he motioned for Jesse to follow him. "Your daddy left a note for you and said to read it b'fore you left my place."

Jesse followed the man to a sagging tool shed which was hardly more than a lean-to, where the farmer dug into an oily smelling chest and pulled out a soiled fold of paper. "Him and the gentleman with the wagon are gone two days already. Seems like he was antsy to get on home, but thanked me and the wife every day for our help."

Jesse studied the paper and saw that it was indeed written in Marcus's hand. It read:

Dear Jesse. I have been fortunate enough to find a way home with an old acquaintance of mine, Mr. W. G. Parks, who used to blacksmith in Murfreesboro. Now that the war is over, he is return-ing and hopes to set up another business. He invited me to ride along with him and drives a fine rig, so it should be a comfortable journey. If you can spare any, please leave another dollar or two with Mr. Shelby for the many kindnesses he showed me. I look forward to seeing you back home when your business in Kentucky is finished. Always, Your Father, Marcus Campbell.

Jesse thanked the farmer and pressed a few more dollars into his callused hand. "Thank you kindly for takin' care of my daddy."

"T'warn't nothin'," the farmer replied, and stood with his hands stuffed into his pockets, watching Jesse all the way down the road.

Lone Oak was one of those disorderly wayside stops thrown together by a populace of dull imaginations, and looked to be the kind of place that would inspire a quick exodus to young people unfortunate enough to be born there. Somehow it ap-peared to have survived in spite of its lack of appeal. He reined his horse in front of a small, seedy-looking store advertising hardware and soft goods, and stepped inside the darkened one room store. It was empty and seemed to have no proprietor.

"Hello?" Jesse called, and was met with dusty silence.

The place looked like the rest of Lone Oak, neglected and sad. He turned to leave, and a shadow fell across the uneven floor as a young woman now stood in the open doorway. Her face was dark, and her unkempt hair tumbled over her shoul-ders, nearly to her waist. She spoke. "What do you want, sol-dier boy? I got it, whatever it is." She moved toward him, swaying as she crossed the room, reaching out a small, trem-bling hand. "I got it all, and you can have it." The hair on the back of Jesse's neck stood straight out. He had seen women like this before, time and again, during his two years in the army. Fools had followed after them and some had returned infected, victims of sowing their wild oats in diseased fields. He shud-dered, almost visibly.

At that moment a short, agitated man darted through the doorway and grabbed her by the arm. "Annie Grace," he hissed at her. "The gentleman don't want favors right now. He's come to shop for nails and such. Get on home!"

Jesse lowered his head, suspecting that the man was the woman's father. She was ushered quickly out the door, but turned one last time and stared at Jesse. Her eyes welled up with a look of melancholy. "Nobody wants love anymore. Nobody wants me but Arthur." Then she disappeared into the brightness of the morning.

The little man addressed Jesse immediately, explaining her away as quickly as possible. "Annie Grace is younger than you'd think, and not all put together. The war made her wanton like that, so I try to keep her in tow. Sometimes she just gets out and says what she feels like. I know you understand." He straightened his shoulders, drawing himself up and recovering his small pride. "Now sir, what can I get for you?"

Jesse's original intent had been to only ask directions to the Beaudine place, but he now felt he owed it to this man to buy something. "I'll have a half pound of coffee beans and a little sugar if you've got it."

Birdlike, the man scooted briskly behind the counter and opened a barrel of wrinkled and dry looking beans. He pulled the scoop out and dumped the beans into a small bag, almost faster than Jesse could see. As the man measured out the sugar lumps, Jesse asked, "Do you know the Beaudines?"

"Beaudines, eh? Who around here don't know the Beaudines!"

He shook his head and continued, "Beaudines used to live just up the road, but they was burned out last winter. Moved up into the hills somewheres."

Jesse nodded his head in absent-minded sympathy. Then he asked, "Did they have a son named Peter?"

The fidgety clerk stooped behind the counter to pick up a stray bag. "Had," he mumbled from below the counter top.

"Ain't come back from the war yet, so I reckon he's dead or

run off by now. How is it you know the Beaudines anyway?"

"I don't know them really. I only uh, met their boy down in Georgia." Jesse was purposely evasive. He wanted to tell the family himself about Peter, but he also wanted to choose the right time. "I didn't know the war reached this far into Kentucky. Was anybody else burned out or anything?"

The clerk picked up a weakly plumed feather duster and set to work on some nearly empty shelves on the wall behind him. "Oh, Beaudines wasn't burned out by the war. Guess Lone Oak didn't have enough goin' for it for the soldiers to do much more than pass through. Their house was set fire by the youngest boy. He's addled, ain't got a lick of sense. Like I said, they's somewhere up in the hills, but the only one of 'em I ever see is the girl. She comes by sometimes to pick up supplies. Her daddy was in the corps of engineers early on, but the damn fool got himself wounded and mustered out. Can't walk real well, so she does most of the work, I reckon. Got a job over to Paducah, though I don't know what she does." He paused for a slight breath, shifted his suspenders, and began another stream of information.

"And don't get me started on the mother! How she ever produced any halfway decent offspring is a shock to anybody who knows her. She's a water witch, she claims, and is as outspoke as I ever seen a female be. She used to stick her nose into everythin' comin' down the pike, and acted like she knowed what the insides of the Almighty was made of. Can't stand her m'self so it's a good thing they stay holed up in the back woods."

As Jesse listened to the man talk, his resolve to offer his apologies to the Beaudines began to dim. They were certainly not the family he had envisioned confessing his war crime to. Still, he had come this far. He might was well finish the thing and be done with it.

"Well, I do have some business with them, so could you direct me to the place where they live now?"

"I ain't rightly sure. I never cared to ask. Like I said, the old lady and me ain't exactly on speakin' terms." Suddenly, Annie Grace spoke from the open doorway. "I can show you where they live. Me and Arthur are friends. I see him sometimes."

Jesse now got a better look at Annie Grace, and saw that with her hair brushed and pulled away from her face she was indeed young. He felt sorry for her and nodded. "Maybe if you can just give me directions I can find it by myself, and not put you to any trouble."

She shook her head vehemently. "No! I got to show you. Show you!"

"Well, then, if it's all right with your folks, I'd be obliged."

The young woman cast a sharp look at the clerk. "Pa?"

Jesse had been right about their kinship. The wiry little man studied Jesse for a long moment, then said, "You seem a decent feller. Keep a rein on her, and send her back directly, and it'll be all right. By the way, she wouldn't mind a copper or so for her time." Jesse's new guide asked him to wait while she got her mule, so he rearranged his supplies and packed away his coffee and sugar.

"Foller me!" Annie Grace shouted to Jesse, and the mule slogged ahead of him. Shortly, she stopped and pointed to the remains of a small dwelling. Chimney bricks stood at the far end, disheveled and gray-looking, cloaked in the new growth of wild morning glory and black marks that gave evidence of fire. The rest of the property was overgrown with weeds and newly sprouted rye grass.

"This here's where Arthur used to live. He burnt it down, but it were not his fault. My daddy don't like him on account of it. But Arthur says my daddy is a mean-spirited man and don't like much of anythin'. I think Arthur's real smart."

As suddenly as she had blurted out this narrative, she stopped. They rode through the remainder of Lone Oak, which had the same stingy look about it as the store as if its up-keep was last on anyone's agenda. A dog, sequestered beneath a hawthorn tree, barked half-heartedly as they loped past, and it seemed to Jesse that even the flies must just loll around in a place like this. Lone Oak was left behind them in five minutes, and they continued through small stands of trees until they reached the open fields. Some of the expanse lay fallow, while other acreage was already furrowed and ready for crops.

Once away from the fields, the terrain began a slight incline, and ahead of them Jesse could see small rises, growing and merging to become good sized hills. Each hillock was densely covered with trees, and the trace they followed was barely perceptible. After a few hundred yards, it disappeared from the landscape altogether, obliterated by the thick canopy of growth.

The last leg of their journey, which was now well into nearly an hour, was along a narrow, one horse path. Jesse continually ducked low, slung branches, and dodged switches from struggling, bent saplings. Annie Grace rode ahead of him, humming a tuneless theme, never once turning to speak.

At last she came to a halt. She dismounted and tied her mule to a small tree trunk. "Foller me!" she announced for the second time, and plunged into the deep woods. Jesse wasn't sure about leaving his mount and supplies in this unfamiliar setting, but he had trusted Annie this far, and things looked all right. He followed her, expecting another long traipse, but found himself almost on the doorstep of a dilapidated clapboard cabin. It seemed to have sprung up out of nowhere.

Annie Grace laughed. She could see the surprise on Jesse's face, had probably anticipated it. "This is where Arthur lives," she announced, as though the cabin were a grand castle. "I'll go find him." She then bolted around to the other side, and Jesse was left alone, confronting this sorry, weather beaten haven for the burned out Beaudines. He wondered what could have possessed them to move so far back into these wooded hills and how they made their way in such solitude.

He waited a few minutes, then walked the weedy path to the other side, following Annie Grace's lead. He was unprepared for what met his eyes. Two people stood a few yards away in the center of a huge and neatly furrowed garden plot. The rich and loamy rows already showed signs of growth where sharp spears of onion pushed out of the earth. Fresh, green, and round, scores of radish leaves sat in one long precise military line, filling their own row. A fence ran in perfect formation alongside the garden, and at ninety degree angles to the north, along the east side and turning sharply south, it delineated the entire yard. Garden tools and seed bags sat neatly in a wooden barrow, and a tin watering bucket overflowed with unwanted weeds.

The two, a man and a woman, turned to him and then to each other, continuing their conversation. He offered a wave and called out. "Annie Grace tells me this is the Beaudine's place. Is it that?"

The couple returned his greeting and walked toward him, dusting garden dirt from themselves and adjusting their hats. The man limped. Jesse was suddenly nervous. How on earth could he really tell these people what he had done? The woman answered him, smiling. "It is that, son. I am Hattie and this here's Clive, my husband. Come on up to the porch and set. Annie Grace told us that you was around back and I scolded her for leavin' you out there. What might be your business so far off the beaten track?"

Jesse cleared his throat and prepared for the worst. "Well, ma'am. I have come with some news about your son Peter, that is, if you are his folks."

Hattie dropped the shovel and clasped Jesse firmly by the shoulders. "Clive! I told you! Didn't I say, we will hear about Pete before the month's out?"

Her eyes were fierce with anticipation of good news and she wore a forced smile. Jesse could see the foreboding she tried to hide behind this brave show and he looked at the silent husband at her side.

"Well, come on, son. Out with the news, be it good or bad. We have been anxious a mighty long time now. What do you know about our boy?"

Jesse lowered his head and shook it slightly. "Well ma'am, and sir. It's not the best."

"But it's not the worst now is it?" Hattie interrupted him, still clinging to the impossible hope all mothers carry. Jesse's heart thumped so heavily in his ribs he thought it would pound its way out of the flesh. He swallowed hard and took a deep breath.

"I'm afraid it is the worst, Mrs. Beaudine. I, uh, saw him die in a prison camp in Georgia."

Hattie's fingers dug into Jesse's shoulders, and her whole frame shook as the finality of his words pried into her mind. Clive reached out to her and rested a dusty hand on her arm.

"Hattie, I know you wanted to believe, but you didn't see what it was out there. Men dyin' right and left." She sat down on the spot and dropped her face to her apron. Her body was still shaking, and her chest heaved as she drew in short breaths. Streaming tears traced little white lines over her cheeks, streaking through the fine garden dust on her skin.

"I can't believe it. I can't believe he's gone." She looked pleadingly at Jesse. "I feel him, right here, every day!" she cried, placing her hand over her breast. "And I see him here, in my mind's eye. Oh, I will be a long time accepting this. My Pete? It can't be!"

Clive lifted Hattie from the ground and said to Jesse, "You've come a mighty long way to tell us this news. Least we can do is offer you some drink. Don't you worry about it, Mama. I'll see to it."

It was uncharacteristic of Hattie to lean on anyone, even Clive, and she straightened herself before walking to the cabin. She passed her big, flat hand across her face, and smeared tear lines over the high cheek bones. They followed Clive's halting step and entered the cabin.

Inside, it was immediately cooler and darker, and touched with the aroma of ground dried lavender, like some city soaps Jesse had smelled. It was neatly laid out, every bit as well as the garden, but with a more feminine touch. Herbs hung from the dark rafters, tied onto pegs with bright bits of ribbon, and fresh picked wildflowers filled a pewter cup by the window. The table was laid with a clean square cloth, the color of bone, edged with pale blue embroidery. Jesse's first thought was that his father would have appreciated the stark contrast of this cabin to the wooded wilds.

"Sit down, young man," said Clive, offering him a chair. "I'll just get the tea fixin's."

Hattie went to the dry sink, poured water from a plain crockery pitcher into the bowl, and washed her hands and face. When she turned to look at Jesse, she said, "I guess you to be about the same age as Pete. That would be twenty-two or three. Where did you come from? Where was it exactly you knew Pete?"

"Ma'am, I came from Tennessee, and I saw him in the prison camp at Andersonville." Jesse stopped his narrative short, his mind in a quandary. Hattie quickly took up the slack. "So, you was a Union man too? I guess bein' from Tennessee you could've gone either way, just like Pete. Did you know him well?"

Jesse told the truth. "No, ma'am, not at all. But after he died I came by this little volume of his, and thought I'd look you up and return it." He placed the dog-eared book into Hattie's shaking hands, and felt the trembling sadness in them. Once more she burst into tears. "It's the Testament Laurel gave him. Wait 'til she sees this. He kept it with him all the time, did he?"

Jesse felt more and more timid and decided to tell her anything she wanted to hear. "I guess he did that, ma'am. He had it with him when he passed."

"How was it he went? Wait! I should know your name first. Tell me, so I don't feel like you're a stranger."

"My name's Jesse Campbell. I just came from Springfield. I went to the ceremonies for Mr. Lincoln."

Clive broke his silence. "Mr. Lincoln? You saw Mr. Lincoln?"

"Well, yes sir. I did."

"How did he look?"

Jesse thought of it as an odd question. How would a man who had been dead at least two weeks look? He reviewed his true impressions of the deceased. Not pretty, not good, not even pretty good. Mr. Lincoln had looked stiff and dead and slightly worn out from the long trip on his back and in his confinement.

He decided for the diplomatic response. "He looked dignified and presidential, sir. And there were thousands who saw him in Springfield alone, not to mention thousands of others all along the route."

Clive brought them tea and sat at the table across from Jesse. "Pete, he believed so strong on the cause. When I come home injured, why, he just practically took the uniform off my back and joined up to take my place. I was proud to see him go, though I saw a bad end in it possible. I didn't try to stop him, for you know what it is when a boy gets it in himself to go off like that. Sure you do. You no doubt did it yourself. Bet your mama was hangin' onto your coat tails before you left. We all want to, you know. Some of us just can't do it, though. Laurel, she was mad as a wet hen when Pete said he was goin'. She hates the war, practically hates all soldiers, and she don't care what side you be on. She flat out hates fightin'. Oh, she's goin' to never get past this. She loved Pete the best of all."

Clive became silent again and shook his head, while tears ran down his cheeks and off the tip of his nose. Jesse felt terrible. He could see what the effect of his own death would have had on Marcus. At least Clive and Hattie had each other and their remaining children to lean on. Marcus would have been alone.

There was silence for a long while.

At last, Jesse asked, "Is Laurel his girl?" He thought of Jen.

Hattie pulled herself together again and cleared her throat. "No, but she might as well have been. Them two was as close as peas in a pod. She's his sister, and it nearly killed her when he went off."

Jesse remembered the clerk in Lone Oak mentioning a sister. "Well, then, I'm glad I could at least bring the Testament back to you. I hope it might help ease the pain." Hattie leaned across the table and touched his hand.

"You have been a godsend, Jesse. Tell me, how did my boy go?"

Jesse sucked in a draught of air and drew his shoulders back. He tried to clear the discomfort from his throat. It felt hot and dry. "He was shot durin' a scuffle. The guards were ordered to fire into any skirmish, and the prisoners were always riled up about somethin' anyway. The food was rotten, and almost everybody had to spend all day outdoors, rain or shine. It was not a good place for anyone, prisoner or guard. I was glad to get away myself. As far as I could see, Pete was a good soldier and just got unlucky, bein' captured. In the end we were all unlucky."

Hattie rose and walked to the door. She gazed out across the slatted porch, and let her eyes rest upon the trim and promising garden. "If you look to the south corner of the garden there, you'll see the worn out trace we first came up to get to this cabin. It was Annie Grace who brought us here after we was burned out. Arthur and Annie's good friends, mainly because they're both touched, and she'd come out here plenty of times before. We wrote and told Pete about it, but we never heard back from him." Her voice broke and she swallowed hard. "I have had it in my mind ever since that we would just keep workin' on the place and I'd look up one afternoon from my chores and see him comin'. Well, I guess that could be just a dream now. Why, it's a good thing Annie didn't bring you up that way today. I mighta seen you through the trees and thought you was Pete."

Jesse was so touched at their grief that he felt compelled to tell her a little more about himself. He'd have been lucky to come to such a place as this, with both of his folks waiting. "It's been just me and my daddy for a long time, and I about forgot what it was like to have a mother." Suddenly he thought he might sound pitiful, like a lost animal with no shelter to go to. "'Course we managed real well. In fact, we started out to Springfield together, but his horse stepped in a gopher hole and fell on him. He went on back to Tennessee before me, and I wanted to come and tell you about your son. I'll join my daddy soon and see about a job at the newspaper."

"Well," said Clive, "there's no reason we can't thank you by offerin' you a bed overnight. I'd like to hear all about the ceremonies for Mr. Lincoln, and it's already gettin' on to sup-pertime. What do you say? We got an extra tick in the back if you're interested." Jesse looked at Hattie, who had turned toward him. Her eyebrows were raised in a sweet, pleading way, and salt water glistened on her lower lids.

"I guess it would be a pleasure, seein' as how I've had few nights of rest on a real bed in the last month." He forgot himself and blurted out his acceptance too late to take it back. How would they feel if they knew that Jesse was the man who fired the shot at Pete and killed him? He vacillated silently. Maybe he could do something for them, maybe give them some solace.

"So, it's decided. I suppose you had a horse? Go on back and get him and we'll brush him down and oat him up." Clive said, slapping Jesse gently on the shoulder. "Hattie makes fine rabbit stew and biscuits."

"Much obliged," Jesse answered, and skirted the back of the cabin once more to retrieve his mount. He wondered what had happened to Annie Grace and if she had found Arthur. He was also having difficulty reconciling the portrait that An-nie's father had painted of Hattie, and thought there might be something more to his dislike of her than he had revealed. All of that would not matter to him by tomorrow night, he fig-ured. He would feel out the situation a little more to determine when it would be necessary to tell them the whole story.

Chapter Twelve

THE FAMILY

The following day was a Tuesday, bright and warm, so good for hoeing and staring up into the patch of blue sky above the clearing. Jesse awoke to peace in his world. The woods were busied by the sounds of birds meddling in the tree tops, and a sweet smell filled his nostrils. Was it jasmine? Was it wild apple blossoms? He rolled out of the tick and immediately heard a small tittering noise to his left. He looked over to see a young man crouching there. His body was developed well, but Jesse knew it must be Arthur, whose mind somehow got left behind.

"Hello, Arthur," he ventured. "I hope I'm not intrudin' on your spot here."

Arthur laughed, and it was more akin to a delighted shriek. "Haw, no! I ain't no wolf that marks his territory. I go just about wherever I please. What's your name?"

"It's Jesse. Annie Grace brought me here yesterday, and your folks invited me to stay over the night."

Arthur wheeled in the dirt and grabbed a low hanging tree branch. "I seen you, but I didn't want to talk to you after you made my ma cry. What did you say to her? She 'most never cries."

"Maybe you should ask her yourself, Arthur. It was kind of bad news." Jesse found himself easing toward the cabin, remembering the agitated woman who had flown at Marcus and Cougar and him on the way to Springfield. It was hard to know what a crazy person might do in the face of great disappointment.

"Did Laurel get kidnapped on her way to the city? I tell her, don't go no more, Laurel, but she just goes on ahead and don't listen to me. Pete, he went to the war and they wouldn't let me go. I'm too young, I guess. He's goin' to come home some night when I'm asleep, mama says. She's 'most always right too."

They reached the front of the cabin to find Hattie pinching newborn weeds from the planted rows. The smell of frying bacon was strong in the air and struck Jesse squarely in the gut. The stew from last night had been delicious and had expanded his stomach, so that morning time brought a new appetite. He wondered exactly what he should do. Hattie solved his slight dilemma.

"Jesse Campbell. How did you sleep? Come on over here and let me show you something."

He could do no more than obey her friendly order.

"Look now at this," she said, pointing to a small spear of green poking its way through the dark earth. "It's an amazement to me every year to see what happens when we plant. This here's only a tiny sprout just now, but come August you'll be able to stand right here and pluck out a great big juicy onion. In them rows over there we got potatoes and yams, and beans, and we'll be eatin' the reddishes in less than a month. Life renews." She fell silent for a moment, then continued. "Some life, that is." Jesse looked away from the earth toward the cabin and saw Clive in the doorway, calling and motioning for them to come to breakfast. They joined with him and Arthur inside. Hattie washed up and took her place at the table. She said a blessing, as she had done the night before, and spoke as if to a close friend. "Lord, you give and you take away, and we thank you now for what is set before us. We accept your blessin's freely and your cursin's too, but are most grateful for the blessin's. Feel free to give us more of the same. Amen."

As they ate, Arthur seemed to have forgotten to ask Hattie what the bad news was that Jesse had brought. Instead the conversation centered on Clive's unfortunate career in the military and a certain plan he had for the property. "I was in the Corps of Engineers," he explained to Jesse. "I knew a little about road buildin' and such and learned a lot more in the army. After we was burned out and come up here, I figured that when Pete got home we could build us a nice roadway, and make travel back and forth a lot easier. Laurel tries to help out, but with her gone all week long and other chores pilin' up, why, we are goin' at it a little slow."

Arthur fidgeted in his chair and sputtered, wanting desperately to say something. Clive invited him to go ahead.

"What's on your mind, son?"

"You know I could help, Pa. I'm strong and I can pull the trees out and heft the stones from the way!"

"Pa never said you couldn't, Arthur," Hattie said to her boy. "But you don't stay with it very long. Pa can't do it alone. He's mighty glad when you do help out though, ain't you, Pa?"

"So glad I can't count the goose bumps on my hind end!" he answered sarcastically, but smiling benevolently at the young man. Arthur beamed, understanding only the smile. Impulsively, Jesse blurted out, "I could probably help, sir. I'm a fair hand with an ax, and I did a little hackin' through the woods myself durin' the war." Three pairs of eyes settled on him, all in amazement, and a slight hint of jealousy registered in Arthur's. Clive spoke first.

"That is real generous of you, Jesse, but surely your daddy expects you back soon. It might be a matter of some weeks before it was finished."

"I could send word. He already knows I had business here in Kentucky. I could just stay long enough to get you started. Then maybe your girl could talk some young buck from town into an assist as well."

Hattie laughed at his remark. "All the young bucks in town has already been told where to jump off the wagon by

106

my Laurel. I doubt there's a man-jack of them that would come out here anyway. The whole place is full of watered down mush eaters, not worth a handful of grain all put together!"

"Now, Hattie, Jesse don't care about the good folks of Lone Oak. I say we accept what help he can give us and be grateful there's such as him in this world."

Jesse cringed inwardly, a victim of his thoughts and true motives. It would be the least he could do if he took Pete's place in this road building work. "Well, then it's settled. I can start whenever you pitch a shovel at me."

Clive grinned and stabbed a thick slice of bacon with his fork. "It don't all have to be done in one day, Jesse. What say we finish off this breakfast first? If you're too slow at it, the bacon will up and walk away, it's that fresh!" Arthur slouched sullenly in his seat and poked at his food with detachment.

Hattie spoke bluntly to him. "Arthur, life would go just as well for you if you stopped your peevishness. Put your nose back in joint and eat up or I'll have to feed your vittles to that bear out in the woods."

"Oh, ma, you know there ain't no bear in the woods. You just made that up to scare me."

"Eat up," she gently commanded him, diverting his mind from the road building. Arthur's saving grace was that thoughts slipped in and out of his mind with such speed he rarely held grudges or remembered insults, even imagined ones. Already he had forgotten that Jesse might take his place in the work planned for the road, and thought for the next few moments on the bear. He worked out a rhyme and repeated it several times silently. Then he opened his mouth, which was still engaged in chewing, and said, "The bear that ain't not there, the bear that ain't not there," uttering it over and over.

Jesse suddenly thought about Annie Grace. He waited for Arthur's rhyming to stop, then asked about her. "Where's Annie Grace? Did she go right back home last night?" An awkward silence passed quickly between Clive and Hattie.

Then Hattie answered in a matter-of-fact tone. "Whenever Annie comes to visit we always invite her to stay the night. There's a little room in the back where she sleeps. I guess she's gone already though, seein' as how she gets up with the roosters."

"Annie Grace and me is friends," Arthur said to no one in particular and smiled to himself.

When their meal was finished, Clive took Jesse around and past the garden to the meager beginnings of his road. It was a narrow path, barely more than a trace, trailing off into the deeper woods. On either side angular scars gouged the trunks of three trees where Arthur had laid into them with a blunt ax. Some wild berry shrubs had been roughly jerked from the sodden earth and lay off to the side at the head of the path. Jesse studied the dense growth all around him and calculated the task. *I don't know if I'd live long enough to do this proper,* he thought, and wondered what it was he'd really promised. "Just how far is it you propose to cut this road, Mr. Beaudine?"

"It's only about a half a mile to a fair size clearin' down south. I don't mean to build no highway here, but somethin' we might drive a one-horse cart through would be nice. It would make haulin' provisions a lot easier, and it would save Laurel some rough goin'." Laurel. Jesse's curiosity was piqued again at the mention of her name. He hadn't thought about this elusive sister of Peter Beaudine since yesterday, and now his mind rested on the graceful handwriting in Peter's Testament. She must be some piece of work, the way Hattie talked about her. A girl brave enough to dare travel on her own, and this far into the woods had to be, well, something of a rugged woman, but the delicacy of her penmanship seemed to portray a different kind of person. He turned to Clive with the obvious question.

"When will she be comin' back?"

Clive jabbed at one of the fallen bushes with a fragile, new branch he'd pulled from a sapling. "She'll be in Friday sometime before sunset, I reckon. She always comes home about that time at week's end. She's a good girl, mind you. Just a little different from your run of the mill filly." He leaned against the slender trunk of a young walnut tree and dropped the green branch. "It's goin' to kill her to hear about Pete. I think it's best if you let me or Hattie tell her. When he went away she shut herself up for two days, wouldn't talk to nobody. A body can't talk to her about the war. She just won't have it."

Jesse nodded silently, for part of him harbored the same feelings. But where Laurel's objections came from a distant observer's views, Jesse's were buried in a bubbling core, a place erupting at odd times and peopling his dreams with the misty dead. Just thinking about it caused a chill to spring from his very hair roots and brought an involuntary shiver. He spoke. "Well, if you'll just point me in the right direction, Mr. Beaudine, I'll have at it as long as I can last."

Clive placed his hand on Jesse's shoulder and the touch of it reminded him of Marcus. "From now on, just call me Clive, if'n you don't mind. Nobody I know of has called me Mr. Beaudine for a coon's age, and that's a mighty long time around here."

"Clive it is, sir." Jesse replied.

Clive laughed out loud. "And you can drop the 'sir' while you're at it. I wasn't ever what you'd call a commissioned officer neither."

Arthur had joined them quietly, and Clive looked at the two young men and swept his arm wide in the direction of the invisible road. "Let's go to it, boys! With three of us layin' in, the trees just might give up and fall over of their own accord."

Arthur laughed heartily. "Pa, you are one funny son of a gun! Son of a gun, son of a gun!" Rhyming again. It was the glue that kept Arthur in touch with himself. Jesse was to hear many such rhymes in the next few weeks.

Wednesday, Thursday, and Friday were spent felling trees and dragging them to the clearing next to the garden plot. Jesse provided the manpower to chop and was joined in turn by Arthur and Clive on the two-man saw. Both afternoons found them drenched with sweat and taking long draughts of spring water from Hattie's old crockery jug. She refilled it at least five times, and at noon she brought a basket of fried chicken and baked yams. By the end of the day all three of the road builders had wearied themselves nearly straight into bed.

As Clive and Hattie turned in that first night, he remarked to her, "Jesse works like a man on fire. He even got Arthur to stick with it. Made him feel good about the work he was doin'. I think Arthur is beginnin' to like him now. Jesse better watch out, or he'll be havin' Arthur tag him home when he leaves. You know how he hangs on to someone he likes."

"I do that," said Hattie, and Annie Grace was in the back of her mind. Aloud, she said, "Maybe with Jesse here, the news about Pete won't hit him so hard." She suddenly choked on her words and turned over, burying her face in the eider tick she had saved from the house fire. Clive reached across her back and squeezed her arm, now shaking with the same grief and once again feeling their fresh loss. It was so hard to take, it was too hard to take, and it felt like a hot, thin sheet of steel searing his skin. They drifted to sleep in each other's arms, a thing which they had not done for many weeks.

Friday morning Hattie got up early and pulled Laurel's bedding out, shaking it gently and hanging it across a heavy twine clothesline to freshen. She picked some later blooming lilac and arranged the blossoms in one of her pewter pitchers, setting it in the middle of the table. Dense clusters of star-shaped purple flowers hung over the pitcher's lip, and their sweet scent permeated the kitchen. Hattie wanted the cabin to look nice when Laurel came in, but she dreaded what must come when her girl heard the news. *It has been an awful blow, but somehow we'll all just have to live with it,* she thought. *There's some things in life you can't change, and death is one of them,* she repeated to herself. *If I could rhyme it, the way Arthur does,* she thought, *maybe it would be easier.* Maybe the repeating of sing-song words would lull her away like it did Arthur, for as Heaven surely knew, she needed some lulling just about now.

Out in the woods and a good deal farther along than they had been yesterday, the three builders hacked away at the thick growth that crowded either side of the narrow trace. Arthur threw his back into the task of dragging the smaller fallen trees as far to the side of the widening path as he could. They would lie there a while until Jesse and Clive could cut them into kindling and fuel for firewood. Some of the really green growth would have to be stacked and let dry for the season.

When Hattie walked toward them with their noon dinner, Jesse noticed the long strides she took, and the determined grace of her step. It seemed somehow familiar. Had his mother walked that way? The thought was gone in a moment when the food appeared, and the three men sat for an hour, eating and talking.

Hattie went immediately back to the cabin to do up Laurel's bedding and start preparing supper. As she tidied the kitchen her gaze wandered to the little shelf where she had placed Pete's Testament. Gingerly, she took it down and let it fall open in her hands. The pages parted naturally to an often read passage, one that was marked not only in pale gray pencil, but by the soiled fingers of her young soldier as he hunkered in his trench. *I'd copy down a thousand of these testaments by hand and in the dark if it would bring my boy back,* she thought. *Now, this is all we have left.* She spent the remainder of the afternoon doing chores mechanically, hoping to numb herself against the heat of pain coming from her insides. Her mind wandered from a dimming remembrance of Pete's happy face, to the sight of him eagerly running off to war, to the unspeakable words coming out of Jesse's mouth. She was struck with the sincerity of feeling that poured from Jesse as he told them the bad news. A body could see that it hurt him to have to tell them. A body could see that he was trying to work the war out of his system, the way a young man might, by throwing himself into a hard labor, into building up instead of tearing down. He seemed to be a decent lad and must have had more than a passable upbringing. As the afternoon became wrapped in a scented spring breeze, Hattie looked up to see Laurel coming up the back way and arriving earlier than usual. The girl looked drawn and sweaty.

"Laurel, honey. You're home early. Now, is somethin' wrong? You don't look too pert." Hattie went out to meet her.

"I feel like death warmed over, Ma. I started with a fever this mornin' and it's just been worsenin' all day. Ruthann let me come on home and I just can't wait to fall into bed."

"Don't you want a bite before? You come a long way, you know."

"I'd upchuck it right over the loft if I ate. I came the back way because it was faster, but I nearly lost my guts right behind the cabin." *Such talk*, thought Hattie, not realizing that her own colorful speech had been Laurel's pattern since the girl's childhood.

"Well, crawl on up there then. Maybe you'll feel a little perkier after a sleep."

The better part of an hour passed before the three woodsmen returned from their work. They were grimy, beat out, and hungry, and they sloshed their hands and forearms heavily in the rain barrel at the side of the cabin. Arthur dumped a full bucket of water on himself and hollered so loudly that the pitch of his voice traveled into the trees and bounced back.

Hattie came quickly to the porch. "You hush it up, young man. Your sister's come home early, sicker'n a dog. I won't have you wakin' her with all that catterwallin'! We can eat out here, so's not to bother her."

"What's the matter, Hattie?" asked Clive, drying himself on his shirt.

"She come home about an hour ago, lookin' like the ash off a campfire and sweatin' like a hog at auction. It might be the ague or somethin' she ate. Anyhow, she went right to bed and I hope," Hattie continued, staring at Arthur, "I hope, she's able to sleep through the night."

"Aw, Ma. I'll be quiet. I didn't know she was here."

Jesse observed Hattie. He thought, *she's as protective as a*

*mother hen and it's a wonder she ever allowed the girl to go off some-
where else to work all week long.* But then, Laurel sounded like the
kind who wouldn't be stopped anyway. It looked as though his
meeting her would be postponed another day.

After supper, there was some brief chatter about how the
day went and how far the road had progressed. Maybe tomorrow they would fish for a while before laying in again. Jesse
agreed, for he hadn't tried fishing since running into Cougar
almost a month ago. Around dusk, everyone settled down and
the cabin became quiet.

In the stillness of the night, Laurel awakened, needing to
go to the cramped one-seater outside by the shed. The moon
was high, so there was no need for a lamp, and she made her
way easily there and back. When she came into the cabin, she
decided a drink of water might be safe, so she poured a swallow from the pitcher and drank slowly. As she set her tin cup
down on the sideboard, she noticed a little black book lying
on the tatted runner. She picked it up, half afraid to open its
cover and see the fly leaf. It looked too familiar and felt too
well worn to be anything but what she feared.

She walked feebly into the moonlight and sat on the step of
the porch. Her hands were shaking as she opened the book and
her eyes brimmed with water the moment she saw her own handwriting. The words, *To Peter Beaudine*, blurred and ran down her
cheeks, as though washed out of her eyes by the blinding tears.

Jesse was awakened from his sound sleep by the most
mournful outcry he had ever heard. It had to have been Laurel. Then Hattie's voice murmured in the night, soothing her
daughter's choking sobs. Jesse's terrible secret was ruining
someone else's life and tomorrow it would be Arthur's, and
every time another person found out about Peter, Jesse's secret
would gnaw at him a little deeper. He would try to make it up
to them all some way, if only by finishing the road, and then
walking away on it before they found out who it was that had
caused their pain. Jesse did not sleep well the rest of the night,
and Laurel went in and lay at her mother's side, weeping.

Chapter Thirteen

THE GIRL

A pale wash of dawn filtered through the trees on the east and crept steadily across the sky, swallowing the stars one by one. Jesse had long given up hope of more sleep that night. Hearing Laurel's anguish, he wondered for a moment if he shouldn't just escape under cover of darkness and leave this family to grieve within their own circle. But his promise to stay and help Clive, at least for a time, stuck in his craw. No, he couldn't do that, not after seeing what a back-breaking job it would be for Clive with only Arthur to work at his side. He decided to walk through the woods for a while and gather his thoughts, away from the path, away from places people had been.

He had pulled his boots on and headed toward the open meadow which he knew was south of the woods. Reaching into his coat pocket, he pulled out his father's journal. He hadn't written anything in it since being in Springfield, and hoped that his daddy wouldn't question the blank pages that might have covered his stay with the Beaudines. How could he write a lie? And that's exactly what he would have to do if he recorded any of his visit with them. Could he write the real feelings which pecked at him, the knowledge that his silence about his wartime allegiance was as good as a lie? Hattie and Clive still thought he had fought with the Union. What would they think if they knew the real truth? Jesse vowed that he would keep that ugly secret inside himself, and go back to Tennessee as soon as the major part of Clive's road building was done.

When he returned to the cabin, he saw smoke rising from the stone chimney, and a hawk circling high above the garden. He stopped at the wooded fringe and followed the hawk's flight with upturned eyes. He remembered trying to picture a bird's eye view of the oddly bustling solemnity in Springfield, trying to imagine such masses. Now, he squinted his gaze against a rising sun, and pictured the woods, the garden, the smoke drifting toward himself as if he were that hawk. As the hawk flew out of sight, Jesse's eye settled on the cabin.

Standing on the wide porch, just outside the door, was the girl. Her long chestnut hair tumbled freely over her shoulders, and the coveralls she wore did not conceal the blooming figure he had seen in the dining room in Paducah. Jesse sucked his breath in through his teeth, and a strange and strong tingle ran down the back of his neck. So this was Laurel!

Jesse's face reddened as he remembered her being in something of a fix and himself, foolishly trying to come to her rescue. She was more than capable of taking care of her own problem that day. And now Jesse found he might be in another clumsy situation. He was an ex-soldier, already an enemy in her eyes, and the bearer of terrible news, perhaps doubly unwelcome on that account. He walked forward, his step hesitant and his breathing uneven. She watched him skirt the garden on the other side of the fence, and followed his movements with much the same eye as the hawk might spy a field mouse.

Hattie appeared behind Laurel in the open doorway and hailed Jesse, smiling at him. "Jesse! Breakfast is set out. Come on in and eat with us."

He waved back and tried to compose himself, wondering what he might say. As he stepped onto the porch, his wondering was put to rest. Laurel came to the point first.

"Mr. Jesse Campbell, I want to thank you for bringin' Pete's Testament back to us. It means a lot that someone thought enough of him to see we found out what happened. Who knows how long it woulda been before the army would let any one of us know?"

Jesse stammered a bit. "Well, I, uh. It was the least I could do, um, since I knew you'd want to know. And, I hope you're feelin' better this mornin', that is, you're not ailin' like yesterday."

"I am, thank you. Maybe just a little squirmy."

There was an awkward silence. Then Clive called from inside, "Grub's gettin' cold here. Let's sit and eat before the eggs hatch on their plates."

As they passed the food around the table, Jesse could see that it would be better for him to wait for someone else to begin the small talk, the talk of hunting and fishing and when to begin the roadwork again. They all ate for a few minutes in silence. Jesse thought he felt the girl staring at him, but he dared not look at her. He wondered if she remembered the incident at the dining room at all.

"Ma told me Pete died in the war," said Arthur in a rush. "We're goin' to miss him, but it's just one of them things that happens, and there ain't nothin' you can do about it." He went on, echoing her earlier remarks to him. He seemed not to realize what he was saying. He continued. "I reckon it's a good thing you come, Jesse, 'cause Pete can't help build no road now."

Laurel's mouth began to twitch and she lay her fork carefully on her plate. Jesse saw her green eyes fill with tears.

"Well, Arthur, it's good that you're here too. You're strong and we couldn't haul the trees without help from a big fellow like you." Jesse hoped to divert the conversation from Pete, for his own sake as much as for Laurel's. Clive said he reckoned Jesse was right, for Arthur was as strong a man as he'd ever seen, even in all his years. Arthur pretended not to hear, but smiled broadly as he gulped his breakfast. He was pleased with himself and forgot to rhyme something about Pete.

"Well, if you boys are huntin' rabbit today, you'd best go soon, for fresh meat has been wantin' lately." Hattie stood up and began to clear the table, practically out from under the four of them. "Come on, Laurel. It's a good thing you're feelin' better 'cause we got to start the washin' sometime before noon, you know!"

"Just as well get up now, Jesse. When Hattie starts clearin' the table she'll wipe the pablum right off your chin if you ain't finished!" Clive laughed and went to find the hunting gear.

"I'm finished now anyway, and thank you, ma'am, for the most tasty breakfast. I'll do my best to plug a rabbit or two to skin."

Hattie's responding laughter was a welcome sound to everyone and helped lighten the mood of the morning. The three men were hustled out of the cabin, and Hattie and Laurel were left to straighten the kitchen together.

"I didn't mean for you to happen onto Pete's Bible like that, honey. I guess I was absent-minded about puttin' it back on the shelf. I guess I'm absent-minded about a lot of things since Jesse told us what happened. I have been tryin' to reconcile myself with it all, but still, in my heart I imagine him steppin' through that door, smilin' in his way, and askin' me what's for supper."

"So Pete and Jesse fought the war together? Jesse was a Union man?" Laurel spoke the words into the dishpan, scrubbing her plate with a slow, deliberate circling motion.

"I got the idea that he didn't really know Pete all that well, but was there when . . . " Hattie paused. Outside the door, a short way into the woods, the staccato of a woodpecker's pounding broke the stillness. Hattie thought of the firing of guns in the Georgia pines for a moment, then continued, "He was there when Pete was wounded. Shot, he said. And must've been gone in a second, so maybe he didn't suffer."

"All of us was wounded by the stupid war and all of us suffer, Ma! Look at Pa. He went away whole and come back almost crippled. It will not likely stop either. Not with Pete, not with us, not with any fool who fights with guns and shells, nor with them they leave behind."

Hattie lay down her work and looked Laurel squarely in the face. "You got to throw off bitterness, child. I've lived a long while, and if there's one thing I've learned, it's that bitterness only eats away at you yourself, and never harms the ones it's aimed at."

Laurel had discovered over the years how to counter her mother, and she knew which spots were sensitive. Without missing a beat, she used that skill now. "That so, Ma? Then, how come you carry such a big grudge against the people down at Lone Oak? Seems to me you have got a mighty big chip on your shoulder when it comes to them."

"I ain't referring to dislikin' jackasses and snakes in the grass." Hattie replied, just as quickly. "That's different. Nobody has to kiss a rattlesnake's fanny or poke a mule from behind to know their kind ain't up to no good. I'm talkin' about things you and me can't help. What I'm sayin' is, don't go blamin' Pete for the whole war, nor Jesse either."

"You like him, don't you, Ma?"

"Jesse? I do, that. And not just because he's helpin' Pa on the road. There's somethin' decent about him I ain't seen in a long while."

"It's funny, though. I recollect seein' him somewheres else myself. I'll put my finger on it before long." Laurel went back to dish washing, pondering Jesse's pleasant features. He was just this side of what she'd call handsome, and something about him was almost pretty. It was right on the tip of her mind, she thought, and she counted on it coming to her before they all got back from fishing. The morning inched by, no rabbits were flushed out or shot. "Guess I'm just bad luck on bunnies," said Jesse, as they returned to the cabin. "It's like the last time I went fishin'. They didn't bite a lick either."

"Never mind about it," said Clive. "It was a good change from fellin' trees."

"I got no bunnies for my honeys. I got no bunnies for my honeys," warbled Arthur, trailing behind the two of them, happily rhyming.

As they stepped up to the porch, Hattie and Laurel were sweeping and shaking rugs. Laurel looked up and suddenly realized where she had seen Jesse. The whole scene played clearly before her. She stared directly at him and said, "Pretty boy hero!"

Even Hattie was shocked and immediately reprimanded her. "Laurel! I never saw you so rude! Jesse, don't mind my girl here. She must still be a little sick." Jesse surprised them all by laughing. He took off his hat and shook his hair loose, letting it fall over one eye.

"Pardon me, Mrs. Beaudine, but it's perfectly all right. I was beginnin' to wonder if I was so washed out that I never made an impression on anybody. Your daughter here is just re-memberin' where she saw me a while back." Hattie and Clive stared open-mouthed at the two of them. Jesse's laugh mellowed to a slow smile, and he continued, looking at Laurel. "I wondered if you lost your job over the decoratin' you gave that soldier. Looks like you really didn't need my help after all."

Hattie was exploding with curiosity. "What are you talkin' about, Jesse?"

"Ma, I never saw you so rude! Don't mind my Ma, here. She's a little nosy!" Laurel smiled at Hattie and nudged her with good nature. "It's a funny story, Ma. Guess I forgot to tell it to you before."

Laurel related the incident, embellishing only slightly, for Jesse's entertainment mostly, and they all had a good laugh over it.

"You better watch out, Laurel honey. Next time you're in trouble maybe there won't be no Jesse around to step in," chided Hattie.

"Well, it appears she didn't need my help anyway. I reckon Miss Laurel can stand up to any man and come off winner." Jesse meant his remark to be a good natured challenge. He should have stopped there and then, but continued. "Especially if he's sittin' down and she's got a bowl of hot gravy in her free hand."

"You sayin' I had the advantage? I could've whupped that little toad with one arm tied behind my back. For that matter, I could probably take you down two out of three wrestles!"

Clive lowered his head and coughed slightly. Hattie reprimanded her gently, "Young ladies don't wrestle, Laurel honey."

Jesse said, "Well now, in that case, maybe she's right. Maybe she could take me down." He was grinning from ear to ear.

"Are you sayin'," countered Laurel, in a raised voice, "that I ain't a lady?"

"Jesse's not sayin' anythin' of the kind, Laurel," said Hattie. "He's just agreein' with you."

"No he ain't! He's agreein' with *you*, just to get my goat!" She slammed the broom to the porch floor, and sputtered. "Maybe Mr. Pretty Boy here is more used to simpy, lily-water petticoats than he is to a real woman!" She stomped into the door yard, turning her back on all of them.

"You better talk to that girl about her manners, Clive," advised Hattie, suddenly afraid that Laurel might scare Jesse off, their road would go unfinished, and her last contact with Pete would be gone. "Go on. She might listen to you."

Clive removed his sweaty hat, ran his hand through his matted hair, and shook his head. "Hattie, I'm not touchin' this one with a ten-foot pole!"

Jesse, on the other hand, was not put off one bit by Laurel's outburst. It was that same spark he had seen and liked in her at the dining room, and just watching her bristle piqued his interest to a curious physical reaction. His blood flowed warmly through him, his arms tingled, and he felt intensely alive. Maybe even alive enough to one day tame a wildcat.

Chapter Fourteen

THE LETTER

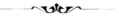

May 15, 1865
To: Hattie and Clive Beaudine
Lone Oak, Kentucky

Dear Mother and Father,
* I most happily inform you that I am still alive. I have been rescued and saved from a dread and dismal death by two very kind people. My wounds are healin' well, tho I was at death's door for many days. They found me in the woods after I was shot. I have been hidden here in their shed and owe my life to them. Soon I will be coming back home and I will bring Amy Sutter and her child back with me. You will like them. I intend to marry Amy, as she is a widow. And a beauty too.*

Amy declined several times to write the last sentence down, but Pete insisted, sayin he didn't want his ma to think he was bringing home a wrinkled old hag dressed in black. It was signed in Pete's shaky hand, *Your Loving Son, Pete.* They sealed the paper with hot wax and handed it over to Jim. The mail was being picked up sporadically at a way station not too far from the mill, so Jim took the letter the next day and left it with the station man. "Can't guarantee when somebody'll be by to pick it up, you know. It ain't as if we was up north, where they're talkin' of railway cars carryin' the

121

mail regular. 'Course it'll be a wagon headin' north that'll take it, since the Union has ripped out any southern tracks to speak of. I'll see it gets on its way soon as I can."

Andrew Slye took the letter from Jim and tossed it casually into a box in the corner. Andrew was fairly new to the area, and his pinched little face did not attract the interest of people thereabout. References to his origins were vague, and he seemed always to wear a salty expression and to be slightly bilious. Though he was a generally sour character, the Sutters had no reason to distrust him.

Friends were in short supply for Andrew. He was slow at finding a niche and didn't seem to get along easily. In his own way he tried, but the only headway he made was with a group of men who managed to get a card game up every week or two. He was grudgingly included when he proved to be a tolerable player.

Life at the way station was boring, full of sad stories and lost equipment and ill kept schedules. Andrew himself felt bored spitless with his own paltry existence, wished he'd been a soldier but couldn't muster the courage, and shuffled from one menial responsibility to another, winding up in this dismal job in the dead-end deep south. The one thing that kept him going at all was his contempt for the Yankees. He silently thrived on it and dreamed and plotted schemes and adventures that featured himself as the conqueror. When Lincoln was killed, Andrew placed himself in the shoes of the assassin, gloried in his vicarious accomplishment, but, unlike John Wilkes Booth, got away with it. He saw himself returning to the south a hero, surrounded by throngs of grateful Confederates.

When the general news failed to excite his imagination, he began doing the one thing a man of integrity would never consider. He opened the packages waiting for delivery and read the letters meant for other eyes. He read Pete's letter that very afternoon.

Andrew's vivid imagination spun out of control during the remainder of the day. He wove lurid tales in his mind about

Amy and Pete. Beaudine, he thought, could be a slave name—and maybe the man was a darkie; maybe he was a Yankee. It could happen, at least in Andrew's fabrications, and he began to devise a plan to uncover the treachery that surely must have taken place at the Sutters'. He decided that Pete's letter must never reach Kentucky, and, in one wild fantastic indulgence, he saw himself in a hand-to-hand battle, bringing this Pete person and the Sutters to some grisly form of justice.

He was bursting for the opportunity to confide his views with the card cronies that night. Dang, it would be sweet. Now they would sit up and take notice. As it happened, his announcement was met with disbelief and laughter. After the game, he returned to the way station, confiscated the letter, and stuffed it into his shirt pocket, intending to show it around the next day. They'd see that he was right!

In the Sutter household the excitement of their newly hatched plans and romantic schemes filled Amy and Pete's next hours. Pete figured he could manage travel after another week and mapped out a rough schedule for their trip north. Jim allowed they could take the wagon and one of the horses.

There had been an old road following the Flint River that would take them northwest and through Atlanta. From there on, Jim didn't know what to advise.

Thus far, they thought, no one knew of Pete's stay at their place, for they had been extremely careful about hiding him. They still feared retaliation from Southern sympathizers. If it were known they harbored a Yankee soldier, suspicions about their underground activities might be raised, and the war was still a fresh and wide open wound. They were not eager to pour any more salt into that wound.

"Pete and me will be married as soon as we get farther north, so nobody here knows or suspects. I guess we'll leave after dark, for safety's sake too." Amy explained their plans to Jim, who sat solemnly absorbing her narrative. Each time he listened to more talk of plans, it was as if their undertaking was new to him. He was having difficulty accepting the idea that Amy and Cotton Two were actually leaving.

"How long you figure it will take to get to your folks' place?" he asked Pete, who was cuddling the sleeping Clary in his good arm.

Pete puckered his lips in a peculiar way he had, and stroked his chin as he calculated the miles between them and Lone Oak. "Far as I can tell, it's about four hundred and some odd miles to Lone Oak. With the horse and wagon and on fair roads, we could make it in maybe a month. Who can tell? Might be we'd even get there before the letter, and really throw the folks into a tizzy." Pete laughed easily at the prospect. "I can just see my Ma now. She'd let out a whoop they could hear clear to Lexington."

"Well, tomorrow we'll start layin' in provisions and check the wagon to make sure it's goin' to get you there safe and sound." Jim stood and tried to muster enthusiasm for Amy's sake. She was acutely aware of his inner turmoil, and spoke to him gently.

"Jim, we meant it when we asked you to come along. I hate to leave you here alone. Please think about it. Clary's goin' to miss you somethin' fierce."

Jim's eyes rested on his sleeping granddaughter. "I thank you, Amy, and Pete, for the invite, but the mill is all I know now. Maybe sometime I'll come on up and visit. Besides, the little codger will forget me soon enough. That's just the way of it."

The following day, Jim took the wagon to Harley Forrest, the blacksmith and one of the players in Andrew Slye's weekly game. In a hurry, he interrupted Harley's conversation with Andrew himself. Jim's timing could not have been worse. "Fix her up good, Harley," he said, in a rush,

"She's been needin' a look-see for a long time." He quickly unhitched the big black mare and saddled her, already late for his shift at the mill. "Let me know what the damages will be," he hollered over his shoulder, and rode away, raising road dust behind him.

Andrew looked sharply at Harley, his eyes squeezed into tight, narrow slits. "What did I tell you boys last night? We got us a Yankee abolitionist right here under our noses. That there wagon is for the girl and the Beaudine fella to sneak off in!"

Harley shook his head, unable to believe Andrew's accusations. "I knowed Jim a long time, Slye. I never suspicioned him bein' a abolitionist, even if his son was."

Andrew's face was reddening and his neck bulged with engorged veins. "What more do you need, man? His son a Union man, the girl from up north, the letter scrawled to some podunk town in Kentucky! The Yankee hid in their shed! Wouldn't surprise me if they ran slaves through there too. No, sir! I say we got snake in the grass abolitionists right here, and they been gettin' away with it while the whole south burns to a cinder!"

Harley shook his head, still turning the thing over in his mind. Andrew pressed forward. "I say we all go out there tonight and rout that Union boy out of Sutter's shed, and get to the bottom of it!"

Harley protested. "You know, for a little squirt you sure got mighty big ideas. And where'd you get the notion he was hid out in their shed anyway?" Andrew chose that moment to draw the folded sheet from his pocket. Harley's jaw dropped in disbelief. "You openin' folks' private letters?"

"The envelope come unsealed. I couldn't help but read it." Andrew paused and opened the letter slowly, for effect. Then he clutched it close to his chest. "You want to see it for yourself, don't you?"

Harley struggled for a brief moment with his conscience, then said, "If'n I do, it'll clear the matter up for me, one way or the other, so I guess it's all right." Now, Harley was a reputable blacksmith. Nobody turned out finer iron than he did, but it might be considered that so many hours spent over the fire had introduced too much carbon and sulfur into his brain, making him highly suggestible to incendiary notions. He read the letter and scratched the back of his neck. "Who'da thought it of Jim Sutter?"

"We got to show this to the others," Andrew said, snatching the letter out of Harley's sooty hands. "If'n you see them today, send 'em on over to the way station, and they can judge for theirselves, just like you did."

"So how come you never showed it to everybody last night?" asked the blacksmith.

"Because, they're just like you. They wouldn't believe it, even with the evidence right in front of them. It was too soon, don't you see? They had to think on it overnight, chew on it, come to their own light. Send 'em over, then." Andrew said, his tone wheedling and slick as the devil himself.

All during the day, one by one, the card players stopped off their beaten tracks at the way station. Each in his turn read the damning letter, injected his own interpretations, and drew the same conclusions that had come from Andrew. One or two of them being riled at having an abolitionist under their noses would have been plenty, Andrew reasoned, but six all together, properly fired up by his harangue, could rid the area of Yankee scum and he could run for election next time around. Later that day they did meet, but not to play cards.

"First off," said Andrew, now glorying in his dubious limelight, "one or two of us has got to sneak out there tonight and get a look at this Beaudine fella. If he's crippled up from bein' shot, so much the better. He'll be easier to take down that way."

"What are you talkin' about, take down?" Harley wanted to know.

"What do you think? Are you thick or somethin'? Get rid of him! Finish the job!" Andrew sputtered.

Another player, Cal, gaped at him. "Kill him?" Andrew looked dumbfounded from face to face. "Why not? Up north, they say the war's over, but I don't see no reason for it to stop as long as one Yankee, or Yankee lover even, is left in our state. Look what they done to us!"

Hank, the lean player, stood up and slapped his hat on his balding head. "It looks like bad business to me. I wash my hands of it. You can count me out."

Andrew responded loudly, "Hank, you're like the old man who dropped his tobacca wad in the chicken yard . . . *confused*. You don't know what you're lookin' at anymore. I'll tell you what we're lookin' at. We're lookin' at a south overrun by Union sympathizers and money grubbers who'll buy up our land for cheap, and take what little we got out from under us!"

The two remaining players sat pondering, rubbing the stubble of their respective chins. Shem, the short one and youngest in the group, nodded his head. "If it's true, and I'm not sayin' yet that it is; if it is, then we ought to go on over to Jim Sutter's place and ask him right out." Andrew was popping at the seams. "Then what? We ask him nice and polite and he nice and polite tells us a bald-face lie. You think he's goin' to fess up just like that? Why a course I'm a Union man and a abolitionist, to boot. War's over now, so what you boys goin' to do about it? And then he laughs hisself silly over us dumb clucks that let him get away with it!"

"She always was stuck up. Looked like she was hidin' somethin' behind that snotty look, too." The speaker was Roger Ward, the one they all called Weasel because of his long, narrow face and small eyes. "She never give nobody the time of day."

The time of day was not all that Weasel had asked of Amy once when he passed her on the street in town. She was quick to put him in his place, and he had resented her ever since. "She must be waitin' for the king or somebody to come along. It ain't natural for a widder that young and pretty to be so up-pity when only a few of the good lookin' men are left," he had said to one of his buddies. "Her and Jim must have somethin' goin'." Weasel's grudge, like a bothersome little animal in the back of his mind, now had fresh fodder for feed. This accusa-tion by Andrew was rich, and dove-tailed neatly into Weasel's previous notions.

"I'm right with you, Andrew. Count me in," he said. Harley was still contending the question, now believing, now doubt-ing. In the end, he decided that Andrew was just too anxious to jump in feet first, without more investigation. He backed out as well, leaving only Andrew and Weasel to conjure some plan against the Sutters. Harley figured the two of them couldn't fight their way out of a burlap bag, so he left, unconcerned that anything might really happen to Jim and Amy.

With everyone else gone, Andrew and Weasel sat staring at one another uneasily for a few moments. Weasel was the first to jump up. "Well, hell! What's wrong with tonight? We could scoot on out there right now, and have a look-see." Confronted so closely here with one who would actually go through with the loosely formed plan, Andrew was somewhat stymied. No one had ever agreed so readily with him before. He had thrust himself forward as leader of a plot, and now that he had a follower, he was in a slight muddle. He thought on it for a second or two.

"We'll wait for another hour or so. Then we'll skirt around the place by way of the woods, so we're comin' from the opposite direction of town. We'll check around their shed and outhouse and see if we cain't get a look in their windows. We got to go it sly though, so they don't catch on. Could be old man Sutter keeps a rifle handy and has a itchy finger."

"Listen," said Weasel. "I got me a jug t'home, if we want a swallow before we head out. It's good stuff, too." A swallow was just what Andrew needed about now, to carry him through the next few hours. He nodded his head and followed Weasel to the little room where the dusty jug was kept. As it happened, the two of them managed to drain the corn squeezings right out of it, and break open a smaller jar for good measure. An hour or more of screwing up their courage left Andrew and Weasel slightly fuzzy about their mission. Every drag on the potent juice enhanced their resolve to do something, but the end result kept wavering. "Let's check the shed" led to "let's bust into the house" to "how about we burn the whole place down."

Candle lighting came upon them suddenly, and during the time that passed while the two men drank, the already scanty sliver of moon hid itself behind black and heavy storm clouds. In the hills to the west of the woods, broad sheets of lightning shimmered above the inky horizon, flashing intermittent summer signals through the night. The downpour that followed fell suddenly, in the wake of furious winds. Andrew first sensed the storm and stuck his head out of Weasel's door. "Damn!" he shouted against the howl. "We couldn't burn a groundhog out of his hole in this. We just goin' to have to wait 'til tomorrow to show them abolitionist dogs!"

Weasel mumbled, almost incoherently, "We'll burn the witch out t'morrow!"

"I got somethin' we can burn tonight, tho'," said Andrew. He drew Pete's letter from his pocket and turned it over in his bony fingers. "Yankee boy ain't never goin' to get home, so his folks won't have no need for this letter. Look at it! He ciphers like a girl anyway. Prob'ly a Nancy-boy on top of it. That stuff about marryin' the Sutter woman is just to cover."

He began to giggle at himself and stared at Weasel. "You ain't no Nancy-boy, are you? 'Cause I got to ride out the storm here in your place. I don't think I could find my way home anyways, feelin' like I do."

"You goin' to be sick? If'n you are, you got to stick your ugly mug outside to do it!" Weasel jumped up but swayed quickly back into his chair.

"What was we drinkin'? It tasted pretty good on the way down, but somethin' tells me the return trip ain't goin' to be no pony ride." Andrew burped and spit generously on Weasel's dirty floor. Then he stood, flapped his arms, and swatted each of his pockets wildly, looking for match sticks.

"Gimme a dish or somethin' to lay this letter in."

"You know what?" observed Weasel. "I cain't see a thing in here. We forgot to light ourself a lantern. I got me one there in the corner."

He stumbled against the table and located his kerosene lantern, sloshing some of the fuel on the floor and down his pant leg. He swore loudly and fell back into the rickety chair. Andrew lit his first match with shaky hands. The feeble flame was blown out immediately by a storm gust slipping through the narrow crack under Weasel's door. Andrew's second try was successful, and he lit the letter before trying the lantern.

On the third match, he kindled the blackened wick, and it burned high, casting a brazen yellow light into the room. The letter was still crackling and turning in its own fire when another breeze lifted it off the table and to the floor. The kerosene trail left by Weasel was instantly ignited, and fire traveled quickly to the corner of the room. Weasel fell to the floor, slapping at the flames with his bare hands and shouting obscenities at the lantern, the storm, and Andrew. Crawling on the floor, he followed the flames too closely, and the kerosene-soaked pant leg caught fire. Andrew watched as if in a trance.

Weasel danced a frantic jig, trying desperately to beat the flames away. He hollered to the stupefied Andrew. "Dammit, Slye! This ain't no frolic here! Put me out! I'm all afire!"

Andrew snapped to it and took Weasel literally, thrusting him into the pelting rain. Weasel's flesh sizzled and stuck tight to his cotton pants when Andrew tried to pull the burned fibers away from his leg.

"Stop it all hell's fire son of a buck! You tryin' to *kill* me? My leg's near burned off. Git me some help!" Weasel was rapidly feeling the effects of shock, but Andrew had turned his attention from his injured card partner to the place Weasel called home. It was little more than a lean-to shed tacked on to the back end of McConnell's barn, and from the looks of things, would soon be nothing more than a heap of ash. Even the downpour did not deter the rapid spread of fire through the barn siding. Old man McConnell's three horses crashed heavy iron hooves against the wood stalls, and their frightened, high pitched whinnies brought people running from the main house.

By now, Weasel's limbs were shaking violently, and he felt chilled, though his leg seemed burned to the bone. Andrew watched him and smelled his flesh and heard him, but stood rooted in his place. It occurred to him in a fuzzy, misty way that he did not want to be found at the site of a fire, that somehow it might have been his fault, and someone might learn that it had been Pete's letter that started it all. He cast one brief glance from the house, to the smoky barn, to Weasel before running behind a water soaked lilac bush to wretch and heave up what was left of his supper. While Andrew staggered home, the fire was extinguished, Weasel was attended by a doctor, and the sodden ashes of Pete's letter became completely and irretrievably a part of the Georgia landscape. Hattie and Clive would never read his words, Laurel would not tuck that precious page between the leaves of his Testament, and Jesse's dreams would still embrace the fallen man just beyond the dead line at Andersonville.

Throughout that same evening, Amy, Pete, and Jim gathered truck to go on the wagon to Kentucky. Amy carefully considered each item before setting it aside for the journey. All the trinkets on the shelves of the whatnot in the corner belonged to her and Clary, so her choices were easy on that wise. But other things which she had shared with Cal she would ask Jim about. The rocking chair in particular had belonged to Cal's mama, but all three of them had rocked Clary to sleep in it, and Jim liked sitting in it of an evening. It traveled a regular path between the kitchen and the dooryard, depending on the weather. She would perhaps wait for him to volunteer that, though it would make a fine keepsake to pass on to the child when she grew older and had her own babies.

She picked up the tin bread box that sat on their sideboard. Cal had fashioned it himself and punched out his own design with an awl one summer day. *I guess Cal really did love hearts,* she thought, as her fingers ran across the symbols of love which served as air holes on this common kitchen piece. She recalled the heart-shaped locket, wondering if it would be proper to cover Cal's likeness with Pete's.

Pete had just finished packing a small box with pins and needles and mending threads when the wind first picked up in the woods. He went to the open door and scanned the sky above the trees. "Laws, it's fixin' to blow a big one. Smell that rain in the air? We'd best close up tight."

"Why, in that case, Mr. Beaudine, you'd best stay the night in this cabin, seein' that the shed leaks like a sieve when it rains around here." Jim spoke, really to the two of them, with a twinkle in his eye. "If you don't travel in your sleep, why, the two of us will do just fine in my bed." Amy and Pete laughed easily with Jim. He knew that they restrained themselves in his presence, but he also remembered how it felt to be young and anxious for loving. He liked to tease them and hoped they were saving man and wife relationships for the marriage bed. They shared his feelings, but it was a sore trial to keep boundaries clear.

"I'm as quiet as a mouse and I sleep like a dead man. Thanks for the offer, Jim, but maybe I'll just roll out on the floor. You got anythin' else to put in this little chest?" A sudden flash of lightning and roll of thunder ushered the full storm into the woods, quickly followed by the slapping of huge raindrops on their roof. Clary was awakened and came crying to her mother.

"Rock me, Mama," she begged, and Amy pulled the rocker close to the hearth, put the child on her lap and hummed softly to her. Jim glanced at the two and loved them silently.

"We have not had a real good thunderstorm like this since you came to us, Pete. Best we just close up shop now and take our rest," Jim advised. "There's blankets in the chest by the wall. Help yourself and sleep good."

Clary raised her head from the shielding cocoon of her mother's arm. "Will we get drownded out, Mama?" Her eyes were bright with childish fear.

"Not in a thousand storms, Honey. This here cabin is sound as a dollar. Grampa Jim built it himself, from the ground up," Amy assured her. She stood up, swinging Clary around a full circle, and plopped her playfully on the braided throw rug. "There now, miss. You crawl on into Mama's bed and I'll be with you real quick." She allowed Pete a brief hug and peck on the lips in front of Jim, then disappeared behind the modesty curtain to her own room. When the lantern was blown out, Pete spoke into the shadows.

"I purely wish I was a fly on my mama's wall when she gets that letter. She'll just plain have a conniption fit waitin' by the door. And Laurel, well, maybe she'll forgive me for goin' off to war when she sees what I'm bringin' home!"

Clary's small voice answered his. "What you bringin' home, Pete?"

Pete propped himself up on one elbow, though no one could see him, and bragged loudly to the wind howling outside. "I'm bringin' the two prettiest girls in the whole Confederacy and Union put together, that's what!"

Amy could not resist a retort in the darkness. "So now I'm only a 'what' and not a 'who'? You goin' to strap me on that wagon like some old bedstead, I suppose."

Pete had no answer for her, except a surprising apology. "Aw, Amy. I was only funnin'. I guess I'm havin' a hard time learnin' woman talk."

Jim felt obliged to add his two bits worth of wisdom. "Pete, you had ought to get used to that, for it ain't likely to change in the next hundred years." Then he rolled over and announced that it was time to go to sleep. The only sound heard after that was the distancing thunder as the storm rumbled through the woods and made its way to the next county.

Chapter Fifteen

Moving On

W easel was out of his head the next day, that was plain to see, so when he babbled to the doctor about Andrew's burning abolitionist letter starting the fire, nobody paid much attention. The country physician loaded him up with additional morphine to kill his pain, and dressed his wounds in such a way that he probably did him more harm than good. Andrew steered clear and lay low, feigning surprise about the fire when Harley mentioned it to him.

"It must of happened after I left off talkin' to him. He asked me to stop on by for a drink, but I come home. I put that letter right back in the box and danged if it weren't picked up this very mornin' by a fella ridin' to the next way station. So, it's gone, see? There ain't no more evidence anyways about Jim Sutter havin' no Yankee stashed out at his place. Guess we'll just let the whole thing drop."

Andrew looked Harley straight in the eye while uttering four of the biggest lies of his career. He still firmly believed that Jim was an abolitionist, and deserved to be punished somehow, but it seemed best to him to keep shut about it. He would have to try to convince Weasel that last night had not happened the way that he recalled it. Upon hearing the news that the letter was on its way north, Harley felt better, cleansed somehow of having read words not meant for his view. He went back to his shop to continue the repairs on Jim's wagon. After Harley was gone, Andrew swallowed a huge dose of pain powders, trying desperately to rid himself of a very unfortunate hangover.

When Amy stepped through her cabin door that morning, she inhaled deeply of the wet pine smell and watched a pair of mockingbirds harass a young squirrel. In turns they would dive at the hapless animal, and finally chased him into some heavy, damp brush. They darted away through the trees, wracking the air with their brazen cries. She would miss these pines that were so much a part of the place she had called home these last four years, and wondered if Clary would remember her days here at all, or if what Jim had said about forgetting was true.

As she stood thinking, Pete slipped up behind her and put his arms around her shoulders. His skin was still warm from sleep, and he nuzzled her neck gently, burying his face in her wonderful hair. "What are you thinkin' about, Punkin?" he murmured into her ear.

She cocked her head slightly and said, "I've been thinkin' how I might miss this little place, and the pines where I found you half in the other world and half in this one. I was also thinkin' about what Jim and me did just over the last two years."

"With the slaves, you mean?"

"Uh huh. I never did tell you much about that, did I?"

Pete turned her slowly around and studied her face.

"No, you didn't, and I'm plain amazed you had the grit to do it. If you'd been caught, it could've gone real bad for you."

"But we didn't get caught, and I know why too. The Lord don't like slavery any more than the Sutters do, so He protected us. I do believe that's why He invented hoop skirts as well."

Pete was puzzled. "What has hoop skirts got to do with anythin'?"

Amy laughed. "Because, Mr. Beaudine, many a little pickaninny has escaped under the hoop skirts of northern sympathizers like myself. Walked right past the whole Confederacy practically, and scooted out from under those hoops like a passel of busy black ants."

"You have one of them skirts and I never saw it?"

"Had one. I shredded it one day for bandages to wrap up a poor wounded courier who was bleedin' like a stuck pig!"

Pete backed away from her, holding her at arm's length. "You cut up your skirt to save me? I can't believe it. What a piece of work you are! My mama is goin' to slosh molasses all over you and eat you up. My whole family is goin' to love you to death!"

"Hold on, Pete. They'll think what they please when they know me better. As long as you like me."

Pete placed his fingers over her lips and said, "*Love* you, as long as I love you everythin' will be all right."

"I hope so, Pete." Amy answered quietly. Her thoughts skipped backward to all the times she and Jim had indeed risked their own safety to escort slaves to freedom. "I just wish Jim would consent to come with us. He could start over again easy. Maybe you could talk to him again about it."

Pete squeezed her to him and replied, "Anythin' you want, Punkin. I do think he'd like Kentucky, and there's sure to be some kinda work there. I'll do my best."

They walked back into the cabin to take their morning meal and pack more of her belongings for the trip. By afternoon, they were down to sifting through Amy's most personal things. She carefully removed some rarely used linens from a crate by her bed. She unfolded them and shook them loose, looking at the fine line embroidery she had done as a young girl. The patterns were simple, but closely stitched, a grape design with vines trailing to the corners, all white threads on white linen.

"My mama showed me how to do this. She was wonderful at it, and one day I'll teach Clary so that part of Mama will live in my child. They never did know one another; Mama died right after I came here. Did you know Clary was named after her?"

"No, I did not, little lady. There's still a lot I don't know about you and your kin. That's what we got a long life together for, you know. To learn all them things and make our own history and our own babies." Pete grinned openly and impishly at Amy, knowing the baby talk would get a rise out of her.

"You'll just be hushin' your mouth about babies until we are properly wed, young man. You know that little pitchers has got big ears around here."

"Clary? She'd be overjoyed at havin' a new little brother or sister. Besides, who's she goin' to tell anyway? I'll say this, all them Beaudine babies will be cute as bugs, if they look like their mama."

"And they'll be rascally as gypsies if they're anythin' like their daddy!"

"Gypsies you will be, by next Sabbath or before." It was Jim, coming home with news from the blacksmith. "Harley says the old wagon wasn't in such bad shape and only needed some work on the axle. We can pick 'er up by Friday, most likely."

Pete made a quick calculation. "We could be eatin' flapjacks at my Mama's table before June is over!" Amy caught his eye and motioned in her father-in-law's direction. He understood the gesture and turned to Jim. "Sir, I'd be pleased if you'd change your mind about comin' with us. Harley'd probably help you sell your place here and people all over are gettin' new starts."

Jim looked at the two youngsters, so full of hope and bright promise, so able to jump into the unknown, and simply shook his head. He had considered leaving with them, but felt he would be riding on their coat tails, so to speak, and he was just too proud to do that. "I thank you both for your kindly invitation, and I do understand it. But I believe I will stay put for now. Maybe right along I'll change my mind and come north and look you up, but I already got my few crops in and things look good at the mill, so I'm goin' to stick around for a while."

Amy heaved a defeated sigh and crossed the room with her arms outstretched to Jim. "I will never forget you, Jim. And I won't let Clary forget you either. We'll always be family."

Jim blinked his eyes and swallowed hard, then reached into his pocket and withdrew a much-creased piece of paper. "This here's a roughed out map of the old trail along the Flint. If you stick to it you should make it up to Atlanta all right. If you need to, you can maybe buy more provisions there and ask better directions than I can give now. By Friday the moon will be on the wane, so the light will be dim, but I can lead you to the river road and you'll be on your way."

"We'll be on our way." Amy repeated the phrase with the ticking regularity of Jim's hand wound watch. Almost the same as going back home, for she had been born and raised just on the north side of the Ohio, in a place behind a small bluff overlooking the river. It was rugged in its way, and green, and she remembered the waters below, and her mother's well-founded fears for Amy's safety. *My knees quiver,* her mother used to say, *when you young 'uns go near the edge, so stay away. That water will suck you under quick as you blink, and you'll come up somewheres along the Mississip!* Amy had been the only girl of three children, born one after the other, smack, smack, smack, and practically out on the road every time. Her father had moved his little brood five times before settling by the river where their last baby, a boy, was born. So, Amy grew through the rough and tumble childhood years, flanked on either side by two sandpaper elbowed boys who teased her and made her strong, who loved her and protected her and made her trusting.

Despite their mother's many warnings, the river drew all of the children to it, and sure as the sun got up every morning, one of them did go too close to the water. It is a hard thing to lose your brother, a boy you thought would grow old right alongside of you, a boy you tried to protect from himself and all other dangers when he was small. And then one night you dream his face becomes a skull and he walks away from you, calm as a summer's day, and you know that somewhere in his future, there will be no more future, and you will be one brother down in life.

But, where the river took away one of the loves in Amy's life, it gifted her with another, that sort which is stronger, more urgent and bears you away from your memories and your roots. Calvin was working the broad Ohio when Amy met him, and he was so full of fire and spit and charm that he wooed her into marriage, far afield of her Ohio family. Never mind. The young can do that, and the old, like her mother and father, just have to stand and kiss them good-bye, with their sad fingers fluttering on the ends of their hands, helpless. After all, they themselves had done the same as youngsters.

Now Amy would be doing it again, this time to Jim. She thought, *Life is just a round of hellos and good-byes and the kissing of loved ones and casting of last looks at familiar sights. Pretty soon,* she mused, *the mind is so full of coming and going that a person must eventually wind up where she started.* She wondered if when her brother died, his spirit came home, and if Calvin did the same. Was he with her all this time anyway, and did he perhaps lead Pete through those woods that early morning, just so Amy would find him? By Thursday their bundling and packing of needed furnishings was finished, and Amy's few precious belongings were tucked safely into chests, all wrapped in cotton scarves. Jim had gone to Harley to ask after progress on the wagon, and had driven it straight back to the woods that very day. With evening came the final task of securing everything in the wagon. Hand over hand they passed the nestled crockery, the patterned bread box, the cherished baby dresses, folded neatly between layers of hoarded wrapping paper, the finely stitched quilt she had brought from up north. A wooden mixing bowl, a cast iron cooking pot and frying pan, numerous long-handle utensils, and a worn tea kettle would serve as her kitchen on the road. It took two of them to load this box. Their bedding was left for tomorrow, so they could have one last night's sleep under a roof. Darkness had crept through the woods while the three worked, and a lamp was lit after they retreated to the cabin. Clary had already fallen asleep on Jim's bed, and so they kept their conversation low, their mood subdued. Amy's handiwork was all stowed away in the wagon, so her fingers would not be busy this last night in Jim Sutter's home. She crawled into Jim's bed next to Clary and drifted off to sleep while Pete and Jim played a short hand of rummy before they finally settled in.

The cooking fire had died out long ago, and the comfortable old rocker sat empty before a cold hearth. Jim glanced up at it and remembered the many hours he had spent there, rocking young Cotton of an evening, crooning to her in his tuneless way. His attention wandered too far from the card game and he lost to Pete. "Guess that's about it for me tonight," he said. "Reckon I'll let those two stay on my bed. I'll just roll out on the floor here and you can take Amy's tick."

Everyone slept. Everyone dreamed in the Sutter cabin. In the back room of the country doctor's office, Weasel struggled with his pain and cursed ever having met the way station man. Andrew, in his own small cubbyhole, thought daring thoughts and devised cunning schemes, more misled in his detachment than ever before. His dreams were drafted of too much drink, too little judgment, and too many delusions. The next morning Andrew grappled with his twisted clothing and dropped out of the low bunk, feeling like "hell on a slow day." His tongue was fuzzed over and his eyeballs were dry and burning in their sockets. There was a familiar density clouding his gray matter, a sort of soft tingling passing back and forth between his ears, a ringing of internal origin. The vigorous shaking of his head produced a pain inside that brought to mind a hot steel ball rolling side to side, front to back. *Stupid!* he thought. *Ought to know better.*

During the day, while Andrew performed his menial duties at the station, elaborate displays bounced around his brain. That he would have to rid Georgia of at least two or three abolitionist dogs by himself was clear to him now, and his fertile mind continued to produce impossible and grandiose tactics. He finally settled on a plan. It was so simple and yet so rich that it caused him to laugh out loud. He could barely wait for darkness to fall. He was not aware that this was the very night Amy and Pete would leave, and his dreams of snaring the Sutters and the Yankee all together would have quite a different outcome than the one he imagined.

Friday morning, Jim went to his work at the mill as usual, though minding the routine job was difficult. Amy and Pete packed their bedding into the wagon and put together the last of their rations. After that, there was little more to do than wander around the two room cabin, steal kisses behind Clary's back, and play games with her. As for Little Cotton, she hadn't grasped the idea that they would be going very far away from Jim, and looked on the trip as something to do until supper time. Then, she imagined, she would play with Bullseye and go to sleep in her own bed, with the dog lying by her side.

When Jim arrived home, Amy was seated in the rocker, with Clary on her lap. The picture was so sweet, so familiar that a pang of regret passed through him, and for the briefest moment he thought again of going with them. The feeling subsided quickly, however, and he did not mention it. After supper, as the sun began its decline above the trees, Jim tossed a tarp over the meager mound of Amy's collectibles, and tied it all down with several lengths of good, strong hemp. "If you get rain, this tarp ought to keep some of the damp off," he said, "and this extra piece you can use for coverin' your own selves and little Cotton as well."

Then he stood back, surveying the load and scratching his chin. "Seems to me there's somethin' missin'. Amy, did you put in all your kitchen stuff?"

"I did. And I left everything you said you needed."

"Did you put in all the flour and sugar we got?"

"I did. Are you thinkin' we need to take some out?"

"Oh, no. Just wonderin'. Are you sure you got everythin' you'll be needin?"

Amy thought for a moment and replied, "Sure as ever I'll be. The only things we didn't pack in was ourselves."

Jim turned to Pete. "Seems to me there's somethin' real important we all forgot. Did you get all of Cotton-two's dolls and playthings?"

"Every one, Jim. Except o'course, the dog." Pete was as puzzled as Amy with Jim's questions. Hadn't he been right there for the loading and securing?

"Still, when I look on that wagon, it looks like there ought to be one more thing on it. Looks to me like there's a space right about here," he said, walking to the rear of the load. "Just big enough to set a rockin' chair!" he continued. "Yes, sir! That was it all along! Pete, go fetch me that rocker and we'll tie it down good and tight."

Amy faced Jim with surprise. "Oh, Jim! That rocker was Cal's mama's. It rightfully belongs to you."

"It rightfully belongs to Cotton-two, you mean. Someday she'll have babies of her own and when she rocks the little fellers, she can say it's in her grandmama's chair, the one that rocked herself and her daddy before her." Pete had brought the chair and hefted it to the back of the wagon.

Amy's eyes welled with tears as she watched the two men tie it securely and fasten off the knots. "I can't thank you enough, Jim. It's the one thing I really wanted."

Now there was no getting around it. Time to go. The waning moon was on the rise, and a few high clouds trailed their filmy streams across the sky. The travelers headed west, away from the woods and the town and toward the Flint River. Pete had tucked Jim's map in his pocket and patted it several times to make sure it was still there. Amy had let Clary ride with Jim on his horse to the point where they would go their separate ways. Bullseye sat between Amy and Pete, lapping the breeze with his long, wet tongue and enjoying the ride.

A good-bye springing from sorrow is one thing, and a good-bye mixed with high anticipation and adventure is another. When they pulled to a halt before the parting of ways, Amy felt as if she were jumping into another skin or riding on the whispers of pines in the wind. All nerves and weightless, all knots and milkweed at once, she kissed Jim's whiskered cheek and brushed the mill dust from his hair.

"I'll write you soon as we get there," she promised and Pete nodded his own farewell.

"I can't never thank you enough, Jim. Maybe someday we'll see you again."

"Maybe," said Jim. He patted Clary's face and became speechless. The little white-haired girl was now drowsing on Amy's lap. He chose not to wake her. He whistled the dog down, then wheeled his horse quickly and sped away, becoming lost in the deep hour, taking with him the jangle of his stirrups and the muffled pounding of hooves.

Owls in the woods and field mice skittering through the damp night went about the business of survival, seeking and hiding, swooping and hugging the earth. Jim rode the same night trail, looking only now for rest, and trying not to consider morning. His return to home was swift, and soon he reined his horse to a halt just outside the barn. He ought to feed the beast something, he thought, and walked to get the oat bucket. Bullseye circled in a curious way through the clearing and began to sniff under the closed cabin door. A few high whining noises sounded from his mouth and soon became short, anxious barks. He stood on his hind legs and began to scratch at the door, turning to look Jim's way every few seconds.

Jim emerged from the barn and slapped the oat bag over his horse's nose. "What's rilin' you, boy?" he whispered to the dog, and advanced toward the cabin. He stopped short of opening the door to listen in the darkness. His hand rested on the dog's muzzle, and Bullseye understood the signal. Now Jim heard no sound except the soft whir of raptor wings through the tree tops and the shoo-shoo of the night owl. Instinct told him, however, that Bullseye had indeed sensed something or someone inside his home. He slipped back to his mount and pulled his rifle off the saddle where he always carried it.

It was very dark by now and the cloud cover had at last obliterated the slivered moon. Jim walked softly back to the cabin, with Bullseye padding cautiously beside him. As they neared the door the dog's hair stood on end and a deep, threatening growl rumbled from far down his throat. He stared intently at the door, stretching the tendons in his neck and bristling from his ears to his tail. Jim lifted the latch and kicked the door in, jabbing the gun through the thick, black, empty space. "Whoever's in there better ease on out before I blast your guts all over the wall, be you man or beast!" In a moment Jim heard a small, quavering voice coming from the corner by the hearth. "Please, Mister. Don't shoot me. I was lost on the road and stopped for shelter. Nobody was t'home, so I just come on in. I didn't mean no harm."

"Step on out, then. Let me see your hands straight to the front of you. Make it quick!"

He saw a figure shuffle quickly to the door, a man it was, hiding his face behind a vest. The man bent while walking, in a further effort to hide himself. "Please, Mister," he repeated in a voice somewhat familiar to Jim, "I didn't mean no harm."

"Don't I know you?" Jim asked sharply, and reached out to take hold of the man's arm. In a flash, the intruder darted across the dooryard and fled towards the woods. Jim briefly considered raising his rifle to fire at him, but pointed it instead to the sky and shot into the trees. He could hear the man crashing through the woods, and wincing as he hurried through the dense growth.

Inside the cabin, Jim lit a lamp and surveyed his home. The only thing out of order was a chair, which the intruder had apparently knocked over. All else seemed to be the same, and nothing was missing. *Well*, thought Jim, *I'm glad Amy and Cotton wasn't here with me. Might have scared the little one.* Then he pictured her asleep in the wagon, bouncing through the night, on her way to another life. He gazed down at Bullseye and patted the dog's tilted head. *Funny how a dog seems to read your mind*, Jim mused. Aloud he said, "Well, boy. Guess we better take that oat bag off the horse before he eats his way through it."

He went out and was back in and sleeping before the half hour had passed.

144

The next day the boys from the card game had to do without Andrew Slye, who had most mysteriously disappeared during the night. Strange, they commented, how he left all of his trappings and just up and evaporated like that. He was a weird duck anyway, and in a day's time they got themselves a replacement at the card table and forgot about Andrew. Jim Sutter was left in peace.

Chapter Sixteen

KENTUCKY CLEARING

R ain's wonderful on the garden, ain't it?" Hattie hunkered before the hearth, stirring the fire to life, making
ready for the morning meal. Clive grunted a rather
surly reply, speaking more around her than to her.

"Roof's leakin' by the front door again. Guess I got to
plug it up better this time."

Should have done it when the weather was good, Hattie wanted
to say, but it wouldn't have done any more than irritate her already testy man. If she had to be cooped up all day in the cabin
with him, she may as well keep shut about the crack in the roof
and get about her business. It was Sunday, one day following
Jesse and Laurel's abrupt clash. After Laurel had stomped away,
Jesse smoothed things over by saying, "Miss Laurel probably
still feels slightly sick, and naturally wouldn't take to teasin'.
I'll try not to upset her that way again." Hattie and Clive had
each smiled secretly at his effort.

They could all feel the rain coming that night, and smell
it in the air. Jesse and Clive had spent a good deal of Saturday
afternoon clearing more trees from the trace, ever widening
and lengthening the roadway down to the meadow. When the
first tang of impending rain came upon them, they packed it
in and headed for the cabin. Arthur was not with them, and
nobody had seen him since after the noon dinner. Jesse had
been told that the boy often wandered off like that, and they

never were seriously concerned about him because he always popped up again around supper time. Last night, however, he had not come in, and they concluded that he must be holed up somewhere, waiting out the storm.

Now, with the morning and the continuing rain, Arthur was in the back of their minds.

One by one, the group filled in, until the four of them were in the warming kitchen. Hattie had built the cooking fire, and Clive was still cogitating on the patching of the roof, while Laurel sat silently mending a tear in her overalls. Jesse tried not to feel useless, so he volunteered to make coffee with the beans he had bought in Lone Oak.

"They look a little puny," he apologized, "but I really did just buy them down in Lone Oak last week."

"Oh, we all know who sold 'em to you. Asa Bitter would sell his grandmaw to the Shawnee if they was buyin', and see if he couldn't get a return when they was finished with her."

Clive retorted, not so much in Asa's defense as in rebuke to Hattie. "Asa's been hard hit by the war, just like everybody else. Can't blame a man for tryin' to make a livin'."

Hattie was not having any of Clive's reasoning. "You see how he sold off other things durin' the war, and don't tell me he didn't. The man's a no-account, low disgrace to the human family!"

"Damn his soul to hell!"

They all turned and stared at Laurel. These were her first words of the morning.

"Laurel!" Hattie said. "There's no need for swearin'!"

"I don't see the difference between thinkin' it, which everybody does, and sayin' it out loud. I'm sure Mr. Jesse here has heard worse than that in the Union army."

"I have indeed, Miss Laurel," Jesse replied, and wanted to add that he had never heard it from such a pretty girl, but thought better of it.

"The coffee'll taste just fine, Jesse. Don't you worry about that," Clive assured him. Then he asked, "How was your sleep last night? Storm keep you up?"

"I slept well, thanks, and the storm did not keep me up. It just feels good to sleep under a roof."

"Speakin' of which, I got to figure out a way to patch this one up before we get washed away."

"I can help out, if you don't mind, sir. Just tell me what to do," Jesse volunteered, rising from the stool to leave the table. His eyes fell on Laurel, and he took note that she quickly averted her gaze, which he was sure, had been in his direction.

"I can help too, Pa," she offered, "soon as I get these coveralls fixed."

"Never you mind about the roof, honey. That's man's work. It's about time you put your mind to more woman's chores."

Hattie winced at Clive's thoughtless remark, for she saw the immediate rise in Laurel. Laurel had been working at Clive's side for years, and now, like Arthur, she felt a sense of rebuff with the young and able bodied Jesse here. She stood up quickly and dropped her spoon into the yellowed crockery bowl. "Well then, I'll just go see to my knittin' and let you and your hired man fix it!"

Silence thick enough to wade through permeated the room, and everyone felt the tension. Hattie glared openly at Clive and berated him inwardly for such a stupid remark. Jesse read the territorial jealousy in Laurel's voice and didn't know what to say. Clive wondered what the sudden outburst amounted to, and Laurel threw on her slicker and headed for the door. "I'm goin' to go see where Arthur might be. Holler when all the man's work is done so I'll know it's safe to come in!"

Jesse kept his silence and left the next remark to a Beaudine. He hoped it wouldn't be Clive, stuffing his foot any farther into his mouth than it already was. Hattie opened her own mouth to speak and was halted by Arthur, who bolted headlong through the door. Laurel was right behind him, her slicker streaked with bright red. Arthur's shoulder was bleeding badly, and the soaking rain had washed blood clear down to his pants.

"Heaven have mercy!" Hattie shouted, finally catching her breath. "Who done this to you, Arthur? What happened?" Arthur fell forward into Jesse's arms, breathing heavily and gasping every intake of air.

"Just settle, boy," said Jesse. "You're gonna be all right."

He lay Arthur gently on the floor and raised the boy's legs slightly. "Put somethin' under his head here," he commanded. "And get a blanket to cover him." Laurel moved quickly to help her brother. Arthur had fainted and could answer none of their questions, so when they examined the wound he did not feel their probing.

"Looks like buckshot to me," said Jesse. "I saw plenty worse from mini balls, and my guess is he can pull through this if we get it out fast."

Hattie had composed herself and began to rifle through a chest where she kept medicinals and such. Laurel ripped Arthur's shirt to expose his shoulder so that they were able to see the blood oozing from several wounds. Hattie set Clive to work tearing long strips of bandaging, and repeating to him the names of various herbs they might use for healing. They pressed forward at a feverish pace to clean as many of the wounds as possible before Arthur came around.

He was not spared pain and had to be subdued by Jesse and Clive and Laurel all together, while Hattie did her best to dig out the shot.

When they were finished, the whimpering Arthur lay in his mother's arms, muttering about the rain storm and finding somewhere to stay. Hattie now persisted in her questioning.

"Who done this to you, son? Did you see? Where did it happen?"

Arthur answered straightforward. "It was Mr. Bitter, Mama. Old Asa seen me and Annie Grace together and chased me down with his gun. Mama, am I goin' to die and go be with Pete? Is Pete in hell, like Mr. Bitter says?" A silent, sharp exchange between Hattie and Clive told Jesse that something like this might have been anticipated long before today. It was not a pleasing thought that Mr. Bitter probably lay in wait for the time he could do harm to simple minded Arthur. "Pete is not in hell, for darn sure, Arthur! As Asa Bitter will sure find that out the minute he gets there himself!" Laurel had taken Arthur's hand and held it tightly, trying to control her own shaking as much as her brother's.

"He will answer for this, the coward!"

"He hollered at me and said to leave Annie Grace alone, and get away b'fore he's goin' to shoot me, and then, he up and started chasin' me."

"He chased you all the way from Lone Oak?" Clive broke his silence with this question.

"No. Me and Annie was in Stetson's old barn, gettin' out of the rain. We go there sometimes."

"That's more than a mile from here," said Laurel. "Whereabouts were you when he fired on you?"

"I was in the meadow, by the edge of the woods." Arthur answered, then moaned loudly and buried his head in Hattie's bosom. He had come a long way, wounded and bleeding, and headed straight up the trace which was becoming the road to home.

Jesse was sickened by the vision of this harmless boy, soaked with rain and blood, stumbling helplessly through the rugged woods. His mind raced back to so many others he had seen doing the same, raced back to himself, running lost and tired through strange territory, just yards ahead of gunfire. It turned his stomach to see Arthur bleeding from his own enemy, in his own private and one-sided war. Yes, Laurel was right. Asa Bitter belonged in hades. Then, ruefully he reflected, perhaps all men who fire on the helpless belong there.

He had a sudden and fearful thought. "Do you suppose I should go and see about Annie Grace? He wouldn't harm her, would he?"

"No more than usual," sneered Hattie. "Like a snot, she ran the other way when Asa took off after Arthur. No, I wouldn't worry about Annie. She has places she can go 'til the old man cools off."

Hattie and Clive spent the remainder of the day absorbed in Arthur's care. The storm dispersed and by afternoon the sun had warmed any chill left by the rain, so Jesse decided to ride down to the meadow. The woods were fresh, and water clung to the leaves, pearling them with glassy drops of light. To look closely at one of them was to see the rainbow repeated in singular perfection. To see them all through the woods was to take in a thousand prisms, and to behold a thousand miniature sunbursts.

Jesse wondered what was to be done now. How would the Beaudines handle such violence against one of their own? It was a double-edged question, with Asa Bitter straddling one fine rim of the sword, and Jesse himself slipping on the other. The difference was only that they knew about Asa's act, and Jesse still cloaked his in silence. He doubted he would ever tell them. No, he would be long gone when this road building business was finished, and they would never be the wiser. Still, a certain feeling gnawed at him; the feeling that he might never be able to let it rest, no matter how many trees he felled or how far the road stretched from Tennessee to this family's home.

He reached the meadow and sat on the horse contemplating the direction from which Arthur had probably come. Gradually he became aware of movement behind him. Shifting in the saddle, he saw Laurel riding from the woods, sitting high and proud on her mare, and coming straight at him. She reined up next to him and spoke in her blunt fashion.

"I've come to apologize for my ignorance. I have been rude on no other account than you was a soldier and brought the bad news about Pete. For all I know you tried to save him, and, well, you did come a long way. I'm most grateful to have his Testament, too. It means a lot to me, to us all." Jesse was caught off guard and tried to suppress a tight cough that gripped his throat. He had hardly thought to hear, or felt that he deserved, praise from her. She had completely unsettled him. He realized he was staring at her like a dumbfounded fool and tried to think of a response.

"It was the least I could do, Miss Laurel. I, uh, should apologize too."

"Maybe we ought to start all over and be friends," she offered her hand to him.

Jesse reached out his own hand and, as the two touched, raised his eyes to meet hers. She had wonderful eyes, he thought, green like the bright spring trees around them, and suddenly warm toward him. She averted her gaze after what he considered too short a time, and spoke of showing him Stetson's barn.

"You can see how far Arthur had to come. Asa must've been on his horse, chasin' my brother like a wild man. We're goin' to catch the sheriff or judge when one of 'em comes around the county circuit and take care of Asa good and proper. My folks don't go for blood reproach, but they'll get him with everythin' else they can." She laughed a strange, throaty laugh. "My mama's sittin' there right now, dreamin' up a curse on the old man's business or somethin'. Mama's wonderful with curses. At least she thinks she is. She's too Christian to do bodily harm, but she ain't above spells and damnations. Once she cast a spell over the preacher down there in Lone Oak, and while he was preachin' at a tent meetin' his very coat tails caught fire. It was a caution! He sat right down in the sanctified water to put himself out. She said she did it because he was preachin' blasphemy and takin' money from the poor to support his bad habits."

Again Jesse was caught off center. Laurel had said so little up to now that he had not realized she could string this many words together at one time. He liked it. He liked her voice and the way her face lit up while talking about her mother's eccentricities. He liked the way she sat straight and tall on her horse, and that her hair was such a wonderful, rich chestnut hue. *No gettin' around it*, he mused. *Laurel was one considerable fine lookin' woman.*

152

"Come on," she challenged, "I'll race you to the barn!" She started to nudge her horse into action, but Jesse was too quick for her. He grabbed the reins and held her back.

"Hold on! Now, that would give you the unfair advantage, Miss Laurel. You already know where the barn is!" This time, Laurel was caught off guard. She restrained her competitive instinct, and let Jesse keep his grip on the reins.

"Unless you're in a real big hurry," he said slowly, "I'd like to just amble along and have a look around. Seems like it's goin' to be a nice day after all."

"Fair enough," she answered. "I can show you some of the prettiest spots in all of Kentucky, right here in my old stompin' grounds."

Across the meadow they spied a red-winged blackbird puffing out his chest as he clung to a slender cattail. Looking at it, Jesse remembered something from his childhood.

"My daddy used to read me a poem when I was a boy, all about that bird. Wish I could recall it. It brought to mind exactly what a person might think seein' a red wing."

"Your daddy? My daddy never read to me. 'Twas always Mama. That's the way it mostly goes."

"Strange though it might seem, it was always him. He is more inclined to reading than my mama was. She did handiwork, mostly, quiltin' and such. She's gone now, but what she made is still as good as new."

"Where's your home, exactly?"

"Tennessee—Murfreesboro—Water Street—exactly."

"So you and him went up to Springfield to see Mr. Lincoln laid out?"

"More than that. Daddy wanted to sort of be a part of somethin' important, some place in history, not just to read about it."

"Too bad he didn't get there, since he set such store by it."

"Oh, he asked me to keep up his journal and write down everythin' I saw for him. It's not the same, but it'll be close."

"Well, what did you put down about Lone Oak and the

Beaudines? Anythin' interestin'?"

"To tell the truth, I have been too busy to record any of my adventures here in Kentucky."

"Ain't we interestin' enough for you?"

"Now, Miss Laurel, I never said such a thing. Just said I was too busy, that's all. Take this afternoon for instance. I could be back at the cabin writin' about all that happened to Arthur, but what's happenin' right now is much more interestin'."

"What is happenin', Mr. Jesse Campbell?"

"Why Miss, I am trottin' along on a fine horse, over a fine meadow, on a fine summer's day."

"Hmmm," she replied. "Well, to me it still looks like a good one for a race. See that stand of poplars over there? Bet money I can get to it before you do!" Jesse was suddenly fired up by her challenge.

"Greenbacks?"

"Whatever you got!" she hollered and dug her feet into the mare's sides. She was off like a shot. Jesse's first thought was to thump her soundly, but he restrained himself instead. He waited long enough and nudged his horse lightly enough that he allowed Laurel to beat him to the mark. Pulling up just slightly behind he hoped it appeared that it had been a real race, since the last thing he wanted to do was spoil the afternoon by getting her riled. She stood high in the stirrups and smiled triumphantly as he brought his horse around to face her.

"Where'd you learn to ride like that?" he asked, only slightly gasping.

"Me and Pete used to race, from the time we was knee high to a grasshopper. When I was little he could always beat me, but by the time he—" she hesitated, then continued, "by the time he left, I could pretty much keep pace and even whip him once in a while." She was reflective for the smallest moment. Then she said, "Come on then, and I'll take you to the barn."

Stetson's barn was dilapidated, the siding grayed from years of weather. The hay loft had completely collapsed, but there was one corner that could afford shelter.

"This is where they most likely were. Like Arthur said, they come here sometimes. Asa knows it. Mama and Daddy know it too, but they can't keep watch on them all day and night, so Arthur and Annie meet out here."

Jesse was not quite getting the full picture, and rather innocently asked, "What harm can come of their bein' together? At least they seem to understand each other."

Laurel looked at him with disbelief. "That was a Clive question if ever I heard one. Ain't you ever had a girlfriend? Arthur and Annie may be addled but they still got feelin's. No doubt they meet here with one thing on their minds, and I don't think it's their ABCs!"

Jesse suddenly felt stupid, and once again speechless. He scratched behind his ear and shook his head before responding. "Well, uh, I just never imagined that people, well, like Arthur . . . "

"Had urges? Wake up, Jesse! People is people. You must've grown up under a box or somethin'." She smiled at his discomfort and continued. "Asa's scared Annie's goin' to pop out a freak or worse."

"If he's so scared that will happen, how is it he let her bring me out here?"

"Maybe because you got money. Maybe because he knew she'd do it anyway. Maybe because he thought Arthur would see you together and get riled at her and they'd have a fight. I wouldn't know."

Laurel shook her head and continued. "If they're lucky, Annie Grace would be barren by now. But Mama says if it ever happened she'd take Annie and the little critter in and raise it up herself."

"Your mama has got a big heart, I guess. I admire her spunk."

"Call it what you want. She holds us all together most of the time. Even if I smart mouth her sometimes, I respect her. Her notion that Pete was goin' to make it home kept her high through some hard times, but I can see now that she is havin' a struggle with the bad news, though she tries not to let it show."

Jesse was touched as he realized how much caring flowed between these two Beaudine women. Laurel's main concern seemed to be her mother's welfare, and Hattie's was for Laurel. They were a strength to each other. Clive and Arthur fit in the picture too, but the energetic undercurrent in the family poured through Hattie and Laurel. He wondered if his father would like them. They were so different from his own mother. Marcus! He was now shocked to realize he hadn't given much thought to his own father since coming here. He should write to Marcus, he reflected, and breaking the train of conversation, remarked, "If I send word to my daddy, would you mail it from Paducah? I should really let him know what's goin' on."

"I would do that. Mail gets picked up on Wednesdays there. We could use Ruthann's boardin' house for return word. Oh, but I suppose that depends on how long you plan on bein' out here."

She looked at him for a moment, then casually plucked the coarse mane on her horse's neck, obviously waiting for an answer.

"Guess I'll be here 'til the road's finished now. Arthur won't be much good with that shoulder shot up. 'Course if you could help out, we'd get it done faster, but you got your job over there."

Laurel nodded quickly. "There's no way I could lose that job just to whack trees down and beat a wider path for myself to travel on. Without that job I wouldn't have nowhere to go anyhow. Besides," she jabbed him just the slightest bit, "that's man's work."

Jesse laughed at the comment and wheeled his horse away from the barn. "You know, now that you showed me where this barn is and I know for myself how to get back to your place, I think another race is in order. What do you say?"

"I'll go it," she answered, "But this time we start together and don't hold back just to make sure I win!" After supper, Jesse chose solitude for the writing of his letter to Marcus. He had torn a sheet from the journal, sharpened the lead pencil with his pocketknife, and sat down to write. So much had happened, it was hard to know where to begin. Deciding to start with Springfield, he gave the barest outline of events, saying that a more detailed account was to be found in Marcus's journal. He did include the incident between Cougar and Neils, knowing it would be a source of satisfaction to his father.

As he described the Beaudines, he found himself wanting to include Pete, almost as a living member of the family. Indeed, he had felt, in a most supernatural way, that Pete was here anyway. He supposed it was the way Laurel spoke of her brother and Hattie's strong feelings that he should have come back. But it remained something more, something inside. Perhaps he had just tried so hard to avoid telling anyone the awful truth, that it was easier to deny it to himself.

He chose instead to write about the wonderful coincidence that the girl at the boarding house was here. He decided not to devote too much space to her, but managed to spell out her name once, just for the pure pleasure of putting it in writing. His father might think he was smitten if he mentioned her too much. He concluded with his intentions to help Clive complete the road.

Since Arthur will be laid up for many days, maybe weeks, I have decided to stay on and lend a hand until the way is finished. Hoping that your recovery is speedy and you are back at the Register, *I remain, Your Son, Jesse.*

Laurel tucked it inside the pocket of her coveralls and assured him it would go in the first mail out of Paducah. She left at sunup the next morning, retracing the path she and Jesse had raced together, feeling the crackle of the crisp paper in her pocket. When the light was fully up, she removed the folded letter and studied its front while she rode. The handwriting was slanted and a little uneven, and the address read: *Mr. Marcus Campbell, 112 Water Street, Murfreesboro, Tennessee.* She wondered about Tennessee and the look of a house on a street named Water, and the feel of the quilts

a woman might have made for Jesse and his father. She suddenly became aware that it was going to be a long week, and
hoped in the vaguest way that there would be enough rain
to slow the work on the road. Men can't work at felling trees
in the rain, now can they?

Chapter Seventeen

THE GOWN

Arthur's recovery was going to be complete, or Hattie would hang up her water-witching and seer-shingle, and pack it in. She hadn't been given these extra sensory gifts for nothing, and it was for darn sure she would use them in her own boy's behalf. She was a praying woman, a Bible-reading soul, and she believed completely in faith healing. But she was practical enough to know that the Good Lord placed herbs and curatives all around us if we just knew where to look. He also gave certain ones a finer tuned feeling for the secrets held close to Mother Earth's bosom and the gift to look at a person and see the hidden workings of his soul. She held that she could discern a man's character by the spirit of him and that people walked with a kind of light around them, and some's light was brighter than other's. In many the light was absent, and seeing them was like looking at folks covered with road dust. As Hattie felt herself to be one of these chosen, she didn't mind letting anyone know. It was, after all, a gift and not something she had worked at acquiring, so it ought to be shared.

Asa Bitter was one with whom she shared some of her insights. He had been told in no uncertain terms and with no holds barred that his was a shriveled and mortgaged soul, for Hattie had perceived in him an evil spirit. When the war came and Annie Grace was a grown girl, big enough to be sold off a little at a time for cash money, Hattie shook her head and asked Asa what good had come of him bargaining Annie with the devil. He had traded his own child for coppers and colored paper and dirtied himself with stains worse than the inks from Old Scratch's press.

Asa countered that men had used the girl without his permission, as if Annie were property anyway. He couldn't chain her to a tree, could he? After all, he was only a single man, doing his best to raise a witless girl in hard times.

Now the despicable ogre had gone after her boy and shot him up, could have taken his life. Hattie thought long and hard about Asa's recompense. The law would soon pass through the territory and she could hope for justice on that wise, but the only eye witnesses against him would be two simple-minded children whose words were never believed anyway. Still, Hattie was a patient woman. She knew that the proper curse would come to her with time, that Arthur would heal by her faith and wisdom, and that somehow all would be made right in heaven.

As it happened, the weather that following week was glorious, and though Laurel's hope for rain was not answered, Clive's dream of a proper road came closer to being. He and Jesse worked day after day, taking advantage of the season, and returning home each evening bone tired. Jesse found that, while he liked Clive and Hattie both, he didn't comprehend their odd match. She was strong-willed, outspoken, perceptive, and had a certain edge. Clive was softer, perhaps as determined but more quiet about it, and ideas that were native to Hattie flew over his head like pixies on gossamer wings, noiseless and airy. He told Jesse that before he went into the Army he was a hard swearing man when provoked, but he had given it up after hearing so much of it there. The Army had changed him in other ways, he said, and made him appreciate things in life he hadn't seen before. Though he seemed slow at times, he was not a stupid person, but his world differed widely from that of his vocal wife. Jesse wondered why people of such opposite dispositions so often married.

He also daydreamed of Laurel. He couldn't help himself. She was there in the woods where he hauled trees, and she was moving about the cabin at suppertime, wearing a white dress, with her wonderful waist cinched tight. He imagined her riding swiftly across the meadow at the end of the trace and letting her hair fly loose and free. He would like to have written about her on a page in the journal, but restrained himself, not knowing exactly what to say. When she was home again the following weekend, they danced around each other in the ways that young people do when they find mutual attraction, picnicking, riding to the meadow together. Another week of heavy work passed. The way was almost being cleared faster than Jesse intended. He wanted more time to shake out his intense feelings for Laurel and to discover how she might respond, if, for instance, he should try to kiss her.

Laurel returned at her usual time the following Friday, just as Jesse and Clive were walking back to the cabin themselves. She jumped down from her horse and walked with them, saying it had been a long ride and she was tired out from sitting in the saddle.

"Daddy," she said, "you can ride her on home if you like. It'll save your leg walkin'."

Miraculously, Clive took the hint and rode ahead of them, leaving the two to walk together the last little distance. Jesse was filled with the pleasant sensation and hope that maybe she had been thinking of him too.

"How's Arthur doin'?" she asked, getting that subject out of the way quickly.

"He seems fair. Your mama stirs up a mean poultice, and she has some stuff to make him sleep. Helps him heal better, she says."

"It also keeps him out of her hair while she dreams up some way to get Asa back," Laurel laughed confidently.

"Looks like you've got the faith in her that she can do it. There must be somethin' to her magic if you believe in it.'"

"You think I'm hard as nails and don't believe in much?"

"Nooo," he drawled slightly. "'I thought maybe since you've been around her your whole life you might not think it was unusual or magic. Myself, I have never known any kind of charmer, so it's all new to me."

"Well, believe me, she can do it and what's more, it always looks natural. She don't stick pins in dolls or anythin' like that, but she has her ways. You wait and see." They walked a little farther in silence, surrounded by the unfolding summer evening. He still wore his army issue pants, but had traded the shirts for civilian styles, and though he was sweaty from the long day's work, he appeared invigorated and fresh. She wore the coveralls again and a blue cotton shirt that had belonged to Pete. On her head was a straw sun hat, and her chestnut hair was pulled only halfway back, framing her face with soft brown wisps. They arrived at the cabin a little before sundown and walked in to the aromas of good food, cooked well. Hattie was just pulling the kettle away from the fire when they came through the door.

"Laurel, honey. I'm so glad to see you. Soon as you two wash up we'll eat. Then I got somethin' to give you." Laurel looked at Jesse with a puzzled expression. Jesse returned her glance with a shrug of his shoulders that said he didn't know himself what Hattie was talking about. Supper talk was mostly of Laurel's week in Paducah and the retelling of funny stories about Ruthann and some of the regulars. There wasn't much to the narration on tree felling, and Arthur's recovery was coming along fine. Hattie's surprise would have to cap the conversation. Laurel asked with more than a little curiosity about it.

"Well, we set and et. Now what do I get?"

"You rhymed it Laurel," Arthur beamed. "Just like me!"

"I did that, Arthur. I guess that makes me almost as smart as you." She smiled warmly at him, sincerely complimenting his gift for rhyme. "So what is it, Mama?" Hattie reached into her trunk by the wall and drew out a skirted garment, a dress made of blue and pink gingham. She held it up and swung it free through the air, at arm's length, letting the skirt sway and settle nicely, the hem barely touching the floor.

"Laws, Mama! That is a beautiful dress!" Laurel was nearly speechless.

"It ain't just a dress, honey. It's a gown. Somethin' you wear on special occasions or to go to church in. I thought it was about time you had one."

"Mama, I don't even go to church. And the only special occasion in my life is bein' home on the weekends."

Jesse spoke quickly, as if in a foreign tongue. "Then, this bein' the weekend and you bein' home, you should put it on right now."

Laurel blushed, another out of character occurrence. The thought of Jesse seeing her displayed right here, so close, caught her up and brought blood to her cheeks. "Oh, I don't know. It's been so long since I put on a dress. Maybe it won't even fit me. Why don't I wait 'til later?"

"Same folks is going' to be here later as is here now, darlin'. Just as well do it now and get it over with."

Clive wore a grin as wide as a barn door, seeing Hattie's purpose.

"Come on, honey." Hattie pulled her toward the other room. "I'll do up the buttons for you."

When Laurel stepped back into the kitchen, it was obvious that she was pleased with her own appearance. Arthur crooned to her immediately. "You are the most prettiest girl I ever seen in that dress."

"Well,'" she laughed nervously, "I am the only girl you ever saw in this dress. I mean, gown."

"I swan, Laurel. If I didn't see you walk in there with your mother, I'd say you was some other girl!" Clive was a master at left-handed compliments, so Laurel took no offense. If it had come from Jesse, her reaction might have been different.

"What do you think of it, Jesse?" Hattie peeked from

behind her daughter's shoulder.

Jesse cleared his throat to forestall the stammer he felt coming. "I, uh . . . I think she looks like a painted picture." He tried to keep his eyes from scanning her up and down, but it was nearly impossible, since he was supposed to be inspecting the dress as well. "That's a real nice dress, Hattie."

"Well, now that we're finished passin' judgment, and Mama I think it's a wonderful gown myself, I'll just go change back." Laurel made a hasty move toward the other room, where her comfortable and baggy coveralls hung.

Jesse jumped to his feet immediately. "Oh, no. Don't do that! We should show it off, out there in the garden. Why, the black-eyed Susans will bust out with envy when they see it. A dress like that deserves to be seen by the man-in-the-moon himself!"

"There ain't no man-in-the-moon, Jesse!" Arthur roared. "You made that up!"

"Well, if'n there is, and he sees my girl in that gown," bragged Hattie, "he'll hope there's a woman in the moon up there with him and that she looks like Laurel. Scoot on out there, you two!" Hattie moved in behind Jesse and Laurel, and hustled them through the door into an evening awash with soft, white moonlight.

"Mind the thistle though," she called from the kitchen.

Jesse and Laurel walked side by side, not too close and not too far from each other. Jesse spoke first. "You sure look different in a dress."

"You'd look different in a dress too. Reckon the last time I wore one was when I went to my granny's funeral. I was about fourteen. I looked like a scarecrow in a field."

"The last time I wore one, I was at my baptism. I don't remember how I looked, since I was just a baby then."

Laurel's laughter warmed the evening even further, and Jesse began to feel a little more comfortable with her. He wanted to ask her many things, talk to her of a thousand thoughts. Instead, the dullest possible question popped out of his mouth.

"So, how long is it you have worked at the boardin' house?"'

It was not the kind of question Laurel wanted to hear either, but she answered politely. "It's goin' on seven months now, ever since we got burned out of our house in town. Nothin' was goin' in Lone Oak, and Daddy had no work, so we just sort of squatted out here and I looked for work where I could. The folks who lived here before went back east and left the place to go to ruin. Mama and Daddy did most of the fix up, and I help out on weekends. Daddy's daydreamed about buildin' that road the whole time."

He watched her out of the corner of his eye, not daring to stare straight at her. He felt like a fool, his thoughts a jumble and his words too simple, but a happy fool at that. He waited for her to continue.

She didn't.

They walked on, slowly and deliberately, she with her head tilted slightly to the side, and he looking everywhere but at her. Suddenly she stopped.

"You don't have to do this, you know. I know what Mama's up to and so do you. If you don't want to be out here walkin' around this stupid garden, we can go back right now."

Jesse was dumbfounded. This was truly the only place in the world he wanted to be at all, and how she could have thought otherwise surprised him. "Well now, Miss Laurel. It was me suggested showin' off the dress, if you recall."

"I figured you was only bein' polite."

"Oh, no," he stammered. "I'm not even a polite person, in fact."

"You are polite enough to stay and put in hard hours on a road that will sooner or later just take you away from this place." She blatantly teased him, batting her eyelashes and shrugging her shoulders. "I can't see you comin' back for regular visits once you get back to Tennessee." Once again, he was stymied. What was it she wanted him to say, anyway? He made a stab at a sensible response.

"When I saw that your daddy was so set on gettin' it done

and how long it would take him and Arthur, I just figured I'd lend a hand before gettin' back to my own life. It was the least I could do . . . " He hesitated only slightly, then continued. "It was the least I could do since I brought the bad news about Pete."

"But it wasn't your fault Pete was killed. It was kind enough that you came out of your way to tell us."

"So then, let's say that I'm not really polite, but I am kind, and leave it at that." Without warning and without thinking, Jesse grabbed Laurel's hand and pulled her forward beside him. He quickened his pace and said, "Let's quit talkin' about me and see how fast your legs can run in that there pretty dress."

She squealed as he tightened his grip, and she lifted one side of the skirt with her free hand. He pulled her faster over the path. "Jesse Campbell! You got legs twice as long as mine! I'm goin' to tear my dress! Stop!"

He didn't stop until they were into the woods and well on the widened roadway. By then, they were both breathless and laughing, swallowing great gulps of air. Jesse felt life coursing through him from head to foot, his heart racing and blood pulsing heavily at his throat. If she looked at him at all, he would just have to kiss her full on the mouth. No matter what, that's what he would have to do. He nearly collapsed when he felt her arms locked tightly around his neck and her mouth pressed precisely over his. At that moment, a voice in the back of his mind fairly shouted: *Jesse, you haven't ever been kissed like this before in your life!* Don't let her go! He answered the voice silently by exchanging twenty or thirty more of the same with the most beautiful girl he had ever seen. There was no need for moonlight on Jesse's road in the woods that night, for Jesse and Laurel saw each other clearly behind closed eyelids.

When they walked back to the cabin, they dropped the hand holding just before entering the kitchen. Hattie looked up to see two young people filling the doorway with the peculiar glow that comes from discovery and mystery combined. She was pleased. She was satisfied that Jesse would do no harm to her girl, and she saw that the gown she had carefully sewn had done its job, just like magic.

Arthur called for Hattie then. Laurel went in to take off her dress, and Clive was already snoring in his deep, untroubled sleep. Jesse excused himself for the night and wondered if he would ever get to sleep again. He would hate to see Laurel leave. They had talked of many things, out there in those woods. He felt sure that these next two days would bring them closer, that his ties with Peter Beaudine would be bound by more than the memory of a young man falling at the end of his rifle. His giddiness overcame any cloud that Peter's name brought to mind. He would just deal with that whole memory later.

Jesse would be good for nothing as far as road building went that weekend. Hattie had suggested to Clive that he give the young people leave to enjoy such a nice warm day, and that he stay around the cabin and get to that roof before the rains came again. Clive at last played into her schemes, and acted as if it had been his idea. If Jesse and Laurel saw through it, they didn't let it be known, and they didn't mind her folks' matchmaking efforts. They were already making efforts of their own.

"I'm goin' to purely hate workin' this week," Laura told Jesse. "I wish I could stay right here and bring you dinner and cook your supper myself. I can't believe you just popped up out of nowhere and found us so easy, and that it was you next to Pete. It all seems so fateful, like Mama would say. She says everythin' happens for a reason. I used to doubt her believin' that, but now I'm beginnin' to consider otherwise. What do you think, Jesse?"

Jesse was winding her hair around his index finger and not particularly interested in talk at the moment, so he responded slowly. He kissed her head and cheek before answering. "I think that whatever you think is the most wonderful thought that was ever thunk."

She laughed and returned kiss for kiss to him. "Will you hate to see me go?"

"I already hate it and you are still here. And guess what? I'll work extra slow this week so the road will take twice as long to finish. Then I'll chop holes all over your daddy's roof so he'll need my help fixin' it. Then I'll knock down the rail fence around the garden so I'll have to split some more rails and put it together again."

Suddenly Laurel puckered her lips and crinkled her forehead. "Would you do all that for me, just to see me on the weekends? Seems like a lot of hard work just to chase around with a poor little country girl for a couple of days at a time."

"If you want me to, I'll tear the whole place down and rebuild it!"

"Now that is stretchin' it. Better watch out what you promise, Jesse Campbell. Maybe I wouldn't be worth it after a bit."

Jesse became serious and gripped her by the shoulders. His eyes swam with emotion. "I can't ever see that day comin'. Not ever!"

Their parting the next Monday morning was almost comical. Jesse got up early to see her off and rode with her to the meadow. There was much turning around and looking back at each other, waving of hands, and finally, standing in the saddle to allow broad swaying of the arms. At last, when they could no longer see one another in the distance, each turned and rode away.

Jesse threw himself into his tasks that day, driving hard to get rid of his pent up energy. Watching him, Clive thought of himself when he was a younger man, and when he had first loved Hattie. Being young was a blessing, he could see now, but for all that, he wouldn't go back and start over. Too many experiences had been too troublesome. Jesse would learn the same as he grew older, and some of the shine would wear off with him and Laurel. *What am I thinkin'?* he asked himself. *They barely knew each other, and already I have them married and dissatisfied. Next thing you know, I'll have them dead and buried. I'm gettin' to be as bad as Hattie,* he mused.

Jesse's energy worked against him the next day, for he pounded the pickax into a tree stump so hard it broke. The force of it rattled his teeth and threw him backwards. The handle was shattered beyond repair and since it was the only one he owned, Clive began to think out loud, looking to alternatives.

"Maybe we can dig out the stumps with the head of the hatchet, or burn 'em. We still got my spade and that might do it."

"I'm real sorry, Clive. I'll give it a go with the shovel, and if it don't work I'll go on into Lone Oak and buy 'nother one, since I broke it."

They talked of replacing the pick at supper, and the progress already made on Clive's road. Hattie jumped into the conversation with her usual vigor. "Don't you dare spend a red cent at Asa Bitter's junk pile of a store. If you insist on buyin' a new one, go on over to Paducah. I got somethin' here you could deliver to Laurel while you're at it." Hattie was becoming more and more transparent, and Clive expected her to offer a dowry for Laurel any minute. Not that he would mind Laurel hitching up with a boy like Jesse. He could see that Jesse was a match for her, and he wouldn't allow the girl to run over him.

Early Wednesday, Jesse headed for Paducah, retracing the way through Lone Oak. He hadn't seen Annie Grace since the first day she led him to the Beaudine's place, so he stopped at the store to inquire after her. Asa was there, puttering behind the counter, fidgeting, just as Jesse had remembered him.

"Mornin', Mr. Bitter. I'm just passin' through and thought I'd ask after Annie Grace. How's she doin'?" He wanted to say that Arthur was mending well, and he was curious as to any reproach Annie might have suffered, but he pulled up short of asking any more. Asa's undersized hand reached for his shotgun and he began to shine the barrel, all the while eyeing Jesse smugly.

"You know her well enough now to call her by name? I reckon you have heard all the tales as long as you've been out there on that cursed property. Let me tell you somethin', young man. If that idiot boy ever comes around my Annie again, there'll be hell to pay, and I won't be no twenty feet behind him with a pea shooter! I reckon I didn't kill him then?"

Jesse tried to control his response. His gut wrenched with the plain ignorance of the man, and the gloating expression on his face.

"I reckon he might be the only kind of person you could kill, Mr. Bitter. Especially from behind. But no, Arthur is not dead. You really ought to watch out carryin' a gun around like that. There's plenty back from the war with itchy fingers just like yours, and a lot better aim."

"That some kind of threat? Are you under the old harpy's spell, or is it the young one? Hattie looked like that when she was a filly, but you'd never guess it to look at her now. I'll tell you somethin' else, boy. A woman's bosom appears soft and invitin', but underneath it's flinty and cold as a gravestone. Maybe you'd best just keep on keepin' on, and head back to wherever it was you come from."

Jesse walked away from him, then came to a standstill at the doorway. "Tell Annie that Jesse stopped by to see her," he said, and disappeared through the open door. He rarely disliked a man on hearsay, and he had heard plenty from Hattie, but Asa's sour spirit had spoken so plainly, that now Jesse believed everything she had told him. He was hard pressed to think of a more despicable character.

The "something" Jesse was carrying for Laurel from her mother appeared to be no more than a bag of herbs and bark, probably a tea mixture. Jesse couldn't figure how it could be of great importance, but he treated it as if it were gold. "I'll see she gets this first thing, Hattie," he had said as he left.

"I do thank you, Jesse. And we'll see you when you get back."

Standing there, watching Jesse leave, Hattie recalled similar words which had been said to Pete. Somehow she still could not put those words to rest. She even dreamed once or twice since Jesse's arrival that Pete came back. She saw him, plain as day, ambling up that wide road Jesse and Clive were finishing. In her dream, the day was brilliant and he was shining. He was the same Pete, only brighter, and his spirit glowed all around him. *Maybe it's me seein' him in Heaven*, she thought. Maybe he's just as happy there and his reward is like a quick-silver happiness, and me dreamin' him is his way of sayin' he's all right, and then some.

She stared after Jesse until he was out of sight.

When he arrived at Paducah, Jesse found the boarding house first thing and arranged with Laurel to meet her when she was off for the evening. He went to the dry goods and hardware store and bought a good, sturdy pickax. He still had a good deal of money with him, for Hattie and Clive had refused to take any for board, even though he offered several times. He was feeling secure and almost childishly happy, and thought that he would take up some of his time that day by writing to Marcus about it all. It was too soon for him to have received a reply to his first letter, but he wouldn't wait for that.

After wandering around for a while, he decided to go back to the boarding house and get some lunch, maybe have a few words with Laurel. As he walked onto the worn porch planks, the door swung wide and a bearded man burst through, nearly knocking Jesse aside. The two looked at each other, and the unshaven man stopped dead still.

"Holy Joe!" he shouted in Jesse's face, his voice all too familiar. The beard had changed his appearance, but the voice and the eyes were the same, and the cocky swagger hadn't changed a bit. It was Cougar Rivers once again, in the flesh and louder than ever.

"Hot damn, it *is* Jesse!" He slapped Jesse on the back and smiled, revealing the gap-toothed grin Neils had given him in Springfield. "I thought you'd be back in Tennessee, married and makin' babies by now."

"And I thought you'd be dead," said Jesse, in the wryest tone he could muster. Bad pennies show up at the worst times, Jesse realized, and his first thought was that his wild and loose handed friend might have spotted Laurel and tried something with her already. "You just passin' through?" he asked, not knowing what he hoped the answer might be.

"Depends on what you mean by passin' through. Manure in a horse is just 'passin' through'. Stayin' for a few days and checkin' out the landscape might be passin' through to some, and to others it might be settlin' down for a spell. I got to see what's available hereabouts before I decide which I'm doin'. What are you up to?"

"I'm, uh, stoppin' by here for a bite. But I guess you already ate, so maybe I'll catch you around town later." Cougar eyed the pickax. "I did just eat, and I can tell you, the meat's tender so you won't need that there pick to cut it. On the other hand, if'n you want to make time with the hired help it might come in handy."

The hair on Jesse's neck fairly crackled, and his stomach churned with anger. Cougar most certainly had seen Laurel! Jesse controlled his voice and answered, "Well, I wouldn't know about that. I'm only here to eat."

Just as he spoke, Laurel came through the door. She smiled with delight when she saw him, and all but threw her arms around his neck. Taking his hand, she pulled closer to him.

"Jesse, you're back! I wasn't expectin' you 'til later."

Then she saw Cougar, and Jesse saw her face darken immediately.

Cougar grinned and purred like a cat with a newly cornered mouse. He had caught the pristine and spotless Jesse in a slight evasion of the truth, a thing which he hadn't dreamed possible before. "Ain't you goin' to introduce me to your friend, Jesse?" he crooned.

Before Jesse could speak, Laurel answered for herself. "I think one run-in with a polecat is all a person needs to smell him the rest of the day. Let's go inside, Jesse."

Jesse allowed Laurel to push him through the open door. Even as they walked to the dining room, they heard Cougar in his best voice call back, "Ask her if'n she's got a sister with a little more gumption. I like 'em lively, myself!"

"How in this world does a half-baked, bone-headed, jackass like him know you?"

172

"Why, he's my twin brother, don't you know?" Jesse teased her, pleased that she was so outspoken and that her first encounter with Cougar had been less than pleasant.

"Actually, he's from roundabout Murfreesboro too. He sort of latched onto me and my daddy when we headed for Springfield. I thought I'd lost him for good along the way."

"Well, I guess a bad apple keeps bobbin' up," Laurel growled.

"I don't know that he's such a bad fellow, but he seems to make poor judgments. But, I don't want to waste my time jawin' about him. How about if I get a nice big bowl of stew and sit here and talk to you?" Laurel smiled and shrugged her shoulders regretfully.

"Stew I can manage, but I can't spend time durin' work for chit-chat. You want biscuits too?"

"Biscuits for sure!"

Jesse felt warm and comfortable at his table, in spite of the butterflies that swarmed through his innards when he was close to Laurel. He had already nearly forgotten Cougar.

Cougar's interest in Jesse, however, was keenly renewed as he watched his friend through the dining room window. Jesse looked flush, taken care of, hard muscled again, and as if he hadn't spent the last few weeks on the road. Cougar considered that maybe there'd be something here for himself if Jesse had found a sweet set-up. And it could be that he had made a mistake being so forward with the girl. Well, hell, how was he to know they knew each other? The spare cogs in his brain began to work and crank out plans and scenes and conversations. Clearly, he would have to revise his actions to gain Jesse's confidence again. As it stood, he was fresh out of the cash he had won at his last card game across the river, a win which had been hotly disputed by the loser, and he was becoming a little weary of high tailing it so often after winning games. Card players sure were a suspicious lot. He didn't actually cheat at every game, only the bigger ones. He guessed that it was the sums of money being lost, not the principle of the thing that rankled losers.

Cougar figured that the sooner he tried to make amends of some sort, the better, so he formed a few mealy mannered words in his mind and went back into the dining room. Jesse did not smile when he raised his eyes and saw Cougar stride through the open door. Nor did he invite him to sit as Cougar pulled up a chair at the table. Cougar rubbed his beard and hung his head, releasing a huge sigh before he spoke. Jesse wanted to be rid of him as quickly as possible.

"Oh, Jesse," Cougar heaved another sigh and began to talk. "I know I musta offended your girl earlier. I'm real sorry about it. I just keep on doin' that to people, but I don't mean no harm. They just take what I say too much to heart. Not everybody's like you, Jesse. You always were my one true friend."

He stole a glance at Jesse's face after his speech and saw that there was not a hint of the desired reaction. Jesse continued eating. Cougar tried again.

"It's sure a good thing we run into each other, Jesse. I'm lookin' for a job, and I was thinkin', since you might have connections here, you might be able to sic me onto somethin' I could stick with. What's your line of work out this way?"

Before Jesse could stop himself, he answered, "I'm buildin' a road."

"Road? Damn if I couldn't do that! I seen it done in the war. Think you can get me on too?" He managed to seem eager.

Jesse answered quickly. "I don't think so. It's a small job, kind of private and, uh, there's others already helpin' out. Maybe you ought to just ask around town."

Cougar's face fell and he shook his head. He would have to change tactics. "Hoo-boy. I'll tell you what, Jesse. I spent my last dollar on what I ate here. Could you maybe lend me a bill to at least get a bed for the night and some breakfast?"

If it would get Cougar out of his hair, Jesse considered the money well spent. He pulled two dollars from his pocket. "This should take you through a couple of days. Good luck."

Cougar arranged his face into a school-boy, thank-you-so-much-ma'am smile, and even managed a slight moist eye for effect. A wad of Yankee money had slipped from its hiding place in Jesse's britches and had not escaped Cougar's glistening eye. "I won't forget this, Jesse. Now, if you'll just apologize to your girl for me, and tell her how sorry I am if I offended her tender sensibilities, I'll get myself back on my feet again and try to do better."

He stood up and backed away, realizing himself that the last little speech was pitifully overdone, and he should have been ashamed of concocting such an outrageous promise. He continued backing away and said loudly, "Well, I'll be seein' you, Jesse. Thanks again."

Jesse kept his eyes focused on the stew and nodded his head slightly. Cougar's show had been embarrassing, for it had attracted the attention of the men at the next table. Jesse felt as if he should have turned his collar around and waved holy water in Cougar's repentant direction.

Laurel's work kept her busy the rest of the afternoon, so Jesse occupied himself by writing to Marcus. He stayed as long as possible before heading back to the Beaudines' and ate his supper in the kitchen with Laurel. They each had put Cougar out of their thoughts and talked of rides in the meadow and the weekend to come. Cougar went to a saloon two streets away and resisted the strong urge to divest a couple of Kentuckians of their means. He planned to wait until evening and get himself a room at the boarding house and sniff around a little. He had decided that whatever Jesse was doing might be good enough to tide him over his own current rough times.

And, he mused that the color of Yankee money suited him very well.

Chapter Eighteen

Snooping

H ardly any man ever made a fuss over Ruthann. She was too old for the young ones, too manly for the genteel ones, too outspoken for the manly ones, and too ugly for all the rest. She had run the boarding house through good times and bad, with her husband early on, and later, without him. He had crossed the great Ohio on a ferry one June morning and never returned. It had happened years and years ago, and now she never thought of him anymore. She always "suspitioned" he married her on a bet anyway, so when he disappeared she figured he was collecting money somewhere up north. Just as well. She never liked him all that much to begin with and assumed that anyone who'd marry a female as ugly as she was had to be a little off center. She had a good head for figures, though, and managed the place well, even through the war.

When the young man with the beard came to her that evening and tried to dicker down the price of her smallest room, she was at first put off. Then, he seemed so sincere and destitute, and honest to goodness embarrassed to have to beg, that she let him have it half price. The fact that she was the spitting image of his departed mother might have swayed her, but only slightly, mind you. Cougar thought himself just blamed lucky, as he followed Ruthann up the back stairs, that she hadn't been there for his run-in with Jesse's girl.

"You have a real nice boardin' house here, ma'am. I reckon you see just about all kinds comin' through this town." Cougar mewed in a most simple minded tone.

"The hell if I hain't. Everthin' from the-ayter people and circus fat ladies to high falootin' preacher men. I seen 'em all, and ketched 'em at their pranks too! I know you might not b'lieve this, but hardly nobody is what they seems to be. I got to step lively to keep ahead of the game. What was it you said you done fer a livin'?"

She stopped in front of the door before handing him the old skeleton key. He hung his head down slightly and said, "Oh, I do any work that comes along, ma'am. But since I come home from the war, good jobs is hard to find. I'm partial to road buildin' if'n you know where that's to be done."

"Road buildin'? You might ask over to the county surveyor in the mornin'."

"Thank you, ma'am. I'll do just that."

He took the key from her and placed it in the lock.

As she turned to leave he said, in an offhand manner. "And by the way, ma'am. I seen your daughter in the dinin' room earlier and I got to say she is a real beauty. You must be real proud of her."

Ruthann reacted with astonishment and shook her head.

"Laurel? She hain't my daughter, though I often wisht she was. She comes from over Lone Oak way and lives clear out in the boonies with her ma and pa. They was no work over that way so she come here. Oh, all the boys likes her all right, but she puts 'em off quick as a jack rabbit."

"Now you won't go tellin' her I was commentin' will you? I'm real shy around pretty girls myself."

"I kin keep shut as good as the next," she assured him.

"Well, thanks again and good night to you," Cougar smiled to himself as he closed the door. If he needed to know more in the morning, he was certain Ruthann would share her wisdom and maybe even directions to Lone Oak, where Jesse must surely be connected.

He got up early the next morning and ate breakfast at another kitchen in town, avoiding the chance of running into Laurel. He figured he'd let his apology settle in a while before approaching her again. On second thought, it might be best not to approach her at all.

Cougar was not what might be called a reflective person, but seeing Jesse had brought him up short. Jesse looked happy and well-fed. He looked almost settled with that girl, and Cougar knew that whatever Jesse put his mind to, he would probably get. Now, Cougar was sorely tempted to tap into whatever resource it was that Jesse had found, not to settle in permanently, but for a short detour off the trail he'd been running.

Walking back toward the boarding house, he stopped a boy of about eight on the street. Offering him a small coin, he said, "I'll give you another one just like this if'n you go over to that boardin' house and find the woman that runs the place and ask her to high tail it here to the hardware store to talk to me. Say it's the poor, shy soldier boy wants to see her."

The young boy's eyes bugged out at the prospect of cash money, so he replied, "Yessir!" and ran straight to the house.

While he was gone, Cougar rummaged in his pockets for an item he had been keeping for some time. He located it and took it out, along with a gray lint ball and some dingy string. Soon he saw Ruthann and the boy approach. He replaced the string, blew away the lint ball, and rubbed the object with his shirt tail, buffing off the pocket dust. He dismissed the boy by discreetly slipping him another coin and patting him on the head. "Little feller reminds me of my younger brother. The one that died in the war." He paused. Ruthann appeared puzzled.

"What was it you wanted?" she asked, pushing her head forward on her shoulders. Cougar thought she looked like a turtle, but for once in his life, suppressed comment.

"Well, Miss Ruthann. I went over to the surveyor's like you said, but nobody was in the office. I'm gettin' desperate for work but I just know that somethin' will turn up. Well, this mornin' while I was out I just thought to myself, that you was so kind to me, I couldn't take off and not offer you somethin' more for takin' me in at half-price." At this point he proffered the old woman a well worn gold ring. "Here. I want you to have this. I carried it with me through the war, but the gal it belonged to is gone now. It's the only thing I can offer and ain't nearly enough for your kindness."

Ruthann was dumbfounded. She had never been offered a ring in her life, not even when she was married. "Why, I cain't take this! Hit's your keepsake!" She returned the ring to his hand and continued, "And I wisht to goodness I had some work for you m'self but I'm already full up with help."

Cougar took the ring back, wearing a most reluctant, but boyishly grateful expression. "Oh, I wouldn't want to put you out, Miss Ruthann. But you know, there *is* somethin' you might be able to do for me."

She cocked her head and asked, "What would that be?"

Cougar leaned forward, as if sharing a confidence. "Yesterday, when I was passin' by the dinin' room, I seen your Laurel girl cozyin' up to a feller. I near fell over when I seen who it was, but he left before I could trace him. I was his mess mate in the war, and I hate to say it, but he was a deserter."

Ruthann drew in a breath of disgust. "Noooo! A deserter after Laurel?"

"Oh, I reckon she'll catch on to him soon enough because he's like you said. He ain't what he appears to be. He told me hisself that he shot a Kentucky man in cold blood. Just aimed and boom! Blew the fella away. That ain't all. Before he deserted, he robbed me blind. There wasn't nothin' I could do about it, what with my wound and everythin', and you know, I'd give my right arm to find him and make him pay me back."

"Cold blood, you say? I heerd about that kind of skunk, and like I said, you got to step lively in this life. What can I do?"

"If you will ask Miss Laurel where that man might be found, I promise to get him away from her and run his hide out of town. That is, after I collect. Honest, I never thought I'd ever see him again." Ruthann was visibly agitated. "I got to warn Laurel right away. Why, she's too good to git mixed up with the likes of a thievin' desertin' killer!"

"Oh, Miss Ruthann, don't! If she throws him over before I find him, why, I'll never get my earnin's back. Don't you see? That would kill my chances sure. Besides, he'll be hot-footin' it anyway when I get through with him."

At this point Cougar slapped his thigh and smiled. "Now that my leg is healed I can run with the best of 'em!"

Ruthann, the wise, the worldly, the hawk-eyed dispenser of rules and advice was suckered in, like a rube at a carnival staring at the snake woman. Cougar savored her parting words. "I see now why you didn't just come into the house to talk to me. She mighta mentioned seein' you and that would tip him off right away. Well, don't you worry none. I'll find out where the low-down swamp rat is stayin' and tell you before noon. What say we meet here again at 11:30?"

"All right, and meantime I'll go back on over to the surveyor's and see about work. Shucks. Maybe he's got an old mule I could ride. I had to sell mine cross the river just for passage on the ferry."

What was one more lie? Cougar had abused the truth for so long he actually believed himself while in the middle of most of his fabrications. He spent the rest of the morning watching a card game and spotting all the moves of two cheats trying to bamboozle each other. He left feeling confident that he could have whipped them both with one hand tied behind his back. Interesting news awaited him.

"She told me all about him. Leastways, what she *thinks* she knows. I was hard pressed to keep shut about the real truth. Says his name's Jesse, prob'ly made up, eh? Anyways, he showed up at their place after the war with word that her brother was dead for sure. Then he started helpin' her pappy on a road through the woods that stands in the way of their cabin. He give her some cock and bull story about wantin' to help with the road on account of her brother bein' dead. Said he'd been up to Springfield and saw Mr. Lincoln. She's took with him though, so you'd best see to it right away. I don't want her no more hurt than need be."

"He's at her place, buildin' a road? That explains the pick-ax I seen. And no wonder he didn't . . . "

Cougar stopped himself short. He had almost blurted too much to her. "So, just where is it she lives?" he asked quickly.

Ruthann withdrew a folded paper from her canvas pants. "I wrote it down soon as she went back to the kitchen. You go on the east road out of town, the big one, that is, not the old trace. Get yourself as fer as Lone Oak and foller the road farther east and a bit south. She says you go a couple mile 'til you come to a big meadow where the trace is worn. Jest foller that 'til you git to the woods and the place is practical straight on ahead. Nobody but her people lives out there. It's all Beaudines, she says, as fer as you kin throw a pig. And the Jesse boy is workin' on the road ever day. Looks like he's puttin' on a pretty good show. You s'pose he's just hidin' out?"

"Ma'am, I don't know what to suppose, except that I wouldn't put nothin' past him. I do thank you. Now," he paused and reached for his pocket. "Are you sure you wouldn't take this little trinket for your trouble?"

She waved her thick hand heavily through the air and laughed. "Not on yer tintype, young man! You hang on to it and one day you'll find yerself a diff'rent gal that's worthy of you. Good luck! I got to git back."

Cougar studied her rough handwriting and concluded that it would be a long walk to Lone Oak and even longer to the Beaudines'. From the way Ruthann had talked, he saw himself wading through Beaudines for days. He would definitely need a horse. The multi-colored mount he had borrowed from Mary many weeks ago had saved his skin across the river after an unfortunate run-in with a better gambler, and he didn't like going shank's mare any farther than needful.

He slipped around behind the boarding house and eyed the horses. Sure was lucky, he thought, that people were so trusting. They'd leave everything on their horse but the oat bag, and not think twice about parking a fine mare just out of sight. He picked one out, slung his haversack over the animal's rump, and rode off as if he had been born on it. He headed east on the main highway and never looked back. Later that day Ruthann walked through the back door of her boarding house, stopped suddenly, and let out a screech that pickled the cucumbers in their crocks.

"Sonofabuck! Some rotten egg-sucker has stole my horse!"

Chapter Nineteen

BENNY

Their first night on the Flint road seemed suspended to Pete and Amy. They felt far removed from the cozy cabin, and almost detached from themselves. It seemed to Amy as though she were floating through some quiet and strange territory, all white and gray shadow, and even her keen senses dimmed in this opaque world. Cotton-two slept on, unaware of distance or change and the peek-a-boo game of cloud and moon above her. Pete guided the horse carefully, then halted the wagon after going about three miles. He leaned over just to kiss Amy's nose.

"I love you," he said to her. "Everything's all right."

They stopped just short of dawn to rest for a few hours before continuing their journey. Toward evening of the next day, seeking a place to eat and rest, they decided to pull off the road by a long stretch of woods. Cotton-two jumped down, eager to stretch her legs and run.

"Don't you go off too far, Clary!" Amy cautioned her. Soon their fire sparked, and a slow curl of smoke eased upward from the dry tinder. Pete added kindling and hauled out the heavy iron frying pan and food box. "We'd best eat this bacon right away so it don't go riesty on us."

Amy peeled potatoes and sliced onions to throw in with the bacon, humming and smiling to herself. It would be good to settle in one day, but just now this seemed wonderful. What an adventure and such a story to share with the children she and Pete would have together. Pete saw to the horse while she finished cooking their meal. Suddenly Amy became aware that Clary was no longer playing within her eyesight. A slight pang of fear nested immediately in her stomach and she jumped up, calling after her.

"Clary! Clary! Where are you? Come here this minute!" Her concern was relieved immediately when she saw the little girl emerge from a thicket at the side of the woods. Clary strolled toward her mother, dragging the worn rag doll they had packed for her.

"I'm just here, Mama."

"Well, you stay right by me and don't go wanderin' off again. You made me worry there for a minute." Amy took Clary into her arms and squeezed her.

"Besides, we're about to eat and you don't want to miss your supper, do you?"

Pete finished with the horse and added his slight reprimand. "It's not always best to hike off by yourself. You might find a bear in the woods. That's what my mama always told me."

"No bears," said Clary, "just people." Amy and Pete exchanged long, hard looks.

"People?" asked Pete. "Where'd you see people?"

"Over there," she answered, pointing to the thicket. Pete walked toward the bushes cautiously, carrying a shotgun at his side. Suddenly two raggedly clad dark men burst through the dense growth. Taking one look at Pete's shotgun, they ran past the campsite and headed for the road.

"Well, they're sure in some kind of hurry!" he declared, returning to the fire.

"Wonder where they're headed and what they were doin' in there," said Amy. Clary spoke up matter-of-factly. "They runned away from the other darkie."

"What other darkie" Amy immediately pulled Clary close by her. She had never feared the slaves she and Jim took in, but out on the highway, you could never tell.

"The big one that's sleepin'," Clary said. Pete approached the thicket more warily this time and strained to hear some sound. As he pulled the bushes aside, he discovered what seemed to be the body of a very large black man. Resting the gun on the ground, he knelt down to check for a pulse. He was just leaning over the man's chest when a huge arm grasped him around the neck and pulled him to the dirt.

Amy heard Pete gasp and jumped immediately to the wagon. She pulled out a pistol and shot it into the air, screaming the whole time. Clary joined her with a piercing screech and the big man reacted by loosing Pete and leaping to his feet.

"Lawd, Ah thought you was one of them boys!"

He raised his shaking arms above his head and quivered, his face written all over with regret. "Ah'm sorry, suh! Ah truly am. Them boys done hit me while ah was down and lef' me fo' dead! Ah fool 'em though, fo' Ah'm still here."

He thumped his big chest, grinned widely, and returned his arms to the surrender position. Pete was still haking from the shock of being taken down so quickly, but managed a weak smile. "It's all right, Amy!" he called. "No need to fire off more shot." He turned to the huge man vibrating in front of him and added, "And you can out your arms down now. We don't mean harm to you."

The two emerged from the thicket to see Amy and Clary wrapped up in each other, standing by the wagon. Amy stared open mouthed at the man. He looked as big as a mountain next to Pete. He had a chest and belly twice as broad as Pete's whole body, and his head was covered with a bush of woolly black knots. She doubted she and Jim could ever have hidden a man that big from anyone for long. He was the largest human being she had ever seen in her life.

He looked at her and Clary, and politely said, "Ma'am, missy."

Pete escorted him to the fire and invited him to sit.

"Pull up a rock and have somethin'." Amy dished up for them.

"What was it happened with the other fellers?" Pete asked.

"Thank y'all. Ah am a might hungry." He dived into the plate Amy had filled and ate for a solid minute until it was completely bare. Then he answered Pete's question.

"Ah was travelin' with them two, but Benny, tha's me, soon finds out, they ain' no good. They wants to rob an' steal from folks what already got nothin'. Benny says it's wrong and they plumb knock me on the head and leave me fo' dead. Benny's jus' comin' round and find them goin' th'ew his pockets. Laws, Benny ain't got nothin' neither but then they heered you' noise and thump me agin. Ah doan know what scared 'em off but when you come around, Benny, he thinks it's them two all ovuh." He paused a moment, staring away from the group. "Or wuss. You coulda bin somebody from the place, chasin' aftuh me with the hounds. Lawd, I bin chased with the hounds befo', an' they pert near tear me to bits. Looka here," he said, rolling his pant leg to the knee. "They done that, my massa's dawgs, fifteen year ago, when Benny was jus' a pup hisself."

He revealed a knotted and scar-ridden leg. A sizable chunk of flesh was missing from his inner calf, and the scars were a shiny pink, running down the length of his calf to the ankle.

Amy turned her head involuntarily. Clary stared hard at the leg and said, "My Bullseye wouldn't never do that. He's a good dog. Mama, where is Bullseye, anyways?"

"Bullseye's back home with Grandpa Jim, honey. He couldn't come with us just now."

Benny nodded his head to Clary. "Das' nice you got a good dawg, Missy. I had me a good dawg onc't too, but massa's dawg, he was mean as a wild hawg."

"Well, I don't reckon they'll be sickin' dogs on you where you're headed," said Pete. "Where are you headed, anyhow?"

"Headed no'th. Folks up no'th set Benny free. Now Benny's goin' to find 'em and go to work fo' 'em. Mus' be lots to do up no'th. They's nothin' down here no more. Plantations is all burned out, fields is tromped to nothin'. Benny's been wantin' to be free a long time now." He stopped talking long enough to refill his plate.

"Now Ah'm free, well, Ah don't know exackly what to do. Mr. Lincoln, he set us free, but never tol' us what we goin' to do aftah. But, it seem to me, they's gotta be somethin' Benny can do!"

He shook his massive head and finished chewing.

"Yassuh. They's gotta be *somethin'* Benny can do!"

By now, the evening was darkening fast. The moon was rising again, illuminating the road as far as the eye could see. Through the woods, the shadows fell in quivering, lacy patterns, and the night was filled with the warm and humid breath of summer. Their fire was reduced to the soft, coral heat of embers, and a wisp of white smoke drifted up from its glowing heart. Clary had fallen asleep on Amy's lap, and Pete and Benny made small talk as Pete pulled out the bedding. Pete introduced himself to the big black man and told him somewhat of their own plans.

Pete offered Benny a blanket, but he refused it.

"Benny'll jus' be movin' on up the road tonight. See, Benny still thinks it's better fo' him to travel in the dark, on account of some folks might *still* think he's a runaway. Bes' not to take a chance. An' then when Ah's up no'th, why, ever'thin' be easy. No runaway, no slave. Yassah, Benny's life goin' t' be all fat and no mo'e lean. Y'all take care now."

They watched Benny lumber down the moon-white road and into the night. Before she slept, Amy pondered Benny's hopes and what his future might hold. The question of his future and the thousands of others who had been freed now played heavily on her mind. She had seen her actions on behalf of the slaves as noble. She had felt the excitement of her part in the so-called underground. But not until now had she considered the end of their journey. Once away from the slave masters, what would they do? What was Benny going to do?

Chapter Twenty

THE CHURCH

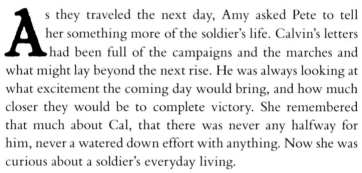

As they traveled the next day, Amy asked Pete to tell her something more of the soldier's life. Calvin's letters had been full of the campaigns and the marches and what might lay beyond the next rise. He was always looking at what excitement the coming day would bring, and how much closer they would be to complete victory. She remembered that much about Cal, that there was never any halfway for him, never a watered down effort with anything. Now she was curious about a soldier's everyday living.

"Well, it wasn't all war and shoutin', although when we got in it, we really got in it! I first went in the infantry, and marched with about two million other boys and twice that many graybacks."

Clary popped onto his lap as he drove. "What's graybacks?"

"Graybacks, my little Miss Cotton, is lice. A louse is the worst bug ever invented, and you can't swat him off, you can't pinch him off, and you can't boil him off either. He thinks your clothes is his house and your hair is his wheat field, and when he brings his relatives in to stay, it's for life. Pretty soon, you got a whole family of lice to support, plus their friends and pets too."

Clary scrunched her shoulders into her neck and made a face.

"How did you get rid of them, then?" Amy asked. "You didn't have any when Jim and me found you in the woods."

"Smoked 'em off my clothes and washed every day I could. Still, I would find one or two at times. Those are the ones I named. I figured they must be extra bright graybacks and so deserved names."

Amy and Clary laughed at the notion and Clary asked, "What names did you give 'em?"

"I named one Hattie and one Clive, after my folks."

Amy slapped him playfully on the arm and scolded, "Pete Beaudine, that is rude! What would your mama think, havin' a bug named after her?"

"She'd love it. I'd just tell her that was the bug lived closest to my heart and she'd swoon right away. My mama loves me so much it makes me crazy."

"Where's your daddy bug live then?" Clary asked.

"Uh, well, I reckon he was the one that lived on my stomach, 'cause my daddy loves to eat."

"So, tell me how you got from the infantry to bein' a courier." Amy was curious beyond the question of graybacks.

"Infantry needs couriers. Ours got the dysentery and went to the hospital and the captain asked who could ride, and I was the first to raise my hand. And it looks like becomin' a courier was the best thing ever happened to me." He leaned over and kissed Amy soundly on the cheek. Suddenly, it seemed a good thing to talk about his days in the army. He had withheld much of his recent experiences because he wished to distance himself from it, but telling Amy felt right. He continued. "I did see a lot of funny shenanigans out there, too. Once, we had this lieutenant that had himself a fancy-dan horse, all dapple gray and sportin' the finest, thickest mane and tail you ever saw. He kept that horse like it was his best dress outfit, shined up and polished. We used to joke that he cleaned the horse's teeth before he did his own. Anyway, one time some boys in the mess two doors down got drunk as skunks and when the lieutenant was asleep, they took the horse and shaved his tail to the nubbin. The lieutenant about had a conniption fit when he got a look at it. It *was* kind of pitiful to see, but everybody knew the hair would grow back in and so we laughed pretty good over that one.

"Another good thing about bein' a courier and havin' a horse was that my shoes didn't wear out so fast. I knew one man that wrote home to his folks to send him some new shoes, for his was worn out. He had a mess-mate draw around his foot on a paper and told his mama to buy a boot bigger so's it would fit him. He was walkin' everywhere barefoot as it was."

"I go barefoot," observed Clary. "I like it."

"Everybody likes it if they're just playin', sweet thing. But if they have to walk twenty miles a day over thistles and rocks, it ain't much like playin'." He related more stories to them as they rode, and Amy could see that the boys must have been bored often as they waited in their camps for the next battle. Pete said there was a lot of card playing and the popular dice throwing game. Chuck-a-luck was big with the boys, though it was declared illegal in many camps. "Once you had your work done and your letters wrote, why, there wasn't always a whole lot more to take up your time. I did go to meetin' when a preacher would come through and some of the boys organized regular meetin's after a bit. We'd have some good singin' and preachin' to keep up our spirits. Sometimes it was real hard, for the war was chock full of hard luck stories. I tried to keep cheerful, even when things got real bad, but it wasn't always easy. The worst times was when mail call came and there was nothin' there. My family was good about writin', but some boys hardly had any mail at all. I reckon their folks couldn't write.

"Well, I would share mine with those kind and try to spark things up for 'em. We surely had some plucky boys in our outfit, I'll say that." Pete chattered freely as they bumped over the road. Most of it was war talk, and he seemed immersed in nothing else. Then suddenly he stood straight up and shouted, "Whee-haw! Look what I see!"

Amy followed the direction of his gaze, and her eye fell upon a small, half charred church building which sat a few hundred feet from the road. There were two people, a man and a woman, hoeing and weeding in a meager garden to the side of it. A sway back mare had rooted herself to a spot by the ruins of an iron picket fence where she nibbled tufts of new grass.

Pete immediately found the turn-off to the church and guided his horse in that direction. "Amy darlin'," he grinned, "I think we just found ourselves a marryin' man." Amy's breath was taken away by the horse's burst of speed, and she held Clary tightly on her lap. It was almost embarrassing, however, to see Pete leap from the wagon, nearly before he reined the horse to a decent standstill. He bounded across the garden, leaving her in the wagon like some onlooker. Well, now, wasn't she supposed to be a part of this marryin' thing too?

Pete approached the man with his hand outstretched and nodded politely to the woman. "Sir, are you the preacher of this here church? Because if you are, I have got a weddin' for you to get on with, right here and now!"

The man appeared to be half startled himself by Pete's exuberant manner. He stuttered slightly and answered, "Yes, I am that. Porter's my name and this is my church. This here's my wife, Mrs. Porter." Pete took two steps toward the round Mrs. Porter and lifted her a foot off the ground, swinging her in a small circle before letting her go. "Well, Mrs. Porter, ma'am, you can be the witness to my marriage and the best man and give the bride away and sing the march if you want. I'm real pleased to meet you. My name is Peter Beaudine, and we are on our way to Kentucky."

"We?" Mr. and Mrs. Porter asked, in one voice.

"What?" Pete looked confused.

Amy got up from her seat and very loudly cleared her throat. She was waiting for him to return and help her and Clary down from the wagon, the way any prospective groom should do. She wore a slightly exasperated look.

"Oh, say! Somebody must've beat me up with a dumb stick. Amy, honey, I'm sorry!"

Pete ran across the plot and lifted Amy from the wagon with enthusiastic grace. Clary followed, jumping into his arms and laughing. The three walked back to Mr. and Mrs. Porter and stood before them, all smiles and youth, remarkable in their freshness. Pete and Amy explained the circumstances of their courtship, their apparent gypsy travel. "You see," said Pete, "we want to do this proper and not travel too far in an unmarried state. It just wouldn't look right, and my mama would skin me alive besides! So, will you do us the honors?"

Mrs. Porter, still flushed from her spin with Pete, insisted they come inside and take some simple refreshment before the ceremony. "I have some flowers growing the other side of the church we might weave through your beautiful hair too. And you wouldn't mind if we all freshened up just the slightest bit, would you? I might have a few ribbons in my trunk you could tie around a little bouquet. Now, wouldn't that be nice? Come on in, sweetie," she continued, taking Clary's hand. "I do believe I saw a piece of hard candy in the dish behind the altar."

Amy was pleased with the extra touches Mrs. Porter was bringing to her wedding ceremony. She had thought they would merely stand before some circuit judge and say the vows, plain and simple, then be on their way. Apparently Mrs. Porter hadn't done a wedding in quite a while, and this was a welcome break for her, or maybe, like the rest of the country, she needed just such a joyful occasion to bring her out of the nightmare of war.

Amy washed her face and Clary's in water from a small bowl provided in an anteroom of the building. The Porters, she was told by the reverend, lived in the church since their home had been destroyed earlier that year. "The only thing saved the church was a very fortunate thunderstorm and a right good size Bible deluge from on high. We feel blessed to have this much. Mrs. Porter and I have sunk our roots here in the south and intend to stay. It may never be the same as before, but we can see that it will prosper again. People need the comfort of their religion now more than ever." After a few minutes of spiffing the young people up, the Porters drew Amy and Pete together for the wedding ritual. Clary stood next to her mother holding a small bouquet of flowers and looking very much like a miniature of the bride herself. It was a short, sweet ceremony which now bound them together as man and wife.

They were both exhilarated, and Clary was awed at the sudden appearance of so much candy after it was over. "Some sweets for your trip," Mrs. Porter said, handing them a large bag of treats. "To remind you to keep your words and actions sweet as candy and keep the sugar in your life."

Amy commenced to protest so large a gift. Mr. Porter gently forced them into her hands and explained, "Mrs. Porter loves to make candy, and I think she does it every time she gets annoyed with me to remind herself of that silly saying. Whatever the case, we always have a lot of candy around, and she always has something good to say to me. Good luck to the both of you, now."

Chapter Twenty-one

Atlanta

———⁓✢⁓———

Within a few more days, Pete and Amy and Clary were inside spitting distance of Atlanta, though they didn't realize it at first. The Atlanta Amy had first seen was a hub of commerce and the progressive southern life. It had been bustling, bursting with dogwood blossom and fresh spring when she and Calvin were there years before. She had almost wished at the time that they would be settling in such a vital city.

Now, the Atlanta which she remembered seemed to have been turned over, like so much plowed earth. Though it was rebuilding remarkably soon, there were vestiges of Sherman's awful assault the year before. Chimneys with no fireplaces, burned out and blackened tree stumps dotted the landscape. Much of the city's remaining grace clung to those forlorn and blackened reminders of a more pleasant past. They spoke in gravest silence. Here, the chimneys said, there once was a fine and spacious home, guarded by the lawn where a family danced on summer nights and clapped fireflies into cupped hands for amusement. Here had stood a home once hemmed all around by a protective iron fence and shaded by a sweeping, giant willow.

Now the lone smokestacks testified that those things were all past and ashes. Pieces of iron, once wrought in curves and fashioned into fences, now lay scattered and broken and bent. Amy was ashamed that such things ever happened. She wondered how this was possible, how men could destroy so easily. She knew that families had been urged by the General to leave this place before the real destruction came and that many had moved out, lock, stock, and barrel, only to return and find their homes in ruins. The Union army was rife with men who destroyed anything that might have been of benefit to the enemy, and evidence of their wanton plunder and demolition still scarred the once beautiful city. She could almost feel the gloom which must have hung over Atlanta in those days immediately following the devastation.

"Mrs. Beaudine! Oh, Mrs. Beaudine!" Pete's voice jarred her back to her senses. "Where have you been? You look like you just saw a ghost."

"I guess I did. I was rememberin' Atlanta the way it was when Calvin and me first rode through. I wonder what can be uglier than war, don't you, Pete?"

"The slavery that caused it was uglier." Pete was quick to respond.

"Do you suppose Benny will find that somethin' he was lookin' for?" she asked. "Will any of them?"

"I can't say for the freed slave. But I can say for you and me. I believe what happened back there in your woods was supposed to happen. I believe I didn't make it through because the Almighty wanted me and you to meet, and even if Benny don't find what he's lookin' for, the Almighty wanted him free, and all the others too. I fought in that war, Amy. I *got* to believe it was the right thing. If it wasn't, then a lot of boys died out there for nothin'. What you and Jim did was right too, and don't you ever think different." Pete reached over and took Amy's hand in his. "Don't you ever think different," he repeated. His reiteration would carry her through the days to come, when they would pass men and women on the roads heading north, ex-slaves whose lives were forever pushed into an uncertain future.

They restocked their water and added honey to the rations before leaving the city. Pete had gotten directions for the best route north, and they decided to camp just on the other side of Atlanta instead of within the city limits. He felt the crush of the southern defeat all around them in the remaining rubble of burned out industrial center,s and it was depressing. It was all depressing: the chimneys, the heaps of brick, the infamous twisted rails dubbed Sherman's neckties, wrapped like licorice sticks around telegraph poles. He wanted to shield Amy from any more such sights.

Leaving Atlanta, he felt a solace in the more open countryside. They watched the little off roads for one that would lead to a farmhouse, figuring on buying eggs or milk for their morning meal. Late in the afternoon they spotted one, so Pete pulled the wagon off the main road, heading toward a dilapidated barn. There was a great commotion coming from inside the pitched building, and they could see two figures thrashing on the straw covered floor.

"Blast you sneakin', chicken stealin', wall-eyed . . . "

A loud crash was heard, as the two men tumbled over a saw horse and into the trough. One man was trying to submerge the other's head in the water, all the while bellowing and howling obscenities.

Pete jumped from the wagon to get a closer look. He immediately recognized the big, clumsy body of Benny, flailing helplessly as the smaller white man overpowered him.

Pete called out and ran into the barn.

"Hey now! What's goin' on here?"

The farmer looked up in astonishment and momentarily loosed Benny. Benny called out Pete's name, gagging at the same time on trough water.

"Mistuh Pete! Ah's sho' glad to see you!"

"Benny," said Pete, "I told you we'd get lost from each other in the big city if you wandered off."

The farmer stared at them dumbfounded. "What in tarnation is this? You two know each other? I just caught this man hidin' in my barn. He's been stealin' my chickens right and left!"

Benny shook his curly head vehemently. "No suh, Ah ain't

stole nuthin'! You doan see *no* chickens nowhere by me and no feathuhs and no chicken *nuthin'* stuck to mah feets. Ah ain't even *see* no chickens. Ah was only restin' mah eyes . . . "

The farmer looked at Pete again.

Pete took Benny by the arm, talking around him to the farmer.

"We got separated in Atlanta. He comes from my wife's daddy's plantation and is headed north with us. I was hopin' we'd catch up to him on the way, bein' practically part of the family as he is."

Amy had climbed down from the wagon with Clary and spoke up. "You about had me in fits, Benny. Why, Daddy would turn over in his grave if he knew we nearly lost you!" Benny played into the charade with ease.

"Ah promise Benny won't do *that* again! Le's just git on out of this place now, and git back on the road."

They turned in the direction of the wagon. The farmer shook his head in disbelief. "Hey, now! Just a minute. What about my chickens?"

"Well, I don't know what about your chickens," said Pete. "What about my man here? You almost drowned him in horse spit. I'd say you owe him some kind of apology or at least directions to where we can buy us some eggs and milk for breakfast."

The farmer's eyebrows shot up in disbelief. "You got cash money?" he asked quickly.

"Enough to buy fresh eggs and milk, I do. Reckon there must be another farm around here where a man can buy such stuff for cash money."

"I got good fresh eggs here myself. And my cow's about due for a milkin'."

"Well, we'd just as soon buy from you if you can bring yourself to apologize to my man here. He's straighter than a hick'ry rod, Benny is, and you can take my word for it."

The farmer lowered his head a notch, shuffled his dusty boots in the straw, and mumbled a barely audible apology.

"Sorry. I musta got you mixed up with some other slave . . . " He hesitated slightly, then continued, "Some other man. Let's go check the hen house for eggs and I'll git my woman to commence milkin'."

The farmer set to the gathering of eggs and the milking of the cow, almost mincing in front of them, overdoing the courtesies he now extended. He gladly took Pete's money and stuffed it quickly into his pocket. Even as Pete took his little band away a few minutes later, an uneasy feeling gripped his chest. He was relieved to quit that place.

That evening, settled once again, they sat beside the cooking fire together, as they had a few days before. Benny helped with the cleanup and couldn't stop laughing about the joke they had played on the farmer. The child Clary giggled with them, finding more pleasure in Benny's deep laughter than in their words.

"Bless me, Mistuh Pete. I cain't b'lieve how fast you was to git me out of that scrape. That man, he was sho' confused."

"Benny, what I want to know is, how did that little runt get you down? You must be twice his size." Benny sat back and smiled slowly. "My mam always teach me, Benny, she says, don't you nevuh hurt nobody what's smaller than you, else you git in big trouble. 'Bout ever'body I see is smaller than me, so I been beat up plenty."

"I don't think she meant that you couldn't defend yourself, Benny," Amy commented. "Everybody has a right to defend himself."

Benny chuckled and lay back, folding his long fingers behind his head and looking up at the sky. "Ah s'pose you right, Miss Amy. From now on, Benny's goin' to do that. An' nobody better come near you or Mistuh Pete or little cotton head neithuh. Not with Benny around. No suh!"

It was apparent now that Benny was to become a part of their travels. Pete was glad for it because he feared, though he didn't tell Benny or Amy, that the next farmer would not hesitate to simply take aim and fire at the big black man. Besides, Benny's physical strength might come in handy on the long journey.

As they pressed northward those next few days, they found themselves traveling past sites which, only a year before, had echoed the fearsome sounds of battle. One such point was at the Kenesaw Mountain battlefield, where Sherman mounted a frontal assault on Joe Johnston's well entrenched Confederates, and counted losses six times greater than that of the enemy. Three thousand Union dead, someone wrote in later history books, to five hundred Confederate. The boys in gray must have shouted many mighty victory cries in those days. Only a summer would pass until the shouts would fade, muffled under the dust trampled by Sherman's indomitable army. It marched from Atlanta to the sea, leveling whatever stood in the path, smacking Georgia right between the eyes and bringing the Confederacy to its knees.

There would be other such sights before they reached the familiar sights in Pete's Kentucky. Nine more days of travel would find them at the Chickamauga-Chattanooga battle-fields. Before reaching this infamous site, they found that traveling with Benny proved to be a blessing and a detriment. To his credit, he always slept a good way from their camp, allowing them a degree of newlywed privacy, and he was always first up and stirred their cooking fire into action. He was most pleasant company and full of jokes and stories.

On the downside were the facts that he was so huge and so hungry. He could out-eat Pete, Amy, and Clary, and the horse combined. Pete began to wonder how long rations could hold if Benny's appetite kept the same gobbling pace. Amy was concerned as well, especially since she had seen Benny stick his huge paw into one of the flour bags and eat the powdery stuff raw. He seemed to have a giant cast iron hole for a stomach and not much regard for their limited supplies. Pete had tried to be subtle about reminding him they only had so much to go on, but subtleties were lost on Benny.

"I'm just goin' to have to come right out and tell him. I hate to do it like that, but he don't seem to get it otherwise." Pete assured Amy that he'd see to it the next morning.

They were a mile or so north of Resaca, and settled for the night under a lightweight cover. Pete was worn out from driving the wagon that day, and Amy had had a difficult time with Clary. Cotton-two was plain wearied from bouncing on the road for so long. Benny found himself a place to doze under a broad elm tree a few yards away. The moon was approaching its half slice stage, covered only slightly now and then by long stretches of gray cloud beard. Night birds called across the treetops, and in the meadows surrounding them, field mice foraged, all the while making their chittering small talk.

Benny was still not accustomed to sleeping at night, and every wild bird and animal sound found a place in his ear. He was staring up into the wide spread limbs of the elm, and fishing around in his mind for the name of the Old Testament giant, when he heard whispers from the road. The murmurings were not from Pete and Amy, for the voices were deeper, the buzz more hurried. He raised himself on one elbow and squinted into the half light. He detected at least three figures skirting the wagon. Hunkered close to one another, each seemed to be armed with some heavy object. He stood, still out of their sight, and studied their motions. Almost before he could react, he watched as one of the men slammed a stone into Pete's shoulder. Pete yelled and tried to jump up, but two of them held him down. The third grabbed Amy and hauled her to her feet, all the while screaming at her.

"White trash, abolitionist nigger-lover!"

Clary, asleep in the wagon, awakened and began to screech. Benny lumbered with staggering speed toward his friends. "Ah's comin', Mistuh Pete! Benny's comin'!"

The man restraining Amy looked up to see Benny's massive form churning up the dust as he charged at him. One of the other assailants called to him, "Hang on, Luther! He's a chicken stealin' coward! You kin take him with one hand!" Before the sentence was finished, Benny had yanked the man off his feet and thrown him into the ashes of their dying fire. The assailant rolled out of the embers and hollered, panic straining his voice. "I'm on fire! I'm burnin' up!"

As the man thrashed on the ground, Benny wheeled and headed toward the other two. Pete had loosed himself from one man's grip, but the other held him fast. Amy ran for the wagon and shielded Clary.

Benny's ponderous fist plowed into the back of the man still holding Pete. Pain shot through his kidneys, and he gave up his grip, howling in agony. The third man, now aware that Benny was thundering toward him, dropped his weapon and turned to run away. The big man caught him by the shirt sleeve and spun him around, picked him up and looked him squarely in the face. "Don't you be callin' Benny no coward no mo'!" Then Benny raised him to eye level and slammed his body flat against the rocky dirt.

Benny looked around eagerly, hardly winded and smiling triumphantly. "Is they any mo', Mistuh Pete?" Pete had grabbed one of the men and pinned his arm behind his back. "Where'd you all come from?" His voice was hoarse and his breath ragged.

The man winced as Pete tightened his grip. "I asked you, where did you come from? You better answer right now, or Benny here will be mighty upset."

"Down south, toward Atlanta. Lemme go!"

Pete quickly remembered the chicken stealing remark. "You wouldn't be related to some dirt grubbin', lame brain, pea farmer down that way, would you?"

"Ah bet they is, Mistuh Pete," said Benny. He now had both of the other men crushed beneath his huge arms and held them fast to his sides. "Seems like a long way to come, jus' to git a free man and them that goes with him."

"We'll see all you abolitionist trash molderin' in the grave with crazy John Brown!" Pete's captive growled between his teeth and hissed on. "Somebody'll catch you one day and even your whore over there will stretch hemp!" Pete's blood boiled at the last remark and he hollered immediately to Amy. "Get some rope!"

"No, Pete! Don't do it!" she said, misunderstanding his intent.

"Don't worry, darlin'. We're just goin' to make sure these fellers stay put for a long time." The men's struggle to be free of Benny's grip was fruitless, and Amy was able to tie his two hostages together by their wrists. Pete had thrown the third man to the ground and sat on him until Amy brought another length of rope. When they were finished, the attackers stood bound to three separate trees, their arms pinned behind them and tied at the elbows and wrists by thick ropes. The final blow came as Benny blindfolded each one. Since night was now full on them, the trio would be a long time standing, and their intended victims would likely be miles away before anyone would pass that way to untie them.

Pete and Benny hastily packed the wagon. Amy climbed up, and as they rumbled into the darkness, she covered Clary's ears against the curses shouted at them. Great trails of dust followed as they sped away. After a few minutes on the road, the tension began to let up and Pete smiled at Benny. "Bet that egg farmer will be surprised when those three tell him what happened. I myself never did see a big feller move that fast. Benny, you got the makin's of a powerful bodyguard. Maybe that's what you ought to do up north—hire yourself out guardin' the new president or some such thing."

"Sho' felt good, Mistuh Pete, to finally knock some heads togethuh. Mah Mam would be su'prise too!" They drove on until about four in the morning, when Pete was too drained to go farther. Making certain to pull a few hundred feet off the road, they concealed themselves well before settling down again.

Over the couple of days Pete and Amy noticed a mix of reactions to their traveling companion. Some people they passed on the road nodded and smiled, seeming to wish them well. Others averted their eyes and moved on in silence. Suspicion clouded the faces of the remainder, and dark scowls brooded over their expressions. The differences did not escape Benny either. He was troubled by them. He thought deeply about them, and finally spoke openly of them.

"Mistuh Pete, Miz Amy, Benny's right pleased to be travelin' with y'all these days, but Ah see that it ain' goin' t' work out, me goin' no'th with y'all. Seem like nobody kin cotton to a black man ridin' along with white folks. Bes' thing is if Benny go his own way and ketch up with some uthuh freemen. Ain' nobody goin' come down on y'all if it's jus' white folks."

Pete felt sorry that he could not protest a little stronger, but he was worried about Amy and Clary himself. Since the night the three intruders had attacked, Clary was full of fear and clung to Amy, refusing to sleep alone. At a crossroad near Chickamauga they parted company. Amy watched Benny lumber away, and it dawned on her that he probably would not be alone for very long. Not with his genuine fondness for visiting and his gentle humor. She just hoped he would remember that it was all right to defend himself and be able to stay out of danger.

Chapter Twenty-two

OTHER FABRICATIONS

R uthann couldn't believe her eyes. She would have believed her ears even less if anyone who told her that such a nice young fellow had ridden off on her horse. Cougar had managed to get through town and disappear down the road with more ease than he could have imagined himself. This was the best horse he'd ever "borrowed," and he almost wished he knew who the unsuspecting sucker was he had lifted it from.

Other thoughts boiled over in his mind. Back in Illinois he had seen the money belt, in spite of Marcus's efforts to hide it from him. It was stuffed with plenty of money, and Cougar knew what Jesse would be like with money—not quite tight, but careful with a buck, especially if it belonged to his daddy. That meant there might still be enough to spread around. Even if the money wasn't there, maybe the girl had a sister.

His ride as far as Lone Oak was uneventful, except for a slight detour he took to investigate some homemade biscuits sitting on the doorstep of a small lopsided house just off the old road. The woman of the place saw him sniffing around the covered tin pan, and confronted him. She was plain, slightly bent, and had fair skin, while her small head was crowned with wispy gray hair. "Smell somethin' interestin', do you?" she quizzed him.

"Oh, ma'am. Them's the best smellin' dodgers I come on since before the war." He lowered his head slightly and coughed a little.

"Ain't dodgers, air good flour biscuits. Made 'em fresh just now," she said, correcting him gently.

"Flour biscuits? My ma used to make flour biscuits when I was a tad. They always was my favorites."

"So, you been to the war?"

"Why, yes'm. I was. Just lucky to get home alive. I was in the infantry." He coughed again and winced, placing his hand on his chest.

"Fought for the Union, did you? 'Twas the only good and true side to be on, warn't it?"

"As you say, ma'am. The way it ended up proved that, for sure."

She studied his young face carefully.

"Was you injured on your face? Is that why you sport such a scraggly beard?"

Cougar shook his head, as if in disbelief. "Ma'am. You see right through me. I took a mighty blow to the head, and it near cost me my jaw. I was hopin' the hair might cover it better. I see it couldn't fool the likes of you."

"Oh, here now. Don't take it hard. And don't think it makes you unsightly neither. You're a fine lookin' young feller. I was only commentin', that's all."

"Well, I guess I better be on my way, b'fore dark hits. I got kin over in Lone Oak, and I have been on the road all night."

"All night? Have you et?" She moved toward the covered pan, and Cougar could see that he would soon be munching some of those biscuits, and be so slobbering grateful he might even make himself groan.

"I ain't had much," he said, lowering his voice a notch and hanging his head a bit further.

"Never let it be said that Tennie Brown ever sent a Union soldier away on a empty stomach. You take all them biscuits you can handle, and welcome to 'em."

Cougar began scooping the hot, fluffy rounds into his hat like a starving child, all the while backing away. "Thank you, ma'am. Thank you, very much. I'll never forget your kindness. Bless you and Old Abe and all of Billy Sherman's babies too!"

He jumped to the horse and galloped away, laughing and stuffing his mouth with the biscuits. Tennie Brown walked back inside her house and thought aloud, "Poor boy. War made some of 'em crazy like that. I guess he won't mind that them biscuits was made with mealy bug flour. He looks too addled to know the difference anyhow."

Lone Oak was not far, and like Jesse, the first place Cougar really noticed was Asa Bitter's dilapidated general store. He jumped from Ruthann's horse and swaggered to the door, feeling certain he could easily smooth talk the rubes out of a drink and some jerky. He was not surprised to see that the place was just as grubby inside as out, and Asa's sour expression cast some doubt on the possibility of striking up a fruitful conversation. *What the hell*, he thought. *I got to try anyway.*

"Afternoon," he said, sauntering across the room. "Looks like you got the rights to the dry goods trade hereabouts. You sell anythin' stronger than tea in this neck of the woods? I got real tired of the swill we could pick up in the infantry."

"Depends on what you're spendin'. Cash money gets you real whiskey. Confederate paper gets you nothin'."

"How about if I'm spendin' time?"

The skin on Asa's forehead crinkled in curiosity. "What's on your mind, boy?"

"Well, I'm fresh out of work at the surveyor's just now, and I could use me a job. I throwed up plenty of roads and bridges the last little while, but I just can't find me a job since the war's over."

"In case it maybe escaped you, there ain't exactly a stampede makin' its way to Lone Oak. I wouldn't go lookin' for no road buildin' in these parts." Asa shook his head. "No, sir. There ain't much of anythin' goin' on around here."

"I heard there was a family name of Beaudine makin'

some road improvements on the other side of town. Thought I might check that out."

"Another one, eh? You come to take Arthur's place, did you?"

Cougar was lost on this turn of the conversation. He switched to another tack.

"I don't know no Arthur, but I do know a feller says he's helpin' build the road. It's him I'm interested in."

"He owe you money?" Asa's eyebrows inched up and his eyes narrowed.

This was too easy, thought Cougar. "As a matter of fact, he does."

"He's out there all right, with the Beaudines. A soldier like yerself. Come through here, actin' the big shot."

"That's him for sure. He owes me plenty. I'm just tryin' to get my due, that's all."

Asa saw a queer sort of ally standing before him. He had disliked Jesse almost from the beginning, and, especially since he was helping the Beaudines. Their run-in yesterday had solidified and increased his feelings of distrust for the whole lot of them. He began to think that this bearded boy could somehow be of use to him.

"Would you be opposed to tradin' some work for your whiskey? I got a tree needs chopped out behind the place here. Have it down by tomorrow night and you got room and board for the day at least."

Cougar thrust his hand into thin air, and Asa took hold of it, smirking. "You got yourself a deal, mister," Cougar said, returning Asa's smile as they shook on it.

Three people passed through the door as the two men released their handshake. Two were old women, eyeing Cougar curiously, and picking their way through the iron-staved barrels of corn meal and flour. The other, Cougar saw, was an easy looking female, wild-haired and blooming, but wary. He was about to open his mouth and speak to them all together when Asa addressed the girl.

"Annie Grace. We got a man here who'll do some chores for trade of a meal and a bed. Go see what you kin rustle up t' home, but find my good ax and bring it first. G'on now." The girl looked suspiciously at Cougar and hurried away. "She's my daughter. She's kinda slow but is a dang fine cook. You kin start right in on that tree soon as she gits back."

"Yessir. Much obliged, Mister . . . ?"

"Bitter. Asa Bitter. And what do you go by?"

"Uh, name's Abraham," lied Cougar, spinning his wheels again. "Abraham Davis."

"G'on!" said Asa, disbelieving the name. "First name of one president and last of the other? How'd you know which side to fight on?" He chuckled and a dry, breathless rattle erupted from his throat. The two women stared at Cougar from beneath identical drab, homesewn bonnets, straining to hear his answer.

"Well, Mr. Bitter," whispered Cougar, just out of their earshot. "Just what side do you figure I shoulda fought on? Which side would you of fought on?"

"Frankly, I'da fought for whoever was winnin' the skirmish b'cause the way I see it, it's every man fer himself," murmured Asa, mimicking Cougar's low voice.

"You got me there!" Cougar grinned, and it was one of his best boyish grins. Now he knew he'd never have to answer to the man about the war. No doubt, thought Cougar, this old Asa feller would have crawled away on his belly, just like I did. He looked up to see Annie Grace lean the ax against the open door and disappear into the evening light. He turned to Asa.

"Lead me to that tree, Mr. Bitter, and watch the chips fly!"

Asa excused himself from the two women for a minute and showed Cougar which tree he wanted chopped down. It was a dried up pine, and didn't look much different than ten other trees standing close by. Cougar stripped off his shirt to lay into the tree, for the early evening was still daytime hot. He had managed a few strong strikes into the trunk before feeling a little winded, and bent to rest against it. From the corner of his eye he saw movement farther into the woods behind the store. He recognized the girl and called to her.

"Hey there! Annie! C'mon over here. I ain't goin' to hurt you."

Annie stopped stone still. Tangles of thick hair fell over her shoulders like the mane of a wild animal. She turned away and as quickly as she had appeared, she vanished into the filigree of woods. An inexplicable chill passed through Cougar, as if, as they say, someone had walked over his grave. He shivered and shook off the feeling, going back to his work. His dislike of physical labor was overcome only by the promise of a meal and a bed, so he made a good show until dusk fell.

At the same hour out in Beaudines' woods, Jesse and Clive finished their continuing task for the day. The new pickax was doing wonders, and the work began to progress again. Arthur came to the road with them, but sat to the side and supervised, smiling and rhyming.

Jesse had now been there four weeks. His travels had brought him to a place of repentance, a place of new hope, and Laurel in his heart. It was more than he had dreamed of, more than he felt he deserved. It was so good that he now promised himself he would never let go of the secret, for unbridled it would surely rob him of all this happiness.

Chapter Twenty-three

UNVEILING

S ome secrets have a way of inching out through unexpected apertures. They are stored all bundled up in one little place, seeming safe and secure, but they soon begin to make barely perceptible sounds, and take minuscule, whispery breaths, and stay alive no matter what you do to bury them. Sometimes the slightest syllable of the smallest word can cause the barest crack in the secret's hiding place, and part of it comes oozing out, so that the tiniest bubble of the syllable lands on an ear. When that happens, the secret is on its way to popping out. You can almost never stop it.

Chapter Twenty-four

HAUNTINGS

Jesse's custom had become spending his day working on Clive's road, eating a good supper, and passing a short while with Hattie and her family before retiring. He slept well and dreamed long. Sometimes his dreams were pleasant, but in spite of channeling his energies on the daily tasks and thinking of his future with Laurel, there were still the dark dreams. He wondered if any of the fighting men would be free of those dreams, or if the images would be forever spun out in their sleep.

The nebulous Pete still haunted him, rising out of dusty, rutted roads and choked woods, and the madness of the Andersonville pen. Relegating Pete's ghost to his dreams did not keep the secret from surfacing in Jesse's mind during the day. When Clive would speak of his boy and Arthur of his brother, it was almost as if Jesse might turn and see the powdery specter leaning against one of the trees he would soon chop down. However, it was Hattie's remarks as she pieced together the remnants of her memories that caused Jesse the rawest pain.

Hattie was perceptive, and Jesse's barely noticeable wincing had not escaped her. She had mulled over many times the possibility that Jesse and Pete had been close friends. Just as often as she considered that, she remembered Jesse saying he didn't know Pete very well. He had never given them specific details, but there he was, in possession of the Testament and a desire so strong to tell them of Pete's passing, she was having a hard time deciphering the depth of his concern.

"It's almost like he feels responsible," she observed to Clive after Jesse returned with the new pickax. "Maybe he thinks he could've done something to save Pete. Maybe . . . " She was stumped. Her mind would take her no further, so she set it aside one more time. "Well, he surely works hard at that road, and you couldn't ask for a more likable boy. I'd be pleased if Laurel married the likes of Jesse Campbell. Yes, I would."

Clive nodded in agreement. "Couldn't do better," he said and took a long draw on his worn and stubby corncob pipe. "That pickax he bought is almost like the end of his own arm already. The road is a lot wider than I intended for it to be, but Jesse gets goin' and you cain't stop him. I doubt Pete could've kept up with him."

Hattie's gaze clouded. She moved into that sphere that Clive did not understand, and her thoughts spun in an orbit beyond his reach. It was as if a fine twined thread still held her tied to the thinnest but most tenacious of hopes that somehow Jesse had been wrong. Clive chided himself inwardly for bringing up Pete's name. *Damn! I'm goin' to have to keep shut about my own boy so as not to set her off again.*

Friday promised to be another hot day, a buggy and sweaty one for the road builders. They started early, planning to leave off for a couple of hours at midday. As they ate their noon meal, Arthur was unusually talkative. He was in the business of praising Jesse these days and made no bones about his admiration for "Pete and Pete's best friend."

"Mama, you purely ought to walk down to the road and have a look-see. It's about wide 'nuf for two wagons to pass, I swear. Jesse is strong as a ox. You purely ought to march on down!"

Clive spoke up and embarrassed Jesse even further.

"That's a fact. I don't know what I'da done without your help, Jesse."

"Sounds like you got some kind of highway goin'. We could maybe throw a shindig and invite the governor to come on over." Hattie joshed them all with welcome good nature.

"You get it wide enough, we'll have Moses and the Israelites pass through arm in arm."

Jesse stood away from the table, smiling at her exaggeration. "Well, I almost hate to say this, now that I have been propped up on a throne, so to speak, but I was wonderin' if we could lay off a little early today and get in some fishin'."

Arthur's face registered absolute delight. "Wish we could fish! Wishin' to go fishin'!" he shouted. "I'll fetch my pole!"

Within seconds he was out of the door and into the steaming sunshine.

Hattie chuckled at her boy. "You know how it hardly takes more than two shakes of a lamb's tail for Arthur to make it to the river. You better hurry and catch up to him, Jesse, else all the fish will be gone. They fairly jump to the shoreline where he stands. It's the dad blamedest thing you ever saw."

He scooted him through the doorway. "Besides, my Laurel loves a good river catch. She cooks them up just so, and they melt in your mouth."

Jesse walked to the river, welcoming the break from road work. A certain coolness pervades the river bed, no matter how hot the field is, and the brilliance of light drops bouncing off the liquid surface bewitches the most troubled of men. Jesse settled on the bank and threw a line into the placid and languid flow. He sat back on the slope to enjoy an afternoon dream. Arthur mimicked him, but was forced to leap up almost immediately, as a tug pulled his line away from his fingers. He drew in a wriggling, whiskered catfish no bigger than a yam, snorted in disgust, and threw the flopping thing back at the river.

"Too small, that's all," he explained to Jesse. Jesse watched the boy as he cast his line most carefully back into the water. It was as if some secret eye of Arthur's could see beneath the glistening skin of the stream and discern fish movements and desires. Jesse wondered if, because he had been shorted on regular understanding, Arthur didn't possess some kind of sixth sense about certain things. If Hattie claimed a connection to the nether world of spells and mountain magic, perhaps some of it had rubbed off on her slow boy. It seemed he lived in an atmosphere invisible to all others much of the time, and the spirit locked in his irregular brain roved about in its own perfection. Jesse doubted that Arthur ever really had physical designs on Annie, in spite of what Laurel had said. His child-like pleasures and possibilities were enclosed in the heart and soul of a ten-year-old-boy, while his body had kept pace with a different time piece. Arthur was, in his own way, an example of purest clarity and noblest intent because he never even tried to execute guile. In truth, Jesse admired and envied Arthur for his simplicity.

The two stretched the fishing expedition to almost three hours before returning to the cabin. Jesse was able to snag a few sizable fish, but it was Arthur who lugged home the fuller string. He made an excuse for his superior catch.

"The fish knows me better, that's all. When they know you, your catch will be just as big as mine, bigger even, you'll see."

Jesse assured him that it was fine if his catch was better. He was beginning to sincerely like Arthur and appreciated the boy's admiration and generosity.

As they skirted the fence along the maturing garden, laughing and swapping gentlemanly brags, Jesse peered around the property, looking for signs of Laurel. Her horse was not tethered in front where it always stood, and Hattie looked up from her weeding, slightly anxious.

"I see Arthur worked his charms on them fish again. Does it every time. You didn't do so bad yourself, Jesse. Hand 'em over and I'll put 'em in some water." Hattie stood and wiped the dirt from her rough hands.

"They're all gutted, Mama. They're wantin' to jump into the fryin' pan! I could eat six or eight by myself." Arthur grinned and displayed obvious pride in himself. He was not shy about taking credit where credit was due. He made for the cooler shade of the house, leaving Jesse and Hattie together.

Hattie said, "Laurel should be here by now. I can't figure what could be keepin' her. I wonder, would you mind ridin' down to the meadow to see if she's comin'?"

Jesse was only too happy to comply. What he hoped would be a short wait at the meadow's edge dragged into a lengthy hour. As the minutes passed, he let his horse wander farther into the meadow, then down the path past Stetson's barn. Dusk was leading him through the countryside and making him progressively uneasy. The disconcerting feeling that something serious might have happened to Laurel dug into the pit of his stomach as he recalled seeing Marcus go down under his horse. He had ridden her path himself and knew of the many stretches where she would be riding alone. Now the sun was dropping behind the hillocks to the west, and Jesse strained to see Laurel's familiar silhouette. His mount sensed tension in Jesse's legs, and became nervous as well. Jesse decided to ride the whole way to Lone Oak or Paducah if he had to, for some sign of her. Dark now had crept across the fields and deep into the woods, wrapping itself around the horse's hooves and penetrating Jesse's sight. The cloud cover was heavy, and the moon, brightly shining on the Georgia river road, was obliterated in this Kentucky county.

The evening was not silent. Crickets, toads, and their frog cousins could be heard sawing and croaking for miles. The air was a constant buzz of life; even the growing grasses seemed to speak under the caressing press of the wind. He had spent many such warm nights in the deep south, but silence never surrounded him then either. Those nights were often filled with the jumble of men's voices, floating across camp from card games, comforting sing alongs, and rowdy story swapping.

He often remembered some of those times with regret. He had known many good and true mess-mates. Some were now gone forever; some had returned home with life-long reminders of battle. Jesse felt lucky. He retained all of his limbs, most of his hair, and some semblance of sanity. He now wished he could have known Pete, could maybe have had a brother like him.

Jesse had just ridden past Asa Bitter's eyeless clapboard store when he heard hoof beats coming fast on the dark street. He peered anxiously into the blackness, and relief washed through him as he made out Laurel's figure riding the oncoming horse.

"Laurel!" he shouted. "Where in creation have you been?"

Laurel reined her mare to a halt in a hail of gravel. She was breathing heavily and nearly shouted at him. "Hell, if I don't know what's got into that crazy Ruthann! Somebody stole her horse yesterday and she had me tearin' around tarnation lookin' for the beast this afternoon. And she kept on blattin' some craziness about watchin' who I hung around and she wouldn't want me to run with the wrong crowd. I don't know. By the time I got out of there, I *knew* I'd be ridin' in the dark and durn, if she didn't know it too. She kept beggin' me to stay overnight, like she didn't want me comin' home. Shoot if I didn't about tell her what to do with her notions *and* her stupid horse!"

Jesse listened as long as he could to Laurel's tirade. Then he jumped off his horse, pulled her from hers, and enveloped the angry girl in his arms.

"Just shut up for a minute, would you? I was worried sick you got hurt on the road." He buried his face in her tumbling, damp hair and was silent for a moment. She raised her face to him, and they shared a long and welcome kiss. "It's goin' to be late when we get back home, but we have to go or your folks will be in fits. Hattie was already pretty worried around suppertime. If we go it slow and we get a crack in the clouds, we should be all right." Jesse ushered her to the resting horse, mounted his own, and they were on their way.

The ride home went slowly as they guided the two horses gingerly through the dimness. The open fields yielded little direction and in the wooded stands, black trunks reached out with sharp unseen twigs and branches to tear at their faces and arms. When Laurel's mount stumbled slightly, Jesse reached over and took her reins. "Come on over to my horse, darlin'. Sit behind me and we'll string yours along behind."

He heard a peep of protest and quickly added, "I'll just feel better if you're right here with me. Come on, now. Put your arms around my waist and keep me company."

"Well," she countered assertively, "I want you to know I could go it by myself if need be. I can ride as good as any man alive!"

Jesse laughed and tugged her closer to his back. "You feel better behind me than so far away on your own horse. And I do know you can ride, almost like the wind. I don't want you gettin' away anyhow. Here now," he continued, "you can kiss my neck anytime you please, too."

"Oh, la-de-da! I *am* the lucky girl!" She grinned and poked his ribs. He looked up to see ragged clouds still covering the face of the moon and smiled to himself. The two young people were in heaven.

Back in Lone Oak, Asa Bitter plotted ways to use this Abraham Davis to his advantage. The bed he tossed and turned in was stony and cold, even on a summer's night. Through the years Asa had come to earn his appellation, hardened by experiences in life which he had not foreseen and was ill prepared to overcome. As a young man he had pursued a beautiful girl, a charming and quick witted girl, one who kept most suitors at arm's length, for she was of an independent mind. She was said to have possessed the power of discernment of spirits, and perpetuated that idea herself as often as possible.

Just when Asa had thought he might be making headway with this desirable object of his affection, she discussed with him what she perceived to be his demerits. She was cruelly outspoken and shattered any illusions he had about their eventual union.

In short, she blasted him out of the saddle. Of course, the girl was Hattie Shane. Her marriage to Clive Beaudine cut Asa Bitter to the quick, and he never forgave either of them. He married the first unwary girl to come along and treated her like a servant. When she died giving birth to Annie Grace, he buried her immediately and never referred to her again. Annie Grace became another source of bitterness and churlishness regarding life. In truth, Asa's disorderly store and sour face were both accurate reflections of his spirit. Hattie had been right all along. Even if she had married him, he would somehow have traveled the same sorry route.

Just how he might utilize this Abraham fellow was still a mystery to him, but for the time being, he offered the boy food and shelter to perform tasks which Asa had put off, some of them for years.

Chapter Twenty-five

BREWINGS

Cougar lay on a cot chewing his nails intensely and brooding, while uneasy and peevish thoughts mingled in his mind. *This old duck is usin' me for a work horse . . . I got to get my hands on some real money . . . I got to flush Jesse out . . . I wonder if I can get me a card game up around here.* And so on, until the gray matter shut down for the night and he began to snore open mouthed into another summer sleep.

Hattie twitched nervously in her troubled napping. The sound of hoof beats snapped her to wakefulness immediately, and she jumped from her chair to look out into the night. Relief spread warmly through her as she made out two horses and saw Laurel slide to the ground from behind Jesse.

"Oh, praise be! You're home safe!" she said, running to the door. "Heaven strike me if I didn't see you dead in some ditch somewhere!" She spoke intently, through clenched and rattling teeth. "You gave us all a turn!"

"Mama, I swear I'm goin' to brain that Ruthann over it! She's makin' me crazy."

The two women embraced. Then Laurel took Jesse's hand.

"Mama, it's a good thing Jesse came along to meet me. I'd probably be out there lost in the dark without he came to get me."

Hattie smiled gratefully at him and said, "I'll fetch us all a cup of herb tea before we settle down for the night."

"Much obliged," Jesse replied and took the two horses to the corral to quickly brush them down. While Jesse tended to the horses, Laurel related to her mother Ruthann's remarks about the company she was keeping and how she kept telling her not to trust a person on account of a pretty face or fancy story.

"I'll tell you, Mama, she kept up her blatherin' and then sent me out after her horse, which she said was stole, but just as likely wandered off. I never saw her act so antsy. I can't imagine what's got into her."

She sipped slowly from her crockery cup until Jesse came in and then motioned for him to sit next to her. Hattie was pleased with the picture they presented. As Jesse drank, Laurel relaxed and rested her head against the boy's muscular shoulder, her hair falling loosely across his chest. They seemed so natural together, and Laurel looked at last contented with a young man at her side. Hattie was left to puzzle Ruthann's remarks as well.

After two days of actual work, Cougar was becoming restless in Lone Oak. The wild looking girl avoided him as if he had running sores, and Asa was beginning to get on what nerves he did possess. He decided to go scouring, a term which he employed when sniffing out a card game or some other way to part a sucker from his money. In the army he'd slickened up his already smooth game moves, and he could palm a card better than most. One glance through Lone Oak and he could see that nothing was going there. Riding back to Paducah was out of the question, since the horse might be recognized, and even here in Kentucky, the locals didn't take kindly to horse "borrowing."

He decided to tell Asa he would probably go and confront Jesse and try to get his money back. "If I had me a mule or some such animal I could ride over on, then he wouldn't see my horse and think I was in the chips. The actual way I come by this horse was, I won him in a card game, fair and square. So I was wonderin' if I couldn't just borrow that scruffy lookin' mule you got out back and see about it."

"And you leave your horse right here, saddle and all?" Asa squinted his right eye in Cougar's direction. Cougar nodded. It seemed to be good enough insurance to Asa that he would get Annie Grace's mule, the only animal he owned, back in one piece.

"All right, then," he said. "You'll be needin' directions, I guess. Annie's been out there plenty of times. She can tell you the way."

"Don't need directions. I got me a little map right here." Cougar displayed the folded paper and tucked it away in his pants pocket. "Wish me luck!"

"Yeah, luck," mumbled Asa, only vaguely wondering where this Abraham fellow had gotten a map to the Beaudine place. Ah well, these were strange times and produced strange happenings. He went back to the half-hearted sifting of weevil from a barrel of flour in the back of the store. It was early Saturday morning, already the third of June, and promising to be hot again. Not a cloud dotted the brilliance of the sky. Cougar swatted pesky gnats from his face and nudged the mule ahead with insistent jabs in the ribs. Annie's mule ambled along at its own pace, never able to interpret urgency in any form, sometimes forgetting it was supposed to be moving forward. After Cougar had arrived at about mid point between Lone Oak and the Beaudine cabin, the mule stopped in the center of the trail and commenced some hawking sounds. Then it simply sat down and refused to get back up.

None of Cougar's colorful bellowings or poor-boy beggings meant anything to the beast, and in the middle of one of his best harangues, the mule proceeded to go to sleep. Cougar aimed his boot at the animal's bony side and let fly a sound kick.

The mule responded by leaping to all fours so fast that the dirt flew under its hooves. Cougar watched despondently and braced his own helplessness with another string of obscenities as the scruffy animal galloped back toward Lone Oak. He would have to walk anyway. Hell!

Hattie was alone when Cougar appeared at the rail fence beside the garden. Clive had gone to the Marystown mill, a few miles east of their home, to buy feed for his animals, and her children and Jesse had headed for the river. He was pulling some bothersome weed away from her fast growing carrot tops and had her mind on far away things, so she was slightly startled.

"Excuse me, ma'am. I am in the way of lookin' for a ex-Confederate soldier boy about my age, name of Jesse Campbell. I heard he might be out here workin' on a road. Is that so?"

Cougar stood a few feet away and affected his most humble look. He had smoothed his hair down and tucked his shirt in, hoping to appear more like Jesse, like somebody less slick than he knew himself to be. Hattie saw a small pistol shoved between his leather belt and worn trousers, and stiffened.

Hattie shielded her eyes from the blaze of sunshine now high in the sky. Confederate? She wondered if she had heard the boy right. She said, "Confederate soldier? Who wants to know? What's your name and how did you get so far off the beaten track?"

"Well, ma'am. My name's . . . " Who should he be, Cougar Rivers or Abraham Davis? He continued. "Let's just say I'm a friend of Jesse's from way back. I was told he'd be out here." He shuffled his feet and leaned over the rail. "Look, ma'am. I come a long way walkin' to find him." Slight hesitation. "I got news about his daddy. Is he around here, then?"

It seemed to him he could see her thawing. *Hoo boy! I am good*, he thought.

"No Confederate that I know of. And what kind of news anyway?" Hattie asked aloud, but reminded herself that Jesse had been with Pete in that infamous Southern prison camp, where Union men were penned up.

"I'm sorry. I can't tell nobody about it but him. 'Twouldn't be right."

"Then tell somebody about yourself. You say you walked clear out here? From where?" Hmmm. Maybe she wasn't thawing that fast.

222

"Other side of town," he lied. "I had me a mule but it died."

"Who told you that this Confederate Jesse person was here?"

"Some woman over in Paducah, some old woman." Hattie's suspicions were growing. She didn't like the look of him, the vagueness about him. She didn't like him saying Jesse had been a Confederate soldier. She stood up to get a better look at him and didn't much like that either. He seemed to be outlined in some kind of drab haze, not unlike the one surrounding Asa Bitter. He projected a certain leaden quality which contrasted heavily with the humble pie intonations she perceived in his voice.

"What does some old woman in Paducah have to do with anybody hereabouts?" she challenged him, Ruthann's remarks sliding around in her mind. Don't trust a person, no matter how good he looks. She wondered what looked good to Ruthann. Cougar was brought up short. Maybe he'd said the wrong thing. Maybe he should have just straight out said he wanted to see Jesse about a loan, or that he himself was looking for work. As he was searching for a new and better lie, Arthur came bounding out of the narrow path from the river.

"Mama! You should see the fish we caught. And Jesse got the biggest! Laurel and him went for a swim, went for a swim, Laurel and him!"

Cougar stared straight into Hattie's eyes and read the disturbed look in them. Then the picture of Jesse and that feisty girl swimming together sparked Cougar's vivid imagination, and he was lost for a moment in thought. Suddenly it struck him that he had caught the woman in a little white one herself, so his own fibs were justified. His lips curved upward in a slow, oily smirk as he turned to Arthur.

"Is that my friend Jesse Campbell you're speakin' of? He always was a Jim-dandy fisherman."

Arthur grinned widely and answered, "That's my best friend, Jesse, all right! He can do just about anythin'!"

Hattie motioned quickly to Arthur. "Come on over here, Arthur, and drop them fish in my basket before they rot. We'll just go on up and take care of this right now."

Then she turned to Cougar and said. "I suppose you can wait for Jesse here if you please, but likely it'll be a while before we see him."

I'll just bet it will, Cougar said to himself. "If you don't mind," he answered most politely. "I'll sit right down in the shade and pass the time until he does come back."

Hattie pulled Arthur into the cabin and whispered to him, giving him important instructions. "You hie yourself to the river by way of the ridge and tell Jesse there's a bearded varmint here lookin' for him. Says he has news about his daddy but can't tell no one but Jesse himself. Tell him I don't like the looks of it and he should come up the ridge instead of the path, and have a look-see through the window where the man can't see him."

Arthur nodded, but still looked a bit confused. Hattie slowly repeated herself and asked him to recite her instructions to be sure he was clear. He did so, word for word, and she knew that he would say it over and over to himself until he reached Jesse.

As Cougar sat under a nearby tree, he rolled the conversation over in his thoughts. The woman—he presumed her to be Laurel's mother—had made a point of questioning his statement about Jesse being a Confederate soldier. He began to consider that maybe Jesse had misled the Beaudines. If that were so, then this visit would turn out to be sweeter than he had planned. The word *blackmail* wandered before his mind's eye. It was something he hadn't yet tried in his illustrious career, and it could prove to be interesting as well as profitable.

Arthur scooted out the back way and scurried through the woods with his important message. When he made the river, he tumbled down the bank, hallooing and wincing all the way. He breathlessly related Hattie's message. Jesse and Laurel had just come out of the water, both dripping and wrapping themselves in dry wool blankets. They guessed immediately that the man must be the bearded Cougar.

"What in the name of Heaven can he want? He can't have news about Marcus, and if he did, why didn't he mention it at the boardin' house?" Jesse was puzzled.

"I can't believe he had the gall to come clear out here!" said Laurel. "And how did he know where to find you in the first place?" Laurel puzzled for only a moment.

"Somethin's makin' sense now. The only person who could've told him is Ruthann. It had to be him she was warnin' me about. Ha! I hope she don't think I'm that dumb!"

"But, Laurel," Arthur reminded his sister. "He was lookin' for Jesse, not you."

Jesse put his arm around Laurel's waist and teased her. "No offense, darlin', but Arthur's probably got a point there. He's been doggin' me since I got back from the war. I just wonder what it is he wants."

"How do you know he wants anythin'?" she asked.

"Because, Laurel sweet, he's always lookin' to get some advantage, whether it's with the ladies or the cards or from somebody else's pocket. My guess is, he's pretty far down on his luck and maybe on the run. This place is far enough away from the Ohio that people wouldn't come lookin' for him."

Laurel snorted in disgust. "Well, I hope he won't suppose he's welcome out here just because we're in the boonies."

"What we'll do is go back the ridge way like Hattie said and see if it *is* him. I'll see what he's up to. With any luck, he'll just give me some sob story and I can send him away with a few dollars to tide him over."

Laurel ran beside him, matching his strides as they moved up the hill to reach the ridge behind the cabin. "I wouldn't give the likes of him one red cent," she growled.

"Me neither," Arthur echoed, panting and huffing his way behind them.

Meantime, Hattie eyed the young man lolling beneath the shade tree. She'd read his spirit and hadn't liked it. He spelled trouble some way, but she couldn't guess how. Naming Jesse a Confederate soldier was sticking almost to the insides of her eyelids and causing unwanted confusion. Jesse hadn't ever actually said he was a Union man. He had said Pete died in the Confederate prison, and intimated that he was with him in that same prison. They had all assumed he had been Pete's fellow prisoner, but Jesse had never really given any detail. She was feeling uneasy and wishing that the young man outside would get up and walk away. Shortly, Jesse, Laurel, and Arthur returned. They shuffled quietly to the lone window at the cabin front. Crowding behind Hattie's only lace curtain, the three of them peered through the wavy grained glass.

"It's him all right!" Laurel whispered. "The skunk!"

Jesse considered what the real purpose of this call might be. He was already settled on the notion that Cougar was after money, but he couldn't imagine what his ploy would be. He guessed he could tolerate wheedling if that's what Cougar had in mind and outright begging would be embarrassing, but he could see Cougar doing it if it meant money he didn't have to work for. He stood up and walked through the door, prepared to part with some bills if it would get rid of this former friend.

"I come to ask for a job." Cougar stated, even before Jesse could get a word out. "That there road buildin' will go a lot faster with another hand workin' on it." Jesse was flabbergasted. He hadn't known Cougar to work at a real job from the time they were both boys in britches.

"Well now, I don't think we're in need of any more straw bosses on this major thoroughfare here. Arthur is doin' a right fine job of that already. But, uh, I wouldn't be the one to say. That would be for Mr. Beaudine to decide. It's his road."

There was a brief silence. Then Jesse continued. "I heard you had news of Marcus. What news would that be?"

"Jesse, I can't lie to you. I only said that because the woman was pretendin' you wasn't here and actin' suspicious. We can tell her I said he's doin' fine and back to work or some such thing. Point is, I need me a job. Now, I know your girl lives out here, and I would stay clean away from her because she don't like me much and I can't blame her. But I am tee-totally down on my luck and I just need a few dollars to get me back on my feet."

"Mr. Beaudine couldn't pay you cash money, Cougar. He's poor like the rest of the county."

"But you must be gettin' somethin' out of it. I seen all them new chopped trees and dug out stumps. You're workin' your rear end off on that road, and for nothin'? What's your angle, Jesse? Would it be a well put together gal? You got someone to snuggle up with on these hot summer nights? How is she anyways?"

Cougar wiggled his eyebrows and smiled knowingly at Jesse. He couldn't see the fist coming at him until it was jammed under his chin, gripping his collar tightly around his neck.

"You'll just shut it up right now!" Jesse hissed at him, and behind the lace curtain three open mouths sucked breath in and swallowed hard.

"I am not like you, Cougar. Usin' women and always lookin' out for number one. It's none of your business what I get out of this, and you couldn't ever hope to understand it anyway." He released the surprised Cougar and stepped back.

"I suggest you cut your losses, get back on that road, and keep movin'."

He reached into his pocket and yanked out a handful of bills, not much money, but enough to stake Cougar to a couple of nights at the boarding house and some meals.

"Jesse, man! I never thought you'd turn on me. If that's the way you want it, fine. I guess you ain't the Jesse I always knew. No, sir." Cougar raised his hand and ran his fingers through the tousled hair. He shook his head and breathed a sigh. "The Jesse I knew wouldn't be leadin' these good people on and makin' 'em think he was a Union man when all along he fought for the See-cesh."

Jesse clinched his fist around the money and demanded angrily, "What are you talkin' about?"

Cougar leaned against the tree, more at ease now. "I had a little conversation with the lady of the house and when I mentioned you and me was Confederates together she got a mite upset, like she didn't believe me. Kept sayin' there wasn't no Confederate soldiers around here. Looked like a cover to me, or else she didn't really know about the one right under her nose."

Jesse's heart sank.

How could he know whether Cougar was telling the truth? He wanted to slam him in the face, as Neils had in Springfield. His stomach churned and he suddenly felt weak.

Through trembling lips he spoke intently.

"What goes on here is none of your business! You will take this money and get out, or by heaven, I will personally find all the gamblers you have cheated and all the women you have used and hunt you down like a dog. Seems like a few of them wouldn't mind seein' you stretch hemp."

In spite of the severity in Jesse's voice, Cougar managed a swagger. He saw that he had hit a very sore spot, and although he couldn't grasp the full magnitude of his position, he realized that he had now become a threat to Jesse. He liked the feeling. He would go back to Lone Oak and mull the situation over for a few days. It was good to see the pure and holy Jesse running scared. He would ponder it on the long walk back to Asa Bitter's store.

Cougar accepted Jesse's money, turned, and stepped onto the road, never looking back. Jesse was shaken and stood for a long minute by the tree, trying to possess his thoughts. For a man accustomed to lying, the solution would have been simple: concoct a lie to cover. Jesse, who had already lived out of character by withholding the truth these last few weeks, felt the weight of his silent lie heavier than ever. His bosom burned with invisible shame, and his spirit shrank. How could he ask Hattie about Cougar's comments without unlocking his secret? He wanted to sink into the ground right then and there.

As soon as Cougar was out of sight, two curious Beaudines rushed from the cabin, while Hattie held back.

"What did he want, Jesse? You looked like you was goin' to kill him!" Arthur jiggled up and down in his childish manner, and laughed loudly. "I wish't you'da hit him!"

Laurel was as curious, but less spirited. "Are you all right, Jesse? Is he comin' back?"

Jesse was trying desperately to calm himself. He shook his head and answered, "I hope for his own sake he skedaddles. He's tryin' to shake anybody he can down for money. Said he'd work on the road, but I know him too well to believe that. He's nothin' but trouble. And I don't like him talkin' trash. I guess that's the worst part."

"You shoulda clobbered him good, Jesse!" declared Arthur, dancing around in a circle, splattering sun dust with his double fists. The three returned to the cabin and assured Hattie that all was well. The troublemaker was gone and she could rest easy. Jesse avoided looking directly at her, for he feared she would delve into Cougar's remark. He wasn't ready to answer that question yet, though he knew it was coming sooner rather than later. He excused himself by offering to go meet Clive over east. Laurel stayed back to help with house chores and Arthur turned his mind to napping.

Hattie went back to the garden and was alone again with her musings. *I suppose if Jesse didn't want to tell us he was a Confederate soldier, he had his reasons,* she thought. I wonder if I dare bring it up or if that scalawag was even tellin' the truth. It *was* funny, the way Jesse showed up, knowing so much and in possession of Pete's Testament, but telling so little when it came down to it. I have trusted him all along and it wouldn't be fair to throw that trust to the wind on account of some stranger's remark. Still, what could the other boy have gained in lying about Jesse's wartime allegiance? Hattie had to admit she was stumped. She would mention it all to Clive when he got back, and maybe they could puzzle it out together.

It was close to noon. There was dinner to be fixed before her husband returned, and other chores to be done, but

Hattie's heart was not in food, nor even in her gardening. She stood straight and stretched her back before going to the cabin. Laurel appeared at the doorway, shaking a rug vigorously in the hot June air and humming casually. Hattie observed her girl and envied her sweet, fresh youth. She decided she would keep her troubled feelings from Laurel for the time being.

Chapter Twenty-six

GIDEON'S DRIVER

On the road and traveling ever northward, Pete and
Amy were facing their own challenges. At about the
same time Cougar ran into Jesse on the doorstep of
the boarding house, the trekkers had been on the road nearly
two weeks. Their adventures with Benny were over, and
it took them the week of traveling plus another day just to
reach Atlanta. When they parted company with Benny, there
remained two more weeks of solid travel, much of it over
rutted, and sometimes rocky, mountain roads.

They established daily routines, almost as if they were setting up housekeeping on the road. Now, the first thing to
come off the wagon each evening was the rocker, to be placed
on a smooth, flat patch of earth, where Clary could be soothed
to sleep in her mother's lap at nightfall. Amy's feet touched
lightly on the worn ground, and she hummed a sing-song
tune, rocking in time to the music of her voice. Pete always
started the fire and Amy commenced the food preparations.
Clary often occupied herself by climbing into the chair and
crooning to her own rag doll. They were occasionally ham-
pered by rain and sought shelter in a grove or an abndoned
shed. Two or three times they had asked for a night's covering
in a farmer's barn. This particular night they were troubled by
an impending storm.

The rain held off, so they were able to start a fire and cook their meal. After supper Clary mentioned Benny. "I miss Benny's stories. I wish we could see him again. Maybe he's with Grampa Jim and Bullseye." Her mother smiled and admitted she missed his stories as well, but both she and Pete had noticed that with no Benny in their party, people were more open and less suspecting. They talked about it after Clary fell asleep.

"It will not ever cease to amaze me that most people think everybody has to fit into one size hole, like so many pegs on a wall," Amy said as she and Pete sat before the fading embers of their fire. "If God had wanted us all like that, he'd have stamped us each out of the same mold. Benny's blackness didn't make him less of a person."

Pete teased her. "God could have made all the women look like you. Then all the men would be as happy as I am."

"Pete, you spoil me."

"Dang right, I do! How many other women's got the chance to travel for a month of Sundays to go live with a bunch of crazy Beaudines, who, by the way, they never laid eyes on before? Show me another new bride who gets to camp out every night and come up with new ways to fix flour and water seven days a week. You are spoiled rotten, for sure!"

"I do feel lucky, Pete. I don't mean to harp on the question, but what does happen to Benny and them like him now? They have nothin', don't know anybody up north, and prejudice runs high in lots of places. I just wish I knew what happened to all the black people Jim and me helped. You know, where they went and what they're doin' now."

"I believe in my heart that what the scripture says is true. In my Testament I had it marked. It was in Matthew, from the Sermon on the Mount if I recollect right. I believe in due time they'll be taken care of."

Amy smiled knowingly. "You mean the part about the fowls of the air and the lilies of the field, how the Heavenly Father feeds them and clothes them."

"Exactly. And the last part goes somethin' like this. 'Take therefore no thought for the morrow, for the morrow shall take thought of the things for itself.'"

"Then what does the very last part mean? 'Sufficient unto the day is the evil thereof?' I always wondered about that."

"I reckon it means you shouldn't go borrowin' trouble from tomorrow, that whatever we got to go through today is plenty enough."

"Sometimes more than enough," Amy murmured, gazing at the black and threatening thunderheads gathering above them. Amy's observation was followed by her tired sigh, and the two travelers turned in, unconsciously crossing off one more day on their journey.

Those same clouds shrouded the dawn as they awoke the next day. The stillness of the preceding night was jarred by stiff winds, and Pete was hesitant about getting back on the already rough and unreliable road in a heavy rain. Bouncing over rocky and irregularly furrowed byways had loosened one of his back wheels, and he hesitated to travel and possibly be stuck in muddy roads. They decided to wait out the storm. When a break in the clouds appeared, Pete informed Amy he would walk a mile or two ahead and see what the road was like and how near the next town might be.

"It shouldn't take me too long just to go a little ways. I want to check out the best way to go. Maybe it's dry enough now you can start a fire and cook up some breakfast for you and Clary."

In two minutes he was gone. Amy was unafraid. She had a pistol and a shotgun with her and knew how to use them both. Pete had walked nearly a mile when he saw a large covered wagon coming toward him. The huge gelding pulling the wagon strained at his bit and the driver, a woman, was struggling to hold him back. She shouted at the animal.

"Hold on! Just hold on, Gideon! Slow up!"

When she spotted Pete she stood straight up in the seat and shouted in his direction. "Don't just stand there! Whack this stupid horse on the skull and help me slow him down! Get a rock and swat him!"

Over the woman's continuing roars and bellowing, Pete calmly approached the animal, gently took hold of the bit, and stopped him in the middle of the road. The woman leaped from the wagon and stumbled once in the ruts before she threw herself against Pete and began to wail. She wrapped her arms around his middle and cried long and loud. Pete stood with his arms opened to each side and let her go until the wail became a sob, the sob became a series of whimpers, and the whimpers flowed into silent tears trickling down her cheeks. She pulled herself away and wiped her face with reddened, trembling hands. One of her palms was bleeding from pulling so tightly against the reins of the monster horse she called Gideon.

Pete offered his neckerchief. "This might help, ma'am."

"Oh, I do thank you!" she said, sniffing and pulling her hair away from her eyes. "I was afraid I'd soon pitch over the side and roll down the hill. Gideon knows we're nearly home, and he was flying like a bird to get there."

"He's a big horse all right. You say you're on your way home?"

She pointed south and tears came again. "Right around the next bend. We've been gone for nearly six months, but you know, a horse doesn't forget. He was anxious to get going, even in the storm this morning."

Pete was a bit hesitant to mention that he had seen no farm or home or anything just around the bend. Still, he thought she ought to be prepared, in case they had been burned out in her absence. "Are you sure you're on the right road, ma'am?"

"I ought to know my own way home. I've been on this road a thousand times."

"You have folks waitin' there, do you?"

"To be sure, they're all there. Three children, my husband, even our old dog, Ezekiel. Oh, yes. None of them have gone anywhere. And Gideon, he can't wait to be back in the old barn. I went away in March, but I felt, now that the war's over,

I should go back. They are my family, after all. It wasn't home up north, no matter what some people said." Pete's hairline shivered with goose bumps as an eerie sensation overpowered him. What woman leaves three children and a husband during war time? Maybe she had ailing parents elsewhere; maybe other things had been pressing. He felt that it might be a good thing to go with her, make certain she got there all right.

"Well, ma'am, if you don't mind, I will just see to it that Gideon don't run you off the road. Show me where to go and I'll take you right to your doorstep."

"Oh, that would be more than kind of you," she said, apparently not giving a thought to his circumstances, not wondering what business he had on the road all alone. And she did not appear to be frightened, except at the prospect of a rollover. She sat on the seat next to him and primped, passing a carved ivory comb through her hair over and over.

"They will be ever so glad to see me again. It's been such a long, long time." She looked eager and stared straight down the road beyond Gideon's head.

"If you don't mind," mentioned Pete, " I'm goin' to stop and tell my wife where I'll be drivin' you. She's waitin' back here with our wagon. We're waitin' for the roads to dry out a little."

"Oh, then bring her along. You can both see them; you can meet my family. They'll be happy to meet you."

Pete pulled back on Gideon's reins and spoke softly.

"Whoa now, boy. Stop here."

They pulled to the edge of the road, and Amy waved to Pete. He called out to her. "The lady here was havin' a bit of trouble with this big old horse so I told her I'd see her home. You and Clary climb on up and we'll get her there in two shakes."

He turned toward the woman, who smiled at Amy and Clary, maintaining her eager expression. "It's only just around the bend there. You'll see it. Maybe your little girl would like to play with mine."

The eerie feeling Pete had felt earlier persisted and grew as they neared the curve in the road. The woman raised herself and leaned on Pete's shoulder, all the while pointing toward what appeared to be a narrow off-road. He had missed it entirely while coming from the south.

The road was narrow but short and soon opened into a small meadow, nestled between two gentle slopes off the mountain side. Amy touched Pete's arm and gripped Clary's hand when the woman's so-called home came into view. It was nothing more than a shack, weather beaten and listing to one side. A small barn stood nearby, its door swinging loosely on one hinge. There was no sign of life, no children scurrying out to meet their mother, no smoke rising from a cooking fire inside. The quiet was broken only by the creaking of the barn door and the careless cawing of two crows perched at the peak of the crumbling roof. The woman dropped quickly from the wagon seat and ran to a scanty grove behind the shack. Pete took Amy's hand and looked at her knowingly.

"She ain't all there, is she Pete?" whispered Amy.

"Either that, or her whole family's run out on her. Nobody's lived here for months from the looks of it."

The woman reappeared immediately, excitement shining in her eyes. Her cheeks were flushed and her voice was high.

"Come, come! I told you they were still here. Everybody, even Ezekiel. Come and see them!"

Pete and Amy hesitated. The woman's smile faded and she murmured an intense supplication. "Please. Please come."

They followed her to the grove, treading softly, as if on sacred ground. She led them to five separate wooden markers, crude headstones, in which coarsely fashioned names had been carved.

"Yes, I was right," the woman said, to no one in particular. "You see, they are still here, every one. There's little Rachel," she continued, pointing out the marker nearest to the shack. "And there's Jeremiah, and Isaiah, and next to him, Ezekiel. John is right here, he's my husband, John."

"Ma'am," said Pete quietly. "Maybe you'd better come on with us. You'd be all alone out here."

"Hush up!" she hissed abruptly, her face contorted in anger. Clary turned her face into Amy's skirt, frightened.

The woman bent down to the child. "Oh, I'm so sorry, little girl. I didn't mean to upset you. It's just that, well, your daddy wants me to leave my babies. I can't do that. Then they'd miss me and it would be all my fault again. I shouldn't have ever left them in the first place. Who's going to take care of them if I'm gone?"

She walked to her husband's marker. "You see how helpless he is without me here? Weeds, weeds, everywhere. Just look. No, they can't do without me. You go on now, and thank you very much for bringing me home."

She fell abruptly to the ground and began tugging at the carpet of overgrown weeds surrounding the graves of her family. Pete pulled Amy and Clary away and they walked quickly down the narrow road, clinging to each other. Even later as they pulled their wagon onto the road and traveled farther north, Amy found it hard to shake the sound of the woman's voice and its repetitive phrase from her ears. Weeds, weeds, she had whispered over and over. Weeds, weeds, weeds. Amy wept for the fragile mind and clutched her own child close to her bosom. She would be glad to get away from this road and the miseries she had encountered on it.

They had gone a mile or two more when a horseman came from the north in a fury. Upon seeing them, he waved them down. He was a man in his mid-forties, dressed in finery such as Pete had never seen in his life. Amy recognized him as one who probably had a profession—doctor, lawyer, something like that. He was agitated and spoke sharply.

"Tell me, have you passed a woman on this road? She would have been driving a wagon, one with a canvas cover. She would probably have been in a hurry. Have you seen her?"

Pete answered quickly, nodding his head. "We have, sure. She's back there, maybe two miles down the road. We rode with her to a place she called her home, due to her havin' trouble with the big gelding pullin' the wagon."

"That would be Gideon. So, you left her at the shanty?"

"Yes, sir, we did. I tried to get her to come away, but she wouldn't have it. I'm afraid she don't quite understand the situation there." Pete was apologetic in his response.

The man shook his head and sighed. "Oh, she understands the situation all right. She's come back at least twice before, to care for her family, as she says. She's my sister. She had been up to visit me and her family was taken ill quite suddenly while she was away. When she returned home she found them all dead, even the mongrel dog. Who knows how long it took for each one to go. A neighbor found her there with them and helped her bury the bodies. I came down and took her back home with me. I believe we'll have to commit her after all. I can't keep coming down here and dragging her back."

"Might be a good thing about now," Pete advised, and immediately felt he had overstepped a delicate line. The man pursed his thin lips and cleared his throat.

"Well, yes."

He patted the sweaty neck of his horse and said, "Thank you for lending her aid. I hope it didn't put you out." Then he reached into his breast pocket and drew out good Yankee bills amounting to twenty dollars, something else neither Pete nor Amy had seen in a long while.

"Take this for your trouble," he insisted. Dropping the money on the wagon seat, he nudged his horse forward and rode south. Pete and Amy exchanged bewildered glances. Amy's furrowed brow indicated some slight distress.

"He was cold as a dead fish. I almost think she'd be better off just wastin' away back with her family. At least she feels like it's home."

Pete was not given to that kind of philosophy at the moment. He examined the money and smiled, shaking his head.

"Well, that just goes to show you, Miss Pretty Face, that all good deeds do *not* go unrewarded!"

Chapter Twenty-seven

FAST AND QUIET

Jesse's presence in her backwoods home made leaving it harder than ever for Laurel. She was completely smitten now, and daydreamed the whole time she was on the road to Paducah. She thought of the hundreds of other ways she would rather spend her hours than loading trays with food at the boarding house and taking guff from smart-mouthed young bucks. The contrast between Jesse and all those others was so evident that she began to think of him as the answer to every adolescent prayer she had ever had, including the eight-year-old's imaginings that she would someday, somehow, be able to marry Pete. Her mother had explained that lots of little girls think they would like to marry their brothers, or their uncles, or some other close relative because they just naturally admire them.

"When you grow up," Hattie had said, "you'll meet somebody who might remind you of Pete, and that will help you make up your mind. That will mean you not only love him, but you'll feel safe with him, just like you do with Pete." Laurel had decided long ago that her mother's advice was good and sound. Lone Oak had not produced anyone remotely like Pete as far as she could see, not so much as a watered down version. Now, she even treasured that first encounter with Jesse as a sign that he was the one for her. She had heard that the course of young love does not always run smooth, and could see how it was true. But she also knew in her heart that there was nothing so sweet and exciting as falling in love with Jesse Campbell and being cuddled in the crook of his arm during an evening. Her mind had wandered far from the boarding house work for many days now. This week, Ruthann cornered her directly after she arrived. The old woman was anxious to find out if the lying, stealing soldier had been discovered and sent packing. Although she tried, her question did not come out delicately.

"How'd yer Satiddy and Sundie go, then?" she asked. "Was they any surprises come up? Any visitors?" She had no gift for subtlety.

Laurel was taken aback. Ruthann had never before asked about her days off. She answered offhandedly. "Well, I guess so. A man came lookin' for Jesse. Said he wanted to work on Daddy's road, but Jesse said all he wanted was money. I reckon Jesse wanted to keep him out of Daddy's hair and he gave him some cash and sent him packin'."

"So, yer sayin' this Jesse gave the man cash money and he went away? What did the man look like?"

"He was youngish. Had a beard. Skinny. Fact is, he came in here last week and bad mouthed me 'til I had to put him in his place. Jesse says it's somebody he knew from way back."

"And him and Jesse never had a fight nor nothin'?"

"Now, why should they fight? Jesse gave him money and sent him skedaddlin'."

"Hmmm" Ruthann stroked the mole and its hair bent under her finger, then flipped straight again. "The stranger, he didn't say nothin' to you about Jesse owin' him money?"

"I never even talked to the man. I saw enough of him that one time last week. Jesse never acted like he owed him the money anyway. I was glad to be rid of him and so was my ma. Excuse me now. I got to get to work."

The subject was dropped and Ruthann judged that the young bearded man must have given up the notion about sending that Jesse boy skedaddling and just felt lucky to get his money back. She skirted the subject of Jesse's trustworthiness several times, but Laurel did not seem to connect two thoughts together any more. The old woman also cross-examined every stranger who passed through her front door, hoping for some clue about her missing horse. Uneasy thoughts mingled in the back of her mind throughout the week as the separate orbs began to merge. She began to wonder vaguely how the bearded young man actually got out to Laurel's place. It was a mighty long walk.

Summer was full upon the woods and fields now, sometimes suffocating people and animals alike in its humidity and simmering heat. The sun, which had been so welcome in the chilly early spring, was fast becoming oppressive, smothering men and women's glistening skin in its great outdoor oven. Shade and water became havens for creeping things and two-legged creatures as well. More often than not Arthur could be found by the river, fishing or staring into the calm pools caught between rocks. Cougar worked sluggishly on Asa Bitter's projects. He was getting room and board for his contributions and slept fitfully in a tiny back room behind the general store. Though he was curious about Asa's very odd daughter, he had not the energy or temperament to pursue her. He found also that the girl stayed far from him. Annie Grace herself was not playing shy with him, but disliked his looks. In truth, she missed the bond she had with Arthur but didn't feel daring enough to try Asa's patience by going to the Beaudine place. Jesse and Clive defied the heat by splashing themselves with buckets of water as they furthered the road. That same road, once a mere trace through the woods, was now nearly finished and permanently nicknamed "Jesse's Highway" by the Beaudine family.

The following weekend found Jesse and Laurel riding in the meadow and strolling along the riverbank, inseparable. Jesse confided to Laurel. "I never dreamed when I came home and found out my girl was married to someone else, that I'd find another even better than her."

"Am I that girl, Jesse?" Laurel asked, astounded herself by the power of emotion she was feeling.

"You are that girl, and then some! I love you like I never loved anyone in my whole life." He pulled her close and bussed her playfully.

"I wish Pete could be here to see us together," she said.

"If Pete was here, chances are I wouldn't ever have come myself," Jesse observed wryly.

"I guess you're right. Then the only memory we would have of each other would be of me spillin' gravy all over that smart-mouth coot and you steppin' out of the crowd."

"I'm just glad you didn't decide to douse me at the same time."

"Truth to tell, I almost did, except that I thought it would be a shame to mess up a fella with such nice eyes."

"You noticed my eyes? "

"Well, only the first two. That one in the middle was closed at the time," she teased, then turned and ran for the river path.

They were as playful as two young puppies. Silent consent kept them from discussing Jesse's next move when the road was finished. It seemed there would be time enough for that when the hour arrived. Jesse's secret surfaced in his mind more frequently now, more determined to be considered, more wilfully seeking disclosure. It was pesky, obstinate, and grievous. What was he going to do about the secret?

In Paducah, the wary Ruthann had digested her many years of experience with humankind. She always thought of herself as seasoned, wise, not needing counsel. Now, doubts marched around daily in her brain. She felt impelled to share her concerns with Laurel, since they involved her in the long run.

The moment Laurel entered the boarding house that next Monday she recognized anxiety in the old woman's face. She could see the cogs cranking slowly behind Ruthann's wrinkled forehead and asked, "What? What? What's back there on your mind?"

"Laurel, honey. I know you're took with that Jesse boy, and you ain't goin' to like what he told me."

"What who told you? Jesse told you somethin'?"

"No. 'Twas the other one, the one with the beard. He said Jesse robbed him of money and such while he was nursin' wounds. He said they was in the army together and he was teetotal shocked when he seen Jesse in the dinin' room with you. He said he needed to foller after him and git his money. Said too, that Jesse was a deserter and kilt some Kentucky man in cold blood."

"So, I was right in thinkin' you told him how to find our place?"

"I was consarned about you! I didn't want fer you to be chasin' around after a liar and a thief."

"So you believed a total stranger? Ruthann! You always think you can spot 'em a mile away, and one comes along and gets so close to your face he skins your nose. If there's a thief and a liar anywhere it's that other fellah. Jesse's as honest as the day is long. I can't believe you!" Ruthann thought briefly about telling Laurel to watch her mouth. "*I'm yer boss here, y' know,*" she might have said, but instead held her tongue, since all week long she chewed on the memory that her horse and the bearded ex-soldier had disappeared from town the same day. If it can be said that the old blush, then Ruthann blushed hot and red. She came closer and closer to the conclusion she had fallen right into that boy's scheme. What if he was the culprit who took her horse? She never did see him with one of his own. It was humiliating to admit gullibility when your self appointed trademark had always been discernment

"Hell's fire, Laurel! You s'pose I was took in by that young humbug?" she moaned.

"I suppose you was, Ruthann. But it looks like Jesse got rid of him, for he went hightailin' it toward Lone Oak last time we saw him."

"Was he ridin' a horse?"

"No. He told my ma that he had a mule, but it died on

him. You don't think . . . ?"

Ruthann lowered her head, still ashamed at having been duped. "Well, it wouldn't stupefy me none to find out he did run off with my horse. Dang, if I don't feel like shucks. Stupid old fool!"

"Don't be so hard on yourself, Ruthann. Maybe it wasn't him took your animal. He's probably clear to heck and gone by now anyway." Laurel felt a twinge of sympathy now for her hoary, aging boss. "Tell you what though. If I can take some time away from the dinin' room, I'll ride back to Lone Oak and check around there. It shouldn't take too awful long."

"You would do that fer me?"

"Bummers like him ought to be run out of the entire county on a rail, just as a general rule. You'll let me go then?"

"I never seen a girl like you in all my born days. Laurel, honey, let 'er rip!"

Laurel leaped to her horse, eager to go after that skinny, good-for-nothing cracker and prove him guilty of horse thieving if she could. It never occurred to her that he might be dangerous, only that he was a worthless bother and had lied to high heaven about the truest love she had ever known.

As she entered Lone Oak, she avoided Asa's store, but let her horse amble through the spread out streets while she looked for Ruthann's animal. The season was doing its best to decorate the miserable little town, and summer's brighter greens were sprinkled over low shrubs and hardwood trees. Still, as she rode she mused that Lone Oak was a pitiful excuse for a stopover, let alone a hometown. In truth, she liked the backwoods better and was glad in the long run that their house had burned down. She was just passing the old place when she heard Annie Grace's timid voice call her name.

"Laurel. I'm here," she said. "Come see me."

Laurel peered at the plot, scanning the overgrown weeds and rubble for a sign of the girl. "I can't see you, Annie. Where're you hidin'?"

"Here, behind the chimbly," she whimpered.

Annie's face, pinched and fretful, popped out beside the crumbling brick. "Come here and see me," she repeated. Laurel alighted and stepped over to her, gingerly avoiding bits of broken glass and charred flooring. She felt as if she were entering a graveyard, a place where the childish ghosts of Pete and Arthur still pulled her hair and teased.

"You should come out of here, Annie. There's glass and splinters and such that could hurt you."

"Never been hurt before. Not here."

"What are you doin'?" Laurel asked again. "Are you playin' hide-and-go-seek?"

"No." Annie picked at her fingers nervously and pulled on her knuckles, popping each one in turn.

"Well then, come on out. Did you want to ask about Arthur?"

"Oh, I know Arthur is all right. My daddy told me so. He was mad Arthur didn't die. He's always mad."

"Is he mad now? Is that why you're out here?"

"No. He ain't mad. He told me to not hang around that other boy, or he would get mad. He hits me when he's mad, and I don't want to get hit, so I stay away."

Annie flinched as she spoke, as if Asa would suddenly materialize beside her and slap her face, a thing which Laurel knew he had done many times.

"What other boy are you talkin' about?" Laurel asked, her suspicions aroused. "What does he look like?"

"He looks bad. He works for my daddy. He watches me and puts me in mind of a wolf. He's all hairy."

"Does he have a beard?"

"Yeah, and he scares me."

"Does he have a horse?"

"He come in on a nice horse, real nice."

"Did you know he rode out to my place Saturday lookin' for Jesse?"

"No, he didn't."

"Oh," said Laurel, disappointed. Maybe she and Annie

were not discussing the same young man.

"He took my mule, but the mule come home without him. He had to walk most all the way. I laughed."

"Where's his horse right now? Do you know?"

"Back of Daddy's store. The boy is choppin' trees out by our shed behind. My mule hates him!"

"Hmmmm," Laurel was pondering, scheming for a way to get a look at that horse. "Suppose I got him to come into the store for five minutes. Do you think you could untie the horse and scoot him on down to the spring real fast?"

"Are you goin' to steal the horse?"

"If I'm right about this, that horse has already been stole once and I mean to take him back to the owner. Do you think you could do that, real fast and real quiet?" Annie gnawed furiously at her thumbnail and rolled her eyes for a minute. Then she smiled, glowing with determination. "Real fast and real quiet! Yeah!"

"All right then. First I'll go around to the back and talk to him. That way I can have a look at the horse too. If it ain't the horse I'm lookin' for I won't get him inside, but if it is . . . "

"I'll take the horse to the spring!"

"Now, scoot on back through the trees and don't let anyone see you. If you see Asa, then don't take any chances. Just stay in the woods."

Annie nodded her head eagerly. This was the first playing she had done since Asa fired at Arthur two weeks before.

Laurel would use the ruse that she accepted Cougar's second hand apology. She would also use the information she got from Ruthann if need be. She tied her horse to a rickety post in front of the store and strolled around to the back. Cougar was resting his arm on the long handled ax when he saw her. He was completely surprised to see the half smile on her face as she walked toward him.

From the corner of her eye she spied the horse in question. It was for hell's sake Ruthann's horse all right, clear down to the saddle and stirrups! *This coot is dumber than I figured him to be,* she thought. Her smile grew larger and she affected a near apologetic tone herself.

"Hello. You remember me? I work at the boardin' house over in Paducah." She looked him straight in the eyes but sensed Annie's presence in the trees behind him.

"Now, I wouldn't be forgettin' a face as purty as yours, even if you *was* my friend's gal," Cougar mewed, cocking his head to the side. "Did he give you my message? For I surely do apologize if I set you off back there. I do get a little crude sometimes, but I blame it on the war. I warn't always like that."

I'll just bet, thought Laurel, as the applesauce oozed out of every pore in Cougar's spindly body. *Well, two can play that game,* she said to herself, and didn't miss a beat.

"I apologize too, for gettin' so huffy. Besides, I've been hearin' things from my boss at the boardin' house about Mr. Jesse that don't put him in any special light. I guess he might not be what I thought he was to begin with." She eased two or three steps closer, looking over his shoulder but seeking out Annie's eye. She nodded her head and went on. "Yes, sir. I guess I need to have a long talk with that boy."

Annie understood the nod and slipped farther into the trees to wait for Laurel's next move. She was eager to advance and slide the tether from the horse, fast and quiet. "Can you leave off work for a minute and answer me some questions? Would it be all right to go inside? It's gettin' powerful hot out here already."

Laurel fanned herself with a white handkerchief she had removed from her bosom ever so slowly, and Cougar nearly tripped over his own swagger while he followed her into the store. Sleeping flies displaced themselves as the two walked through the door, and Asa looked up, startled to see them together.

Laurel nodded to him. "Mr. Bitter," she addressed him respectfully. "I hope you don't mind me takin' a minute or two of your help's time."

She immediately wanted to bite her tongue. What if he

asked her how she knew he was working for Asa? She hurried on, directing her remarks to Cougar and batting her eyelashes.

"That is, I guess you must be workin' here, since I happened by and saw you out back."

"I'm lendin' a hand, that's right."

She could see he hadn't like being called Asa's "help." "What I mean to find out is everythin' you know about Jesse. He says you're friends from way back?"

Cougar hesitated. What had he told Ruthann? Sorting out his most recent lies, it came to him and he answered, shaking his head. "I suppose you could call the war way back if you was of a mind. It does seem a long time ago about now. Me and Jesse served together in the Ninetieth Tennessee." Was there such a regiment? He didn't know. "I got myself wounded tryin' to save the lieutenant, and one night whilst I was restin' my eyes, nursin' a tore up leg, I seen Jesse shuffle through my haversack. He cleaned me out, proper. There was nothin' I could do, for I was loaded up with morphine and couldn't holler."

Laurel wanted to scream in his face, *if you were loaded up with morphine how do you know it was him?* Instead, she shook her head and whispered, "I just knew he seemed too good to be true. Ruthann warned me, but I couldn't go on her say so alone."

Asa's ears burned from across the room as he struggled to hear their words. He sensed that they shared bad news or something similar. She caught him glancing their way and invited him into the conversation.

"Mr. Bitter, could you tell me what you might think of that fella, Jesse? He came here before showin' up at our place."

Asa tried to appear calm, but fairly scrambled from behind his counter to join them. "What kind of thing was you wantin' to know?"

"Oh, just if he acted a little too pure maybe. Or did he seem like a regular fella? You know, honest and respectable."

Asa was boggled. He had no idea Laurel cared for any

248

opinions he might entertain. Maybe she wasn't as bad a Beaudine as he thought.

"Well, Miss Laurel, I did think he was a tad uppity, and then when he come through here last, he practical threatened me with a gun. He seemed to think I had filled your brother with buckshot a while back. I don't know where he come up with that notion."

Laurel concentrated on dividing her attention between these two weasels with their pack of lies and the faint rustling of movement from outside. Cougar was launching into another string of improbabilities when she suddenly stood up and brushed off her coveralls. She stamped her foot for effect.

"Well, that's about all I need to know! And imagine what time it must be! I got to get back home and warn Mama and Daddy to send that Jesse packin'!" She stomped to the door and turned dramatically at the threshold. "I do thank you, gentlemen, for straightenin' me out!" She quickly untied her horse and headed east in the direction of her home, then circled around behind the woods to the spring, where she met Annie. Annie had ridden as fast as she could, after gently coaxing Ruthann's horse away from the store, and arrived just ahead of Laurel. Inside the store the two men were left somewhat puzzled at Laurel's sudden departure, and Cougar began imagining hot meals at Hattie's table and entertaining nights with Laurel. He had always fancied himself a better ladies' man than Jesse and saw himself stepping lightly into Jesse's courting shoes.

By the time Cougar finished lolling around chatting with Asa about Jesse's upcoming comeuppance, Laurel had Ruthann's horse well in tow and was on the road to Paducah. Cougar blinked his way back outside and did not miss the horse immediately. He ambled over to the waiting ax and hefted it to strike a blow on yet another tree for Asa. It was on the down swing that he noticed an emptiness where the horse had stood. His arms drooped in mid-swing, nearly allowing the ax to fall into his leg. From inside the dank little store Asa heard

Cougar's outraged bellow and ensuing epithets.

Asa feared the worst, that Cougar, or Davis as he knew him, had injured himself with the ax. He ran out of the building and around to the back, where Cougar was hopping up and down from leg to leg, cursing.

"What in tarnation is up yer fanny?" Asa saw no signs of blood, and Cougar was obviously not groveling in physical pain.

Cougar finished with his spouting of vulgarities and pointed his finger to the spot where the horse had been.

"While I was in there jawin' with that woman somebody come and let my horse loose. Damn it! Now what am I goin' to do?" He had not come as far as suspecting Laurel in the disappearance.

Asa ran his hand over the bald spot which was now reddening in the sun. "Horses sometimes just wander off. He'll most likely show up again when he gits hungry. If he don't, then maybe we kin arrange somethin' with Annie's mule."

"Oh, that there would be just peachy! That mule hates my guts and has tried to kick me two or three times when I come near it. Besides that, I don't fancy gettin' dumped off in the boondocks any more. The stupid thing ought to be shot!"

His tirade was interrupted by a tittering sound from the little stand of trees nearby. Asa recognized Annie Grace's laughter and called to her. "What are you doin' in there, girl? Git on out here!"

Annie was never obedient as a rule and did not see this as the time to begin. She turned and ran for the old Beaudine place to hide behind the chimney again and chuckle over the bearded boy's fit. Soon she would go to Arthur's and share this story with him, and they would both laugh at the stupidity of bad people.

It wasn't until later in the day that Cougar started putting two and two together; the girl's unexpected friendliness, sudden doubt about Jesse, her abrupt departure, and Annie laughing at him from the woods. He would get to the feeble-minded Annie and squeeze the truth out of her if necessary.

Ruthann was beside herself with delight when Laurel returned with the horse, but angry at having been humbugged by that sneaking horse thief. "I'll pickle that boy's lyin' tongue if'n I git holt of him. He'll wish he never set eyeballs on old Ruthann and never, no way, ever tuck off with my horse!"

"Don't you worry, Ruthann. We'll come up with some stunt to get him back. I think Annie and me already fixed his wagon for a while anyway."

The old woman slapped her hat against her thigh and cawed loudly. "Laws, if'n you didn't! I'll bet his innards is still puckered!"

Puckered indeed. Cougar was never one to do a slow boil, and his reactions to losing the horse were to burn on high and strike on hot. Asa protested the notion that Laurel had anything to do with the horse's disappearance.

"What does she want another horse for? Unless she was the one you beat out of it in the first place, I can't see no reason for her to hie off with it. As fer Annie, she's so addled she couldn't spell shucks, even if she was chokin' on it. No sir, Davis. I say the horse just got loose. He gits hungry. He'll be back, like I said."

That night Cougar waited for Annie's return. It was long past dusk, long enough Annie thought, to hide and be hungry and have to go in the woods instead of your own one-seater in the back, when she finally ventured home. She was quiet about approaching the house, and slipped easily to her small window. She entered the unshuttered opening, relieved to be inside again. Suddenly, Cougar's newly callused hand covered her mouth, and his free arm clamped her body against his. He whispered hoarsely into her ear, his words menacing and frightful.

"I know you and that girl got my horse, and you better tell me where it is before I rip it outta you!" Annie struggled viciously against him, kicking and attempting to scream. He could feel her curves and softness beneath his iron grip, and nearly was sorry they were going to be enemies. He dragged Annie down to the floor and clutched a handful of her thick hair in his fist, banging her head against the planks.

"Tell me where that horse is!" he hissed. When she answered nothing, he slammed her against the floor again. She became quiet and went limp after the second hit, and Cougar crouched over her, breathing heavily, staring dumbly at her still form. He listened for any response from Asa, whose room was in another corner of the house. There was none. Asa was a heavy sleeper, he guessed.

Annie's mute shell lay on the plank floor, washed in the palest of moonlight, quiet as death. Cougar watched her for any sign of movement. It seemed he stared for an eternity before sensing motion in her body. Barely perceptible were the risings and fallings of her bosom, telling Cougar she was alive after all. He was so relieved to see he hadn't killed her that he gave up the questioning.

She began the slow process of coming around, and in so doing, awakened to splintering pains in her head. At the first sounds of moans from Annie's throat, Cougar crept out through the window, slipped to the store where his things were and headed east, back to the Beaudine place or somewhere between Lone Oak and there for the night.

Chances of spending more time in Lone Oak were wiped away in that one rash action. Annie would tell Asa what had happened, and his name would be mud. But it was too late to go back and do differently. Maybe he could stick Jesse for more money if he threatened to reveal to Laurel that he had fought for the Confederacy. Then he would just have to be on his way and keep running from mistakes. He would just have to "borrow" another horse and find another game.

Annie's groans went unheeded until she stumbled into her father's room and wakened him. Blood had oozed from the back of her head and stuck, glistening black, in her tangled hair. Her eyes and ears and jaws were splitting with pain.

"He hit me, Daddy. That boy hit me and banged me on

the floor."

Asa was half awake, and his puny, mean heart was thundering in its brittle cage. Instead of sympathy, Annie received a barrage of questions.

"Why'd he come and beat you up? Did you take that horse, like he said? What was you and that Laurel girl thinkin', to steal a man's horse?" Slap! His hand automatically flew to her face. The sting withered her and she crumpled into a chair and whimpered. "Dumb girl, stupid Annie! Now, who's going to help out with clearing the trees? Who's going to do the heavy work?"

Defeated, she crawled back to her bed and curled into one corner, as she had done so many times before. She was in too much pain to stir up a plan, but a voice far in the recesses of her mind would come to her in the morning and demand to be heard. Annie would run away and never come back.

Tuesday saw Jesse and Clive peering at a somber, iron colored sky. "Summer's boilin'" Clive observed, rubbing liniment on a throbbing elbow. "Fixin' to wash us out today. I felt it comin' last night in my arm here. Looks like we got the day off."

Jesse watched the scudding clouds make haste across the face of the larger gray thunderheads. "Looks like Noah's flood all right. Is everythin' snug as it should be? I can quick slap some boards on the roof if you need."

"We're all right, and thanks, Jesse." Clive said.

"Thanks, Jesse," Arthur repeated. He had joined them in the door yard and now with the first large drops plopping on the dust, he ran into the open turnaround and let the water splash against his flattened tongue. "I wish Annie was here to play. I feel like playin' again," he shouted, running and laughing in the wind.

"You just go on ahead and play without her, Arthur. But when you see the lightnin', come on back inside." Hattie stood in the doorway, thinking it was just like a bunch of men to stand outside in the rain. "Meantime, breakfast is ready for whoever wants it."

Arthur stayed, playing and prancing around as the rain began to fall harder. Clive and Jesse sat with Hattie and she prayed. "Dear Lord, we thank you again for what's set before us. We're askin' you to watch over our girl and bless the work we do and keep us in your way. Amen."

Arthur bounded through the door after the first thunderclap. He had news. "They's a man comin' up the road. Looks like the feller that was here a while back." The three at the table turned toward the door, curious. A soaking Cougar stood on the long plank porch, dripping and grinning, as if he were the hometown boy come back from war.

Clive got up and spoke first. "Looks like you've come a long way, young man. We'll find you some dry clothes and you can wait it out here."

Jesse cringed as he realized that Clive didn't know who Cougar was. He felt chilled and slightly sick to his stomach, envisioning the proverbial viper in the nest.

"Cougar," he said, acknowledging his old acquaintance.

"Jesse. Miz Beaudine, and you must be Mr. Beaudine,"

Cougar responded, nodding to the parents. Clive, surrounded by his usual cloud, registered surprise. "So, how is it you know names, seein' as you're a stranger in these parts? You two friends?"

"We know each other, yes." replied Jesse. Hattie marked the strained exchange between the two young men. She felt an undercurrent which made her uneasy. She trusted her instincts on this encounter but did not like what they told her. Something was wrong, she could see for certain, and it was wrong with Jesse. She wished that the young soaking wet boy would turn around and walk away.

"Well, get on out of them wet duds and set down to some breakfast."

Clive was the soul of congeniality, unaware that this man whom he was befriending held another key to disappointment for the Beaudine family. The viper eased slowly into the nest indeed, keenly appreciative of his position, and eyed Jesse with a cold expression. Jesse turned away, suddenly void of appetite.

In the ensuing conversation, Cougar danced around any discussion of the war, encroaching purposely on the subject, then retreating. He proposed to make Jesse squirm, partly because it was Jesse's friend Neils who had done damage to his face, and partly because it made him feel superior. Hattie observed with the keenness of a hawk, noting any nuances in Jesse's reactions, counting the times Cougar lighted on the subject of the Confederacy like a moth bouncing off a lantern and quickly flying away. Jesse felt like a man being drawn closer to a precipice, similar to a traveler peering over an inevitable gulf. His mind retraced the events that had brought him to the Beaudine household—the reeking stink-hole prison, the unfortunates who inhabited it, the luckless stiffs who guarded it. The travesty of war struck him anew as he recalled the ball tearing through Pete's neck, a neck so haplessly placed in the path of unaimed shot, by what power Jesse couldn't guess, and now, for what purpose he had no idea. He envisioned the ragged preacher who had flung the testament far over the dead line, and heard the testimony, damning him further into his future and in a different way than he had thought it would. He remembered when the notion first came to him to seek out Peter Beaudine's family and make restitution for their loss, at least make confession if there was no repayment possible. How could he have thought, sitting in his room alone, that anyone could replace a mother's absent boy, a sister's lost soulmate, a father's diminished seed? Now too, he regretfully remembered sharing his design in coming here with Cougar.

As Cougar chattered on and on, Jesse's mind began to clear. The bearded man had become his nemesis and would certainly force him to make the confession he had purposed in the first place. Jesse might contrive a way to get around the confederate soldier issue. He could call Cougar a liar, which, in the general sense was always true, but he could not escape the truth that lay inside himself. He had misled the Beaudines, not so much by word, as by silence. In his heart of hearts he knew that one day it would come to this, for an unspoken lie screams just as loudly as a spoken one, and sooner or later, it eats away at its keeper.

Cougar, having tested the waters and discovered that Jesse was firmly entrenched and admired hereabouts, would wait for the right time to speak to him alone. He ran sums over and over in his mind, scheming how much to ask for the ransom of Jesse's reputation. Having guessed the secret about Pete, he would press for all he could get. He had convinced himself by now that Jesse owed him, and not only did Jesse owe him, but the horse stealing Laurel owed him as well. He now inquired about her whereabouts.

"She's over to Paducah, at her job, since yesterday mornin'," Clive informed him.

"So, you ain't seen her since she left then?"

"Not hide nor hair. She'll likely not get back until Friday."

Cougar congratulated himself. She had lied to him about going home. She had not been back yesterday. *Well, tit for tat, young lady. You steal my horse (possession being nine tenths of the law, Cougar believed the horse was lately his), I will steal your future.* He would stay silent about her taking that horse, at least until he had blackmailed a hefty sum from Jesse.

"I always tell her, Laurel, don't you go work in that city. Some bummers will come and knock you over the head." Arthur spoke loudly to find a place in the conversation. He was roundly ignored by Cougar, who was always ill at ease with people who were addled or strange. He somehow had the feeling that their afflictions would rub off on himself, and he might wake up one day and discover he had become what they were. He had looked upon Annie as inferior but not threatening in the same sense as Arthur. His impression of Arthur was born of ignorance and fear, though he did not think of himself as ignorant or fearful. Arthur was big, dumb, and not to be tolerated or noticed. It was as simple as that.

Arthur, on the other hand, was not as slow as Cougar figured. He had been ignored and shut out enough times to know when people were put off by him. He knew but he never understood. Perhaps, in the long run, it was better for him that way. He was not in the mood to subject himself to the malice of silence, so he simply melted through the open doorway and disappeared behind the cabin. Jesse too was uneasy in Cougar's presence and wanted to escape it, but he felt he dared not leave him alone with Hattie and Clive. If they were going to learn the truth, it might as well be the whole story, and it might as well be from his own mouth. Cougar sensed the charge in the air and invited Jesse to step outside to speak of the good old days.

"We don't want to bore you folks with little boy tales."

The rain still fell, but in gentler showers, and Jesse was overwhelmed with the good and fresh air that greeted him. Impossibly happy birds frolicked in the bright green woods and pecked the ground for worms, untroubled by nothing more than babies in some high nest. He waited patiently for Cougar to spill whatever it was he had on his miserable little mind. Cougar began speaking in quiet but intense undertones.

"You got a good thing goin' here, Jesse. Wish't I was in your shoes, but since I ain't I'd just as soon be in your pocketbook. You're smart enough to know already that I'm after a stake now. That piddly handful of bills you gave me the other day wouldn't get me across the state line. I need more, Jesse. I figure that by coverin' your rear about the See-cesh army, I could come out way ahead, say to the tune of a couple hundred? I figure too, that the poor sucker you blasted at the prison belongs to these folks, am I right ? And you ain't told 'em yet, am I right? They just about think you're Holy Joe junior by now, don't they? What they goin' to do if I tell 'em you was the Confederate soldier that killed their boy?"

"What makes you think they don't already know?"

"They ain't mentioned it, for one thing. 'Course it's not like that's a fit subject for polite conversation and you don't really expect it to come up over breakfast." Cougar began to titter and chuckle as he spoke. "Oh, yeah, Jesse. Tell us some more about how it was you shot our boy. Did you use cannon or a pea shooter? Speakin' o' peas, we're havin' some for supper. Won't you join us and, oh, by the way, here's our daughter in the parcel to boot!"

Jesse reached out quickly, attempting to grab Cougar's shirt, but the bearded man was fast this time and dodged away. Cougar smirked menacingly and backed off.

A moment later Clive appeared on the porch and said to Jesse, "Looks like the flood is stayed after all and it's slowin' down enough to where we could do some work on the road. What say you join us while your clothes gets dry?" He directed the last remark to Cougar.

Cougar recouped a boyish manner and answered quickly.

"Why, sure enough. That'd be a good way to repay you yer kind hospitality and the breakfast."

He slapped Jesse's shoulder playfully and smiled at him.

"Let's go, buddy! It'll be like old times, the two of us workin' together."

"I calculate," said Clive, "That only a couple more days are needed to finish out the work. Don't suppose you'd be willin' to stay on another day, would you?" He looked at Cougar, who gloried in the way the older man had played into his plans. He would have Jesse hopping like a frog on a hot skillet and enjoy every minute of it.

"I'd be more'n happy to, Mr. Beaudine. By the way, my name's Rivers. I don't guess we was intoduced proper before. Just call me Cougar."

"How is it you got out here, son?" asked Clive.

"Why, I had me a horse, but danged if it warn't stole practically out from under my nose. I walked from that feeble excuse for a town over west of here. I come lookin' for the one true friend I got in the world."

His contemptible grin turned Jesse's stomach.

"Well, if we're goin' to work," said Jesse, heading for the ax that leaned against the house, "we'd best get started. Cougar, why don't you help Arthur drag stumps off the road?"

"Where is that boy anyway?" Clive looked around for his youngest. "He's always wanderin' off. We'll just have to start without him."

Wander off Arthur had, but not so far that he had not heard the conversation between Jesse and Cougar. It caused him to shiver in the moist heat of that summer day. Cougar's words swam and submerged in his brain, then surfaced again. Their implications were not lost, even on Arthur's simple mind. Could Jesse really be the killer of his heroic and legendary brother? It was unthinkable, yet Jesse had not denied it, Jesse had not yelled at Cougar that it was not true. Arthur was afraid of what might happen now. He would go to Hattie and see what she said. Hattie could always make him feel better.

On that same Tuesday, June 13, Laurel received a letter for Jesse Campbell, addressed care of Laurel Beaudine at Ruthann's Boarding House. She was excited for Jesse to hear from his daddy, for she knew how long it had been and how it would please him. Only a few more days and she would greet him with letter in hand, smiling. She would sit by his side while he read and ask if he could share any news. The next letter Jesse wrote home could possibly contain her name, and might include her in his future.

Chapter Twenty-eight

MR. AND MRS. BEAUDINE

T he twenty dollars that wafted from the man's fingers to their wagon seat was so unexpected and so welcome that Amy nearly cried. A sum like that would see them through the time remaining on their journey to Kentucky, and they could probably contribute some to the family sugar bowl when they arrived at Pete's home. As she rode along the monotonous route, she placed herself again and again in the scenes that would follow their arrival. She had formed a vague notion of Hattie, Clive, Arthur, and Laurel, and attributed certain physical characteristics to each one. Hattie was tall and strong. Clive limped but displayed the noble bearing of a returned soldier. Arthur was a gangly fourteen-year-old, though she knew he was actually older. Laurel was a spunky and tomboyish young woman, full of grit, and they would become instant friends. She had pictured them many times in the last few weeks and was eager to meet them. She imagined how they awaited Pete and her as well. What must they have thought after reading the letter written in Pete's words, but by her hand?

She would be proud to show Clary off to her new relatives, and she visualized them doting over the girl as Jim had. She would write to him and describe in detail the everyday aspects of their life in Kentucky. The first home she would share with Pete would be not much more than the very wagon they traveled in, but they would have sufficient bedding, kitchen tools, and the cherished Sutter rocking chair.

Amy traveled many miles engaged in such projections. She had tired of scenery long ago, and the beauty of a lush countryside faded behind the groanings of wagon wheels and the constancy of drudgery on the road. At the end of each day she fell exhausted into her bed of quilts and slept soundly next to her husband.

Pete pushed their horse to the limit as they traveled, eager to be home, to set up his own housekeeping, and begin life as thousands of other returning soldiers had. He was careful with the money, keeping it close and not spending any. He figured it would make a nice little nest egg to begin with. On that June day, just as Jesse Campbell contemplated revealing his secret to Laurel and her family, the new Mr. and Mrs. Beaudine continued on the northward road, straining toward home. It would only be a few more days until they arrived.

"Lone Oak ain't much," Pete told Amy, "but none of us has to stay there. We could move the whole kit and kaboodle anywhere you want if you don't like it."

"Pete," she answered, "I will like it any place the floor don't move all day long under us! I never dreamed I'd get so tired of sittin' on a wagon seat. I feel blistered and callused all over my backside."

Pete grinned at her and patted her hip. "Well, you don't feel blistered to me."

She slapped him soundly on the arm.

"Just you hush up! The walls have ears, you know!"

"I don't see no walls, but I do see a little girl with ears. Hey, Clary. Do you think your mama's backside is blistered?"

Clary popped up from between the seat and their belongings.

"Blistered is what she says I'll be when I'm bad. If she was bad, I reckon she might be blistered."

"How long 'til we get there, Pete?"

"What do you say to three more days? If we keep pushin' hard, I figure three days, no more, no less."

"By golly, I'll stand the rest of the way if that's all we got!" Amy said, encouraged.

As she stood to make her point, the wagon suddenly lurched and threw her off balance. Amy tumbled from the seat, and Pete reached out desperately, grabbing for her arm. The horse veered, causing a precarious shift in weight on the wagon bed. The right rear wheel ran off the road and hung over the slight embankment. It was impossible for Pete to maintain any control, and the best he could do was pull Clary close to him and roll beyond the rig as it slid to its side. Amy had fallen clear a few yards behind them, and Pete watched with despair as their belongings pitched down into the shallow grassy trench. Their horse had been scratched when he rolled on his side, but was otherwise unharmed. Almost immediately, a man and his wife and son were on the scene. They had witnessed the accident as they approached from the opposite direction, each on horseback.

The woman ran to Amy.

"Air you all right, Missy?" She fussed and fretted, looking more nervous about the mishap than Amy herself.

"Maybe you should ought to stay quiet. Air any bones broke?"

Amy dusted herself and winced from the stinging pain in her arm. She examined it and found a large gash splitting the flesh from elbow to wrist. The wound was not deep but bled freely and needed immediate washing. The woman volunteered water from a small canteen she carried.

"Where's my baby?" Amy asked, frantic about Clary.

She saw the man, his son, and Pete coming toward her. Pete carried Clary in his arms. Little Cotton looked none the worse for her tumble, but was pointing at the wagon and calling for her doll.

The man was speaking. "Looks to me like yer axle is busted and both them wheels has spokes that is smashed to smithereens. You just as well build you a fire out'n it as try to use it without a blacksmith fixes you up."

Pete allowed a discouraged groan to escape his lips. "I can't believe this happened so close to home," he lamented.

"Don't get your bowels in no uproar, son. They's a smithy over yonder about a mile." He indicated the direction from which he and his family had just come. "I'll take ye there and my woman can stay here with yor'n 'til we git back. Dilly, you come on with us." He called to his son and invited Pete to mount the third horse. "You can ride Lulabelle. That's my wife's nag. Where you folks headed anyway?"

"Lone Oak. My family lives there. They're expectin' us any time now. I promised my wife we'd be home in three days. Now it looks like it might be more like a week. We're pretty beat out from the road and want to get off it soon as possible."

"I ain't familiar with Lone Oak. Just been in these parts a few months. Come from over Caroliny way, we did. Let's ride on, then."

Pete followed the man and his boy to a little spread less than a half mile away. Just over a small green knoll lay a house, a lean-to shed, and a sturdy stone outbuilding, which Pete guessed to be the smithy's shop. Blown by a wayward breeze, a curl of smoke floated lazily from its chimney, wafting this way and that. Farm tools and a wagon stood by the stone structure. There appeared to be no one about.

"Looks like nobody's here," said Pete.

"Somebody's here all right. We are!" smiled Dilly. Pete wondered if he was being led on a wild goose chase and if he should have left Amy and Clary with that woman. He looked around suspiciously. "Where's the blacksmith anyway?" he asked.

"Why, it's me, son!" The man grinned broadly at him.

"Although I ain't much for doin' that kind of work. Fact is, I hate it. It's back breakin' toil and I'd ruther be raisin' pigs or somethin'."

"Well, what if you can't fix my wagon? How come you

dragged me over here then tell me you're a poor blacksmith?"

The man tilted his head to one side and answered. "I didn't say I wasn't a good blacksmith. I just said I didn't like it. Now, I can see that it's goin' to take some days runnin' to mend that rig of yor'n, and I was just thinkin' that maybe we could work out some kind of trade or sale to get you into that buggy of mine. Then you could be on yer way quick as a wink."

"How do I know your rig is sound?" Pete questioned, suspicious.

"You ever know a blacksmith with a bum wagon?" the man countered. "Go on, just have a look-see. It's sound as airy a dollar. Ye could drive to Timbuktu and back in it if need be!"

Pete alighted from Lulabelle and walked to the wagon. It appeared to be in good shape, as the man had assured him. He asked what the blacksmith had in mind in the way of trade.

"Well, o' course, there'd be your rig, which is pretty much useless to you now anyway. And then, I did have me a look at the traps you carried and noticed some nice cookin' pots and a real fine lookin' rocker. I noticed too, that it don't seem to be busted from the fall neither. I'd take them things along with the wagon." Pete mulled the offer over and saw that he was not in much of a position to dicker if he wanted to be home soon. One cooking pot would suffice until they reached their destination, and he did not see that any of those utensils were dear to Amy. The rocker, however, was out of the question. He himself was attached to it, if only for Amy's sake.

"You wouldn't consider money instead of the rocker, would you?" he asked the man.

Thinking of the cash, he reasoned with himself, *Easy come, easy go.*

"Money's better'n a rocker, Pa!" Dilly interjected with enthusiasm.

"How much?" his father asked, not missing a beat.

"I got twenty dollars, Yankee."

"Sold! And you kin keep the pots!" The blacksmith declared. "Let's hitch Lulabelle up and head on back!"

So it was that Pete and Amy retained the Sutter rocking chair but parted with the "Gideon" money. Pete had done right, Amy said to him later. If a person thought of the rocker as part of the family instead of just a piece of furniture to be bought or sold, it didn't hurt to let go of the money. A person could always get more money, but the wooden rockers and carved back of the chair had braced three generations of Sutters already, and soothed fussy babies to sleep. Money wouldn't ever buy the grain that was worn and polished by family hands or purchase the hours of peace the chair had provided over the years. Yes, Pete had bargained well, and come out on top. They were on their way again, closer than ever to a home of their own.

Chapter Twenty-nine

BAD NEWS

Arthur wanted to talk to Hattie, needed to talk to her. Clive's insistent calling for him brought the boy out of the woods, nervous as a cat, fumbling and besieged with terrible knowledge that sent his heart racing. He was flustered. How could Jesse be friends with a person who accused him of lies and killing? Why did he not just punch the bearded man and yell at him that he had not killed Pete? Why were they now going to work on the highway together? In his bewildered state of mind, Arthur decided to follow and listen, in hopes of uncovering the real truth. He would speak with his mother later.

Annie escaped Asa's steely eye as he lay sleeping through the early morning rain. The storms would not deter her, because they were no bother to Annie. She sometimes felt as if she were sister to the showers, for Asa would hardly venture out to look for her until the rains stopped. She threw on a rubber slicker, led her mule away from their ramshackle house quietly, and shivered with the thrill of knowing she would never return. She would simply stay at Arthur's. That was her plan, and she had no doubt the Beaudines would take her in forever. She saw it as simple and direct, knowing that Hattie had sympathy for her, that Arthur was her special friend, and that the rain would protect her from Asa until she made it to the safe haven. Annie urged her mule forward through the storm until she reached Stetson's barn, where she decided to take some shelter and rest the mule a short while.

When the heavier rain dwindled to a slow summer shower, she took to the trace again. This trip was more than just the moving ahead of rider and mule, more than one girl running away from a sour and detestable parent. It was a pilgrimage to a new life, although Annie could not have spoken of it as eloquently as that. She was beginning to feel the freedom of making a final decision. It settled on her like warming sunshine, caused her to feel light and airy, and brought to mind how it must feel to be a wood sprite or a brownie.

As the mule carried her across the meadow and closer to the nearly finished road, Annie saw four figures at work. Her blood chilled and enthusiasm melted as she recognized the fourth hand to be her attacker from the previous night. *Not the wolf!* She mouthed to herself. She could not go there as long as that hairy wild man was near. Having escaped Asa, she had no desire to jump from the frying pan into the fire. That man would accuse her again and perhaps hit her when no one was around. The safety she had just felt dissolved before her eyes and she halted the mule abruptly. She walked the animal to a place behind some wild berry bushes, determined to work out a plan.

The men did not see Annie's approach and continued with their task. Most of the talking was between Cougar and Clive. Jesse remained silent out of contempt for Cougar, and Arthur kept his peace as well, mostly due to confusion. Annie waited a long while for them to break away from the job. When it appeared they were at last packing up their tools, she devised a way to get Arthur's attention. A sharp thwack on her beast's flank sent it whinnying from behind the bushes. Arthur saw the mule and immediately recognized it. "That's Annie's mule!" he shouted. "Come on back here, you hinny. Where's Annie Grace?" He ran into the meadow, pursuing the animal and waving his arms.

Cougar took one look at the four-legged ruffian and turned away. "That there is a wild and de-ranged critter. He probably run away from home." Even as he spoke, the same eerie, shivery feeling he had when he first glimpsed Annie passed over him. He was uneasy from it, for it produced a stranger fear than any he had experienced as a soldier.

Clive ventured, "It looks like Annie's mule all right. She comes and visits betimes if the mule's around, she's close by and Arthur will catch up to her sooner or later. Let's get on back to the house." Cougar reflected on what a large fly Annie would be in his bottle of ointment. "Maybe I'll just go help Arthur catch that there mule," he said, and broke away from Jesse and Clive at a run.

Clive shook his head and chuckled. "Your friend seems a little off, Jesse. And if you don't mind me sayin' so, it don't seem like you two are really that friendly."

"Well, I never said we were friends. I only said we knew each other," Jesse commented wryly. They made their way slowly back to the cabin, as Jesse delayed his steps to keep pace with Clive. His mind was still made up about telling Hattie and Clive everything, but it sickened him to think how soon it would be and what the consequences would be. Cougar caught sight of Arthur and Annie as they walked across the meadow in the opposite direction of the new road. He followed at a prudent distance and several times screened himself behind berry bushes or ducked low in the long grass. Arthur and Annie were gesturing wildly, and their raised voices were carried away with the wind. Cougar guessed correctly that they were talking about him. He followed them to Stetson's barn, recognizing the dilapidated and weary old place he himself had passed on his way to the Beaudine place. He continued to hide after they entered, found their usual corner, and sat to talk.

Annie was extremely agitated in retelling the whole story of Laurel and the horse. She laughed hysterically as she admitted they had gotten away with it and that she had played such an important part in the abduction. She grimaced as she remembered how hungry she was while she waited until dark to return home.

"I never thought the wolf man would come at me like that. He banged my head on the floor and hurt me bad. See?" Arthur's face was covered with dismay as he examined the gash on Annie's head. The rain had washed some of the blood away, but the wound was still red and angry looking. Then she told him that Asa had slapped her for stealing the horse.

"That's when I thought I would just run away and never go back."

"They shouldn't never hurt you, Annie. Him and Asa are bad people."

"What's he doin' here anyway? Why's he helpin' on that road?"

"He told my daddy he's friends with Jesse, but I don't believe it. He says Jesse was the one what killed Pete in the war."

Annie was dumbfounded. "Jesse wouldn't never do that! He's good!"

"But, Annie! Jesse never said he didn't, not even when that man was sayin' it! He acted like it might be so! I was goin' to tell Ma, but I ain't yet. She'll know what to do, that's sure."

Annie grasped Arthur's hand in hers and they both trembled. "What are we goin' to do?" she asked.

"You two numskulls are not goin' to do anythin'! Yer too dumb to find the way to the outhouse, let alone make trouble for me!"

The taunting voice belonged to Cougar. Before Arthur could rise clumsily to his feet, Cougar hoisted a thick board from the dirt floor and swung it into the boy's head. Arthur fell to the earth, stunned. Annie began to scream. A wild, high pitch escaped her mouth as she repeated Arthur's name again and again.

Just beyond the barn, Asa Bitter plowed through the towering, thick weeds, wielding a loaded shotgun. "I'll get you this time, you half-witted dunce. I'll teach you mess with my Annie!" he howled. Tramping through the wet morning had increased the already foul mood he felt. He figured Annie had come out this way, and was determined to force her back to Lone Oak. He saw only that Annie was struggling against a larger figure and burst ahead.

He let fire at the man's body before realizing his error. Cougar staggered forward and released his own weapon, firing directly into Asa's heart. Asa dropped like ballast onto the clay floor.

Annie's screams did not cease until Arthur revived a minute or two later.

"They's dead! They killed each other, Arthur! Now, what are we goin' to do?"

Arthur gingerly examined Asa and listened for breathing or gurgling noises.

"Your daddy's gone all right. Shot clean through!" He turned his attention to Cougar, who lay writhing on his side. "He ain't dead. Not yet anyways. We got to go tell somebody about this!"

After a moment's thought, Arthur decided. "You get on your mule and high tail it to Hattie. Get Jesse and them to come and do somethin', I don't know what! I'll stay here and see he don't get away."

Annie scrambled to her feet and nodded, allowing tears to flow freely. She mumbled over and over, "Asa's dead, Asa's dead," and urged the mule to the meadow.

Cougar lay shivering in the smothering heat of that Kentucky summer day. In delirium he felt the uncanny pressure of footsteps walking over the place he would soon sleep—his final rest, his grave. The footsteps had belonged to Annie all along. He faded, and only the jogging of transport to the Beaudine cabin roused him slightly.

"He's pretty bad off," said Hattie after examining him. "He lost a lot of blood out there and he's shot up somethin' awful. I'll do what I can, but maybe we ought to send for Doc Martin."

"Doc Martin ain't in Lone Oak any more, Miss Hattie. He

took off last month." Annie stopped shaking long enough to make that much sense.

"Well, it looks like we're his only hope, don't it?" Hattie cast a quick look at Jesse. "Clive, maybe you and Arthur ought to help Annie out and see to Asa, take him back to town in the wagon. I expect somebody there'll help with the buryin'."

Hattie had seen wounds before, most recently Arthur's, but Cougar's were the worst she had been called upon to doctor. In spite of her pessimistic feelings about the young man, she knew she would do her best to help him, and began giving Jesse instructions. He followed her orders with exactness, exuding outward control, however twisted he felt inside. Jesse knew full well that Cougar's death would mean freedom from shackling blackmail or exposure. A dead Cougar would be a silent Cougar. Still, he could not outright wish it. It was against his nature. Hattie's tongue seemed to be rattling from subject to subject as they cleaned Cougar's wounds, dug out shot, and attempted to check the pulsating flow of Cougar's life blood.

"Hot as it is today, Asa woulda started collectin' flies in no time. Annie's free of him now and likely she'll come here for good. I don't know what about the store, for the place belongs to Asa out-and-out and Annie could in no way run it. Time will tell, I reckon. Hand me that strip of linsey, would you? Tarnation! I never saw such bleedin'!"

Jesse had, and plenty of times. It sickened him here as much as it had during battle. Cougar's breathing was shallow and erratic, and was now producing a sorry rattle. Jesse always heard it referred to as Mr. Death dancing around in your rib cage, with hobnails on his boots. Suddenly, Cougar coughed, and up came the blood, the bright red and bubbling water of life. His eyes opened wide, and a surprisingly strong hand gripped Hattie's wrist. Cougar's eyes burned with high fever, and he felt as though his sockets were shriveling all around the orbs. His body was a blood blister needing puncture, a quivering mass of shredded organs, but his mind was crystallized glass. He would get Jesse now, and get him good.

"You goin' to tell 'em, ain't you, Jess?" He spoke Jesse's name, but stared straight at Hattie. Her eyes were riveted on his parched, twisted lips.

"Tell 'em, Jess. Was you killed their boy down there." His gaze wandered to Hattie's face. "Jesse did it. He told me so. Killed a Kentucky man . . . in prison. He was a Reb guard."

Cougar then looked at Jesse, struggling with the next few words. They were his last.

"If you go back, tell Mary I'm sorry I stole her horse."

One last convulsive shiver racked Cougar's body, and then the iron hand released its grip on Hattie and dropped to the blood-soaked porch.

It was hot in the afternoon sun, but chills passed through Jesse and Hattie both. She searched his face for some sign of denial, some protest that Cougar had lied, been out of his head, or been mistaken. She saw none of this in Jesse's eyes. She rose and wiped crimson from her shaking hands. The silence was long and heavy. Jesse knelt beside Cougar, unable to find his voice or words of explanation.

"I have blood on my hands," she lamented. Then came the question they both dreaded. "Do you have Pete's blood on yours, Jesse, like he said?"

Jesse's absolute quiet was all the answer Hattie needed and she continued speaking, matter-of-factly.

"There's no undertaker in Lone Oak. We'll have to bury him here, somewhere a ways off. I don't reckon we need to wait for any crowd. I'd just as soon see him under ground as quick as possible anyway."

"I'll get the spade," Jesse offered and walked to the lean-to shed. When he came back, he saw that she had pulled two blankets from the trunk and laid them out for wrapping the body. "Where do you want to put him?" he asked.

"Someplace high, away from any water source. I have been over all the ground around here and there's a little rise just south I think we can sling him on your horse and get it done as soon as a place is dug."

"If you don't mind, Hattie, just show me where it is and I'll do the diggin' myself."

"It's your choice, Jesse. I'd help if you needed."

They walked together in earnest silence, leading Jesse's horse through a section of woods and across a small stream. Cougar's limp arms swayed with the loping pace of the big animal, the only horse he had ridden since the war that was not stolen. His face was covered, but the hands and wrists flopped white and slack, exposed from beneath the blanket. The sun was beginning its slow descent beyond the trees and open fields, however, darkness would not be upon them until much later. There would be time enough for Jesse to dig a shallow grave, to mound it over with earth and rocks, and walk back under cover of night. In the morning he would decide when to leave.

Hattie left him to scrape the earth and dig the abominable hole alone. She walked under a heavy cloud of confusion and distress over Jesse. She had begun to think of him as one of her own a short few days after he arrived; he was that charming and that accommodating. Oh, he never had curried favor, but worked hard for his keep and proved himself. The question of his silence about the war was answered easily enough. She knew that many men who had been to war preferred to forget it as soon as possible. If Pete had lived and come back to her, she had vowed she would not press him for more than he wanted to share. War, the public debate and battle, was, in the end, a private thing, touching people in mighty strange ways.

She decided she would wait, reserve judgment on her young friend. She was concerned about the effect such news would have on Laurel. Hattie's mind then wandered to Cougar, truly the devil's advocate as far as she could see. What reason had he to malign Jesse on his death bed, to lay open a man he called friend? She was bewildered. Could be to repay an old wound, could be he had seen it happen? There were so many things it might have been. She knew she must have an answer before Laurel returned. Jesse's dark, telling silence now cut her to the quick, as she realized what he must have been living with all these weeks.

She knew Clive and Arthur would probably stay the night in Lone Oak, and, by the time they returned, Asa Bitter would be stone cold in the ground. Asa's hateful attitude had at last turned on him, she mused. He and Cougar had canceled each other out, just about a fitting end to that chapter. Hattie sat on her porch, indifferently knitting a coverlet, while she awaited Jesse's return. When darkness clouded her vision, she lit a kerosene lamp and placed it on the planks of the porch, which were still warm from the day. She was weary now, sapped of energy and resolve. Her feet were sore, so she loosened the latchets on her high boots, wiggling her toes against the worn leather. The whole business had been a burden, ever since the bearded man showed up. Her dislike of him seemed to have roots in something dark from the beginning, and even his working on the road did not serve to polish that leaden aura he carried. She wanted desperately for it to be last week again. *I must be gettin' old,* she thought, *to wish for such a recent past.* The moon appeared, a bleached saucer of white bone, suspended by filmy threads of cloud. The stars occurred, like small events across the time line of night. Still, Jesse was not there. Hattie removed her boots and walked gingerly across the porch, fearing splinters. Instead, her feet passed over the damp swath her cloth had made while washing off Cougar's spilt blood. It made her flesh crawl, and she jumped away quickly. She suddenly and unexpectedly felt very alone and almost frightened. What if Jesse had decided to stay away until she slept? Maybe take his horse straight off the hill and keep going?

To her relief, Jesse approached the cabin at that moment. He spoke first.

"Well, he's buried. I covered him pretty good with rocks, so the animals shouldn't disturb the place too much. I feel pretty bushed," he continued apologetically. "So I was wonderin' if it's all right for me to stay here until sunup. I can be leavin' then."

"To be sure, you can stay the night. I don't much cotton to bein' out here alone anyway, what with the newly dead just yonder. I'm certain Clive and Arthur won't be comin' back until tomorrow."

Jesse's features were chiseled by sharp moonlight as he stood before Hattie.

The sweat of his labor stood out on his face, though he had wiped it away several times. Up on that knoll, he had dug as a man possessed, scraping and plunging the spade into the earth, opening the wide mouth that would smile at Cougar and swallow him whole. He had hefted the mid-size and large rocks with his hands and, with his body force, walked the huge stones into place. By then it was night, but the sky was cast over with a steady glimmer from the moon. He welcomed his shadow as another living thing on the swell of earth, and looked out over the surrounding landscape. It was ghostly, all washed in that pale glow, and the trees stood placidly, as if asleep in the night.

Now he stood before Hattie, knowing he must say something more than that he was tired, and that the burying was finished. It was difficult to find the words, so he turned and looked out into the garden. Hattie waited. Jesse began at last, "I guess I can talk about it now, but it's hard."

Hattie replied softly. "Jesse, we are friends. Friends hear each other out." Jesse moved to the porch and sat on the edge of it, relaxing his muscles and leaning against his knees. Hattie sat a few feet from him.

"When I first came here, I thought to just tell it outright and ask if you could forgive me. I don't know why I figured it would be easy, and I thought maybe you knew already that he was dead. I at least wanted to give you the Testament so's you'd have somethin' that was his from the war. But when I saw your face and how hard it was for you to take, well, I was not sure you should know right away it was me did it."

"Were you protectin' us or yourself?" It was a gritty question, but Hattie felt she had to ask it.

"I guess I was lookin' out for myself. I thought maybe I could just do somethin' to smooth my own conscience and go on my way. Then, the road business came up, and I guessed that would be a good way to make some of it right. I was wrong about that. I want you to know that I never did aim at anybody. My commanding officer was standin' right there and ordered me to fire into the rowdies or be punished. I was hopin' nobody would get hurt, but they were all so crowded together."

The image of the crushing humanity that was Andersonville rushed back on him. He shook his head to dispell it, but it would not go away. He saw them all again—thousands, sick and dying, black-faced, scarecrows flapping in the fetid wind off the filthy sinks. The smell, his neckerchief, the heat, the hopelessness. Hattie respected the silence that fell for a few minutes.

"How did you come by the Testament, then?" she asked.

"It was the man they all called the preacher. He dug it out of Pete's breast pocket and threw it over the dead line to me. He said I should read the name inside and never forget what I did there. After I met Laurel and realized how much she loved Pete and hated the war, I was scared to bring it up. I felt lucky that she got over me bein' a soldier in the first place."

"How is it you never corrected us about bein' a Confederate man?"

"I guess I thought it didn't make any difference by now. I guess I turned out to be a liar, just like Cougar. That's somethin' I never thought I'd be. Was Cougar all that bad? Yes, he was, but no matter how bad a man is, he can always tell the truth at least once. Even the devil does that, just to gain your confidence. I got to tell the truth now, but the worst part is that I don't know if ever I would have done it but for Cougar speakin' out." Jesse fell silent for a moment. Then he said, "That does not change the fact that I misspoke. I hid the truth by bein' quiet. It's the same thing, just as bad."

Hattie's burden was not as great as Jesse's, but chagrin and disappointment weighed her down. She felt suddenly drained. She stood and spoke. "We'd best talk some more in the mornin'.

I'm all frayed from ponderin' and I need to sleep. You do the same and we'll see what tomorrow brings."

At nine o'clock that Wednesday night, a knock on his door awakened the one official in Lone Oak. He was Zeke Madsen, the sometime preacher, sometime mortician, sometime mayor. He had not really been elected or trained that well, but appointed himself for such occasions as would need an official. A burying was one of those occasions. This night, Clive Beaudine stood at his door.

"Sorry to wake you, Zeke. But I don't rightly know what to do with Asa Bitter."

"What's he up to now? Did he beat on his girl again? You know, there's nothing we can do about domestic squabbles."

Zeke was still half asleep and talking in a muddle.

"No, that ain't it," Clive went on. "Asa's dead and it's still mighty warm out here. We need to get him planted, and I mean soon as possible." Zeke's faculties were roused in quick fashion. "Asa, dead meat? What happened?" He stepped outside in his loose nightshirt and scratched through a handful of tousled hair. Asa dead. An amusing thought. Zeke had not much cared for Asa either.

"He got himself shot out at Stetson's barn. Fella that shot him got it from Asa too, and is likely dyin' out at my place. Point is, we want to take care of this soon as possible."

Zeke nodded his head. "I see what you mean. None of us ever liked the smell of Asa while he was living anyway. Maybe we'd best round up some men right now and get it over with."

"How many do you reckon we need?"

"Two more ought to do it. Wait. I'm forgetting your bum leg. We'll get three more."

Annie agreed to putting Asa in the ground as soon as possible. While the men were excavating Mr. Bitter's resting place, Annie and Arthur sat against a stone marker a few yards away, fascinated by the sight of diggers working in the combined lights of the moon and a flickering kerosene lamp.

Asa's remains lay on the wagon bed, covered by a stiff, gray canvas. "He cannot bother you no more," Arthur assured the wide-eyed Annie.

"And he cannot bother you no more neither," she answered, not quite believing. They sat together, patting one another's hands and stroking each other's hair, playing the peculiar games of innocents, until Zeke called to them. "Your Daddy's in his pit here, Annie, and we're going to say a few words over him. Care to join in?"

Annie jumped up, now nervous. "Can I see him? Can I throw dirt in? I want to see for sure he's there." Cold chills passed over all the men present. Asa must have been even more cruel than they imagined to the girl, for they noticed there was not a tear for him, only her plea for reassurance.

"Annie, you can be the first." Clive handed her a shovel filled with fresh earth. Only after she had pitched the dirt over Asa did she seem to relax a little. She turned and smiled at the small gathering. "Say whatever you want. It won't be no skin off my nose no more."

"Lord," Zeke began, "here is Brother Asa, coming home sooner than he thought."

He was interrupted by Arthur, whose propensity for rhyme was surfacing. "He thought he wasn't shot, thought he wasn't shot, shot right in the pot, he was shot a lot!"

Annie began to giggle and Arthur grinned with pride. A couple of men stifled a snigger behind their dirty hands. Zeke and Clive smiled in spite of themselves, but nobody tried to stop Arthur.

"So much for ceremony," said Zeke.

While Arthur rhymed, the men threw dirt, and soon the grave was filled in. Clive found a withered stick under a nearby tree and thrust it into the soft, newly turned clay.

"Until somebody marks this place proper, this stick will have to serve. God have mercy on his soul. Thank you, gentlemen."

The party dispersed and Clive, Arthur, and Annie retired for the night in the Bitter house. While Arthur and Clive slept, Annie slipped out and walked to the little graveyard. They would have wondered at her lack of fear, out there in the dark all alone, had they realized she was gone. She took with her some sulfur matches and tinder from the box next to the hearth. She went straight to the gravesite, yanked the dry shoot marking Asa's plot from its mooring, and snapped it into three pieces. She walked a short way from the new mound of earth and dropped the broken marking stick into the pile of tinder. Humming softly and swaying as she knelt by the tiny wood stack, she struck match after match and dropped each one into it. When the pyre had burned itself to ash, she got up and walked back to the house, calm as a summer's morning.

The following day Clive readied himself to return to the cabin in the woods. Arthur and Annie refused to ride along with him, saying they wanted to play in the store and change things around to suit Annie. Clive only shook his head and smiled, reckoning they could be left in peace for a while. He snapped the reins above the horse's back and was on his way home.

Clive traveled during mid-morning. He felt too good, he reflected, to have just buried an old acquaintance. Maybe though, it was looking at death that made the contrast. Having looked into that awful, inevitable face, life around him took on a keener glint and a clearer pitch. Nearing home, he saw that his road became a broad and sweeping highway. The trees above suggested a lacy canopy, shot through with bursts of sunlight. By heaven, it was good to be alive. He wanted to share that sentiment with Hattie as soon as he got back. Hattie was not as eager to pronounce life a good gift as Clive was, a thing which he saw as soon as he looked on her face. She was in the garden, rooting out weeds again. It seemed to be her eternal lot, and ordinarily she did not mind. Today was different. She raised up and asked him how everything went.

"Tolerable for all. We got help from Zeke and some others and just buried him straight away. Short and sweet. Annie and Arthur stayed behind to mind some things at the store. I guess they'll be along sooner or later. What's goin' on with the other one?"

"He died last night. Jesse buried him up on the knoll south of here. Clive, there's things you got to know about Jesse before he goes."

"Before he goes? Where's he goin'? I thought maybe him and Laurel would get together. Did they have a fallin' out?" Clive was obviously still in the dark about the situation.

"He's in the back, gettin' himself ready. Go talk to him."

Hattie's abrupt manner suggested to Clive that she was upset, and he was trying to determine what he had done this time. The whole thing was a puzzle. His joyful mood was ruined, and suddenly it was another hot, worrisome day. He turned to retreat to the cabin, when he saw Jesse come from the woods behind it. Clive walked toward him, and the two went to the porch and sat to talk. Jesse repeated his confession to Clive, and the full impact of it settled like a stone in the older man's heart. He longed to offer full forgiveness, but something held him back. Only when Jesse suggested that he was ready to leave did Clive find words enough to respond.

"I think you ought to at least tell Laurel face to face. It's the manly thing to do. And, Jesse, maybe we could work it through anyway. I was there. I know what the war was. I know what duty was. Some things you can't help."

Jesse was less ready to forgive himself. "Lyin' is one thing you can help. I can't see any reason for that, not even with the good excuses I thought I had."

"Listen, Jesse. I think you ought to tell Laurel when she comes back and maybe by then you'll feel better yourself. Now, I ain't sayin' I'm happy that my boy was killed, even less that it was you who done it, but I can't condemn you for followin' orders. Pete just happened to be in the wrong place. It could have been the other way around, you know."

Jesse was amazed at Clive. One minute the man seems thick as mud, the next, he offers uncommon charity. Jesse could only respond in one way. "I will stay then, if Hattie won't mind. I will finish the last little bit of the road. I can do it by myself, too. In fact, that's what I'd like. You can attend to things here and not worry about that." Clive wanted to embrace the sorrowing young man he had grown to care for, but he restrained himself. Instead, he rubbed his own knees and nodded approval.

"Then, it's settled. I'll tell Hattie."

As they spoke together, Hattie and Clive had difficulty finding words to express their feelings. They, who had been married twenty-five years, almost felt like strangers on this issue. Each feared taking the wrong direction, forgiving not enough, forgiving too much. Finally, Hattie voiced the thing that sorrowed her most. "I nearly feel like I've lost another son. For the longest time in my life I held that everything happens for a reason, and now I can't think that Jesse only came here to build that road and then leave. Maybe if he'd have told us right off that it was him did it, we wouldn't have welcomed him in. But, what then?"

"We'd not have known him, we'd not have the road, likely Asa wouldn't be dead, and we wouldn't be sittin' here pinin' over the whole case. My thought is this. It might take a while, but I think we can do it. I think we can forgive Jesse. I don't know what about Laurel, but I could. Maybe we don't have to tell her at all."

Hattie reflected on Clive's words and added, "That'd be for Jesse to decide. I got a feelin' he won't let it go, though. It's too deep in him, the lie. No, I think Laurel is goin' to have to face this square. Jesse won't have it no other way."

All day Thursday and the morning of Friday, Jesse dug in to finish the road, agonizing over telling Laurel the truth. Under such unbroken skies, life should have been joyful for him, but his load was heavy and he sat down often in the woods, trying to clear his mind. He knew it would not happen until he could see Laurel's response. At noon, Hattie and Clive appeared with food for him, an offering of sorts, to demonstrate their willingness to forgive and forget.

"The road looks mighty fine, Jesse. It's as near finished as it will likely ever need to be." Hattie complimented him, and Clive nodded in agreement. They ate in relative silence.

At last, Jesse said, "I'm scared to tell Laurel." Hattie and Clive stared at him over their tin cups, hardly knowing what to say. They knew it was a matter of his conscience and the question of ongoing trust with their daughter.

"The only advice I can give is that you'll know what to say when the time comes. The Lord will provide you a way." Hattie's words sounded wise at the moment, so Jesse decided to let his tongue be guided by Providence when he confronted Laurel.

None of them could know that Providence was already taking care of the news for Laurel. Ruthann had let her leave early that day, and as she rode through Lone Oak, she happened on Annie and Arthur while they stood outside Asa's store. They flagged her down and she was surprised to see them together so close to Asa Bitter's property. Annie was energized in telling her about the shootings, and while she spoke, Arthur acted out all the parts. He fell to the ground after knocking himself out. He grabbed Annie and shook her around as he portrayed Cougar. He ran at his invisible self as he mimicked Asa, running and firing a loaded stick. He fell two more times, dying once for Asa and receiving severe wounds as Cougar. They told of Arthur staying with the wounded men while Annie hit it lickety split back to the cabin to get help. Laurel begged them to slow down the storytelling and make sense.

"We *are* makin' sense, Laurel. It's everybody else that don't make sense!"

Arthur's expression was agitated. "That bearded one, he said Jesse was the one killed Pete, and Jesse never said no, it wasn't! Never even hit him nor nothin'!" Laurel strained to get the gist of Arthur's rantings. She asked him to repeat himself, and this time try to tell the truth.

"I am tellin' the truth. I heard it with these here ears.

282

He says to Jesse, 'you was the Confederate soldier who shot their boy,' and Jesse says, 'what makes you think they don't already know.' And then, Jesse, he don't talk hardly anymore to him."

"The wolf!" cried Annie. "I'm glad he's shot! He knocked me down and hurt me." The conversation was now more of a muddle than ever.

"You're tellin' me, Arthur, that Jesse shot Pete?" She attempted to get at least one clear conclusion from him.

"He never said he didn't. That's what I'm tellin' you."

Annie rattled on about Asa being buried last night, about burning some stick in the cemetery, about how she was the owner of the store now and had to stay with it so no one would steal from her. Laurel's ears were stopped by Arthur's words ringing in her head. It couldn't be! Jesse would have told her. Jesse would not lie.

"I got to go," she said suddenly, and jumped on her horse. Arthur realized he had upset her and followed after, calling out to his sister, "Laurel, wait for me." She turned and saw him running after her, determined to catch up. She reined the animal in and waited for him. "Jump on behind then, and be quick. I'm just goin' to find out what all this horsewhip is about!"

Arthur begged Laurel to stop by Stetson's barn before they came to the meadow. The bloody stains belonging to Asa and Cougar had soaked into the dirt floor but could still be made out. "That's where I got knocked over and Asa went down right there, and that other one, he was sprawled right there. I like to wet myself when I seen them."

"It's ugly!" said Laurel, turning her lip involuntarily. She moved away from the barn quickly and went to the horse. "Come on, Arthur. This place reeks of the dead."

Laurel dug her heels into the big animal's sides and urged him forward. *I'll get this straightened out right away,* she thought. *Then Jesse will sit down with me and we will read his daddy's letter together.* When she galloped into the woods, she could see that the road was finished. The way was broad and the path smooth, which meant no more ducking tree branches or watching for stumps in her path. Suddenly, it seemed a bad omen. If the road was finished, Jesse could be gone any time. What really was to hold him here? Could her love and affection do it?

Approaching the cabin, she saw the three of them ahead, walking back together. Clive's limp was almost painful to watch, Hattie's stride was shorter, and Jesse's beloved, now familar gait had lost its swing. What was wrong? The beat of hooves and Arthur's whooping brought them to a halt. Hattie turned first.

"It's Laurel," she said, her voice nearly a whisper.

Laurel's gaze traveled from her mother to her father, and finally to Jesse. When their eyes at length met, Jesse's were full of sad anticipation. Laurel was stunned, for she read gloom in them. Quickly, she said, "Is it true about Asa and your friend? Where is he now?"

"The other one is dead too. Jesse buried him last night. Yes, it's all true," Clive answered her.

"Is it really all true, what Arthur told me? He said he over-heard the other man and Jesse talkin'. Is it true what he said about Pete?" Laurel's head was shaking and her heart pounded furiously. Her fingers gripped the reins with fierce strength. Arthur slipped to the ground and stood numbly beside the horse.

"What was it more Arthur told you, honey?" This time, Hattie spoke.

Laurel could not bring herself to say the words. They screamed in her head, but would not form in her mouth. She wanted to cry aloud, say it's not so, Jesse! Jesse's face was ashen, his eyes downcast, and his shoulders slumped. His whole body shouted that what Arthur had told her was true.

"Oh, no," she sighed, and bit her quivering lip. She fumbled in her pocket and pulled out Marcus's letter and handed it to Hattie. Burning tears stung her eyes and a terrible, searing ache closed her throat. She could not bring herself to look at Jesse. Wordless and raw, she wheeled the horse, entered the road once more, and did not look back. Jesse took the letter from Hattie's big, rough hand and could not see the inscription on it for the tears that welled in his own eyes. Arthur began to moan and clung to Hattie. "Mama, I didn't know what to do. The words just come out like I heard 'em from Jesse and the wolf. Did I do wrong?" Then, Jesse realized Arthur must have heard them talking outside the house when Cougar brought the shooting up.

"No, honey. You didn't do wrong. Laurel was goin' to find out anyway. Jesse was goin' to tell her. Just go on in the kitchen and get yourself a biscuit or somethin'. We'll talk about it later."

Hattie tried to soothe Arthur, but knew that Jesse and Laurel were the souls needing balm just now. Balm of Gilead, it was called in the Bible, and she knew that for each of them, it would have to come from inner strength and love. Whether they possessed enough of both to see them through this, she did not know. "I'll go look for Laurel. Maybe I can help."

Jesse reached out and restrained her. "Please, Hattie. Don't go. I'll wait for her to come back and talk to her myself. She needs to be alone right now. I guess I do too."

Jesse walked to the river alone, silently hoping that he might see her on the way. He did not. Sitting beneath the tree that shaded their bathing spot, he took out the letter from Marcus. It read:

Dear Son,

I was elated to hear from you. I am on the mend and doing very well. I take it the trip to Springfield did not disappoint, with the exception of seeing Cougar Rivers again perhaps. I am eager to hear your accounts firsthand. I have read many other accounts in the papers, but I feel you will add dimensions they have not touched. I have been able to return to my work on a half day basis, having to stop after a few hours due to the discomfort in my knee. We certainly could use you as soon as you return. Which brings to mind the question itself. Do you know how soon you will be coming home? I am anxious to see you again. Is your work there finished yet?

The remainder of the letter was devoted to catching Jesse up on hometown news and mentioning the names of three girls who were available, due to circumstances in the war. Marcus was clearly enthused about Jesse returning to Murfreesboro, getting married, and settling down there. Jesse contemplated his father's questions and feared that he would be returning sooner than he had planned and empty hearted as well. He remained at the riverside, reviewing the many paths that had led to this place, to the happiness he found here, to the beautiful Laurel. It had been a long journey, a tenuous one, a journey whose end was never really in sight. Well, he had finished it now, he thought, with no one to blame but himself, and he had learned a bitter lesson along the way. In the dimming light, Jesse read his father's last line: *I look forward to your homecoming when your business in Kentucky is finished.*

Darkness crept in and dropped a curtain of deep stillness over Jesse. Certain that Laurel would have returned by now, he made his way back to the cabin. When he entered the kitchen and read the faces of her family, he saw plainly that she was not there.

"Where do you suppose she might be?" he asked, disquieted.

Hattie put down her work with the ongoing coverlet.

"Hard to say. But, I wouldn't worry too much. She's got friends roundabout. Any number of folks would take her in for the night. Then too, maybe she went back to Lone Oak to be with Annie."

Jesse sat up far into the night, waiting for some sound of Laurel's return. Creatures of the night crept through the woods and invaded Hattie's garden, chawing at root and green, dining on her efforts. He heard them scuttling about, rustling through the succulent plants. At last, sleep overcame him, stealing heavily over his eyes and clouding his thoughts. He slept hard and awoke to strong sunlight and clear skies.

Refusing breakfast, he told Hattie and Clive he would go looking in Lone Oak for signs of Laurel. In his heart, he knew that if he did not find her there, he probably would not come back. He had decided that much last night. He had seen such sadness and disappointment in all of their faces that he judged none of them, including himself, could probably ever truly overcome it.

He packed his few things on his horse and tried to summon a calm face in front of them. Hattie read through him and offered a few words. "Jesse, what was meant to be was meant to be. No matter what happens, you'll always be a part of us. Every time we ride along that highway yonder, we'll remember what you did here. I hope it all works out."

He replied, "Thank you," simply and quietly.

Turning his mount, he let the animal lope past the garden and down to the road. Behind him, Clive scratched the back of his neck and lowered his head. There was a peculiar tight feeling in his throat, and he tried to dispell it by swallowing. Arthur had emerged from his sleep and watched intently, trying to think of a rhyme. None came. Hattie squinted into the sky and sought to blink back certain tears, without success. It was one of the few times in her life that she frankly did not know what to do.

Jesse allowed his horse to amble through the woods, and he studied the finished work of what Hattie had referred to as that highway yonder. The labor had been hard and had rebuilt sinew and muscle in him, but the clearing of it was not as wrenching as riding down it for the last time. At length, he faced the long stretch of meadow where he and Laurel had first exchanged flirtations and raced together. It was covered with high grass and brown-eyed Susans, and brushed by the ever present vagrant wind. Red-winged blackbirds still called to each other over the tops of cattails by the stream, and Jesse saw himself and Laurel riding across the open field once again. It was too much. He jabbed the sides of the beast with his boots and, leaning forward in the saddle, rode hell-bent-for-leather into the grassland.

On such a pristine morning, a young girl should not have to stand sequestered in a dense growth of woods, watching her hopes and dreams disappear into the distance and be swallowed up in high grass. Still, pristine mornings do not always make promises of happy days ahead. Laurel observed the beloved figure of Jesse Campbell ride out of her life, and then she headed for home and Hattie. If he did not come back, she vowed, she would never forget the Jesse she had loved, and never forgive the Jesse who had lied.

Halfway between the Beaudine cabin and Lone Oak, Jesse spied a loaded wagon on the road. A young man about his own age guided the horse, and on the wagon seat next to him sat a yellow-haired woman and a tin-type little girl copy of her. As they neared each other, Jesse nodded in solemn greeting. The young man spoke to him, asking directions. The woman stared intently at him, making him a little uneasy.

"Do you know of a road back there in the woods, goin' to the Beaudine place?" Pete asked.

"I do," said Jesse. "Just keep on goin' east and follow this one. You'll come to a meadow soon enough and see the woods across the way. Road's at the edge of it. You can't miss it."

"Much obliged," Pete replied, and brushed the brim of his hat in farewell.

Jesse rode on, wondering who it was wanted to see the Beaudines. Still immersed in his own world, he rehearsed any words he might speak to Laurel, should he see her in Lone Oak. They all seemed to work out into a jumble, and sound like paltry excuses for his mistakes. He found the door of Asa's store closed, but knocked anyway, in hopes of finding Annie there and asking about Laurel.

After a few moments, a wide-eyed Annie Grace stared through the window and, seeing that it was Jesse, unhooked the latch and swung the door open. She told him to come in and be quick about it.

"There's spirits outside," she whispered, pulling Jesse into the dark room.

"Spirits? Are you thinkin' Asa's come back to haunt you?"

"Twere not Asa. But maybe soon. I'm scared, Jesse!"

She was visibly shaken and her speech came in spasms.

Jesse took her by the arm and gently sat her down.

"Now, I'm goin' to light a lamp in here, and we can talk more about this. Just wait a minute and calm down. Tell me what happened. Just what spirits did you see?"

"I was inside here, lookin' at stuff my daddy said I could never have. Pretty stuff, good smellin' stuff. All of a sudden I seen a face in the window. They was a halo around its head, bright yellow and blindin' like the sun. Pretty soon, another was behind it and then they went away. I went to the window and seen them walk away with the ghost. I judge them two was angels."

"Was it dark in here then? Did they see you, do you think?"

"They couldn't see me, for I was clear in the back, but I seen them plain as day."

"What ghost was it?" Jesse recalled the young man and two cotton-haired travelers beside him in the wagon. He assumed it was these three riders that Annie had seen.

"Ooooh, Jesse, maybe he's lookin' for you!" Annie shrieked in terror. "Maybe that's what he's doin' here!" Jesse gripped the girl's shoulders lightly and waited for her to quiet down.

Presently, she raised her head and looked into his eyes. In a hushed voice she uttered, "It was Pete Beaudine! He's come back from the dead!"

Back from the dead was exactly the way Pete felt when he drew the wagon to a halt in front of the old burned out homesite. He and Amy had stopped briefly the night before about five miles from Lone Oak, resting only for a few hours so they could arrive at the Beaudines in the morning. Now they exchanged anxious looks, both wondering what had happened there, and where Pete's family might be. "I'm sure as shootin' this is our old house, or what used to be it. I can't believe I have been gone so long that I'd forget how to get here. There's the Stowe place and across the way is where Zeke Madsen lives. You two jump on down and stretch your legs and I'll go see Zeke and find out what's goin' on."

When Zeke answered his door, he nearly fell backwards. Pete approached him and held out his hand in greeting. "Zeke," he said, "Maybe you can help me out."

"Is it Pete? Gosh, I thought you was dead. I heard you was dead. Asa Bitter told me he had it on good authority you was shot in the war. Excuse me! I near leaped out of my skin seeing you at my door! What a way to start off my day!"

"You heard I was dead? How can that be, seein' that I'm standin' right here in front of you? How would Asa Bitter know somethin' like that anyway? Why, I sent my folks a letter back five or six weeks ago. They should surely have it by now."

Pete shook his head in confusion. "Wait a minute. First, tell me what happened to my house. Where's my family?"

By this time, Amy and Clary had joined them on the doorstep. "This here's my wife and her child. We come a long way from Georgia and I got to find my family."

"Come on in and set," said Zeke. "I got some stories to tell you."

Zeke's narrative unfolded to an amazed Pete. "Back a few months ago, I think it was in the winter. Yep, it was. Anyway, your brother, Arthur, was left home alone and got to horsing around with a stick or some such thing, stirring up the fire and first thing you know, he drops hot coals on a rag rug. Your folks and sister were coming up the road and saw the smoke. They all ran in and started pulling stuff out fast as they could, but a lot of truck was burned up. They were out on the street then, with all that was left of their worldly goods. Now, you remember Annie Grace, Asa Bitter's addled daughter? She was always good friends with Arthur."

He turned to Amy and added this aside. "On account of them both being underdeveloped, you see."

He continued, looking at Pete. "Anyway, Annie Grace told them she knew of a place out in the woods that was abandoned. Nobody ever went there except for her, I suppose when she was trying to get away from Asa. Remember, he used to mistreat her? Well, the upshot was, your family moved lock, stock, and barrel

290

into the woods and we have not seen much of them since."

Pete was astounded, but urged Zeke to continue. "Tell me about how it was Asa heard I was dead. Does my family think the same?"

"Well, here's how I got it from Asa. Seems a young fellow came riding through one day, looking for your folks, saying he had private business with them. Now, you know, there was no love lost between Asa and Hattie, so he never had a high opinion of the Beaudines. Personally, I hold that he never got past her throwing him over for Clive. When this man came along wanting to find the Beaudines, Asa said at first he was of a mind to send him on a wild goose chase, so they'd never know what his business was. Then he changed his thinking, being nosy as he is, er, was, and decided to let Annie show the man the way. Since Annie and Arthur were so chummy, Asa figured he'd find out what was going on through her. Now this young man, I forget his name, told the Beaudines that he saw you shot and killed during the war. He even brought back a Testament that your sister gave you." A sharp chill ran up Amy's spine. "You don't suppose it's Tommy Jackson, do you Pete? Why would he come all the way up here? Why, he was nothin' but a low down raider! It must've been him that took your Testament in the woods!"

"Well, this one, he didn't act low down, from what I heard around. He could still be out there for all I know. He helped your daddy build a road through the woods, clear up to the cabin, and was doing some courting on the side. You know, your sister has growed up to be a beauty." Zeke managed a sly grin and winked at Pete.

Pete ignored the wink and said, "Whew! That is an earful. So you reckon my folks never got my letter? Wait a minute! What if that *is* Tommy Jackson courtin' my sister? We got to get out there right now! How do I get there? Which road do I take?"

"I think you just stay on the road that goes right through town and head east. Annie Grace could tell you for sure, maybe even take you there herself. Asa is not around any-more to tell her yea or nay."

Pete looked puzzled, so Zeke went on to explain.

"Seems Asa followed Annie out to Stetson's barn, where she and Arthur always met, and he thought he was firing on Arthur, to finally blow him away. He never liked Arthur, see, because . . . " Looking at Amy, he discontinued the direction of his remarks. "That is, because, he was a Beaudine. At any rate, turns out it wasn't Arthur, although Arthur was there. Turns out it was a vagrant that Asa himself took in a couple of weeks ago. He fires at the vagrant, and the vagrant whips out a pistol and downs Asa with one shot, clean through the heart. Heard this all from your daddy last night when we buried Asa."

"You know, we always used to say that nothin' ever hap-pened in Lone Oak. Much obliged, Zeke, for all the informa-tion. I believe we'll be on our way and you can tell anybody you see from now on that Pete Beaudine is alive and kickin'!"

"It'll purely be a pleasure, Pete, and nice meeting you, Mrs. Beaudine."

Pete shuffled his little family into the wagon and turned back toward Asa's store. "Let's see if Annie Grace is there before we head out." So it was, that Clary and Amy peered through the window into the darkened one room store, and seeing no one, turned away.

Later, when they passed Jesse on the way to the meadow, Amy examined his face closely to see if he looked like Tommy or any of the raiders. She told Pete that she was satisfied that the handsome young man who gave them directions was none of those marauders. They would just have to wait and see who was out in the woods with his family and go from there.

"Annie!" Jesse now insisted. "People don't come back from the dead! There's no such thing as a ghost! You couldn't have seen Pete!"

"Yes, yes, I did! It was him!"

"What did he look like?" A small suspicion was aroused in Jesse. What if, by some ironic twist, Pete really was back? Did the man he shot have light hair or dark? Was he tall or short? Thin or bulky? Jesse remembered as if it was yesterday. Dark, short, rounded.

Annie was dead sure of her description. Pete looked almost the same as when he left. His hair was light, but not as yellow as the angel's. He was tallish, like Laurel and Hattie. No, he was not chunky. Jesse's heart leaped as he pictured the young man driving the wagon and asking directions. It had to have been Pete!

"Annie," he said. "I truly think you did see angels, just like you said, and if you are right, neither of us will ever have to worry about ghosts again!" He kissed her soundly on the forehead and ran through the doorway.

Chapter Thirty

HOME ON THE HIGHWAY

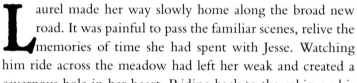

L aurel made her way slowly home along the broad new road. It was painful to pass the familiar scenes, relive the memories of time she had spent with Jesse. Watching him ride across the meadow had left her weak and created a cavernous hole in her heart. Riding back to the cabin on his highway burned her soul, clear down to her fingertips and soles of her feet. *I'm going to die,* she thought.

As soon as she spied Hattie, she slid off the horse and ran to her. She wailed loudly, unashamed to be so full of sorrow. Hattie cried with her and felt helpless to soothe this child of hers. When the crying was finished, Laurel gathered her words at last.

"Did he really shoot Pete, Mama?"

"Yes, honey, he did. It was part of the war though, and he hadn't much choice. Pete was a prisoner in the camp where Jesse was standin' guard and there was a tousle in the prison yard. Sometimes men have to behave like soldiers whether they want to or not. It's just a fact of war."

"But, Mama. He let on like he was Union. He lied about so many things."

"Well, he didn't exactly lie. He just left out a lot of infor-mation."

"Why? Why, did he have to come along any way, and have me fall in love with him and trust him?"

"Honey, we all fell in love with him and trusted him. I think that's one reason he didn't tell us after time. He was afraid of it, because he loved us too. He's real hard on himself, Laurel, harder than we are, maybe. So, he never did catch up to you?"

"No. I stayed in the woods and I watched him leave. It was all I could do not to run after him."

"He was lookin' for you. He said he was goin' to go find Annie to see if she knew where you were."

Laurel picked up a corner of Hattie's well-worn apron and wiped her eyes on it, gulping back tears and trying to pull herself together. Hattie simply ran her sleeve along her nose and sniffed. She slid her other arm around Laurel's waist, and they headed for the cabin. Suddenly, they heard shouting from the direction of the road. It was Arthur.

"Mama! Mama! It's a miracle! He's back!"

Thinking it was Jesse returning to her, Laurel ran to Arthur. "Jesse's back? Where did you see him?"

"No, not Jesse! Not Jesse!"

She became angry, her temper flaring. "Then who? What are you blubberin' about?"

"Pete's back! Pete's comin' on the road! I seen him!"

"Damn it, Arthur! Stop your stupid games! Go stick your head in the river!"

Hattie looked past her two arguing children to see a wagon in the distance. Her head told her it was impossible, but her heart insisted it could be. A tall figure stood straight up on the wagon seat, shouting the mare forward, while two tow-headed people bounced on the seat beside him.

Only deafness would have prevented Hattie from recognizing Pete's voice. She dashed around Laurel and Arthur, raising her skirts high to allow her to run. The astonished brother and sister hurried after her, and all of them reached the wagon at the same time. Pete leaped off the seat and embraced the whole lot of them at once, dancing up and down all the while. Amy thought she had never witnessed such a happy reunion, so full of laughter and tears and squeezing. She hugged Clary sitting beside her, just to share in the feeling. No wonder Pete was burning to get home. He was obviously much beloved here.

Pete loosened himself from the embraces of his family and ran to the wagon, hoisted Amy and Clary from the seat, and displayed each one proudly. He smiled happily as he introduced them.

"Mama, Laurel, Arthur, this here's Amy Beaudine and her child, Clary Sutter. I wrote you about them, but I guess the letter got lost in the mail somewhere. Zeke told me about the house and the fire and all. I never dreamed you didn't know I was alive. Amy and her father-in-law saved my life. It's such a story. Where's Daddy? He's all right, ain't he?"

Pete's words poured like a stream of water. More tears, more smiles went around again. This time, Amy received them as well, and Hattie picked Clary up as if she had known her forever. In the excitement, several minutes passed before Laurel realized the full impact of her brother's present state of health. "Hell's fire, Pete! You *are* alive! That means Jesse never killed you at all! We got to find him and stop him!"

"I don't rightly know what you're talkin' about, Laurel, but this ain't the first confusin' story I've heard since I come home." Pete smiled broadly at his young and beautiful sister.

Hattie fairly hollered in Laurel's face. "Get on your horse and beat it to Lone Oak. Maybe he's still there!"

"We passed a man headed that way a while back. Nice lookin' fella, brown hair, keen eyes, on a black mare," Amy said. "He told us how to get here."

"That's Jesse, all right! What a sight, what a sight!" Arthur was suddenly back to rhyming.

"What's goin' on, Mama?" Pete asked. "Is she talkin' about the man that helped Daddy build the new road?"

"She is, that!" Hattie grinned. "That's a good story too. Come on. Let's go scare the daylights out of your father. I don't believe he's ever seen a ghost before." Hattie ran before Pete and Amy, calling triumphantly. "Resurrection day is here! Our boy is home!"

Clive was crawling feet first from under the trough out back where the supper chicken had fled. He missed the commotion of Pete's arrival due to the squawking and scratching of the soon-to-be sacrificed poultry. He emerged in a flurry of feathers and dirt, limping and subduing the lively bird. As soon as he saw Pete and Amy, he let loose of the fowl and tried to regain some thread of dignity, but with chicken droppings streaming down his shirt, dignity was a little difficult to manage. Pete ran to him and nearly lifted him off the ground with a huge bear hug, chicken droppings and all.

"Daddy! You look just the way I remember you!"

"With fertilizer all over my front? That ain't much to recommend a man."

Then Clive, holding Pete at arm's length, burst into unchecked tears and cried like a woman. Arthur slapped Pete again and again across the back and hollered at Hattie.

"Mama, you was always right! Pete did come home just like you said and he come home on mine and Jesse's highway."

Carrying Clary, Hattie joined them. She gathered Pete and Amy into her arms and answered, smiling, "Maybe he was just waitin' for the road to be finished."

EPILOGUE

Lone Oak was not so far away from the Beaudine place that two swift riders would take all day to meet somewhere in the middle. Laurel rode at top pace to catch Jesse if she could. Her heart was racing and pounding, fearful that she would miss him, that he had not stopped off to see Annie. In her wildest thoughts she imagined herself trekking to Murfreesboro, looking for the house on Water Street. If she had to do it, she would go all that way alone, and ride the distance bareback if necessary.

Thundering across the countryside, Jesse spurred his horse toward the cabin in the wood, aware that he could finally put the shadow of war behind him, and lay to rest the ghost of Peter Beaudine. He knew he would never identify the prisoner who died from the last shot he took, but now he understood that he did not need to know. The dimness and uncertainty that clouded his mind was lifted, and the clarity of hope carried him along.

In the heights above this road that came and went at the same time, as all roads do, a hawk cast his eyes and ears to the scene below. What strange creatures these were, always earth-bound and fettered by legs, and how they tried to hurry. While the hawk circled and floated on a draft, they struggled along dusty paths and through high grasses. The hawk, with any real feelings, would feel sorry for such living things, that they were so constrained to the bosom of the earth. Today, the hawk looked down and saw two of them, mounted on clumsy beasts, come together in an extraordinary dance, throwing their arms around each other and smiling, the sounds of their laughter rising to meet the keen ears of all the circling birds. At that instant, the horizon called to him and the hawk was gone. He did not see the two ride off side by side.

Jesse and Laurel were on their way home, beginning the journey along their own highway, together. In answer to the last question in Marcus's letter, "Is your business in Kentucky finished, Jesse?" Jesse wrote, "No, I think it has just started. Will keep you advised." Two months later, Marcus received notice of Jesse and Laurel's impending marriage.

In time, Annie Grace turned her father's store over to Pete and Amy, who shared their profits generously with her and paid Arthur a sum to deliver goods to people in the area roundabout. Hattie and Clive stayed in the woods and visited Lone Oak every Sabbath, and Pete said it was mostly to see the grandchildren that came along. Jesse and Laurel moved to Murfreesboro and lived in the little house on Water Street until Marcus died. Four years after they left Lone Oak, they moved back, started the first weekly newspaper in the county, and called it the *Register*. One of the first obituaries Jesse composed was for a fiery circuit preacher, who lay down to sleep one night and never woke up. His name was Davis Chancellor.

ABOUT THE AUTHOR

On the living room floor of an Ohio walkup apartment some years ago, Barbara Miller came forth a squalling new infant on the pages of the Halloween edition of the *Columbus Dispatch*. For lack of a crib, she spent some baby time in an empty dresser drawer. These events no doubt account for her interest in the written word and a slight case of claustrophobia. While growing up in the Midwest drawing in the margins of her ChildCraft books and composing less than free verse, Barbara learned early that a good sense of humor will see you a long way through life.

Barbara has been an illustrator and editor and a participant in many humanitarian efforts, often using her ability to defend herself in Spanish.

After forty years of marriage, child rearing, and doggedly pursuing these artistic interests, she acknowledges her family as her greatest love, her faith as her greatest anchor, and her husband, Ron, as her best friend. As a woman of a certain age, Barbara also gives credit to her hair stylist, Roberta North; her dentist, Dr. Mike VanLeeuwen; and her orthopedic surgeon, Dr. Kim Bertin. Without these people she would not be the woman she is today.